PUFFIN BOOKS

THE BFG

The BFG is no ordinary bone-crunching giant. He is far too nice and jumbly, and it's lucky for Sophie that he is. Had she been snitched from her bed by Fleshlumpeater, Bone-cruncher, Childchewer, Gizzardgulper or any of the other giants, she wouldn't have stood a chance, but would have been guzzled like a whiffswhiddle before you could say rack jobinson.

Whisked off to giant land, Sophie is shocked and horrified by the BFG's repulsive neighbours. When she hears that they are flushbunking off to England that very night to swollomp a few nice little English chiddlers, she decides she must put a stop to them at once.

This is a wildly funny, wickedly inventive, golden phizz-wizard of a book and will be enjoyed by children of all ages.

Roald Dahl was born in Wales of Norwegian parents. He spent his childhood in England and was educated at Repton. At eighteen he joined the Shell Oil Company in Africa, and when World War II broke out he joined the RAF and became a fighter pilot, serving in Syria and Greece. In 1942 he went to Washington as Assistant Air Attaché and it was there he started to write short stories. He now lives in Buckinghamshire.

Roald Dahl

THE BFG

Illustrations by Quentin Blake

PUFFIN BOOKS

in association with Jonathan Cape

Puffin Books, Penguin Books Ltd, Harmondsworth, Middlesex, England
Viking Penguin Inc., 40 West 23rd Street, New York, New York 10010, U.S.A.
Penguin Books Australia Ltd, Ringwood, Victoria, Australia
Penguin Books Canada Limited, 2801 John Street, Markham, Ontario, Canada L3R 1B4
Penguin Books (N.Z.) Ltd, 182–190 Wairau Road, Auckland 10, New Zealand

First published by Jonathan Cape Ltd 1982
Published in the U.S.A. by Farrar, Straus and Giroux 1982
Published in Puffin Books 1984
Reprinted 1984 (twice), 1985 (four times), 1986 (five times), 1987

LIBRARY OF CONGRESS CATALOG CARD NUMBER: 85-566

Made and printed in Great Britain by
Richard Clay (The Chaucer Press) Ltd, Bungay, Suffolk
Filmset in Monophoto Baskerville by
Northumberland Press Ltd, Gateshead

For Olivia

20 April 1955–17 November 1962

Contents

The characters in this book are:

HUMANS:

THE QUEEN OF ENGLAND
MARY, the Queen's maid
MR TIBBS, the Palace butler
THE HEAD OF THE ARMY
THE HEAD OF THE AIR FORCE
And, of course, SOPHIE, *an orphan*

GIANTS:

THE FLESHLUMPEATER
THE BONECRUNCHER
THE MANHUGGER
THE CHILDCHEWER
THE MEATDRIPPER
THE GIZZARDGULPER
THE MAIDMASHER
THE BLOODBOTTLER
THE BUTCHER BOY
And, of course, THE BFG

The Witching Hour

Sophie couldn't sleep.

A brilliant moonbeam was slanting through a gap in the curtains. It was shining right on to her pillow.

The other children in the dormitory had been asleep for hours.

Sophie closed her eyes and lay quite still. She tried very hard to doze off.

It was no good. The moonbeam was like a silver blade slicing through the room on to her face.

The house was absolutely silent. No voices came up from downstairs. There were no footsteps on the floor above either.

The window behind the curtain was wide open, but nobody was walking on the pavement outside. No cars went by on the street. Not the tiniest sound could be heard anywhere. Sophie had never known such a silence.

Perhaps, she told herself, this was what they called the witching hour.

The witching hour, somebody had once whispered to her, was a special moment in the middle of the night when every child and every grown-up was in a deep deep sleep, and all the dark things came out from hiding and had the world to themselves.

The moonbeam was brighter than ever on Sophie's pillow. She decided to get out of bed and close the gap in the curtains.

You got punished if you were caught out of bed after lights-out. Even if you said you had to go to the lavatory, that was not accepted as an excuse and they punished you just the same. But there was no one about now, Sophie was sure of that.

She reached out for her glasses that lay on the chair beside her bed. They had steel rims and very thick lenses, and she could hardly see a thing without them. She put them on, then she slipped out of bed and tip-toed over to the window.

When she reached the curtains, Sophie hesitated. She longed to duck underneath them and lean out of the window to see what the world looked like now that the witching hour was at hand.

She listened again. Everywhere it was deathly still.

The longing to look out became so strong she couldn't resist it. Quickly, she ducked under the curtains and leaned out of the window.

In the silvery moonlight, the village street she knew so well seemed completely different. The houses looked bent and crooked, like houses in a fairy tale. Everything was pale and ghostly and milky-white.

Across the road, she could see Mrs Rance's shop, where you bought buttons and wool and bits of elastic. It didn't look real. There was something dim and misty about that too.

Sophie allowed her eye to travel further and further down the street.

Suddenly she froze. *There was something coming up the street on the opposite side.*

It was something black ...

Something tall and black ...

Something very tall and very black and very thin.

Who?

It wasn't a human. It couldn't be. It was four times as tall as the tallest human. It was so tall its head was higher than the upstairs windows of the houses. Sophie opened her mouth to scream, but no sound came out. Her throat, like her whole body, was frozen with fright.

This was the witching hour all right.

The tall black figure was coming her way. It was keeping very close to the houses across the street, hiding in the shadowy places where there was no moonlight.

On and on it came, nearer and nearer. But it was moving in spurts. It would stop, then it would move on, then it would stop again.

But what on earth was it doing?

Ah-ha! Sophie could see now what it was up to. It was stopping in front of each house. It would stop and peer into the upstairs window of each house in the street. It actually had to bend down to peer into the upstairs windows. That's how tall it was.

It would stop and peer in. Then it would slide on to the next house and stop again, and peer in, and so on all along the street.

It was much closer now and Sophie could see it more clearly.

Looking at it carefully, she decided it *had* to be some

kind of PERSON. Obviously it was not a human. But it was definitely a PERSON.

A GIANT PERSON, perhaps.

Sophie stared hard across the misty moonlit street. The Giant (if that was what he was) was wearing a long BLACK CLOAK.

In one hand he was holding what looked like a VERY LONG, THIN TRUMPET.

In the other hand, he held a LARGE SUITCASE.

The Giant had stopped now right in front of Mr and Mrs Goochey's house. The Goocheys had a greengrocer's shop in the middle of the High Street, and the family lived above the shop. The two Goochey children slept in the upstairs front room, Sophie knew that.

The Giant was peering through the window into the room where Michael and Jane Goochey were sleeping. From across the street, Sophie watched and held her breath.

She saw the Giant step back a pace and put the suitcase down on the pavement. He bent over and opened the suitcase. He took something out of it. It looked like a glass jar, one of those square ones with a screw top. He unscrewed the top of the jar and poured what was in it into the end of the long trumpet thing.

Sophie watched, trembling.

She saw the Giant straighten up again and she saw him poke the trumpet in through the open upstairs window of the room where the Goochey children were sleeping. She saw the Giant take a deep breath and *whoof*, he blew through the trumpet.

No noise came out, but it was obvious to Sophie that whatever had been in the jar had now been blown through the trumpet into the Goochey children's bedroom.

What could it be?

As the Giant withdrew the trumpet from the window and bent down to pick up the suitcase he happened to turn his head and glance across the street.

In the moonlight, Sophie caught a glimpse of an enormous long pale wrinkly face with the most enormous ears. The nose was as sharp as a knife, and above the nose there were two bright flashing eyes, and the eyes were staring straight at Sophie. There was a fierce and devilish look about them.

Sophie gave a yelp and pulled back from the window. She flew across the dormitory and jumped into her bed and hid under the blanket.

And there she crouched, still as a mouse, and tingling all over.

The Snatch

Under the blanket, Sophie waited.

After a minute or so, she lifted a corner of the blanket and peeped out.

For the second time that night her blood froze to ice and she wanted to scream, but no sound came out. There at the window, with the curtains pushed aside, was the enormous long pale wrinkly face of the Giant Person, staring in. The flashing black eyes were fixed on Sophie's bed.

The next moment, a huge hand with pale fingers came snaking in through the window. This was followed by an arm, an arm as thick as a tree-trunk, and the arm, the hand, the fingers were reaching out across the room towards Sophie's bed.

This time Sophie really did scream, but only for a second because very quickly the huge hand clamped down over her blanket and the scream was smothered by the bedclothes.

Sophie, crouching underneath the blanket, felt strong fingers grasping hold of her, and then she was lifted up from her bed, blanket and all, and whisked out of the window.

If you can think of anything more terrifying than that happening to you in the middle of the night, then let's hear about it.

The awful thing was that Sophie knew exactly what was going on although she couldn't see it happening. She knew that a Monster (or Giant) with an enormous long pale wrinkly face and dangerous eyes had plucked her from her bed in the middle of the witching hour and was now carrying her out through the window smothered in a blanket.

What actually happened next was this. When the Giant had got Sophie outside, he arranged the blanket so that he could grasp all the four corners of it at once in one of his huge hands, with Sophie imprisoned inside. In the other hand he seized the suitcase and the long trumpet thing and off he ran.

Sophie, by squirming around inside the blanket, managed to push the top of her head out through a little gap just below the Giant's hand. She stared around her.

She saw the village houses rushing by on both sides. The Giant was sprinting down the High Street. He was running so fast his black cloak was streaming out behind

him like the wings of a bird. Each stride he took was as long as a tennis court. Out of the village he ran, and soon they were racing across the moonlit fields. The hedges dividing the fields were no problem to the Giant. He simply strode over them. A wide river appeared in his path. He crossed it in one flying stride.

Sophie crouched in the blanket, peering out. She was being bumped against the Giant's leg like a sack of potatoes. Over the fields and hedges and rivers they went, and after a while a frightening thought came into Sophie's head. *The Giant is running fast,* she told herself, *because he is hungry and he wants to get home as quickly as possible, and then he'll have me for breakfast.*

The Cave

The Giant ran on and on. But now a curious change took place in his way of running. He seemed suddenly to go into a higher gear. Faster and faster he went and soon he was travelling at such a speed that the landscape became blurred. The wind stung Sophie's cheeks. It made her eyes water. It whipped her head back and whistled in her ears. She could no longer feel the Giant's feet touching the ground. She had a weird sensation they were flying. It was impossible to tell whether they were over land or sea. This Giant had some sort of magic in his legs. The wind rushing against Sophie's face became so strong that she had to duck down again into the blanket to prevent her head from being blown away.

Was it really possible that they were crossing oceans? It certainly felt that way to Sophie. She crouched in the blanket and listened to the howling of the wind. It went on for what seemed like hours.

Then all at once the wind stopped its howling. The pace began to slow down. Sophie could feel the Giant's feet pounding once again over the earth. She poked her head up out of the blanket to have a look. They were in a country of thick forests and rushing rivers. The Giant had definitely slowed down and was now running more normally, although normal was a silly word to use to describe a galloping giant. He leaped over a dozen rivers. He went rattling through a great forest, then down into a valley and up over a range of hills as bare as concrete, and soon he was galloping over a desolate wasteland that was not quite of this earth. The ground was flat and pale yellow. Great lumps of blue rock were scattered around, and dead trees stood everywhere like skeletons. The moon had long since disappeared and now the dawn was breaking.

Sophie, still peering out from the blanket, saw suddenly ahead of her a great craggy mountain. The mountain was dark blue and all around it the sky was gushing and glistening with light. Bits of pale gold were flying among delicate frosty-white flakes of cloud, and over to one side the rim of the morning sun was coming up red as blood.

Right beneath the mountain, the Giant stopped. He was puffing mightily. His great chest was heaving in and out. He paused to catch his breath.

Directly in front of them, lying against the side of the mountain, Sophie could see a massive round stone. It was as big as a house. The Giant reached out and rolled the stone to one side as easily as if it had been a football, and now, where the stone had been, there appeared a vast black hole. The hole was so large the Giant didn't even have to duck his head as he went in. He strode into the black hole still carrying Sophie in one hand, the trumpet and the suitcase in the other.

As soon as he was inside, he stopped and turned and rolled the great stone back into place so that the entrance to his secret cave was completely hidden from outside.

Now that the entrance had been sealed up, there was not a glint of light inside the cave. All was black.

Sophie felt herself being lowered to the ground. Then the Giant let go the blanket completely. His footsteps moved away. Sophie sat there in the dark, shivering with fear.

He is getting ready to eat me, she told herself. He will probably eat me raw, just as I am.

Or perhaps he will boil me first.

Or he will have me fried. He will drop me like a rasher of bacon into some gigantic frying-pan sizzling with fat.

A blaze of light suddenly lit up the whole place. Sophie blinked and stared.

She saw an enormous cavern with a high rocky roof.

The walls on either side were lined with shelves, and on the shelves there stood row upon row of glass jars. There were jars everywhere. They were piled up in the corners. They filled every nook and cranny of the cave.

In the middle of the floor there was a table twelve feet high and a chair to match.

The Giant took off his black cloak and hung it against the wall. Sophie saw that under the cloak he was wearing a sort of collarless shirt and a dirty old leather waistcoat that didn't seem to have any buttons. His trousers were faded green and were far too short in the legs. On his bare feet he was wearing a pair of ridiculous sandals that for some reason had holes cut along each side, with a large hole at the end where his toes stuck out. Sophie, crouching on the floor of the cave in her nightie, gazed back at him through thick steel-rimmed glasses. She was trembling like a leaf in the wind, and a finger of ice was running up and down the length of her spine.

'Ha!' shouted the Giant, walking forward and rubbing his hands together. 'What has us got here?' His booming voice rolled around the walls of the cave like a burst of thunder.

The BFG

The Giant picked up the trembling Sophie with one hand
and carried her across the cave and put her on the table.

Now he really is going to eat me, Sophie thought.

The Giant sat down and stared hard at Sophie. He had
truly enormous ears. Each one was as big as the wheel of
a truck and he seemed to be able to move them inwards
and outwards from his head as he wished.

'I is hungry!' the Giant boomed. He grinned, showing
massive square teeth. The teeth were very white and very
square and they sat in his mouth like huge slices of white
bread.

'P . . . please don't eat me,' Sophie stammered.

The Giant let out a bellow of laughter. 'Just because I
is a giant, you think I is a man-gobbling cannybull!' he
shouted. 'You is about right! Giants is all cannybully and
murderful! And they *does* gobble up human beans! We is
in Giant Country now! Giants is everywhere around! Out
there us has the famous Bonecrunching Giant! Bonecrunching Giant crunches up two wopsey whiffling
human beans for supper every night! Noise is earburst-
ing! Noise of crunching bones goes crackety-crack for
miles around!'

'Owch!' Sophie said.

'Bonecrunching Giant only gobbles human beans from

Turkey,' the Giant said. 'Every night Bonecruncher is galloping off to Turkey to gobble Turks.'

Sophie's sense of patriotism was suddenly so bruised by this remark that she became quite angry. 'Why Turks?' she blurted out. 'What's wrong with the English?'

'Bonecrunching Giant says Turks is tasting oh ever so much juicier and more scrumdiddlyumptious! Bone-cruncher says Turkish human beans has a glamourly flavour. He says Turks from Turkey is tasting of turkey.'

'I suppose they would,' Sophie said.

'Of course they would!' the Giant shouted. 'Every human bean is diddly and different. Some is scrum-diddlyumptious and some is uckyslush. Greeks is all full of uckyslush. No giant is eating Greeks, ever.'

'Why not?' Sophie asked.

'Greeks from Greece is all tasting greasy,' the Giant said.

'I imagine that's possible too,' Sophie said. She was wondering with a bit of a tremble what all this talking about eating people was leading up to. Whatever happened, she simply *must* play along with this peculiar giant and smile at his jokes.

But were they jokes? Perhaps the great brute was just working up an appetite by talking about food.

'As I am saying,' the Giant went on, 'all human beans is having different flavours. Human beans from Panama is tasting very strong of hats.'

'Why hats?' Sophie said.

'You is not very clever,' the Giant said, moving his great ears in and out. 'I thought all human beans is full of brains, but your head is emptier than a bundongle.'

'Do you like vegetables?' Sophie asked, hoping to steer

26

the conversation towards a slightly less dangerous kind of food.

'You is trying to change the subject,' the Giant said sternly. 'We is having an interesting babblement about the taste of the human bean. The human bean is not a vegetable.'

'Oh, but the bean *is* a vegetable,' Sophie said.

'Not the *human* bean,' the Giant said. 'The human bean has two legs and a vegetable has no legs at all.'

Sophie didn't argue any more. The last thing she wanted to do was to make the Giant cross.

'The human bean,' the Giant went on, 'is coming in dillions of different flavours. For instance, human beans from Wales is tasting very whooshey of fish. There is something very fishy about Wales.'

'You means *whales*,' Sophie said. 'Wales is something quite different.'

'Wales is whales,' the Giant said. 'Don't gobblefunk around with words. I will now give you another example. Human beans from Jersey has a most disgustable woolly tickle on the tongue,' the Giant said. 'Human beans from Jersey is tasting of cardigans.'

'You mean jerseys,' Sophie said.

'You are once again gobblefunking!' the Giant shouted. 'Don't do it! This is a serious and snitching subject. May I continue?'

'Please do,' Sophie said.

'Danes from Denmark is tasting ever so much of dogs,' the Giant went on.

'Of course,' Sophie said. 'They taste of great danes.'

'Wrong!' cried the Giant, slapping his thigh. 'Danes

from Denmark is tasting doggy because they is tasting of *labradors!*'

'Then what do the people of Labrador taste of?' Sophie asked.

'Danes,' the Giant cried, triumphantly. 'Great danes!'

'Aren't you getting a bit mixed up?' Sophie said.

'I is a very mixed up Giant,' the Giant said. 'But I does do my best. And I is not nearly as mixed up as the other giants. I know one who gallops all the way to Wellington for his supper.'

'Wellington?' Sophie said. 'Where is Wellington?'

'Your head is full of squashed flies,' the Giant said. 'Wellington is in New Zealand. The human beans in Wellington has an especially scrumdiddlyumptious taste, so says the Welly-eating Giant.'

'What do the people of Wellington taste of?' Sophie asked.

'Boots,' the Giant said.

'Of course,' Sophie said. 'I should have known.'

Sophie decided that this conversation had now gone on long enough. If she was going to be eaten, she'd rather get it over and done with right away than be kept hanging around any more. 'What sort of human beings do *you* eat?' she asked, trembling.

'*Me!*' shouted the Giant, his mighty voice making the glass jars rattle on their shelves. 'Me gobbling up human beans! This I never! The others, yes! All the others is gobbling them up every night, but not me! I is a freaky Giant! I is a nice and jumbly Giant! I is the only nice and jumbly Giant in Giant Country! I is THE BIG FRIENDLY GIANT! I is the BFG. What is *your* name?'

'My name is Sophie,' Sophie said, hardly daring to believe the good news she had just heard.

The Giants

'But if you are so nice and friendly,' Sophie said, 'then why did you snatch me from my bed and run away with me?'

'Because you saw me,' the Big Friendly Giant answered. 'If anyone is ever seeing a giant, he or she must be taken away hipswitch.'

'Why?' asked Sophie.

'Well, first of all,' said the BFG, 'human beans is not really *believing* in giants, is they? Human beans is not *thinking* we exist.'

'I do,' Sophie said.

'Ah, but that is only because you has seen me!' cried the BFG. 'I cannot possibly allow *anyone*, even little girls, to be seeing me and staying at home. The first thing you would be doing, you would be scuddling around yodelling the news that you were actually seeing a giant, and then a great giant-hunt, a mighty giant look-see, would be starting up all over the world, with the human beans all rummaging for the great giant you saw and getting wildly excited. People would be coming rushing and bushing after me with goodness knows what and they would be catching me and locking me into a cage to be stared at. They would be putting me into the zoo or the bunkumhouse with all those squiggling hippodumplings and crocadowndillies.'

Sophie knew that what the Giant said was true. If any person reported actually having seen a giant haunting the streets of a town at night, there would most certainly be a terrific hullabaloo across the world.

'I will bet you,' the BFG went on, 'that *you* would have been splashing the news all over the wonky world, wouldn't you, if I hadn't wiggled you away?'

'I suppose I would,' Sophie said.

'And that would never do,' said the BFG.

'So what will happen to me now?' Sophie asked.

'If you do go back, you will be telling the world,' said the BFG, 'most likely on the telly telly bunkum box and the radio squeaker. So you will just have to be staying here with me for the rest of your life.'

'Oh no!' cried Sophie.

'Oh yes!' said the BFG. 'But I am warning you not

ever to go whiffling about out of this cave without I is with you or you will be coming to an ucky-mucky end! I is showing you now who is going to eat you up if they is ever catching even one tiny little glimp of you.'

The Big Friendly Giant picked Sophie off the table and carried her to the cave entrance. He rolled the huge stone to one side and said, 'Peep out over there, little girl, and tell me what you is seeing.'

Sophie, sitting on the BFG's hand, peeped out of the cave.

The sun was up now and shining fiery-hot over the great yellow wasteland with its blue rocks and dead trees.

'Is you seeing them?' the BFG asked.

Sophie, squinting through the glare of the sun, saw several tremendous tall figures moving among the rocks about five hundred yards away. Three or four others were sitting quite motionless on the rocks themselves.

'This is Giant Country,' the BFG said. 'Those is all giants, every one.'

It was a brain-boggling sight. The giants were all naked except for a sort of short skirt around their waists, and their skins were burnt brown by the sun. But it was the sheer size of each one of them that boggled Sophie's brain most of all. They were simply colossal, far taller and wider than the Big Friendly Giant upon whose hand she was now sitting. And oh how ugly they were! Many of them had large bellies. All of them had long arms and big feet. They were too far away for their faces to be seen clearly, and perhaps that was a good thing.

'What on earth are they doing?' Sophie asked.

'Nothing,' said the BFG. 'They is just moocheling and footcheling around and waiting for the night to come. Then they will all be galloping off to places where *people* is living to find their suppers.'

'You mean to Turkey,' Sophie said.

'Bonecrunching Giant will be galloping to Turkey, of course,' said the BFG. 'But the others will be whiffling off to all sorts of flungaway places like Wellington for the booty flavour and Panama for the hatty taste. Every giant is having his own favourite hunting ground.'

'Do they ever go to England?' Sophie asked.

'Often,' said the BFG. 'They say the English is tasting ever so wonderfully of crodscollop.'

'I'm not sure I quite know what that means,' Sophie said.

'Meanings is not important,' said the BFG. 'I cannot be right all the time. Quite often I is left instead of right.'

'And are all those beastly giants over there really going off again tonight to eat people?' Sophie asked.

'All of them is guzzling human beans every night,' the BFG answered. 'All of them excepting me. That is why you will be coming to an ucky-mucky end if any of them should ever be getting his gogglers upon you. You would be swalloped up like a piece of frumpkin pie, all in one dollop!'

'But eating people is horrible!' Sophie cried. 'It's frightful! Why doesn't someone stop them?'

'And who please is going to be stopping them?' asked the BFG.

'Couldn't you?' said Sophie.

'Never in a pig's whistle!' cried the BFG. 'All of those

man-eating giants is enormous and very fierce! They is all at least two times my wideness and double my royal highness!'

'Twice as high as you!' cried Sophie.

'Easily that,' said the BFG. 'You is seeing them in the distance but just wait till you get them close up. Those giants is all at least fifty feet tall with huge muscles and cockles alive alive-o. I is the titchy one. I is the runt. Twenty-four feet is puddlenuts in Giant Country.'

'You mustn't feel bad about it,' Sophie said. 'I think you are just great. Why even your toes must be as big as sausages.'

'Bigger,' said the BFG, looking pleased. 'They is as big as bumplehammers.'

'How many giants are there out there?' Sophie asked.

'Nine altogether,' answered the BFG.

'That means,' said Sophie, 'that somewhere in the world, every single night, nine wretched people get carried away and eaten alive.'

'More,' said the BFG. 'It is all depending, you see, on how big the human beans is. Japanese beans is very small, so a giant will need to gobble up about six Japanese before he is feeling full up. Others like the Norway people and the Yankee-Doodles is ever so much bigger and usually two or three of those makes a good tuck-in.'

'But do these disgusting giants go to every single country in the world?' Sophie asked.

'All countries excepting Greece is getting visited some time or another,' the BFG answered. 'The country which a giant visits is depending on how he is feeling. If it is very warm weather and a giant is feeling as hot as a sizzlepan, he will probably go galloping far up to the frisby north to get himself an Esquimo or two to cool him down. A nice fat Esquimo to a giant is like a lovely ice-cream lolly to you.'

'I'll take your word for it,' Sophie said.

'And then again, if it is a frotsy night and the giant is fridging with cold, he will probably point his nose towards the swultering hotlands to guzzle a few Hotten-tots to warm him up.'

'How perfectly horrible,' Sophie said.

'Nothing hots a cold giant up like a hot Hottentot,' the BFG said.

'And if you were to put me down on the ground and I was to walk out among them now,' Sophie said, 'would they really eat me up?'

'Like a whiffswiddle!' cried the BFG. 'And what is more, you is so small they wouldn't even have to chew you. The first one to be seeing you would pick you up in his fingers and down you'd go like a drop of drain-water!'

'Let's go back inside,' Sophie said. 'I hate even watching them.'

The Marvellous Ears

Back in the cave, the Big Friendly Giant sat Sophie down once again on the enormous table. 'Is you quite snuggly there in your nightie?' he asked. 'You isn't fridgy cold?'

'I'm fine,' Sophie said.

'I cannot help thinking,' said the BFG, 'about your poor mother and father. By now they must be jipping and skumping all over the house shouting "Hello hello where is Sophie gone?"'

'I don't have a mother and father,' Sophie said. 'They both died when I was a baby.'

'Oh, you poor little scrumplet!' cried the BFG. 'Is you not missing them very badly?'

'Not really,' Sophie said, 'because I never knew them.'

'You is making me sad,' the BFG said, rubbing his eyes.

'Don't be sad,' Sophie said. 'No one is going to be worrying too much about me. That place you took me from was the village orphanage. We are all orphans in there.'

'You is a norphan?'

'Yes.'

'How many is there in there?'

'Ten of us,' Sophie said. 'All little girls.'

'Was you happy there?' the BFG asked.

'I hated it,' Sophie said. 'The woman who ran it was

called Mrs Clonkers and if she caught you breaking any of the rules, like getting out of bed at night or not folding up your clothes, you got punished.'

'How is you getting punished?'

'She locked us in the dark cellar for a day and a night without anything to eat or drink.'

'The rotten old rotrasper!' cried the BFG.

'It was horrid,' Sophie said. 'We used to dread it. There were rats down there. We could hear them creeping about.'

'The filthy old fizzwiggler!' shouted the BFG. 'That is the horridest thing I is hearing for years! You is making me sadder than ever!' All at once, a huge tear that would have filled a bucket rolled down one of the BFG's cheeks and fell with a splash on the floor. It made quite a puddle.

Sophie watched with astonishment. What a strange and moody creature this is, she thought. One moment he is telling me my head is full of squashed flies and the next moment his heart is melting for me because Mrs Clonkers locks us in the cellar.

'The thing that worries *me*,' Sophie said, 'is having to stay in this dreadful place for the rest of my life. The orphanage was pretty awful, but I wouldn't have been there for ever, would I?'

'All is my fault,' the BFG said. 'I is the one who kidsnatched you.' Yet another enormous tear welled from his eye and splashed on to the floor.

'Now I come to think of it, I won't actually be here all that long,' Sophie said.

'I is afraid you will,' the BFG said.

'No, I won't,' Sophie said. 'Those brutes out there are bound to catch me sooner or later and have me for tea.'

'I is *never* letting that happen,' the BFG said.

For a few moments the cave was silent. Then Sophie said, 'May I ask you a question?'

The BFG wiped the tears from his eyes with the back of his hand and gave Sophie a long thoughtful stare. 'Shoot away,' he said.

'Would you please tell me what you were doing in our village last night? Why were you poking that long trumpet thing into the Goochey children's bedroom and then blowing through it?'

'Ah-ha!' cried the BFG, sitting up suddenly in his chair. 'Now we is getting nosier than a parker!'

'And the suitcase you were carrying,' Sophie said. 'What on earth was *that* all about?'

The BFG stared suspiciously at the small girl sitting cross-legged on the table.

'You is asking me to tell you whoppsy big secrets,' he said. 'Secrets that nobody is ever hearing before.'

'I won't tell a soul,' Sophie said. 'I swear it. How could I anyway? I am stuck here for the rest of my life.'

'You could be telling the other giants.'

'No, I couldn't,' Sophie said. 'You told me they would eat me up the moment they saw me.'

'And so they would,' said the BFG. 'You is a human bean and human beans is like strawbunkles and cream to those giants.'

'If they are going to eat me the moment they see me, then I wouldn't have time to tell them anything, would I?' Sophie said.

'You wouldn't,' said the BFG.

'Then why did you say I might?'

'Because I is brimful of buzzburgers,' the BFG said.

'If you listen to everything I am saying you will be getting earache.'

'Please tell me what you were doing in our village,' Sophie said. 'I promise you can trust me.'

'Would you teach me how to make an elefunt?' the BFG asked.

'What *do* you mean?' Sophie said.

'I would dearly love to have an elefunt to ride on,' the BFG said dreamily. 'I would so much love to have a jumbly big elefunt and go riding through green forests picking peachy fruits off the trees all day long. This is a sizzling-hot muckfrumping country we is living in. Nothing grows in it except snozzcumbers. I would love to go somewhere else and pick peachy fruits in the early morning from the back of an elefunt.'

Sophie was quite moved by this curious statement.

'Perhaps one day we will get you an elephant,' she said. 'And peachy fruits as well. Now tell me what you were doing in our village.'

'If you is really wanting to know what I am doing in your village,' the BFG said, 'I is blowing a dream into the bedroom of those children.'

'*Blowing a dream?*' Sophie said. 'What *do* you mean?'

'I is a dream-blowing giant,' the BFG said. 'When all the other giants is galloping off every what way and which to swollop human beans, I is scuddling away to other places to blow dreams into the bedrooms of sleeping children. Nice dreams. Lovely golden dreams. Dreams that is giving the dreamers a happy time.'

'Now hang on a minute,' Sophie said. 'Where do you get these dreams?'

'I collect them,' the BFG said, waving an arm towards

41

all the rows and rows of bottles on the shelves. 'I has billions of them.'

'You can't *collect* a dream,' Sophie said. 'A dream isn't something you can catch hold of.'

'You is never going to understand about it,' the BFG said. 'That is why I is not wishing to tell you.'

'Oh, please tell me!' Sophie said. 'I *will* understand! Go on! Tell me how you collect dreams! Tell me everything!'

The BFG settled himself comfortably in his chair and crossed his legs. 'Dreams,' he said, 'is very mysterious things. They is floating around in the air like little wispy-misty bubbles. And all the time they is searching for sleeping people.'

'Can you see them?' Sophie asked.

'Never at first.'

'Then how do you catch them if you can't see them?' Sophie asked.

'Ah-ha,' said the BFG. 'Now we is getting on to the dark and dusky secrets.'

'I won't tell a soul.'

'I is trusting you,' the BFG said. He closed his eyes and sat quite still for a moment, while Sophie waited.

'A dream,' he said, 'as it goes whiffling through the night air, is making a tiny little buzzing-humming noise. But this little buzzy-hum is so silvery soft, it is impossible for a human bean to be hearing it.'

'Can *you* hear it?' Sophie asked.

The BFG pointed up at his enormous truck-wheel ears which he now began to move in and out He performed this exercise proudly, with a little proud smile on his face. 'Is you seeing these?' he asked.

'How could I miss them?' Sophie said.

'They maybe is looking a bit propsposterous to you,'
the BFG said, 'but you must believe me when I say they
is very extra-usual ears indeed. They is not to be coughed
at.'

'I'm quite sure they're not,' Sophie said.

'They is allowing me to hear absolutely every single
twiddly little thing.'

'You mean you can hear things I can't hear?' Sophie
said.

'You is *deaf as a dumpling* compared with me!' cried the
BFG. 'You is hearing only thumping loud noises with
those little earwigs of yours. But I am hearing *all the secret
whisperings of the world!*'

'Such as what?' Sophie asked.

'In your country,' he said, 'I is hearing the footsteps of a ladybird as she goes walking across a leaf.'

'*Honestly?*' Sophie said, beginning to be impressed.

'What's more, I is hearing those footsteps *very loud*,' the BFG said. 'When a ladybird is walking across a leaf, I is hearing her feet going *clumpety-clumpety-clump* like giants' footsteps.'

'Good gracious me!' Sophie said. 'What else can you hear?'

'I is hearing the little ants chittering to each other as they scuddle around in the soil.'

'You mean you can hear ants talking?'

'Every single word,' the BFG said. 'Although I is not exactly understanding their langwitch.'

'Go on,' Sophie said.

'Sometimes, on a very clear night,' the BFG said, 'and if I is swiggling my ears in the right direction,' – and here he swivelled his great ears upwards so they were facing the ceiling – 'if I is swiggling them like this and the night is very clear, I is sometimes hearing faraway music coming from the stars in the sky.'

A queer little shiver passed through Sophie's body. She sat very quiet, waiting for more.

'My ears is what told me you was watching me out of your window last night,' the BFG said.

'But I didn't make a sound,' Sophie said.

'I was hearing your heart beating across the road,' the BFG said. 'Loud as a drum.'

'Go on,' Sophie said. 'Please.'

'I can hear plants and trees.'

'Do *they* talk?' Sophie asked.

'They is not exactly talking,' the BFG said. 'But they

is making noises. For instance, if I come along and I is picking a lovely flower, if I is twisting the stem of the flower till it breaks, then the plant is screaming. I can hear it screaming and screaming very clear.'

'You don't mean it!' Sophie cried. 'How awful!'

'It is screaming just like you would be screaming if someone was twisting *your* arm right off.'

'Is that really true?' Sophie asked.

'You think I is swizzfiggling you?'

'It *is* rather hard to believe.'

'Then I is stopping right here,' said the BFG sharply. 'I is not wishing to be called a fibster.'

'Oh no! I'm not calling you anything!' Sophie cried. 'I believe you! I do really! Please go on!'

The BFG gave her a long hard stare. Sophie looked right back at him, her face open to his. 'I believe you,' she said softly.

She had offended him, she could see that.

'I wouldn't ever be fibbling to you,' he said.

'I know you wouldn't,' Sophie said. 'But you must understand that it isn't easy to believe such amazing things straightaway.'

'I understand that,' the BFG said.

'So do please forgive me and go on,' she said.

He waited a while longer, and then he said, 'It is the same with trees as it is with flowers. If I is chopping an axe into the trunk of a big tree, I is hearing a terrible sound coming from inside the heart of the tree.'

'What sort of sound?' Sophie asked.

'A soft moaning sound,' the BFG said. 'It is like the sound an old man is making when he is dying slowly.'

He paused. The cave was very silent.

45

'Trees is living and growing just like you and me,' he said. 'They is alive. So is plants.'

He was sitting very straight in his chair now, his hands clasped tightly together in front of him. His face was bright, his eyes round and bright as two stars.

'Such wonderful and terrible sounds I is hearing!' he said. 'Some of them you would never wish to be hearing yourself! But some is like glorious music!'

He seemed almost to be transfigured by the excitement of his thoughts. His face was beautiful in its blaze of emotions.

'Tell me some more about them,' Sophie said quietly.

'You just ought to be hearing the little micies talking!' he said. 'Little micies is always talking to each other and I is hearing them as loud as my own voice.'

'What do they say?' Sophie asked.

'Only the micies know that,' he said. 'Spiders is also talking a great deal. You might not be thinking it but spiders is the most tremendous natterboxes. And when they is spinning their webs, they is singing all the time. They is singing sweeter than a nightingull.'

'Who else do you hear?' Sophie asked.

'One of the biggest chatbags is the cattlepiddlers,' the BFG said.

'What do they say?'

'They is argying all the time about who is going to be the prettiest butteryfly. That is all they is ever talking about.'

'Is there a dream floating around in here now?' Sophie asked.

The BFG moved his great ears this way and that, listening intently. He shook his head. 'There is no dream in here,' he said, 'except in the bottles. I has a special place to go for catching dreams. They is not often coming to Giant Country.'

'How do you catch them?'

'The same way you is catching butteryflies,' the BFG answered. 'With a net.' He stood up and crossed over to a corner of the cave where a pole was leaning against the wall. The pole was about thirty feet long and there was a net on the end of it. 'Here is the dream-catcher,' he said, grasping the pole in one hand. 'Every morning I is going out and snitching new dreams to put in my bottles.'

Suddenly, he seemed to lose interest in the conversation. 'I is getting hungry,' he said. 'It is time for eats.'

Snozzcumbers

'But if you don't eat people like all the others,' Sophie said, 'then what *do* you live on?'

'That is a squelching tricky problem around here,' the BFG answered. 'In this sloshflunking Giant Country, happy eats like pineapples and pigwinkles is simply not growing. Nothing is growing except for one extremely icky-poo vegetable. It is called the snozzcumber.'

'The snozzcumber!' cried Sophie. 'There's no such thing.'

The BFG looked at Sophie and smiled, showing about twenty of his square white teeth. 'Yesterday,' he said, 'we was not believing in giants, was we? Today we is not believing in snozzcumbers. Just because we happen not to have actually *seen* something with our own two little winkles, we think it is not existing. What about for instance the great squizzly scotch-hopper?'

'I beg your pardon?' Sophie said.

'And the humplecrimp?'

'What's that?' Sophie said.

'And the wraprascal?'

'The what?' Sophie said.

'And the crumpscoddle?'

'Are they animals?' Sophie asked.

'They is *common* animals,' said the BFG contemptuously. 'I is not a very know-all giant myself, but it seems to me that you is an absolutely know-nothing human bean. Your brain is full of rotten-wool.'

'You mean cotton-wool,' Sophie said.

'What I mean and what I say is two different things,' the BFG announced rather grandly. 'I will now show you a snozzcumber.'

The BFG flung open a massive cupboard and took out the weirdest-looking thing Sophie had ever seen. It was about half as long again as an ordinary man but was much thicker. It was as thick around its girth as a perambulator. It was black with white stripes along its length. And it was covered all over with coarse knobbles.

'Here is the repulsant snozzcumber!' cried the BFG, waving it about. 'I squoggle it! I mispise it! I dispunge it! But because I is refusing to gobble up human beans like the other giants, I must spend my life guzzling up icky-poo snozzcumbers instead. If I don't, I will be nothing but skin and groans.'

'You mean skin and *bones*,' Sophie said.

'I *know* it is bones,' the BFG said. 'But please under-stand that I cannot be helping it if I sometimes is saying things a little squiggly. I is trying my very best all the time.' The Big Friendly Giant looked suddenly so forlorn that Sophie got quite upset.

'I'm sorry,' she said. 'I didn't mean to be rude.'

'There never was any schools to teach me talking in Giant Country,' the BFG said sadly.

'But couldn't your mother have taught you?' Sophie asked.

'My *mother!*' cried the BFG. 'Giants don't have mothers! Surely you is knowing *that*.'

'I did *not* know that,' Sophie said.

'Whoever heard of a *woman* giant!' shouted the BFG, waving the snozzcumber around his head like a lasso. 'There never was a woman giant! And there never will be one. Giants is always men!'

Sophie felt herself getting a little muddled. 'In that case,' she said, 'how were you born?'

'Giants isn't born,' the BFG answered. 'Giants *appears* and that's all there is to it. They simply *appears*, the same way as the sun and the stars.'

'And when did you appear?' Sophie asked.

'Now how on earth could I be knowing a thing like that?' said the BFG. 'It was so long ago I couldn't count.'

'You mean you don't even know how *old* you are?'

'No giant is knowing that,' the BFG said. 'All I is knowing about myself is that I is very old, very very old and crumply. Perhaps as old as the earth.'

'What happens when a giant dies?' Sophie asked.

'Giants is never dying,' the BFG answered. 'Sometimes and quite suddenly, a giant is disappearing and nobody is ever knowing where he goes to. But mostly us giants is simply going on and on like whiffsy time-twiddlers.'

The BFG was still holding the awesome snozzcumber in his right hand, and now he put one end into his mouth and bit off a huge hunk of it. He started crunching it up and the noise he made was like the crunching of lumps of ice.

'It's filthing!' he spluttered, speaking with his mouth full and spraying large pieces of snozzcumber like bullets in Sophie's direction. Sophie hopped around on the table-top, ducking out of the way.

'It's disgusterous!' the BFG gurgled. 'It's sickable! It's rotsome! It's maggotwise! Try it yourself, this foulsome snozzcumber!'

'No, thank you,' Sophie said, backing away.

'It's all you're going to be guzzling around here from now on so you might as well get used to it,' said the BFG. 'Go on, you snipsy little winkle, have a go!'

Sophie took a small nibble. 'Ugggggggggh!' she spluttered. 'Oh no! Oh gosh! Oh help!' She spat it out quickly. 'It tastes of frogskins!' she gasped. 'And rotten fish!'

'Worse than that!' cried the BFG, roaring with laughter. 'To me it is tasting of clockcoaches and slime-wanglers!'

51

'Do we really have to eat it?' Sophie said.

'You do unless you is wanting to become so thin you will be disappearing into a thick ear.'

'Into *thin air*,' Sophie said. 'A thick ear is something quite different.'

Once again that sad winsome look came into the

BFG's eyes. 'Words,' he said, 'is oh such a twitch-tickling problem to me all my life. So you must simply try to be patient and stop squibbling. As I am telling you before, I know exactly what words I am wanting to say, but somehow or other they is always getting squiff-squiddled around.'

'That happens to everyone,' Sophie said.

'Not like it happens to me,' the BFG said. 'I is speaking the most terrible wigglish.'

'I think you speak beautifully,' Sophie said.

'You do?' cried the BFG, suddenly brightening. 'You really do?'

'Simply beautifully,' Sophie repeated.

'Well, that is the nicest present anybody is ever giving me in my whole life!' cried the BFG. 'Are you sure you is not twiddling my leg?'

'Of course not,' Sophie said. 'I just love the way you talk.'

'How wondercrump!' cried the BFG, still beaming. 'How whoopsey-splunkers! How absolutely squiffling! I is all of a stutter.'

'Listen,' Sophie said. 'We don't *have* to eat snozzcumbers. In the fields around our village there are all sorts of lovely vegetables like cauliflowers and carrots. Why don't you get some of those next time you go visiting?'

The BFG raised his great head proudly in the air. 'I is a very honourable giant,' he said. 'I would rather be chewing up rotsome snozzcumbers than snitching things from other people.'

'You stole *me*,' Sophie said.

'I did not steal you very much,' said the BFG, smiling gently. 'After all, you is only a tiny little girl.'

The Bloodbottler

Suddenly, a tremendous thumping noise came from outside the cave entrance and a voice like thunder shouted, 'Runt! Is you there, Runt? I is hearing you jabbeling! Who is you jabbeling to, Runt?'

'Look out!' cried the BFG. 'It's the Bloodbottler!' But before he had finished speaking, the stone was rolled aside and a fifty-foot giant, more than twice as tall and wide as the BFG, came striding into the cave. He was naked except for a dirty little piece of cloth around his bottom.

Sophie was on the table-top. The enormous partly eaten snozzcumber was lying near her. She ducked behind it.

The creature came clumping into the cave and stood towering over the BFG. 'Who was you jabbeling to in here just now?' he boomed.

'I is jabbeling to myself,' the BFG answered.

'Pilfflefizz!' shouted the Bloodbottler. 'Bugswallop!' he boomed. 'You is talking to a human bean, that's what I is thinking!'

'No no!' cried the BFG.

'Yus yus!' boomed the Bloodbottler. 'I is guessing you has snitched away a human bean and brought it back to your bunghole as a pet! So now I is winkling it out and guzzling it as extra snacks before my supper!'

The poor BFG was very nervous. 'There's n-no one in here,' he stammered. 'W-why don't you l-leave me alone?'

The Bloodbottler pointed a finger as large as a tree-trunk at the BFG. 'Runty little scumscrewer!' he shouted. 'Piffling little swishfiggler! Squimpy little bottle-wart! Prunty little pogswizzler! I is now going to search the primroses!' He grabbed the BFG by the arm. 'And you is going to help me do it. Us together is going to winkle out this tasteful little human bean!' he shouted.

The BFG had intended to whisk Sophie off the table as soon as he got the chance and hide her behind his back, but now there was no hope of doing this. Sophie peered around the chewed-off end of the enormous snozz-cumber, watching the two giants as they moved away down the cave. The Bloodbottler was a gruesome sight. His skin was reddish-brown. There was black hair sprouting on his chest and arms and on his stomach. The hair on his head was long and dark and tangled. His foul face was round and squashy-looking. The eyes were tiny black holes. The nose was small and flat. But the mouth was huge. It spread right across the face almost ear to ear, and it had lips that were like two gigantic purple frank-furters lying one on top of the other. Craggy yellow teeth stuck out between the two purple frankfurter lips, and rivers of spit ran down over the chin.

It was not in the least difficult to believe that this ghastly brute ate men, women and children every night.

The Bloodbottler, still holding the BFG by the arm, was examining the rows and rows of bottles. 'You and your pibbling bottles!' he shouted. 'What is you putting in them?'

'Nothing that would interest you,' the BFG answered.

'You is only interested in guzzling human beans.'

'And you is dotty as a dogswoggler!' cried the Blood-bottler.

Soon the Bloodbottler would be coming back, Sophie told herself, and he was bound to search the table-top. But she couldn't possibly jump off the table. It was twelve feet high. She'd break a leg. The snozzcumber, although it was as thick as a perambulator, was not going to hide her if the Bloodbottler picked it up. She examined the chewed-off end. It had large seeds in the middle, each one as big as a melon. They were embedded in soft slimy stuff. Taking care to stay out of sight, Sophie reached forward and scooped away half a dozen of these seeds. This left a hole in the middle of the snozzcumber large enough for her to crouch in so long as she rolled herself up into a ball. She crawled into it. It was a wet and slimy hiding-place, but what did that matter if it was going to save her from being eaten.

The Bloodbottler and the BFG were coming back towards the table now. The BFG was nearly fainting with fear. Any moment, he was telling himself, Sophie would be discovered and eaten.

Suddenly, the Bloodbottler grabbed the half-eaten snozzcumber. The BFG stared at the bare table. Sophie, where is you? he thought desperately. You cannot possibly be jumpelling off that high table, so where is you hiding, Sophie?

'So this is the filthing rotsome glubbage you is eating!' boomed the Bloodbottler, holding up the partly eaten snozzcumber. 'You must be cockles to be guzzling such rubbsquash!'

For a moment, the Bloodbottler seemed to have forgotten about his search for Sophie. The BFG decided to lead him further off the track. 'That is the scrumdiddly-umptious snozzcumber,' he said. 'I is guzzling it gleefully every night and day. Is you never trying a snozzcumber, Bloodbottler?'

'Human beans is juicier,' the Bloodbottler said.

'You is talking rommytot,' the BFG said, growing braver by the second. He was thinking that if only he could get the Bloodbottler to take one bite of the repulsive vegetable, the sheer foulness of its flavour would send him bellowing out of the cave. 'I is happy to let you sample it,' the BFG went on. 'But please, when you see how truly glumptious it is, do not be guzzling the whole thing. Leave me a little snitchet for my supper.'

The Bloodbottler stared suspiciously with small piggy eyes at the snozzcumber.

Sophie, crouching inside the chewed-off end, began to tremble all over.

'You is not switchfiddling me, is you?' said the Blood-bottler.

'Never!' cried the BFG passionately. 'Take a bite and I am positive you will be shouting out oh how scrum-diddlyumptious this wonderveg is!'

The BFG could see the greedy Bloodbottler's mouth beginning to water more than ever at the prospect of extra food. 'Vegitibbles is very good for you,' he went on. 'It is not healthsome always to be eating meaty things.'

'Just this once,' the Bloodbottler said, 'I is going to taste these rotsome eats of yours. But I is warning you that if it is filthsome, I is smashing it over your sludgy little head!'

He picked up the snozzcumber.

He began raising it on its long journey to his mouth, some fifty feet up in the air.

Sophie wanted to scream *Don't!* But that would have been an even more certain death. Crouching among the slimy seeds, she felt herself being lifted up and up and up.

Suddenly, there was a *crunch* as the Bloodbottler bit a huge hunk off the end. Sophie saw his yellow teeth clamping together, a few inches from her head. Then there was utter darkness. She was in his mouth. She caught a whiff of his evil-smelling breath. It stank of bad meat. She waited for the teeth to go *crunch* once more. She prayed that she would be killed quickly.

'*Eeeeeowtch!*' roared the Bloodbottler. 'Ughbwelch! Ieeeech!' And then he spat.

All of the great lumps of snozzcumber that were in his mouth, as well as Sophie herself, went shooting out across the cave.

If Sophie had struck the stony wall of the cave, she would most certainly have been killed. Instead, she hit the soft folds of the BFG's black cloak hanging against the wall. She dropped to the ground, half-stunned. She crawled under the hem of the cloak and there she crouched.

'You little swinebuggler!' roared the Bloodbottler. 'You little pigswiller!' He rushed at the BFG and smashed what was left of the snozzcumber over his head. Fragments of the filthy vegetable splashed all over the cave.

'You is not loving it?' the BFG asked innocently, rubbing his head.

'Loving it!' yelled the Bloodbottler. 'That is the most disgusterous taste that is ever touching my teeth! You must be buggles to be swalloping slutch like that! Every night you could be galloping off happy as a hamburger and gobbling juicy human beans!'

'Eating human beans is wrong and evil,' the BFG said.

'It is guzzly and glumptious!' shouted the Blood-bottler. 'And tonight I is galloping off to Chile to swobble a few human Chile beans. Is you wishing to know why I is choosing Chile?'

'I is not wishing to know anything,' the BFG said, very dignified.

'I is choosing Chile,' the Bloodbottler said, 'because I is fed up with the taste of Esquimos. It is important I has plenty of cold eats in this scuddling hot weather, and the next coldest thing to an Esquimo is a Chile bean. Human beans from Chile is very chilly.'

'Horrible,' the BFG said. 'You ought to be ashamed.'

'Other giants is all saying they is wanting to gallop off to England tonight to guzzle school-chiddlers,' the

Bloodbottler said. 'I is very fond indeed of English school-chiddlers. They has a nice inky-booky flavour. Perhaps I will change my mind and go to England with them.'

'You is disgusting,' the BFG said.

'And you is an insult to the giant peoples!' shouted the Bloodbottler. 'You is not fit to be a giant! You is a squinky little squiddler! You is a pibbling little pitsqueak! You is a ... cream puffnut!'

With that, the horrible Bloodbottling Giant strode out of the cave. The BFG ran to the cave entrance and quickly rolled the stone back into place.

'Sophie,' he whispered. 'Sophie, where is you, Sophie?'

Sophie emerged from under the hem of the black cloak. 'I'm here,' she said.

The BFG picked her up and held her tenderly in the palm of his hand. 'Oh, I is so happy to be finding you all in one lump!' he said.

'I was in his mouth,' Sophie said.

'You was *what!*' cried the BFG.

Sophie told him what had happened.

'And there I was telling him to eat the filthsome snozz-cumber and you was all the time inside it!' the BFG cried.

'Not much fun,' Sophie said.

'Just look at you, you poor little chiddler!' cried the BFG. 'You is all covered in snozzcumber and giant spit.' He set about cleaning her up as best he could. 'I is hating those other giants more than ever now,' he said. 'You know what I should like?'

'What?' Sophie said.

'I should like to find a way of disappearing them, every single one.'

'I'd be glad to help you,' Sophie said. 'Let me see if I can't think up a way of doing it.'

Frobscottle and Whizzpoppers

By now Sophie was beginning to feel not only extremely hungry, but very thirsty as well. Had she been at home she would have finished her breakfast long ago.

'Are you sure there's nothing else to eat around here except those disgusting smelly snozzcumbers?' she asked.

'Not even a fizzwinkel,' answered the Big Friendly Giant.

'In that case, may I please have a little water?' she said.

'Water?' said the BFG, frowning mightily. 'What is water?'

'We drink it,' Sophie said. 'What do you drink?'

'Frobscottle,' announced the BFG. 'All giants is drinking frobscottle.'

'Is it as nasty as your snozzcumbers?' Sophie asked.

'Nasty!' cried the BFG. 'Never is it nasty! Frobscottle is sweet and jumbly!' He got up from his chair and went to a second huge cupboard. He opened it and took out a glass bottle that must have been six feet tall. The liquid inside it was pale green, and the bottle was half full.

'Here is frobscottle!' he cried, holding the bottle up proud and high, as though it contained some rare wine. 'Delumptious fizzy frobscottle!' he shouted. He gave it a shake and the green stuff began to fizz like mad.

'But look! It's fizzing the *wrong way!*' Sophie cried. And indeed it was. The bubbles, instead of travelling upwards

64

and bursting on the surface, were shooting downwards and bursting at the bottom. A pale green frothy fizz was forming at the bottom of the bottle.

'What on earth is you meaning *the wrong way?*' asked the BFG.

'In our fizzy drinks,' Sophie said, 'the bubbles always go up and burst at the top.'

'*Upwards* is the *wrong way!*' cried the BFG. 'You mustn't ever be having the bubbles going upwards! That the most flushbunking rubbish I ever is hearing!'

'Why do you say that?' Sophie asked.

'You is asking me *why?*' cried the BFG, waving the enormous bottle around as though he were conducting an orchestra. 'You is actually meaning to tell me you cannot see *why* it is a scrotty mistake to have the bubbles flying up instead of down?'

'You said it was flushbunking. Now you say it's scrotty. Which is it?' Sophie asked politely.

'Both!' cried the BFG. 'It is a flushbunking *and* a scrotty mistake to let the bubbles go upwards! If you can't see why, you must be as quacky as a duckhound! By ringo, your head must be so full of frogsquinkers and buzzwangles, I is frittered if I know how you can think at all!'

'Why shouldn't the bubbles go upward?' Sophie asked.

'I will explain,' said the BFG. 'But tell me first what name is you calling *your* frobscottle by?'

'One is Coke,' Sophie said. 'Another is Pepsi. There are lots of them.'

'And the bubbles is *all* going up?'

'They all go up,' Sophie said.

'Catasterous!' cried the BFG. 'Upgoing bubbles is a catasterous disastrophe!'

'Will you *please* tell me why?' Sophie said.

'If you will listen carefully I will try to explain,' said the BFG. 'But your brain is so full of bugwhiffles, I doubt you will ever understand.'

'I'll do my best,' Sophie said patiently.

'Very well, then. When you is drinking this cokey drink of yours,' said the BFG, 'it is going straight down into your tummy. Is that right? Or is it left?'

'It's right,' Sophie said.

'And the *bubbles* is going also into your tummy. Right or left?'

'Right again,' Sophie said.

'And the bubbles is fizzing upwards?'

'Of course,' Sophie said.

'Which means,' said the BFG, 'that they will all come swishwiffling up your throat and out of your mouth and make a foulsome belchy burp!'

'That is often true,' Sophie said. 'But what's wrong with a little burp now and again? It's sort of fun.'

'Burping is filthsome,' the BFG said. 'Us giants is never doing it.'

'But with *your* drink,' Sophie said, 'what was it you called it?'

'Frobscottle,' said the BFG.

'With frobscottle,' Sophie said, 'the bubbles in your tummy will be going *downwards* and that could have a far nastier result.'

'Why nasty?' asked the BFG, frowning.

'Because,' Sophie said, blushing a little, 'if they go down instead of up, they'll be coming out somewhere else with an even louder and ruder noise.'

'A whizzpopper!' cried the BFG, beaming at her. 'Us giants is making whizzpoppers all the time! Whizzpopping is a sign of happiness. It is music in our ears! You surely is not telling me that a little whizzpopping is forbidden among human beans?'

'It is considered extremely rude,' Sophie said.

'But you is whizzpopping, is you not, now and again?' asked the BFG.

'Everyone is whizzpopping, if that's what you call it,' Sophie said. 'Kings and Queens are whizzpopping. Presidents are whizzpopping. Glamorous film stars are whizzpopping. Little babies are whizzpopping. But where I come from, it is not polite to talk about it.'

'Redunculous!' said the BFG. 'If everyone is making whizzpoppers, then why not talk about it? We is now having a swiggle of this delicious frobscottle and you will see the happy result.' The BFG shook the bottle vigorously. The pale green stuff fizzed and bubbled. He removed the cork and took a tremendous gurgling swig.

'It's glummy!' he cried. 'I love it!'

For a few moments, the Big Friendly Giant stood quite still, and a look of absolute ecstasy began to spread over his long wrinkly face. Then suddenly the heavens opened and he let fly with a series of the loudest and rudest noises Sophie had ever heard in her life. They reverberated around the walls of the cave like thunder and the glass jars rattled on their shelves. But most astonishing of all, the force of the explosions actually lifted the enormous giant clear off his feet, like a rocket.

'*Whoopee!*' he cried, when he came down to earth again. 'Now *that* is whizzpopping for you!'

Sophie burst out laughing. She couldn't help it.

'Have some yourself!' cried the BFG, tipping the neck of the enormous bottle towards her.

'Don't you have a cup?' Sophie said.

'No cups. Only bottle.'

Sophie opened her mouth, and very gently the BFG tipped the bottle forward and poured some of the fabulous frobscottle down her throat.

And oh gosh, how delicious it was! It was sweet and refreshing. It tasted of vanilla and cream, with just the faintest trace of raspberries on the edge of the flavour. And the bubbles were wonderful. Sophie could actually feel them bouncing and bursting all around her tummy. It was an amazing sensation. It felt as though hundreds of tiny people were dancing a jig inside her and tickling her with their toes. It was lovely.

'It's lovely!' she cried.

'Just wait,' said the BFG, flapping his ears.

Sophie could feel the bubbles travelling lower and

lower down her tummy, and then suddenly, inevitably
... the explosion came. The trumpets sounded and she
too made the walls of the cavern ring with the sound of
music and thunder.

'Bravo!' shouted the BFG, waving the bottle. 'You is
very good for a beginner! Let's have some more!'

Journey to Dream Country

After the mad frobscottle party was over, Sophie settled herself again on top of the enormous table.

'You is feeling better now?' asked the Big Friendly Giant.

'Much better, thank you,' Sophie said.

'Whenever I is feeling a bit scrotty,' the BFG said, 'a few gollops of frobscottle is always making me hopscotchy again.'

'I must say it's quite an experience,' Sophie said.

'It's a razztwizzler,' the BFG said. 'It's gloriumptious.' He turned away and strode across the cave and picked up his dream-catching net. 'I is galloping off now,' he said, 'to catch some more whoppsy-whiffling dreams for my collection. I is doing this every day without missing. Is you wishing to come with me?'

'Not me, thank you very much!' Sophie said. 'Not with those other giants lurking outside!'

'I is snuggling you very cosy into the pocket of my waistcoat,' the BFG said. 'Then no one is seeing you.'

Before Sophie could protest, he had picked her up off the table and popped her into the waistcoat pocket. There was plenty of room in there. 'Is you wishing for a little hole to peep out from?' he asked her.

'There's one here already,' she said. She had found a small hole in the pocket, and when she put one eye close to it, she could see out very well indeed. She watched the BFG as he bent down and filled his suitcase with empty glass jars. He closed the lid, picked up the suitcase in one hand, took the pole with the net on the end in the other hand, and marched towards the entrance of the cave.

As soon as he was outside, the BFG set off across the great hot yellow wasteland where the blue rocks lay and the dead trees stood and where all the other giants were skulking about.

Sophie, squatting low on her heels in the pocket of the leather waistcoat, had one eye glued to the little hole. She saw the group of enormous giants about three hundred yards ahead.

'Hold your breaths!' the BFG whispered down to her. 'Cross your figglers! Here we go! We is going right past all these other giants! Is you seeing that whopping great one, the one nearest to us?'

'I see him,' Sophie whispered back, quivering.

'That is the horriblest of them all. And the biggest of them all. He is called the Fleshlumpeating Giant.'

'I don't want to hear about him,' Sophie said.

'He is fifty-four feet high,' the BFG said softly as he jogged along. 'And he is swolloping human beans like they is sugar-lumps, two or three at a time.'

'You're making me nervous,' Sophie said.

'I is nervous myself,' the BFG whispered. 'I always gets as jumpsy as a joghopper when the Fleshlumpeating Giant is around.'

'Keep away from him,' Sophie pleaded.

'Not possible,' the BFG answered. 'He is galloping easily two times as quicksy as me.'

'Shall we turn back?' Sophie said.

'Turning back is worse,' the BFG said. 'If they is seeing me running away, they is all giving chase and throwing rocks.'

'They would never *eat* you though would they?' Sophie asked.

'Giants is never guzzling other giants,' the BFG said. 'They is fighting and squarreling a lot with each other, but never guzzling. Human beans is more tasty to them.'

The giants had already spotted the BFG and all heads were turned, watching him as he jogged forward. He was aiming to pass well to the right of the group.

Through her little peep-hole, Sophie saw the Fleshlumpeating Giant moving over to intercept them. He didn't hurry. He just loped over casually to a point where the BFG would have to pass. The others loped after him. Sophie counted nine of them altogether and she recognized the Bloodbottler in the middle of them. They were bored. They had nothing to do until nightfall. There was an air of menace about them as they loped slowly across the plain with long lolloping strides, heading for the BFG.

'Here comes the runty one!' boomed the Fleshlumpeater. 'Ho-ho there, runty one! Where is you splatch-winkling away to in such a hefty hurry?' He shot out an enormous arm and grabbed the BFG by the hair. The BFG didn't struggle. He simply stopped and stood quite still and said, 'De so kind as to be letting go of my hair, Fleshlumpeater.'

The Fleshlumpeater released him and stepped back a pace. The other giants stood around, waiting for the fun to start.

72

'Now then, you little grobsquiffler!' boomed the Flesh-lumpeater. 'We is all of us wanting to know where you is galloping off to every day in the daytime. Nobody ought to be galloping off to anywhere until it is getting dark. The human beans could easily be spotting you and starting a giant hunt and we is not wanting that to happen, is we not?'

'We is not!' shouted the other giants. 'Go back to your cave, runty one!'

'I is not galloping to any human bean country,' the BFG said. 'I is going to other places.'

'I is thinking,' said the Fleshlumpeater, 'that you is catching human beans and keeping them as pets!'

'Right you is!' cried the Bloodbottler. 'Just now I is hearing him chittering away to one of them in his cave!'

'You is welcome to go and search my cave from frack to bunt,' the BFG answered. 'You can go looking into every crook and nanny. There is no human beans or stringy beans or runner beans or jelly beans or any other beans in there.'

Sophie crouched still as a mouse inside the BFG's pocket. She hardly dared breathe. She was terrified she might sneeze. The slightest sound or movement would give her away. Through the tiny peep-hole she watched the giants clustering around the poor BFG. How revolting they were! All of them had piggy little eyes and enormous mouths with thick sausage lips. When the Fleshlumpeater was speaking, she got a glimpse of his tongue. It was jet black, like a slab of black steak. Every one of them was more than twice as tall as the BFG.

Suddenly, the Fleshlumpeater shot out two enormous

73

hands and grabbled the BFG around the waist. He tossed him high in the air and shouted, 'Catch him, Manhugger!'

The Manhugger caught him. The other giants spread out quickly in a large circle, each giant about twenty yards from his neighbour, preparing for the game they were going to play. Now the Manhugger threw the BFG high and far, shouting 'Catch him, Bonecruncher!'

The Bonecruncher ran forward and caught the tumbling BFG and immediately swung him up again. 'Catch him, Childchewer!' he shouted.

And so it went on. The giants were playing ball with the BFG, vying with each other to see who could throw him the highest. Sophie dug her nails into the sides of the pocket, trying to prevent herself from tumbling out when she was upside down. She felt as though she were in a barrel going over the Niagara Falls. And all the time there was the fearful danger that one of the giants would fail to catch the BFG and he would go crashing to the ground.

'Catch him, Meatdripper!' . . .

'Catch him, Gizzardgulper!' . . .

'Catch him, Maidmasher!' …

'Catch him, Bloodbottler!' …

'Catch him! … Catch him! … Catch him! …'

In the end, they got bored with this game. They dumped the poor BFG on the ground. He was dazed and shattered. They gave him a few kicks and shouted, 'Run, you little runt! Let us be seeing how fast you is galloping!' The BFG ran. What else could he do? The giants picked up rocks and hurled them after him. He managed to dodge them. 'Ruddy little runt!' they shouted. 'Troggy little twit! Shrively little shrimp! Mucky little midget!

Squaggy little squib! Grobby little grub!'

At last the BFG got clear of them all and in another couple of minutes the pack of giants was out of sight over the horizon. Sophie popped her head up from the pocket. 'I didn't like that,' she said.

'Phew!' said the BFG. 'Phew and far between! They was in a nasty crotching mood today, was they not! I is sorry you was having such a whirlgig time.'

'No worse than you,' Sophie said. 'Would they ever *really* hurt you?'

'I isn't ever trusting them,' the BFG said.

'How do they actually catch the humans they eat?' Sophie asked.

'They is usually just sticking an arm in through the bedroom window and snitching them from their beds,' the BFG said.

'Like you did to me.'

'Ah, but I isn't eating you,' the BFG said.

'How else do they catch them?' Sophie asked.

'Sometimes,' the BFG said, 'they is swimmeling in from the sea like fishies with only their heads showing above the water, and then out comes a big hairy hand and grabbles someone off the beach.'

'Children as well?'

'Often chiddlers,' the BFG said. 'Little chiddlers who is building sandcastles on the beach. That is who the swimmeling ones are after. Little chiddlers is not so tough to eat as old grandmamma, so says the Childchewing Giant.'

As they talked, the BFG was galloping fast over the land. Sophie was standing right up in his waistcoat pocket now and holding on to the edge with both hands.

Her head and shoulders were in the open and the wind was blowing in her hair.

'How else do they catch people?' she asked.

'All of them is having their own special ways of catching the human bean,' the BFG said. 'The Meatdripping Giant is preferring to pretend he is a big tree growing in the park. He is standing in the park in the dusky evening and he is holding great big branches over his head, and there he is waiting until some happy families is coming to have a picnic under the spreading tree. The Meatdripping giant is watching them as they lay out their little picnic. But in the end it is the Meatdripper who is having the picnic.'

'It's too awful!' Sophie cried.

'The Gizzardgulping Giant is a city lover,' the BFG went on. 'The Gizzardgulper is lying high up between the roofs of houses in the big cities. He is lying there snuggy as a sniggler and watching the human beans walking on the street below, and when he sees one that looks like it has a whoppsy-good flavour, he grabs it. He is simply reaching down and snitching it off the street like a monkey taking a nut. He says it is nice to be able to pick and choose what you is having for your supper. He says it is like choosing from a menu.'

'Don't people *see* him doing it?' Sophie asked.

'Never is they seeing him. Do not forget it is dusky-dark at this time. Also, the Gizzardgulper has a very fast arm. His arm is going up and down quicker than squinkers.'

'But if all these people are disappearing every night, surely there's some sort of an outcry?' Sophie said.

'The world is a whopping big place,' the BFG said. 'It has a hundred different countries. The giants is clever.

They is careful not to be skididdling off to the same country too often. They is always switchfiddling around.'

'Even so . . .' Sophie said.

'Do not forget,' the BFG said, 'that human beans is disappearing everywhere all the time even *without* the giants is guzzling them up. Human beans is killing each other much quicker than the giants is doing it.'

'But they don't *eat* each other,' Sophie said.

'Giants isn't eating each other either,' the BFG said. 'Nor is giants *killing* each other. Giants is not very lovely, but they is not killing each other. Nor is crockadowndillies killing other crockadowndillies. Nor is pussy-cats killing pussy-cats.'

'They kill mice,' Sophie said.

'Ah, but they is not killing their own kind,' the BFG said. 'Human beans is the only animals that is killing their own kind.'

'Don't poisonous snakes kill each other?' Sophie asked. She was searching desperately for another creature that behaved as badly as the human.

'Even poisnowse snakes is never killing each other,' the BFG said. 'Nor is the most fearsome creatures like tigers and rhinostossterisses. None of them is ever killing their own kind. Has you ever thought about that?'

Sophie kept silent.

'I is not understanding human beans at all,' the BFG said. '*You* is a human bean and you is saying it is grizzling and horrigust for giants to be eating human beans. Right or left?'

'Right,' Sophie said.

'But human beans is squishing *each other* all the time,' the BFG said. 'They is shootling guns and going up in aerioplanes to drop their bombs on each other's heads every week. Human beans is always killing other human beans.'

He was right. Of course he was right and Sophie knew it. She was beginning to wonder whether humans were actually any better than giants. 'Even so,' she said, defending her own race, 'I think it's rotten that those foul giants should go off every night to eat humans. Humans have never done *them* any harm.'

'That is what the little piggy-wig is saying every day,' the BFG answered. 'He is saying, "I has never done any harm to the human bean so why should he be eating me?"'

'Oh dear,' Sophie said.

'The human beans is making rules to suit themselves,' the BFG went on. 'But the rules they is making do not suit the little piggy-wiggies. Am I right or left?'

'Right,' Sophie said.

'Giants is also making rules. Their rules is not suiting the human beans. Everybody is making his own rules to suit himself.'

'But you don't like it that those beastly giants are eating humans every night, do you?' Sophie asked.

'I do not,' the BFG answered firmly. 'One right is not making two lefts. Is you quite cosy down there in my pocket?'

'I'm fine,' Sophie said.

Then suddenly, once again, the BFG went into that magical top gear of his. He began hurtling forward with phenomenal leaps. His speed was unbelievable. The landscape became blurred and again Sophie had to duck down out of the whistling gale to save her head from being blown off her shoulders. She crouched in the pocket and listened to the wind screaming past. It came knifing in through the tiny peep-hole in the pocket and whooshed around her like a hurricane.

But this time the BFG didn't stay in top gear long. It seemed as though he had had some barrier to cross, a vast mountain perhaps or an ocean or a great desert, but having crossed it, he once again slowed down to his normal gallop and Sophie was able to pop her head up and look out once more at the view.

She noticed immediately that they were now in an altogether paler country. The sun had disappeared above a film of vapour. The air was becoming cooler every minute. The land was flat and treeless and there seemed to be no colour in it at all.

Every minute, the mist became thicker. The air became colder still and everything became paler and paler until soon there was nothing but grey and white all around them. They were in a country of swirling mists and ghostly vapours. There was some sort of grass underfoot but it was not green. It was ashy grey. There was no sign of a living creature and no sound at all except for the soft thud of the BFG's footsteps as he hurtled on through the fog.

Suddenly he stopped. 'We is here at last!' he announced. He bent down and lifted Sophie from his pocket and put her on the ground. She was still in her nightie and her feet were bare. She shivered and stared around her at the swirling mists and ghostly vapours.

'Where are we?' she asked.

'We is in Dream Country,' the BFG said. 'This is where all dreams is beginning.'

Dream-Catching

The Big Friendly Giant put the suitcase on the ground. He bent down low so that his enormous face was close to Sophie's. 'From now on, we is keeping as still as winky little micies,' he whispered.

Sophie nodded. The misty vapour swirled around her. It made her cheeks damp and left dewdrops in her hair.

The BFG opened the suitcase and took out several empty glass jars. He set them ready on the ground, with their screw tops removed. Then he stood up very straight. His head was now high up in the swirling mist and it kept disappearing, then appearing again. He was holding the long net in his right hand.

Sophie, staring upwards, saw through the mist that his colossal ears were beginning to swivel out from his head. They began waving gently to and fro.

Suddenly the BFG pounced. He leaped high in the air and swung the net through the mist with a great swishing sweep of his arm. 'Got him!' he cried. 'A jar! A jar! Quick quick quick!' Sophie picked up a jar and held it up to him. He grabbed hold of it. He lowered the net. Very carefully he tipped something absolutely invisible from the net into the jar. He dropped the net and swiftly clapped one hand over the jar. 'The top!' he whispered. 'The jar top quick!' Sophie picked up the screw top and handed it to him. He screwed it on tight and the jar was closed. The BFG was very excited. He held the jar close to one ear and listened intently.

'It's a winksquiffler!' he whispered with a thrill in his voice. 'It's ... it's ... it's ... it's even better. It's a phizz-wizard! It's a golden phizzwizard!'

Sophie stared at him.

'Oh my, oh my!' he said, holding the jar in front of him. 'This will be giving some little tottler a very happy night when I is blowing it in!'

'Is it really a good one?' Sophie asked.

'A *good one?*' he cried. 'It's a golden phizzwizard! It is not often I is getting one of these!' He handed the jar to Sophie and said, 'Please be still as a starfish now. I is thinking there may be a whole swarm of phizzwizards up here today. And do kindly stop breathing. You is terribly noisy down there.'

'I haven't moved a muscle,' Sophie said.

'Then don't,' the BFG answered sharply. Once again he stood up tall in the mist, holding his net at the ready. Then came the long silence, the waiting, the listening, and at last, with surprising suddenness came the leap and the swish of the net.

'Another jar!' he cried. 'Quick quick quick!'

When the second dream was safely in the jar and the top was screwed down, the BFG held it to his ear.

'Oh *no!*' he cried. 'Oh mince my maggots! Oh swipe my swoggles!'

'What's the matter?' Sophie asked.

'It's a trogglehumper!' he shouted. His voice was filled with fury and anguish. 'Oh, save our solos!' he cried. 'Deliver us from weasels! The devil is dancing on my dibbler!'

'What *are* you talking about?' Sophie said. The BFG was getting more distressed every moment.

'Oh, bash my eyebones!' he cried, waving the jar in the air. 'I come all this way to get lovely golden dreams and what is I catching?'

'What *are* you catching?' Sophie said.

'I is catching a frightsome trogglehumper!' he cried. 'This is a *bad bad dream!* It is worse than a bad dream! It is a *nightmare!*'

'Oh dear,' Sophie said. 'What will you do with that?'

'I is never never letting it go!' the BFG cried. 'If I do, then some poor little tottler will be having the most curdbloodling time! This one is a real kicksy bog-thumper! I is exploding it as soon as I get home!'

'Nightmares are horrible,' Sophie said. 'I had one once and I woke up sweating all over.'

'With this one you would be waking up *screaming* all over!' the BFG said. 'This one would make your teeth stand on end! If this one got into you, your blood would be freezing to icicles and your skin would go creeping across the floor!'

'Is it as bad as that?'

'It's worse!' cried the BFG. 'This is a real whoppsy grobswitcher!'

'You said it was a trogglehumper,' Sophie told him.

'It *is* a trogglehumper!' cried the exasperated BFG. 'But it is also a *bogthumper* and a *grobswitcher*! It is all three riddled into one! Oh, I is so glad I is clutching it tight. Ah, you wicked beastie, you!' he cried, holding up the jar and staring into it. 'Never more is you going to be bunk-doodling the poor little human-beaney tottlers!'

Sophie, who was also staring into the glass jar, cried out, 'I can see it! There's something in there!'

'Of course there is something in there,' the BFG said. 'You is looking at a frightsome trogglehumper.'

'But you told me dreams were invisible.'

'They is always invisible until they is *captured*,' the BFG told her. 'After that they is losing a little of their invisibility. We is seeing this one very clearly.'

Inside the jar Sophie could see the faint scarlet outline of something that looked like a mixture between a blob of gas and a bubble of jelly. It was moving violently, thrashing against the sides of the jar and forever changing shape.

'It's wiggling all over the place!' Sophie cried. 'It's fighting to get out! It'll bash itself to bits!'

'The nastier the dream, the angrier it is getting when it is in prison,' the BFG said. 'It is the same as with wild animals. If an animal is very fierce and you is putting it in a cage, it will make a tremendous rumpledumpus. If it is a nice animal like a cockatootloo or a fogglefrump, it will sit quietly. Dreams is exactly the same. This one is a nasty fierce bogrotting nightmare. Just look at him splashing himself against the glass!'

'It's quite frightening!' Sophie cried.

'I would be hating to get this one inside me on a darksome night,' the BFG said.

'So would I!' Sophie said.

The BFG started putting the bottles back into the suitcase.

'Is that all?' Sophie asked. 'Are we going?'

'I is so upset by this trogglehumping bogthumping grobswitcher,' the BFG said, 'that I is not wishing to go on. Dream-catching is finished for today.'

Soon Sophie was back in the waistcoat pocket and the BFG was racing home as fast as he could go. When, at last, they emerged out of the mist and came again on to the hot yellow wasteland, all the other giants were sprawled out on the ground, fast asleep.

A Trogglehumper for the Fleshlumpeater

'They is always having fifty winks before they goes scumpering off to hunt human beans in the evening,' the BFG said. He stopped for a few moments to let Sophie have a better look. 'Giants is only sleeping every then and now,' he said. 'Not nearly as much as human beans. Human beans is crazy for sleeping. Is it ever occurring to you that a human bean who is fifty is spending about *twenty* years sleeping fast?'

'I must admit that never occurred to me,' Sophie said.

'You should *allow* it to occur to you,' the BFG said. 'Imagine it please. This human bean who says he is fifty has been fast asleep for twenty years and is not even knowing where he is! Not even *doing* anything! Not even thinking!'

'It's a funny thought,' Sophie said.

'Exunckly,' the BFG said. 'So what I is trying to explain to you is that a human bean who says he is fifty is not fifty, he is only thirty.'

'What about me?' Sophie said. 'I am eight.'

'You is not eight at all,' the BFG said. 'Human bean babies and little chiddlers is spending half their time sleeping, so you is only four.'

'I'm eight,' Sophie said.

'You may *think* you is eight,' the BFG said, 'but you has only spent four years of your life with your little eyes open. You is only four and please stop higgling me. Titchy little snapperwhippers like you should not be higgling around with an old sage and onions who is hundreds of years more than you.'

'How much do giants sleep?' Sophie asked.

'They is never wasting much time snozzling,' the BFG said. 'Two or three hours is enough.'

'When do *you* sleep?' Sophie asked.

'Even less,' the BFG answered. 'I is sleeping only once in a blue baboon.'

Sophie, peeping out from her pocket, examined the nine sleeping giants. They looked even more grotesque now than when they were awake. Sprawled out across the yellow plain, they covered an area about the size of a football field. Most of them were lying on their backs with their enormous mouths wide open, and they were snoring like foghorns. The noise was awful.

Suddenly the BFG gave a jump in the air. 'By gumfrog!' he cried. 'I is just having the most whoppsy-whiffling idea!'

'What?' Sophie said.

'Wait!' he cried. 'Hold your horsefeathers! Keep your skirt on! Just you wait to see what I is going to bring about!' He galloped off fast to his cave with Sophie hanging on tight to the rim of the pocket. He rolled back the stone. He entered the cave. He was very excited. He was moving quickly. 'You stay where you is in my pocket, huggybee,' he said. 'We is doing this lovely bit of buck-swashling both together.' He laid aside the dream-catching net but hung on to the suitcase. He ran across to the other side of the cave and grabbed the long trumpet thing, the one he had been carrying when

Sophie had first seen him in the village. With the suitcase in one hand and the trumpet in the other, he dashed out of the cave.

What *is* he up to now, Sophie wondered.

'Peep your head up good,' the BFG said, 'then you will get a fine winkle of what is going on.'

When the BFG came near to the sleeping giants, he slowed his pace. He began moving softly. He crept on his toes towards the ugly brutes. They were still snoring loudly. They looked repulsive, filthy, diabolical. The BFG tip-toed around them. He went past the Gizzardgulper, the Bloodbottler, the Meatdripper, the Childchewer. Then he stopped. He had reached the Fleshlumpeater. He pointed at him, then he looked down at Sophie and gave her a big wink.

He knelt on the ground and very quietly he opened the suitcase. He took out of it the glass jar containing the terrible nightmarish trogglehumper.

At that point, Sophie guessed what was going to happen next.

Owtch, she thought. This could be rather dangerous. She crouched lower in the pocket so that only the top of her head and her eyes were showing. She wanted to be ready to duck out of sight very fast should anything go wrong.

They were about ten feet away from the Fleshlump-eater's face. The snoring-snorting noise he was making was disgusting. Every now and again a big bubble of spit formed between his two open lips and then it would burst with a splash and cover his face with saliva.

Taking infinite care, the BFG unscrewed the top of the glass jar and tipped the squiggling squirming faintly

89

scarlet trogglehumper into the wide end of his long trumpet. He put the other end of the trumpet to his lips. He aimed the instrument directly at the Fleshlump-eater's face. He took a deep breath, puffed out his cheeks and then *whoof*! He blew!

Sophie saw a flash of pale red go darting towards the giant's face. For a split second it hovered above the face. Then it was gone. It seemed to have been sucked up the giant's nose, but it had all happened so quickly, Sophie couldn't be sure.

'We had better be skiddling away quick to where it is safe,' the BFG whispered. He trotted off for about a hundred yards, then he stopped. He crouched low to the earth. 'Now,' he said, 'we is waiting for the gun and flames to begin.'

They didn't have long to wait.

The air was suddenly pierced by the most fearful roar Sophie had ever heard, and she saw the Fleshlumpeater's body, all fifty-four feet of it, rise up off the ground and fall back again with a thump. Then it began to wriggle and twist and bounce about in the most violent fashion. It was quite frightening to watch.

'Eeeow!' roared the Fleshlumpeater. 'Ayeee! Oooow!'

'He's still asleep,' the BFG whispered. 'The terrible trogglehumping nightmare is beginning to hit him.'

'Serves him right,' Sophie said. She could feel no sympathy for this great brute who ate children as though they were sugar-lumps.

'Save us!' screamed the Fleshlumpeater, thrashing about madly. 'He is after me! He is getting me!'

The thrashing of limbs and the waving of arms became

more violent by the second. It was an awesome thing to watch such a massive creature having such mighty convulsions.

'It's Jack!' bellowed the Fleshlumpeater. 'It's the grueful gruncious Jack! Jack is after me! Jack is wackcrackling me! Jack is spikesticking me! Jack is splashplunking me! It is the terrible frightswiping Jack!' The Fleshlumpeater was writhing about over the ground like some colossal tortured snake. 'Oh, spare me, Jack!' he yelled. 'Don't hurt me, Jack!'

'Who is this Jack he's on about?' Sophie whispered.

'Jack is the only human bean all giants is frightened of,' the BFG told her. 'They is all absolutely terrified of Jack. They is all hearing that Jack is a famous giant-killer.'

'Save me!' screamed the Fleshlumpeater. 'Have mercy on this poor little giant! The beanstalk! He is coming at me with his terrible spikesticking beanstalk! Take it away! I is begging you, Jack, I is praying you not to touch me with your terrible spikesticking beanstalk!'

'Us giants,' the BFG whispered, 'is not knowing very much about this dreaded human bean called Jack. We is knowing only that he is a famous giant-killer and that he is owning something called a beanstalk. We is knowing also that the beanstalk is a fearsome thing and Jack is using it to kill giants.'

Sophie couldn't stop smiling.

'What is you griggling at?' the BFG asked her, slightly nettled.

'I'll tell you later,' Sophie said.

93

The awful nightmare had now gripped the great brute
to such an extent that he was tying his whole body into
knots. 'Do not do it, Jack!' he screeched. 'I was not eating
you, Jack! I is never eating human beans! I swear I has
never gobbled a single human bean in all my wholesome
life!'

'Liar,' said the BFG.

Just then, one of the Fleshlumpeater's flailing fists
caught the still-fast-asleep Meatdripping Giant smack in
the mouth. At the same time, one of his furiously thrashing legs kicked the snoring Gizzardgulping Giant right in
the guts. Both the injured giants woke up and leaped to
their feet.

'He is swiping me right in the mouth!' yelled the Meatdripper.

'He is bungswoggling me smack in the guts!' shouted the Gizzardgulper.

The two of them rushed at the Fleshlumpeater and began pounding him with their fists and feet. The wretched Fleshlumpeater woke up with a bang. He awoke straight from one nightmare into another. He roared into battle, and in the bellowing thumping rough and tumble that followed, one sleeping giant after another either got stepped upon or kicked. Soon, all nine of them were on their feet having the most almighty free-for-all. They punched and kicked and scratched and bit and butted each other as hard as they could. Blood flowed. Noses went crunch. Teeth fell out like hailstones. The giants roared and screamed and cursed, and for many minutes the noise of battle rolled across the yellow plain.

The BFG smiled a big wide smile of absolute pleasure. 'I is loving it when they is all having a good tough and rumble,' he said.

'They'll kill each other,' Sophie said.

'Never,' the BFG answered. 'Those beasts is always bishing and walloping at one another. Soon it will be getting dusky and they will be galloping off to fill their tummies.'

'They're coarse and foul and filthy,' Sophie said. 'I hate them!'

As the BFG headed back to the cave, he said quietly, 'We certainly was putting that nightmare to good use though, wasn't we?'

'Excellent use,' Sophie said. 'Well done you.'

Dreams

The Big Friendly Giant was seated at the great table in his cave and he was doing his homework.

Sophie sat cross-legged on the table-top near by, watching him at work.

The glass jar containing the one and only good dream they had caught that day stood between them.

The BFG, with great care and patience, was printing something on a piece of paper with an enormous pencil.

'What are you writing?' Sophie asked him.

'Every dream is having its special label on the bottle,' the BFG said. 'How else could I be finding the one I am wanting in a hurry?'

'But can you really and truly tell what sort of a dream it's going to be simply by listening to it?' Sophie asked.

'I can,' the BFG said, not looking up.

'But *how*? Is it by the way it hums and buzzes?'

'You is less or more right,' the BFG said. 'Every dream in the world is making a different sort of buzzy-hum music. And these grand swashboggling ears of mine is able to read that music.'

'By music, do you mean tunes?'

'I is not meaning tunes.'

'Then what *do* you mean?'

'Human beans is having their own music, right or left?'

'Right,' Sophie said. 'Lots of music.'

97

'And sometimes human beans is very overcome when they is hearing wonderous music. They is getting shivers down their spindels. Right or left?'

'Right,' Sophie said.

'So the music is saying something to them. It is sending a message. I do not think the human beans is knowing what that message is, but they is loving it just the same.'

'That's about right,' Sophie said.

'But because of these jumpsquiffling ears of mine,' the BFG said, 'I is not only able to *hear* the music that dreams is making but I is *understanding* it also.'

'What do you mean *understanding* it?' Sophie said.

'I can read it,' the BFG said. 'It talks to me. It is like a langwitch.'

'I find that just a little hard to believe,' Sophie said.

'I'll bet you is also finding it hard to believe in quogwinkles,' the BFG said, 'and how they is visiting us from the stars.'

'Of course I don't believe that,' Sophie said.

The BFG regarded her gravely with those huge eyes of his. 'I hope you will forgive me,' he said, 'if I tell you that human beans is thinking they is very clever, but they is not. They is nearly all of them notmuchers and squeakpips.'

'I *beg* your pardon,' Sophie said.

'The matter with human beans,' the BFG went on, 'is that they is absolutely refusing to believe in anything unless they is actually seeing it right in front of their own schnozzles. Of course quogwinkles is existing. I is meeting them oftenly. I is even chittering to them.' He turned away contemptuously from Sophie and resumed his writing. Sophie moved over to read what he had written so far. The letters were printed big and bold, but were not very well formed. Here is what it said:

THIS DREAM IS ABOUT HOW I IS SAVING MY TEECHER FROM DROWNING. I IS DIVING INTO THE RIVER FROM A HIGH BRIDGE AND I IS DRAGGING MY TEECHER TO THE BANK AND THEN I IS GIVING HIM THE KISS OF DEATH ...

'The kiss of *what?*' Sophie asked.

The BFG stopped writing and raised his head slowly. His eyes rested on Sophie's face. 'I is telling you once before,' he said quietly, 'that I is never having a chance to go to school. I is full of mistakes. They is not my fault. I do my best. You is a lovely little girl, but please remember that *you* is not exactly Miss Knoweverything yourself.'

'I'm sorry,' Sophie said. 'I really am. It is very rude of me to keep correcting you.'

The BFG gazed at her for a while longer, then he bent his head again to his slow laborious writing.

'Tell me honestly,' Sophie said. 'If you blew this dream into my bedroom when I was asleep, would I really and truly start dreaming about how I saved my teacher from drowning by diving off the bridge?'

'More,' the BFG said. 'A lot more. But I cannot be squibbling the whole gropefluncking dream on a titchy bit of paper. Of course there is more.'

The BFG laid down his pencil and placed one massive ear close to the jar. For about thirty seconds he listened intently. 'Yes,' he said, nodding his great head solemnly up and down. 'This dream is continuing very nice. It has a very dory-hunky ending.'

'How does it end?' Sophie said. '*Please* tell me.'

'You would be dreaming,' the BFG said, 'that the morning after you is saving the teacher from the river, you is arriving at school and you is seeing all the five hundred pupils sitting in the assembly hall, and all the teachers as well, and the head teacher is then standing up and saying, "I is wanting the whole school to give three cheers for Sophie because she is so brave and is saving the life of our fine arithmatic teacher, Mr Figgins, who was unfortunately pushed off the bridge into the river by our gym-teacher, Miss Amelia Upscotch. So three cheers for Sophie!" And the whole school is then cheering like mad and shouting bravo well done, and, for ever after that, even when you is getting your sums all gungswizzled and muggled up, Mr Figgins is always giving you ten out of ten and writing *Good Work Sophie* in your exercise book. Then you is waking up.'

'I like that dream,' Sophie said.

'Of course you like it,' the BFG said. 'It is a phizz-wizard.' He licked the back of the label and stuck it on the jar. 'I is usually writing a bit more than this on the labels,' he said. 'But you is watching me and making me jumpsy.'

'I'll go and sit somewhere else,' Sophie said.

'Don't go,' he said. 'Look in the jar carefully and I think you will be seeing this dream.'

Sophie peered into the jar and there, sure enough, she saw the faint translucent outline of something about the size of a hen's egg. There was just a touch of colour in it, a pale sea-green, soft and shimmering and very beautiful. There it lay, this small oblong sea-green jellyish thing, at the bottom of the jar, quite peaceful, but pulsing gently, the whole of it moving in and out ever so slightly, as though it were breathing.

'It's moving!' Sophie cried. 'It's alive!'

'Of course it's alive.'

'What will you feed it on?' Sophie asked.

'It is not needing any food,' the BFG told her.

'That's cruel,' Sophie said. 'Everything alive needs food of some sort. Even trees and plants.'

'The north wind is alive,' the BFG said. 'It is moving. It touches you on the cheek and on the hands. But nobody is feeding it.'

Sophie was silent. This extraordinary giant was disturbing her ideas. He seemed to be leading her towards mysteries that were beyond her understanding.

'A dream is not needing anything,' the BFG went on. 'If it is a good one, it is waiting peaceably for ever until it is released and allowed to do its job. If it is a bad one, it is always fighting to get out.'

The BFG stood up and walked over to one of the many shelves and placed the latest jar among the thousands of others.

'Please can I see some of the other dreams?' Sophie asked him.

The BFG hesitated. 'Nobody is ever seeing them before,' he said. 'But perhaps after all I is letting you have a little peep.' He picked her up off the table and stood her on the palm of one of his huge hands. He carried her towards the shelves. 'Over here is some of the good dreams,' he said. 'The phizzwizards.'

'Would you hold me closer so I can read the labels,' Sophie said.

'My labels is only telling bits of it,' the BFG said. 'The dreams is usually much longer. The labels is just to remind me.'

Sophie started to read the labels. The first one seemed long enough to her. It went right round the jar, and as she read it, she had to keep turning the jar. This is what it said:

TODAY I IS SITTING IN CLASS AND I DISCOVER
THAT IF I IS STARING VERY HARD AT MY TEECHER
IN A SPHESHAL WAY, I IS ABLE TO PUT HER TO
SLEEP. SO I KEEP STARING AT HER AND IN THE END
HER HEAD DROPS ON TO HER DESK AND SHE GOES
FAST TO SLEEP AND SNORKLES LOUDLY. THEN IN
MARCHES THE HEAD TEACHER AND HE SHOUTS
'WAKE UP MISS PLUMRIDGE! HOW DARE YOU GO
TO SLEEP IN CLASS! GO FETCH YOUR HAT AND COTE
AND LEAVE THIS SCHOOL FOR EVER! YOU IS
SACKED!' BUT IN A JIFFY I IS PUTTING THE HEAD
TEECHER TO SLEEP AS WELL, AND HE JUST
CRUMPLES SLOWLY TO THE FLOOR LIKE A LUMP OF
JELLY AND THERE HE LIES ALL IN A HEAP AND
STARTS SNORKELLING EVEN LOWDER THAN MISS
PLUMRIDGE. AND THEN I IS HEARING MY MUMMY'S
VOICE SÀYING WAKE UP YOUR BREKFUST IS
REDDY.

'What a funny dream,' Sophie said.

'It's a ringbeller,' the BFG said. 'It's whoppsy.'

Inside the jar, just below the edge of the label, Sophie
could see the putting-to-sleep dream lying peacefully on
the bottom, pulsing gently, sea-green like the other one,
but perhaps a trifle larger.

'Do you have separate dreams for boys and for girls?'
Sophie asked.

'Of course,' the BFG said. 'If I is giving a girl's dream to a boy, even if it was a really whoppsy girl's dream, the boy would be waking up and thinking what a rot-bungling grinksludging old dream that was.'

'Boys would,' Sophie said.

'These here is all girls' dreams on this shelf,' the BFG said.

'Can I read a boy's dream?'

'You can,' the BFG said, and he lifted her to a higher shelf. The label on the nearest boy's-dream jar read as follows:

I IS MAKING MYSELF A MARVELUS PAIR OF SUCTION BOOTS AND WHEN I PUT THEM ON I IS ABEL TO WALK STRATE UP THE KITSHUN WALL AND ACROSS THE CEILING. WELL, I IS WALKING UPSIDE DOWN ON THE CEILING WEN MY BIG SISTER COMES IN AND SHE IS STARTING TO YELL AT ME AS SHE

ALWAYS DOES, YELLING WOT ON EARTH IS YOU
DOING UP THERE WALKING ON THE CEILING AND I
LOOKS DOWN AT HER AND I SMILES AND I SAYS I
TOLD YOU YOU WAS DRIVING ME UP THE WALL AND
NOW YOU HAS DONE IT.

'I find that one rather silly,' Sophie said.

'Boys wouldn't,' the BFG said, grinning. 'It's another ringbeller. Perhaps you has seen enough now.'

'Let me read another boy's one,' Sophie said.

The next label said:

THE TELLYFONE RINGS IN OUR HOUSE AND MY
FATHER PICKS IT UP AND SAYS IN HIS VERY
IMPORTANT   TELLYFONE   VOICE   'SIMPKINS
SPEAKING'. THEN HIS FACE GOES WHITE AND HIS
VOICE GOES ALL FUNNY AND HE SAYS '*WHAT!
WHO?*' AND THEN HE SAYS 'YES SIR I UNDERSTAND
SIR BUT SURELY IT IS *ME* YOU IS WISHING TO SPEKE
TO SIR NOT MY LITTLE SON?' MY FATHER'S FACE IS
GOING FROM WHITE TO DARK PURPLE AND HE IS
GULPING LIKE HE HAS A LOBSTER STUCK IN HIS
THROTE AND THEN AT LAST HE IS SAYING 'YES SIR
VERY WELL SIR I WILL GET HIM SIR' AND HE TURNS
TO ME AND HE SAYS IN A RATHER RESPECKFUL
VOICE 'IS YOU KNOWING THE PRESIDENT OF THE
UNITED STATES?' AND I SAYS 'NO BUT I EXPECT HE
IS HEARING ABOUT ME.' THEN I IS HAVING A LONG
TALK ON THE FONE AND SAYING THINGS LIKE 'LET
ME TAKE CARE OF IT, MR PRESIDENT. YOU'LL
BUNGLE IT ALL UP IF YOU DO IT YOUR WAY'. AND MY
FATHER'S EYES IS GOGGLING RIGHT OUT OF HIS

HEAD AND THAT IS WHEN I IS HEARING MY
FATHER'S REAL VOICE SAYING GET UP YOU LAZY
SLOB OR YOU WILL BE LATE FOR SKOOL.

'Boys are crazy,' Sophie said. 'Let me read this next
one.' Sophie started reading the next label:

I IS HAVING A BATH AND I IS DISCOVERING THAT
IF I PRESS QUITE HARD ON MY TUMMY BUTTON A
FUNNY FEELING COMES OVER ME AND SUDDENLEY
MY LEGS IS NOT THERE NOR IS MY ARMS. IN FACT I
HAS BECOME ABSOLOOTLY INVISIBLE ALL OVER. I
IS STILL THERE BUT NO ONE CAN SEE ME NOT EVEN
MYSELF. SO MY MUMMY COMES IN AND SAYS 'WHERE
IS THAT CHILD! HE WAS IN THE BATH A MINIT AGO
AND HE CAN'T POSSIBLY HAVE WASHED HIMSELF
PROPERLY!' SO I SAYS 'HERE I IS' AND SHE SAYS
'WHERE?' AND I SAYS 'HERE' AND SHE SAYS
'WHERE?' AND I SAYS 'HERE!' AND SHE YELLS
'HENRY! COME UP QUICK!' AND WHEN MY DADDY
RUSHES IN I IS WASHING MYSELF AND MY DADDY

SEES THE SOAP FLOATING AROUND IN THE AIR BUT OF CORSE HE IS NOT SEEING ME AND HE SHOUTS 'WHERE ARE YOU BOY?' AND I SAYS 'HERE' AND HE SAYS 'WHERE?' AND I SAYS 'HERE' AND HE SAYS '*WHERE?*' AND I SAYS '*HERE!*' AND HE SAYS 'THE SOAP, BOY! THE SOAP! IT'S FLYING IN THE AIR!' THEN I PRESS MY TUMMY BUTTON AGAIN AND NOW I IS VISIBLE. MY DADDY IS SQUIFFY WITH EX-CITEMENT AND HE SAYS 'YOU IS THE INVISIBLE BOY!' AND I SAYS 'NOW I IS GOING TO HAVE SOME FUN,' SO WHEN I IS OUT OF THE BATH AND I HAVE DRIED MYSELF I PUT ON MY DRESSING-GOWN AND SLIPPERS AND I PRESS MY TUMMY BUTTON AGAIN TO BECOME INVISIBLE AND I GO DOWN INTO THE TOWN AND WALK IN THE STREETS. OF CORSE ONLY ME IS INVISIBLE BUT NOT THE THINGS I IS WEARING SO WHEN PEEPLE IS SEEING A DRESSING GOWN AND SLIPPERS FLOATING ALONG THE STREET WITH NOBODY IN IT THERE IS A PANIC WITH EVERYBODY YELLING 'A GHOST! A GHOST!' AND PEEPLE IS SCREAMING LEFT AND RIGHT AND BIG STRONG POLICEMEN IS RUNNING FOR THEIR LIVES AND BEST OF ALL I SEE MR GRUMMIT MY ALGEBRA

TEECHER COMING OUT OF A PUB AND I FLOAT UP
TO HIM AND SAY 'BOO!' AND HE LETS OUT A
FRIGHTSOME HOWL AND DASHES BACK INTO THE
PUB AND THEN I IS WAKING UP AND FEELING
HAPPY AS A WHIFFSQUIDDLER.

'Pretty ridiculous,' Sophie said. All the same, she
couldn't resist reaching down and pressing her own
tummy button to see if it worked. Nothing happened.

'Dreams is very mystical things,' the BFG said.
'Human beans is not understanding them at all. Not even
their brainiest prossefors is understanding them. Has you
seen enough?'

'Just this last one,' Sophie said. 'This one here.'

She started reading:

I HAS RITTEN A BOOK AND IT IS SO EXCITING
NOBODY CAN PUT IT DOWN. AS SOON AS YOU HAS
RED THE FIRST LINE YOU IS SO HOOKED ON IT YOU
CANNOT STOP UNTIL THE LAST PAGE. IN ALL THE
CITIES PEEPLE IS WALKING IN THE STREETS
BUMPING INTO EACH OTHER BECAUSE THEIR
FACES IS BURIED IN MY BOOK AND DENTISTS IS
READING IT AND TRYING TO FILL TEETHS AT THE
SAME TIME BUT NOBODY MINDS BECAUSE THEY IS
ALL READING IT TOO IN THE DENTIST'S CHAIR.
DRIVERS IS READING IT WHILE DRIVING AND CARS
IS CRASHING ALL OVER THE COUNTRY. BRAIN
SURGEONS IS READING IT WHILE THEY IS
OPERATING ON BRAINS AND AIRLINE PILOTS IS
READING IT AND GOING TO TIMBUCTOO INSTEAD
OF LONDON. FOOTBALL PLAYERS IS READING IT ON

THE FIELD BECAUSE THEY CAN'T PUT IT DOWN
AND SO IS OLIMPICK RUNNERS WHILE THEY IS
RUNNING. EVERYBODY HAS TO SEE WHAT IS GOING
TO HAPPEN NEXT IN MY BOOK AND WHEN I WAKE
UP I IS STILL TINGLING WITH EXCITEMENT AT
BEING THE GREATEST RITER THE WORLD HAS
EVER KNOWN UNTIL MY MUMMY COMES IN AND SAYS
I WAS LOOKING AT YOUR ENGLISH EXERCISE BOOK
LAST NITE AND REALLY YOUR SPELLING IS
ATROSHUS SO IS YOUR PUNTULASHON.

'That's enough for now,' the BFG said. 'There is
dillions more but my arm is getting tired holding you up.'

'What are all those over there?' Sophie said. 'Why
have they got such tiny labels?'

'That,' the BFG said, 'is because one day I is catching
so many dreams I is not having the time or energy to
write out long labels. But there is enough to remind me.'

'Can I look?' Sophie said.

The long-suffering BFG carried her across to the jars she was pointing to. Sophie read them rapidly, one after the other:

I IS CLIMBING MOUNT EVERAST WITH JUST MY PUSSY-CAT FOR CUMPANY.

I IS INVENTING A CAR THAT RUNS ON TOOTH-PASTE.

I IS ABLE TO MAKE THE ELEKTRIK LITES GO ON AND OFF JUST BY WISHING IT.

I IS ONLY AN EIGHT YEAR OLD LITTLE BOY BUT
I IS GROWING A SPLENDID BUSHY BEARD AND ALL
THE OTHER BOYS IS JALOUS.

I IS ABEL TO JUMP OUT OF ANY HIGH WINDOW
AND FLOTE DOWN SAFELY.

I HAS A PET BEE THAT MAKES ROCK AND ROLL
MUSIK WHEN IT FLIES.

'What amazes me,' Sophie said, 'is how you ever learned to write in the first place.'

'Ah,' said the BFG. 'I has been wondering how long it is before you is asking me that.'

'Considering you never went to school, I think it's quite marvellous,' Sophie said. 'How *did* you learn?'

The BFG crossed the cave and opened a tiny secret door in the wall. He took out a book, very old and tattered. By human standards, it was an ordinary sized book, but it looked like a postage stamp in his huge hand.

'One night,' he said, 'I is blowing a dream through a window and I sees this book lying on the little boy's bedroom table. I wanted it so very badly, you understand. But I is refusing to steal it. I would never do that.'

'So how did you get it?' Sophie asked.

'I *borrowed* it,' the BFG said, smiling a little. 'Just for a short time I borrowed it.'

'How long have you had it?' Sophie asked.

'Perhaps only about eighty years,' the BFG said. 'Soon I shall be putting it back.'

'And that's how you taught yourself to write?' Sophie asked him.

'I is reading it hundreds of times,' the BFG said. 'And I is still reading it and teaching new words to myself and how to write them. It is the most scrumdiddlyumptious story.'

Sophie took the book out of his hand. '*Nicholas Nickleby*,' she read aloud.

'By Dahl's Chickens,' the BFG said.

'By *who?*' Sophie said.

Just then, there came a tremendous noise of galloping feet from outside the cave. 'What's that?' Sophie cried.

'That is all the giants zippfizzing off to another country to guzzle human beans,' the BFG said. He quickly popped Sophie into his waistcoat pocket, then hurried to the cave entrance and rolled back the stone.

Sophie, peeping out of her spy-hole, saw all nine of the fearsome giants coming past at full gallop.

'Where is you off to tonight?' shouted the BFG.

'We is all of us flushbunking off to England tonight,' answered the Fleshlumpeater as they went galloping past. 'England is a luctuous land and we is fancying a few nice little English chiddlers.'

'I,' shouted the Maidmasher, 'is knowing where there is a gigglehouse for girls and I is guzzling myself full as a frothblower!'

'And I knows where there is a bogglebox for boys!' shouted the Gizzardgulper. 'All I has to do is reach in and grab myself a handful! English boys is tasting extra lickswishy!'

In a few seconds, the nine galloping giants were out of sight.

'What *did* he mean?' Sophie said, poking her head out of the pocket. 'What is a gigglehouse for girls?'

'He is meaning a girls' school,' the BFG said. 'He will be eating them by the bundle.'

'Oh no!' cried Sophie.

'And boys from a boys' school,' said the BFG.

'It mustn't happen!' Sophie cried out. 'We've got to stop them! We can't just sit here and do nothing!'

'There's not a thing we can do,' the BFG said. 'We is helpless as horsefeathers.' He sat down on a large craggy blue rock near the entrance to his cave. He took Sophie from his pocket and put her beside him on the rock. 'It is now quite safe for you to be outside until they is coming back,' he said.

The sun had dipped below the horizon and it was getting dark.

The Great Plan

'We've absolutely *got* to stop them!' Sophie cried. 'Put me back in your pocket quick and we'll chase after them and warn everyone in England they're coming.'

'Redunculus and *um*-possible,' the BFG said. 'They is going two times as fast as me and they is finishing their guzzle before we is halfway.'

'But we can't just sit here doing nothing!' Sophie cried. 'How many girls and boys are they going to eat tonight?'

'Many,' the BFG said. 'The Fleshlumpeating Giant alone has a most squackling whoppsy appetite.'

'Will he snatch them out of their beds while they're sleeping?'

'Like peas out of a poddle,' the BFG said.

'I can't bear to think of it!' Sophie cried.

'Then don't,' the BFG said. 'For years and years I is sitting here on this very rock every night after night when they is galloping away, and I is feeling so sad for all the human beans they is going to gobble up. But I has had to get used to it. There is nothing I can do. If I wasn't a titchy little runty giant only twenty-four feet high then I would be stopping them. But that is absolutely out of the window.'

'Do you always know where they're going?' Sophie asked.

'Always,' the BFG said. 'Every night they is yelling at

me as they go bootling past. The other day they was yelling "We is off to Mrs Sippi and Miss Souri to guzzle them both!"'

'Disgusting,' Sophie said. 'I hate them.'

She and the Big Friendly Giant sat quietly side by side on the blue rock in the gathering dusk. Sophie had never felt so helpless in her life. After a while, she stood up and cried out, 'I can't stand it! Just think of those poor girls and boys who are going to be eaten alive in a few hours time! We can't just sit here and do nothing! We've got to go after those brutes!'

'No,' the BFG said.

'We must!' Sophie cried. 'Why won't you go?'

The BFG sighed and shook his head firmly. 'I has told you five or six times,' he said, 'and the third will be the last. I is *never* showing myself to human beans.'

'Why ever not?'

'If I do, they will be putting me in the zoo with all the jiggyraffes and cattypiddlers.'

'Nonsense,' Sophie said.

'And they will be sending *you* straight back to a norphanage,' the BFG went on. 'Grown-up human beans is not famous for their kindnesses. They is all squifflerotters and grinksludgers.'

'That simply isn't true!' Sophie cried angrily. 'Some of them are very kind indeed.'

'Who?' the BFG said. 'Name one.'

'The Queen of England,' Sophie said. 'You can't call her a squifflerotter or a grinksludger.'

'Well . . .' the BFG said.

'You can't call her a squeakpip or a notmucher either,' Sophie said, getting angrier and angrier.

'The Fleshlumpeater is longing dearly to guzzle her up,' the BFG said, smiling a little now.

'Who, the *Queen*?' Sophie cried, aghast.

'Yes,' the BFG answered. 'Fleshlumpeater says he is never eating a queen and he thinks perhaps she has an especially scrumdiddlyumptious flavour.'

'How dare he!' Sophie cried.

'But Fleshlumpeater says there is too many soldiers around her palace and he dursent try it.'

'He'd better not!' Sophie said.

'He is also saying he would like very much to guzzle one of the soldiers in his pretty red suit but he is worried about those big black furry hats they is wearing. He thinks they might be sticking in his throat.'

'I hope he chokes,' Sophie said.

'Fleshlumpeater is a very careful giant,' the BFG said.

Sophie was silent for a few moments. Then suddenly, in a voice filled with excitement, she cried out, 'I've got it! By golly, I think I've got it!'

'Got what?' asked the BFG.

'The answer!' cried Sophie. 'We'll go to the Queen! It's a terrific idea! If I went and told the Queen about these disgusting man-eating giants, I'm sure she'd do something about it!'

The BFG looked down at her sadly and shook his head. 'She is never believing you,' he said. 'Never in a month of Mondays.'

'I think she would.'

'Never,' the BFG said. 'It is sounding such a wonky tall story, the Queen will be laughing and saying "What awful rubbsquash!"'

'She would not!'

'Of course she would,' the BFG said. 'I has told you before that human beans is simply not *believing* in giants.'

'Then it's up to us to find a way of *making* her believe in them,' Sophie said.

'And how is you getting in to see the Queen anyway?' the BFG asked.

'Now hold on a sec,' Sophie said. 'Just you hold on a sec because I've got another idea.'

'Your ideas is full of crodswoggle,' the BFG said.

'Not this one,' Sophie said. 'You say that if we tell the Queen, she would never believe us?'

'I is certain she wouldn't,' the BFG said.

'But we aren't *going* to tell her!' Sophie said excitedly. 'We don't *have* to tell her! We'll make her *dream* it!'

'That is an even more frothbungling suggestion,' the BFG said. 'Dreams is lots of fun but nobody is believing in dreams either. You is only believing in a dream while you is actually dreaming it. But as soon as you is waking up you is saying "Oh thank goodness it was only a dream".'

'Don't you worry about that part of it,' Sophie said. 'I can fix that.'

'Never can you fix it,' the BFG said.

'I can! I swear I can! But first of all, let me ask you a very important question. Here it is. Can you make a person dream absolutely anything in the world?'

'Anything you like,' the BFG said proudly.

'If I said I wanted to dream that I was in a flying bathtub with silver wings, could you make me dream it?'

'I could,' the BFG said.

'But how?' Sophie said. 'You obviously don't have exactly that dream in your collection.'

'I do not,' the BFG said. 'But I could soon be mixing it up.'

'How could you mix it up?'

'It is a little bit like mixing a cake,' the BFG said. 'If you is putting the right amounts of all the different things into it, you is making the cake come out any way you want, sugary, splongy, curranty, Christmassy or grobs-witchy. It is the same with dreams.'

'Go on,' Sophie said.

'I has dillions of dreams on my shelfs, right or left?'

'Right,' Sophie said.

'I has dreams about bathtubs, lots of them. I has dreams about silver wings. I has dreams about flying. So all I has to do is mix those dreams together in the proper way and I is very quickly making a dream where you is flying in a bathtub with silver wings.'

'I see what you mean,' Sophie said. 'But I didn't know you could mix one dream with another.'

'Dreams *like* being mixed,' the BFG answered. 'They is getting very lonesome all by themselves in those glassy bottles.'

'Right,' Sophie said. 'Now then, do you have dreams about the Queen of England?'

'Lots of them,' the BFG said.

'And about giants?'

'Of course,' the BFG said.

'And about giants eating people?'

'Swiggles of them,' the BFG said.

'And about little girls like me?'

'Those is commonest of all,' the BFG said. 'I has bottles and bottles of dreams about little girls.'

'And you could mix them all up just as I want you to?' Sophie asked, getting more and more excited.

'Of course,' the BFG said. 'But how is this helping us? I think you is barking up the wrong dog.'

'Now hold on,' Sophie said. 'Listen carefully. I want you to mix a dream which you will blow into the Queen of England's bedroom when she is asleep. And this is how it will go.'

'Now hang on a mintick,' the BFG said. 'How is I possibly going to get near enough to the Queen of

England's bedroom to blow in my dream? You is talking dumbsilly.'

'I'll tell you that later,' Sophie said. 'For the moment please listen carefully. Here is the dream I want you to mix. Are you paying attention?'

'Very close,' the BFG said.

'I want the Queen to dream that nine disgusting giants, each one about fifty feet tall, are galloping to England in the night. She must dream their names as well. What are their names again?'

'Fleshlumpeater,' the BFG said. 'Manhugger. Bonecruncher. Childchewer. Meatdripper. Gizzardgulper. Maidmasher. Bloodbottler. And the Butcher Boy.'

'Let her dream all those names,' Sophie said. 'And let her dream that they will be creeping into England in the depths of the witching hour and snatching little boys and girls from their beds. Let her dream that they will be reaching into the bedroom windows and pulling the little boys and girls out of their beds and then ...' Sophie paused. 'Do they eat them on the spot or do they carry them away first?' she asked.

'They is usually just popping them straight into their mouths like popcorn,' the BFG said.

'Put that in the dream,' Sophie said. 'And then ... then the dream must say that when their tummies are full, they will go galloping back to Giant Country where no one can find them.'

'Is that all?' the BFG said.

'Certainly not,' Sophie said. 'You must then explain to the Queen in her dream that there is a Big Friendly Giant who can tell her where all those beasts are living, so that she can send her soldiers and her armies to capture them once and for all. And now let her dream one last and very important thing. Let her dream that there is a little girl called Sophie sitting on her window-sill who will tell her where the Big Friendly Giant is hiding.'

'Where is he hiding?' asked the BFG.

'We'll come to that later,' Sophie said. 'So the Queen dreams her dream, right?'

'Right,' the BFG said.

'Then she wakes up and the first thing she thinks is oh what a horrid dream. I'm so glad it *was* only a dream. And then she looks up from her pillow and what does she see?'

'What *does* she see?' the BFG asked.

'She sees a little girl called Sophie sitting on her window-sill, right there in real life before her very eyes.'

'How is you going to be sitting on the Queen's window-sill, may I beg?' the BFG said.

'*You* are going to put me there,' Sophie said. 'And that's the lovely part about it. If someone *dreams* that there is a little girl sitting on her window-sill and then she wakes up and sees that the little girl *really is* sitting there, that is a dream come true, is it not?'

'I is beginning to see where you is driving to,' the BFG said. 'If the Queen is knowing that part of her dream is true, then perhaps she is believing the rest of it is true as well.'

'That's about it,' Sophie said. 'But I shall have to convince her of that myself.'

'You said you is wanting the dream to say there is a Big Friendly Giant who is also going to talk to the Queen?'

'Absolutely,' Sophie said. 'You must. You are the only one who can tell her where to find the other giants.'

'How is I meeting the Queen?' asked the BFG. 'I is not wanting to be shooted at by her soldiers.'

'The soldiers are only in the front of the Palace,' Sophie said. 'At the back there is a huge garden and there are no soldiers in there at all. There is a very high wall with spikes on it around the garden to stop people climbing in. But you could simply walk over that.'

'How is you knowing all this about the Queen's Palace?' the BFG asked.

'Last year I was in a different orphanage,' Sophie said. 'It was in London and we used to go for walks all around there.'

'Is you helping me to find this Palace?' the BFG asked. 'I has never dared to go hide and sneaking around London in my life.'

'I'll show you the way,' Sophie said confidently.

'I is frightened of London,' the BFG said.

'Don't be,' Sophie said. 'It's full of tiny dark streets and there are very few people about in the witching hour.'

The BFG picked Sophie up between one finger and a thumb and placed her gently in the palm of the other hand. 'Is the Queen's Palace very big?' he asked.

'Huge,' Sophie said.

'Then how is we finding the right bedroom?'

'That's up to you,' Sophie said. 'You're supposed to be an expert at that sort of thing.'

'And you is absolutely sure the Queen will not put me in a zoo with all the cattypiddlers?'

'Of course she won't,' Sophie said. 'You'll be a hero. And you'll never have to eat snozzcumbers again.'

Sophie saw the BFG's eyes widen. He licked his lips.

'You mean it?' he said. 'You really mean it? No more disgustive snozzcumbers?'

'You couldn't get one if you wanted to,' Sophie said. 'Humans don't grow them.'

That did it. The BFG got to his feet. 'When is you wanting me to mix this special dream?' he asked.

'Now,' Sophie said. 'At once.'

'When is we going to see the Queen?' he said.

'Tonight,' Sophie said. 'As soon as you've mixed the dream.'

'Tonight?' the BFG cried. 'Why such a flushbunking flurry?'

'If we can't save tonight's children, we can anyway save tomorrow's,' Sophie said. 'What is more, I'm getting famished. I haven't had a thing to eat for twenty-four hours.'

'Then we had better get crackling,' the BFG said, moving back towards the cave.

Sophie kissed him on the tip of his thumb. 'I knew you'd do it!' she said. 'Come on! Let's hurry!'

Mixing the Dream

It was dark now. The night had already begun. The BFG, with Sophie sitting on his hand, hurried into the cave and put on those brilliant blinding lights that seemed to come from nowhere. He placed Sophie on the table. 'Stay there please,' he said, 'and no chittering. I is needing to listen only to silence when I is mixing up such a knotty plexicated dream as this.'

He hurried away from her. He got out an enormous empty glass jar that was the size of a washing machine. He clutched it to his chest and hurried towards the shelves on which stood the thousands and thousands of smaller jars containing the captured dreams.

'Dreams about giants,' he muttered to himself as he searched the labels. 'The giants is guzzling human beans ... no, not that one ... nor that one ... here's one! ... And here's another! ...' He grabbed the jars and un-screwed the tops. He tipped the dreams into the enor-mous jar he was clutching and as each one went in, Sophie caught a glimpse of a small sea-green blob tumbling from one jar into the other.

The BFG hurried towards another shelf. 'Now,' he muttered, 'I is wanting dreams about gigglehouses for girls ... and about boggleboxes for boys.' He was becom-ing very tense now. Sophie could almost see the excite-ment bubbling inside him as he scurried back and forth

among his beloved jars. There must have been fifty
thousand dreams altogether up there on the shelves, but
he seemed to know almost exactly where every one of
them was. 'Dreams about a little girl,' he muttered. 'And
dreams about me ... about the BFG ... come on, come
on, hurry up, get on with it ... now where in the wonky
world is I keeping those? ...'

And so it went on. In about half an hour the BFG had found all the dreams he wanted and had tipped them into the one huge jar. He put the jar on the table. Sophie sat watching him but said nothing. Inside the big jar, lying on the bottom of it, she could clearly see about fifty of those oval sea-green jellyish shapes, all pulsing gently in and out, some lying on top of others, but each one still a quite separate individual dream.

'Now we is mixing them,' the BFG announced. He went to the cupboard where he kept his bottles of frobscottle, and from it he took out a gigantic egg-beater. It was one of those that has a handle which you turn, and down below there are a lot of overlapping blades that go whizzing round. He inserted the bottom end of this contraption into the big jar where the dreams were lying. 'Watch,' he said. He started turning the handle very fast.

Flashes of green and blue exploded inside the jar. The dreams were being whisked into a sea-green froth.

'The poor things!' Sophie cried.

'They is not feeling it,' the BFG said as he turned the handle. 'Dreams is not like human beans or animals. They has no brains. They is made of zozimus.'

After about a minute, the BFG stopped whisking. The whole bottle was now full to the brim with large bubbles. They were almost exactly like the bubbles we ourselves blow from soapy water, except that these had even brighter and more beautiful colours swimming on their surfaces.

'Keep watching,' the BFG said.

Quite slowly, the topmost bubble rose up through the neck of the jar and floated away. A second one followed. Then a third and a fourth. Soon the cave was filled with hundreds of beautifully coloured bubbles, all drifting gently through the air. It was truly a wonderful sight. As Sophie watched them, they all started floating towards the cave entrance, which was still open.

'They're going out,' Sophie whispered.

'Of course,' the BFG said.

'Where to?'

'Those is all little tiny dream-bits that I isn't using,' the BFG said. 'They is going back to the misty country to join up with proper dreams.'

'It's all a bit beyond me,' Sophie said.

'Dreams is full of mystery and magic,' the BFG said. 'Do not try to understand them. Look in the big bottle and you will now see the dream you is wanting for the Queen.'

Sophie turned and stared into the great jar. On the

bottom of it, something was thrashing around wildly, bouncing up and down and flinging itself against the walls of the jar. 'Good heavens!' she cried. 'Is that it?'

'That's it,' the BFG said proudly.

'But it's ... it's horrible!' Sophie cried. 'It's jumping about! It wants to get out!'

'That's because it's a trogglehumper,' the BFG said. 'It's a nightmare.'

'Oh, but I don't want you to give the Queen a nightmare!' Sophie cried.

'If she is dreaming about giants guzzling up little boys and girls, then what is you expecting it to be except a nightmare?' the BFG said.

'Oh, no!' Sophie cried.

'Oh, yes,' the BFG said. 'A dream where you is seeing little chiddlers being eaten is about the most frightsome trogglehumping dream you can get. It's a kicksy bog-thumper. It's a whoppsy grobswitcher. It is all of them riddled into one. It is as bad as that dream I blew into the Fleshlumpeater this afternoon. It is worse.'

Sophie stared down at the fearful nightmare dream that was still thrashing away in the huge glass jar. It was much larger than the others. It was about the size and shape of, shall we say, a turkey's egg. It was jellyish. It had tinges of bright scarlet deep inside it. There was something terrible about the way it was throwing itself against the sides of the jar.

'I don't want to give the Queen a nightmare,' Sophie said.

'I is thinking,' the BFG said, 'that your Queen will be happy to have a nightmare if having a nightmare is going to save a lot of human beans from being gobbled up by filthsome giants. Is I right or is I left?'

'I suppose you're right,' Sophie said. 'It's got to be done.'

'She will soon be getting over it,' the BFG said.

'Have you put all the other important things into it?' Sophie asked.

'When I is blowing that dream into the Queen's bedroom,' the BFG said, 'she will be dreaming every single little thingalingaling you is asking me to make her dream.'

'About me sitting on the window-sill?'

'That part is very strong.'

'And about a Big Friendly Giant?'

'I is putting in a nice long gobbit about him,' the BFG said. As he spoke, he picked up one of his smaller jars and very quickly tipped the struggling thrashing troggle-humper out of the large jar into the small one. Then he screwed the lid tightly on to the small jar.

'That's it,' he announced. 'We is now ready.' He fetched his suitcase and put the small jar into it.

'Why bother to take a great big suitcase when you've only got one jar?' Sophie said. 'You could put the jar in your pocket.'

The BFG looked down at her and smiled. 'By goggles,' he said, taking the jar out of the suitcase, 'your head is not quite so full of grimesludge after all! I can see you is not born last week.'

'Thank you, kind sir,' Sophie said, making a little curtsey from the table-top.

'Is you ready to leave?' the BFG asked.

'I'm ready!' Sophie cried. Her heart was beginning to thump at the thought of what they were about to do. It really was a wild and crazy thing. Perhaps they would both be thrown into prison.

The BFG was putting on his great black cloak.

He tucked the jar into a pocket in his cloak. He picked up his long trumpet-like dream-blower. Then he turned and looked at Sophie who was still on the table-top. 'The dream-bottle is in my pocket,' he said. 'Is you going to sit in there with it during the travel?'

'Never!' cried Sophie. 'I refuse to sit next to that beastly thing!'

'Then where is you going to sit?' the BFG asked her.

Sophie looked him over for a few moments. Then she said, 'If you would be kind enough to swivel one of your lovely big ears so that it is lying flat like a dish, that would make a very cosy place for me to sit.'

'By gumbo, that is a squackling good idea!' the BFG said.

Slowly, he swivelled his huge right ear until it was like a great shell facing the heavens. He lifted Sophie up and placed her into it. The ear itself, which was about the size of a large tea-tray, was full of the same channels and crinkles as a human ear. It was extremely comfortable.

'I hope I don't fall down your earhole,' Sophie said, edging away from the large hole just beside her.

'Be very careful not to do that,' the BFG said. 'You would be giving me a cronking earache.'

The nice thing about being there was that she could whisper directly into his ear.

'You is tickling me a bit,' the BFG said. 'Please do not jiggle about.'

'I'll try not to,' Sophie said. 'Are we ready?'

'Oweeee!' yelled the BFG. 'Don't *do* that!'

'I didn't do anything,' Sophie said.

'You is talking too *loud!* You is forgetting that I is hearing every little thingalingaling fifty times louder than usual and there you is shouting away right inside my ear!'

'Oh gosh,' Sophie murmured. 'I forgot that.'

'Your voice is sounding like tunder and thrumpets!'

'I'm so sorry,' Sophie whispered. 'Is that better?'

'No!' cried the BFG. 'It sounds as though you is shootling off a bunderbluss!'

'Then how can I talk to you?' Sophie whispered.

'Don't!' cried the poor BFG. 'Please don't! Each word is like you is dropping buzzbombs in my earhole!'

Sophie tried speaking right under her breath. 'Is this better?' she said. She spoke so softly she couldn't even hear her own voice.

'That's better,' the BFG said. 'Now I is hearing you very nicely. What is it you is trying to say to me just now?'

'I was saying are we ready?'

'We is off!' cried the BFG, heading for the cave entrance. 'We is off to meet Her Majester the Queen!'

Outside the cave, he rolled the large round stone back into place and set off at a tremendous gallop.

Journey to London

The great yellow wasteland lay dim and milky in the moonlight as the Big Friendly Giant went galloping across it.

Sophie, still wearing only her nightie, was reclining comfortably in a crevice of the BFG's right ear. She was actually in the outer rim of the ear, near the top, where the edge of the ear folds over, and this folding-over bit made a sort of roof for her and gave her wonderful protection against the rushing wind. What is more, she was lying on skin that was soft and warm and almost velvety. Nobody, she told herself, had ever travelled in greater comfort.

Sophie peeped over the rim of the ear and watched the desolate landscape of Giant Country go whizzing by. They were certainly moving fast. The BFG went bouncing off the ground as though there were rockets in his toes and each stride he took lifted him about a hundred feet into the air. But he had not yet gone into that whizzing top gear of his, when the ground became blurred by speed and the wind howled and his feet didn't seem to be touching anything but air. That would come later.

Sophie had not slept for a long time. She was very tired. She was also warm and comfortable. She dozed off.

She didn't know how long she slept, but when she woke up again and looked out over the edge of the ear, the landscape had changed completely. They were in a green country now, with mountains and forests. It was still dark but the moon was shining as brightly as ever.

Suddenly and without slowing his pace, the BFG turned his head sharply to the left. For the first time during the entire journey he spoke a few words. 'Look quick-quick over there,' he said, pointing his long trumpet.

Sophie looked in the direction he was pointing. Through the murky darkness all she saw at first was a great cloud of dust about three hundred yards away.

'Those is the other giants all galloping back home after their guzzle,' the BFG said.

Then Sophie saw them. In the light of the moon, she saw all nine of those monstrous half-naked brutes thundering across the landscape together. They were galloping in a pack, their necks craned forward, their arms bent at the elbows, and worst of all, their stomachs bulging. The strides they took were incredible. Their speed was unbelievable. Their feet pounded and thundered on the ground and left a great sheet of dust behind them. But in ten seconds they were gone.

'A lot of little girlsies and boysies is no longer sleeping in their beds tonight,' the BFG said.

Sophie felt quite ill.

But this grim encounter made her more than ever determined to go through with her mission.

It must have been about an hour or so later that the BFG began to slow his pace. 'We is in England now,' he said suddenly.

Dark though it was, Sophie could see that they were in a country of green fields with neat hedges in between the fields. There were hills with trees all over them and occasionally there were roads with the lights of cars moving along. Each time they came to a road, the BFG was over it and away, and no motorist could possibly have seen anything except a quick black shadow flashing overhead.

All at once, a curious orange-coloured glow appeared in the night sky ahead of them.

'We is coming close to London,' the BFG said.

He slowed to a trot. He began looking about cautiously.

Groups of houses were now appearing on all sides. But there were still no lights in their windows. It was too early for anyone to be getting up yet.

'Someone's bound to see us,' Sophie said.

'Never is they seeing me,' the BFG said confidently. 'You is forgetting that I is doing this sort of thing for years and years and years. No human bean is ever catching even the smallest wink of me.'

'I did,' Sophie whispered.

'Ah,' he said. 'Yes. But you was the very first.'

During the next half-hour, things moved so swiftly and so silently that Sophie, crouching in the giant's ear, was unable to understand exactly what was going on. They were in streets. There were houses everywhere. Sometimes there were shops. There were bright lamps in the streets. There were quite a few people about and there were cars with lights on. But nobody ever noticed the BFG. It was impossible to understand quite how he did it. There was a kind of magic in his movements. He seemed to melt into the shadows. He would glide – that was the only word to describe his way of moving – he would glide noiselessly from one dark place to another, always moving, always gliding forward through the streets of London, his black cloak blending with the shadows of the night.

It is quite possible that one or two late-night wanderers might have thought they saw a tall black shadow skimming swiftly down a murky sidestreet, but even if they had, they would never have believed their own eyes. They would have dismissed it as an illusion and blamed themselves for seeing things that weren't there.

Sophie and the BFG came at last to a large place full of trees. There was a road running through it, and a lake. There were no people in this place and the BFG stopped for the first time since they had set out from his cave many hours before.

'What's the matter?' Sophie whispered in her under-the-breath voice.

'I is in a bit of a puddle,' he said.

'You're doing marvellously,' Sophie whispered.

'No, I isn't,' he said. 'I is now completely boggled. I is lost.'

'But why?'

'Because we is meant to be in the middle of London and suddenly we is in green pastures.'

'Don't be silly,' Sophie whispered. 'This *is* the middle of London. It's called Hyde Park. I know exactly where we are.'

'You is joking.'

'I'm not. I swear I'm not. We're almost there.'

'You mean we is nearly at the Queen's Palace?' cried the BFG.

'It's just across the road,' Sophie whispered. 'This is where *I* take over.'

'Which way?' the BFG asked.

'Straight ahead.'

The BFG trotted forward through the deserted park.

'Now stop.'

The BFG stopped.

'You see that huge roundabout ahead of us just outside the Park?' Sophie whispered.

'I see it.'

'That is Hyde Park Corner.'

Even now, when it was still an hour before dawn, there was quite a lot of traffic moving around Hyde Park Corner.

Then Sophie whispered, 'In the middle of the round-about there is an enormous stone arch with a statue of a horse and rider on top of it. Can you see that?'

The BFG peered through the trees. 'I is seeing it,' he said.

'Do you think that if you took a very fast run at it, you could jump clear over Hyde Park Corner, over the arch and over the horse and rider and land on the pavement the other side?'

'Easy,' the BFG said.

'You're sure? You're absolutely sure?'

'I promise,' the BFG said.

'Whatever you do, you mustn't land in the middle of Hyde Park Corner.'

'Don't get so flussed,' the BFG said. 'To me that is a snitchy little jump. There's not a thingalingaling to it.'

'Then *go!*' Sophie whispered.

The BFG broke into a full gallop. He went scorching

across the Park and just before he reached the railings that divided it from the street, he took off. It was a gigantic leap. He flew high over Hyde Park Corner and landed as softly as a cat on the pavement the other side.

'Well *done!*' Sophie whispered. 'Now quick! Over that wall!'

Directly in front of them, bordering the pavement, there was a brick wall with fearsome-looking spikes all along the top of it. A swift crouch, a little leap and the BFG was over it.

'We're there!' Sophie whispered excitedly. 'We're in the Queen's back garden!'

The Palace

'By gumdrops!' whispered the Big Friendly Giant. 'Is this really it?'

'There's the Palace,' Sophie whispered back.

Not more than a hundred yards away, through the tall trees in the garden, across the mown lawns and the tidy flower-beds, the massive shape of the Palace itself loomed through the darkness. It was made of whitish stone. The sheer size of it staggered the BFG.

'But this place is having a hundred bedrooms at least!' he said.

'Easily, I should think,' Sophie whispered.

'Then I is boggled,' the BFG said. 'How is I possibly finding the one where the Queen is sleeping?'

'Let's go a bit closer and have a look,' Sophie whispered.

The BFG glided forward among the trees. Suddenly he stopped dead. The great ear in which Sophie was sitting began to swivel round. 'Hey!' Sophie whispered. 'You're going to tip me out!'

'Ssshh!' the BFG whispered back. 'I is hearing something!' He stopped behind a clump of bushes. He waited. The ear was still swinging this way and that. Sophie had to hang on tight to the side of it to save herself from tumbling out. The BFG pointed through a gap in the bushes, and there, not more than fifty yards away, she saw a man padding softly across the lawn. He had a guard-dog with him on a leash.

The BFG stayed as still as a stone. So did Sophie. The man and the dog walked on and disappeared into the darkness.

'You was telling me they has no soldiers in the back garden,' the BFG whispered.

'He wasn't a soldier,' Sophie whispered. 'He was some sort of a watchman. We'll have to be careful.'

'I is not too worried,' the BFG said. 'These wacksey big ears of mine is picking up even the noise of a man *breathing* the other side of this garden.'

'How much longer before it begins to get light?' Sophie whispered.

'Very short,' the BFG said. 'We must go pell-mell for leather now!'

He glided forward through the vast garden, and once again Sophie noticed how he seemed to melt into the shadows wherever he went. His feet made no sound at all, even when he was walking on gravel.

Suddenly, they were right up close against the back wall of the great Palace. The BFG's head was level with the upper windows one flight up, and Sophie, sitting in his ear, had the same view. In all the windows on that floor the curtains seemed to be drawn. There were no lights showing anywhere. In the distance they could hear the muted sound of traffic going round Hyde Park Corner.

The BFG stopped and put his other ear, the one Sophie wasn't sitting in, close to the first window.

'No,' he whispered.

'What are you listening for?' Sophie whispered back.

'For breathing,' the BFG whispered. 'I is able to tell if it is a man human bean or a lady by the breathing-voice. We has a man in there. Snortling a little bit, too.'

He glided on, flattening his tall, thin, black-cloaked body against the side of the building. He came to the next window. He listened.

'No,' he whispered.

He moved on.

'This room is empty,' he whispered.

He listened in at several more windows, but at each one he shook his head and moved on.

When he came to the window in the very centre of the Palace, he listened but did not move on. 'Ho-ho,' he whispered. 'We has a lady sleeping in there.'

Sophie felt a little quiver go running down her spine. 'But who?' she whispered back.

The BFG put a finger to his lips for silence. He reached up through the open window and parted the curtains ever so slightly.

The orange glow from the night-sky over London crept into the room and cast a glimmer of light on to its walls. It was a large room. A lovely room. A rich carpet. Gilded chairs. A dressing-table. A bed. And on the pillow of the bed lay the head of a sleeping woman.

Sophie suddenly found herself looking at a face she had seen on stamps and coins and in the newspapers all her life.

For a few seconds she was speechless.

'Is that her?' the BFG whispered.

'Yes,' Sophie whispered back.

The BFG wasted no time. First, and very carefully, he started to raise the lower half of the large window. The

BFG was an expert on windows. He had opened thousands of them over the years to blow his dreams into children's bedrooms. Some windows got stuck. Some were wobbly. Some creaked. He was pleased to find that the Queen's window slid upward like silk. He pushed up the lower half as far as it would go so as to leave a place on the sill for Sophie to sit.

Next, he closed the crack in the curtains.

Then, with finger and thumb, he lifted Sophie out of his ear and placed her on the window-ledge with her legs dangling just inside the room, but behind the curtains.

'Now don't you go tip-toppling backwards,' the BFG whispered. 'You must always be holding on tight with both hands to the inside of the window-sill.'

Sophie did as he said.

It was summertime in London and the night was not cold, but don't forget that Sophie was wearing only her thin nightie. She would have given anything for a dressing-gown, not just to keep her warm but to hide the whiteness of her nightie from watchful eyes in the garden below.

The BFG was taking the glass jar from the pocket of his cloak. He unscrewed the lid. Now, very cautiously, he poured the precious dream into the wide end of his trumpet. He steered the trumpet through the curtains, far into the room, aiming it at the place where he knew the bed to be. He took a deep breath. He puffed out his cheeks and *pooff*, he blew.

Now he was withdrawing the trumpet, sliding it out very very carefully, like a thermometer.

'Is you all right sitting there?' he whispered.

'Yes,' Sophie murmured. She was quite terrified, but

determined not to show it. She looked down over her
shoulder. The ground seemed miles away. It was a nasty
drop.

'How long will the dream take to work?' Sophie
whispered.

'Some takes an hour,' the B F G whispered back. 'Some
is quicker. Some is slower still. But it is sure to find her in
the end.'

Sophie said nothing.

'I is going off to wait in the garden,' the B F G whispered. 'When you is wanting me, just call out my name
and I is coming very quick.'

'Will you hear me?' Sophie whispered.

'You is forgetting these,' the BFG whispered, smiling and pointing to his great ears.

'Goodbye,' Sophie whispered.

Suddenly, unexpectedly, the BFG leaned forward and kissed her gently on the cheek.

Sophie felt like crying.

When she turned to look at him, he was already gone. He had simply melted away into the dark garden.

The Queen

Dawn came at last, and the rim of a lemon-coloured sun rose up behind the roof-tops somewhere behind Victoria Station.

A while later, Sophie felt a little of its warmth on her back and was grateful.

In the distance, she heard a church clock striking. She counted the strikes. There were seven.

She found it almost impossible to believe that she, Sophie, a little orphan of no real importance in the world, was at this moment actually sitting high above the ground on the window-sill of the Queen of England's bedroom, with the Queen herself asleep in there behind the curtain not more than five yards away.

The very idea of it was absurd.

No one had ever done such a thing before.

It was a terrifying thing to be doing.

What would happen if the dream didn't work?

No one, least of all the Queen, would believe a word of her story.

It seemed possible that nobody had ever woken up to find a small child sitting behind the curtains on his or her window-sill.

The Queen was bound to get a shock.

Who wouldn't?

With all the patience of a small girl who has something

important to wait for, Sophie sat motionless on the window-sill.

How much longer? she wondered.

What time do Queens wake up?

Faint stirrings and distant sounds came to her from deep inside the belly of the Palace.

Then, all at once, beyond the curtains, she heard the voice of the sleeper in the bedroom. It was a slightly blurred sleep-talker's voice. 'Oh no!' it cried out. 'No! Don't – Someone stop them! – Don't let them do it! – I can't bear it! – Oh please stop them! – It's horrible! – Oh, it's ghastly! – No! No! No! . . .'

She is having the dream, Sophie told herself. It must be really horrid. I feel so sorry for her. But it has to be done.

After that, there were a few moans. Then there was a long silence.

Sophie waited. She looked over her shoulder. She was terrified that she would see the man with the dog down in the garden staring up at her. But the garden was deserted. A pale summer mist hung over it like smoke. It was an enormous garden, very beautiful, with a large funny-shaped lake at the far end. There was an island in the lake and there were ducks swimming on the water.

Inside the room, beyond the curtains, Sophie suddenly heard what was obviously a knock on the door. She heard the doorknob being turned. She heard someone entering the room.

'Good morning, Your Majesty,' a woman was saying. It was the voice of an oldish person.

There was a pause and then a slight rattle of china and silver.

'Will you have your tray on the bed, ma'am, or on the table?'

'Oh Mary! Something awful has just happened!' This was a voice Sophie had heard many times on radio and television, especially on Christmas Day. It was a very well-known voice.

'Whatever is it, ma'am?'

'I've just had the most frightful dream! It was a nightmare! It was awful!'

'Oh, I am sorry, ma'am. But don't be distressed. You're awake now and it will go away. It *was* only a dream, ma'am.'

'Do you know what I dreamt, Mary? I dreamt that girls and boys were being snatched out of their beds at boarding-school and were being eaten by the most ghastly giants! The giants were putting their arms in through the dormitory windows and plucking the children out with their fingers! One lot from a girls' school and another from a boys' school! It was all so ... so *vivid*, Mary! It was so *real*!'

There was a silence. Sophie waited. She was quivering with excitement. But why the silence? Why didn't the other one, the maid, why didn't she say something?

'What on earth's the matter, Mary?' the famous voice was saying.

There was another silence.

'Mary! You've gone as white as a sheet! Are you feeling ill?'

There was suddenly a crash and a clatter of crockery which could only have meant that the tray the maid was carrying had fallen out of her hands.

'Mary!' the famous voice was saying rather sharply. 'I

think you'd better sit down at once! You look as though you're going to faint! You really mustn't take it so hard just because I've had an awful dream.'

'That ... that ... that isn't the reason, ma'am.' The maid's voice was quivering terribly.

'Then for heaven's sake what *is* the reason?'

'I'm very sorry about the tray, ma'am.'

'Oh, don't worry about the *tray*. But what on earth was it that made you drop it? Why did you go white as a ghost all of a sudden?'

'You haven't seen the papers yet, have you, ma'am?'

'No, what do they say?'

Sophie heard the rustling of a newspaper as it was being handed over.

'It's like the very dream you had in the night, ma'am.'

'Rubbish, Mary. Where is it?'

'On the front page, ma'am. It's the big headlines.'

'Great Scott!' cried the famous voice. 'Eighteen girls vanish mysteriously from their beds at Roedean School! Fourteen boys disappear from Eton! Bones are found underneath dormitory windows!'

Then there was a pause punctuated by gasps from the famous voice as the newspaper article was clearly being read and digested.

'Oh, how ghastly!' the famous voice cried out. 'It's *absolutely* frightful! Bones under the windows! What *can* have happened? Oh, those *poor* children!'

'But ma'am ... don't you see, ma'am ...'

'See what, Mary?'

'Those children were taken away almost exactly as you dreamt it, ma'am!'

'Not by giants, Mary.'

'No, ma'am. But the bit about the girls and boys disappearing from their dormitories, you dreamt it so clearly and then it actually happened. That's why I came over all queer, ma'am.'

'I'm coming over a bit queer myself, Mary.'

'It gives me the shakes, ma'am, when something like that happens, it really does.'

'I don't blame you, Mary.'

'I shall get you some more breakfast, ma'am, and have this mess cleared up.'

'No! Don't go, Mary! Stay here a moment!'

Sophie wished she could see into the room, but she didn't dare touch the curtains. The famous voice began speaking again. 'I really *did* dream about those children, Mary. It was clear as crystal.'

'I know you did, ma'am.'

'I don't know how *giants* got into it. That was rubbish.'

'Shall I draw the curtains, ma'am, then we shall all feel better. It's a lovely day.'

'Please do.'

With a swish, the great curtains were pulled aside.

The maid screamed.

Sophie froze to the window-ledge.

The Queen, sitting up in her bed with *The Times* on her lap, glanced up sharply. Now it was *her* turn to freeze. She didn't scream as the maid had done. Queens are too self-controlled for that. She simply sat there staring wide-eyed and white-faced at the small girl who was perched on her window-sill in a nightie.

Sophie was petrified.

Curiously enough, the Queen looked petrified, too. One would have expected her to look surprised, as you or I would have done had we discovered a small girl sitting on our window-sill first thing in the morning. But the Queen didn't look surprised. She looked genuinely frightened.

The maid, a middle-aged woman with a funny cap on the top of her head, was the first to recover. 'What in the name of heaven do you think you're doing in here?' she shouted angrily to Sophie.

Sophie looked beseechingly towards the Queen for help.

The Queen was still staring at Sophie. Gaping at her would be more accurate. Her mouth was slightly open, her eyes were round and wide as two saucers, and the whole of that famous rather lovely face was filled with disbelief.

'Now listen here, young lady, how on earth did you get into this room?' the maid shouted furiously.

'I don't believe it,' the Queen was murmuring. 'I simply don't believe it.'

'I'll take her out, ma'am, at once,' the maid was saying.

'No, Mary! No, don't do that!' The Queen spoke so sharply that the maid was quite taken aback. She turned and stared at the Queen. What on earth had come over her? It looked as though she was in a state of shock.

'Are you all right, ma'am?' the maid was saying.

When the Queen spoke again, it was in a strange strangled sort of whisper. 'Tell me, Mary,' she said, 'tell me quite truthfully, is there *really* a little girl sitting on my window-sill, or am I still dreaming?'

'She is sitting there all right, ma'am, as clear as daylight, but heaven only knows how she got there! Your Majesty is certainly not dreaming it this time!'

'But that's exactly what I *did* dream!' the Queen cried out. 'I dreamt that *as well*! I dreamt there would be a little girl sitting on my window-sill in her nightie and she would talk to me!'

The maid, with her hands clasped across her starched white bosom, was staring at her mistress with a look of absolute disbelief on her face. The situation was getting beyond her. She was lost. She had not been trained to cope with this kind of madness.

'Are you real?' the Queen said to Sophie.

'Y-y-yes, Your Majesty,' Sophie murmured.

'What is your name?'

'Sophie, Your Majesty.'

'And how did you get up on to my window-sill? No, don't answer that! Hang on a moment! I dreamed that part of it, too! I dreamed that a giant put you there!'

'He did, Your Majesty,' Sophie said.

The maid gave a howl of anguish and clasped her hands over her face.

'Control yourself, Mary,' the Queen said sharply. Then to Sophie she said, 'You are not serious about the giant, are you?'

'Oh yes, Your Majesty. He's out there in the garden now.'

'Is he indeed,' the Queen said. The sheer absurdity of it all was helping her to regain her composure. 'So he's in the garden, is he?' she said, smiling a little.

'He is a *good* giant, Your Majesty,' Sophie said. 'You need not be frightened of him.'

'I'm delighted to hear it,' said the Queen, still smiling.

'He is my best friend, Your Majesty.'

'How nice,' the Queen said.

'He's a lovely giant, Your Majesty.'

'I'm quite sure he is,' the Queen said. 'But why have you and this giant come to see me?'

'I think you have dreamed that part of it, too, Your Majesty,' Sophie said calmly.

That pulled the Queen up short.

It took the smile right off her face.

She certainly *had* dreamed that part of it. She was remembering now how, at the end of her dream, it had said that a little girl and a big friendly giant would come and show her how to find the nine horrible man-eating giants.

But be careful, the Queen told herself. Keep very calm. Because this is surely not very far from the place where madness begins.

'You *did* dream that, didn't you, Your Majesty?' Sophie said.

The maid was out of it now. She just stood there goggling.

'Yes,' the Queen murmured. 'Yes, now you come to mention it, I did. But how do *you* know what I dreamed?'

'Oh, that's a long story, Your Majesty,' Sophie said. 'Would you like me to call the Big Friendly Giant?'

The Queen looked at the child. The child looked straight back at the Queen, her face open and quite serious. The Queen simply didn't know what to make of it. Was someone pulling her leg, she wondered.

'Shall I call him for you?' Sophie went on. 'You'll like him very much.'

The Queen took a deep breath. She was glad no one except her faithful old Mary was here to see what was going on. 'Very well,' she said. 'You may call your giant. No, wait a moment. Mary, pull yourself together and give me my dressing-gown and slippers.'

The maid did as she was told. The Queen got out of bed and put on a pale pink dressing-gown and slippers.

'You may call him now,' the Queen said.

Sophie turned her head towards the garden and called out, 'BFG! Her Majesty The Queen would like to see you!'

The Queen crossed over to the window and stood beside Sophie.

'Come down off that ledge,' she said. 'You're going to fall backwards any moment.'

Sophie jumped down into the room and stood beside the Queen at the open window. Mary, the maid, stood behind them. Her hands were now planted firmly on her hips and there was a look on her face which seemed to say, 'I want no part of this fiasco.'

'I don't see any giant,' the Queen said.

'Please wait,' Sophie said.

'Shall I take her away now, ma'am?' the maid said.

'Take her downstairs and give her some breakfast,' the Queen said.

Just then, there was a rustle in the bushes beside the lake.

Then out he came!

Twenty-four feet tall, wearing his black cloak with the grace of a nobleman, still carrying his long trumpet in one hand, he strode magnificently across the Palace lawn towards the window.

The maid screamed.

The Queen gasped.

Sophie waved.

The BFG took his time. He was very dignified in his approach. When he was close to the window where the three of them were standing, he stopped and made a slow graceful bow. His head, after he had straightened up again, was almost exactly level with the watchers at the window.

'Your Majester,' he said. 'I is your humbug servant.' He bowed again.

Considering she was meeting a giant for the first time in her life, the Queen remained astonishingly self-composed. 'We are very pleased to meet you,' she said.

Down below, a gardener was coming across the lawn

157

with a wheelbarrow. He caught sight of the BFG's legs over to his left. His gaze travelled slowly upwards along the entire height of the enormous body. He gripped the handles of the wheelbarrow. He swayed. He tottered. Then he keeled over on the grass in a dead faint. Nobody noticed him.

'Oh, Majester!' cried the BFG. 'Oh, Queen! Oh Monacher! Oh, Golden Sovereign! Oh, Ruler! Oh, Ruler of Straight Lines! Oh, Sultana! I is come here with my little friend Sophie ... to give you a ...' The BFG hesitated, searching for the word.

'To give me *what?*' the Queen said.

'A *sistance,*' the BFG said, beaming.

The Queen looked puzzled.

'He sometimes speaks a bit funny, Your Majesty,' Sophie said. 'He never went to school.'

'Then we must send him to school,' the Queen said. 'We have some very good schools in this country.'

'I has great secrets to tell Your Majester,' the BFG said.

'I should be delighted to hear them,' the Queen said. 'But not in my dressing-gown.'

'Shall you wish to get dressed, ma'am?' the maid said.

'Have either of you had breakfast?' the Queen said.

'Oh, *could we?*' Sophie cried. 'Oh, *please!* I haven't eaten a thing since yesterday!'

'I was about to have mine,' the Queen said, 'but Mary dropped it.'

The maid gulped.

'I imagine we have more food in the Palace,' the Queen said, speaking to the BFG. 'Perhaps you and your little friend would care to join me.'

'Will it be repulsant snozzcumbers, Majester?' the BFG asked.

'Will it be *what?*' the Queen said.

'Stinky snozzcumbers,' the BFG said.

'What *is* he talking about?' the Queen said. 'It sounds like a rude word to me.' She turned to the maid and said, 'Mary, ask them to serve breakfast for three in the ... I think it had better be in the Ballroom. That has the highest ceiling.' To the BFG, she said, 'I'm afraid you will have to go through the door on your hands and knees. I shall send someone to show you the way.'

The BFG reached up and lifted Sophie out of the window. 'You and I is leaving Her Majester alone to get dressed,' he said.

'No, leave the little girl here with me,' the Queen said. 'We'll have to find something for her to put on. She can't have breakfast in her nightie.'

The BFG returned Sophie to the bedroom.

'Can we have sausages, Your Majesty?' Sophie said. 'And bacon and fried eggs?'

'I think that might be managed,' the Queen answered, smiling.

'Just you wait till you taste it!' Sophie said to the BFG. 'No more snozzcumbers from now on!'

The Royal Breakfast

There was a frantic scurry among the Palace servants when orders were received from the Queen that a twenty-four-foot giant must be seated with Her Majesty in the Great Ballroom within the next half-hour.

The butler, an imposing personage named Mr Tibbs, was in supreme command of all the palace servants and he did the best he could in the short time available. A man does not rise to become the Queen's butler unless he is gifted with extraordinary ingenuity, adaptability, versatility, dexterity, cunning, sophistication, sagacity, discretion and a host of other talents that neither you nor I possess. Mr Tibbs had them all. He was in the butler's pantry sipping an early morning glass of light ale when the order reached him. In a split second he had made the following calculations in his head: if a normal six-foot man requires a three-foot-high table to eat off, a twenty-four-foot giant will require a twelve-foot-high table.

And if a six foot man requires a chair with a two-foot-high seat, a twenty-four-foot giant will require a chair with an eight-foot-high seat.

Everything, Mr Tibbs told himself, must be multiplied by four. Two breakfast eggs must become eight. Four rashers of bacon must become sixteen. Three pieces of toast must become twelve, and so on. These calculations about food were immediately passed on to Monsieur Papillion, the royal chef.

Mr Tibbs skimmed into the ballroom (butlers don't walk, they skim over the ground) followed by a whole army of footmen. The footmen all wore knee-breeches and every one of them displayed beautifully rounded calves and ankles. There is no way you can become a royal footman unless you have a well-turned ankle. It is the first thing they look at when you are interviewed.

'Push the grand piano into the centre of the room,' Mr Tibbs whispered. Butlers never raise their voices above the softest whisper.

Four footmen moved the piano.

'Now fetch a large chest-of-drawers and put it on top of the piano,' Mr Tibbs whispered.

Three other footmen fetched a very fine Chippendale mahogany chest-of-drawers and placed it on top of the piano.

'That will be his chair,' Mr Tibbs whispered. 'It is exactly eight feet off the ground. Now we shall make a table upon which this gentleman may eat his breakfast in comfort. Fetch me four very tall grandfather clocks. There are plenty of them around the Palace. Let each clock be twelve feet high.'

Sixteen footmen spread out around the Palace to find the clocks. They were not easy to carry and required four footmen to each one.

'Place the four clocks in a rectangle eight feet by four alongside the grand piano,' Mr Tibbs whispered.

The footmen did so.

'Now fetch me the young Prince's ping-pong table,' Mr Tibbs whispered.

The ping-pong table was carried in.

'Unscrew its legs and take them away,' Mr Tibbs whispered. This was done.

'Now place the ping-pong table on top of the four grandfather clocks,' Mr Tibbs whispered. To manage this, the footmen had to stand on stepladders.

Mr Tibbs stood back to survey the new furniture. 'None of it is in the classic style,' he whispered, 'but it will have to do.' He gave orders that a damask table-cloth should be draped over the ping-pong table, and in the end it looked really quite elegant after all.

At this point, Mr Tibbs was seen to hesitate. The footmen all stared at him, aghast. Butlers never hesitate, not even when they are faced with the most impossible problems. It is their job to be totally decisive at all times.

'Knives and forks and spoons,' Mr Tibbs was heard to mutter. 'Our cutlery will be like little pins in his hands.'

But Mr Tibbs didn't hesitate for long. 'Tell the head gardener,' he whispered, 'that I require immediately a brand new unused garden fork and also a spade. And for a knife we shall use the great sword hanging on the wall in the morning-room. But clean the sword well first. It was last used to cut off the head of King Charles the First and there may still be a little dried blood on the blade.'

When all this had been accomplished, Mr Tibbs stood near the centre of the Ballroom casting his expert butler's eye over the scene. Had he forgotten anything? He certainly had. What about a coffee cup for the large gentleman?

'Fetch me,' he whispered, 'the biggest jug you can find in the kitchen.'

A splendid one gallon porcelain water-jug was brought in and placed on the giant's table beside the garden fork and the garden spade and the great sword.

So much for the giant.

Mr Tibbs then had the footmen move a small delicate table and two chairs alongside the giant's table. This was for the Queen and for Sophie. The fact that the giant's table and chair towered far above the smaller table simply could not be helped.

All these arrangements were only just completed when the Queen, now fully dressed in a trim skirt and cashmere cardigan, entered the Ballroom holding Sophie by the hand. A pretty blue dress that had once belonged to one of the Princesses had been found for Sophie, and to make her look prettier still, the Queen had picked up a superb sapphire brooch from her dressing-table and had pinned it on the left side of Sophie's chest. The Big Friendly Giant followed behind them, but he had an awful job getting through the door. He had to squeeze himself through on his hands and knees, with two footmen pushing him from behind and two pulling from the front. But he got through in the end. He had removed his black cloak and got rid of his trumpet, and was now wearing his ordinary simple clothes.

As he walked across the Ballroom he had to stoop quite a lot to avoid hitting the ceiling. Because of this he failed to notice an enormous crystal chandelier. *Crash* went his head right into the chandelier. A shower of glass fell upon the poor BFG. 'Gunghummers and bogswinkles!' he cried. 'What was that?'

'It *was* Louis the Fifteenth,' the Queen said, looking slightly put out.

'He's never been in a house before,' Sophie said.

Mr Tibbs scowled. He directed four footmen to clear up the mess, then, with a disdainful little wave of the hand, he indicated to the giant that he should seat himself on top of the chest-of-drawers on top of the grand piano.

'What a phizz-whizzing flushbunking seat!' cried the BFG. 'I is going to be bug as a snug in a rug up here.'

'Does he always speak like that?' the Queen asked.

'Quite often,' Sophie said. 'He gets tangled up with his words.'

The BFG sat down on the chest-of-drawers-piano and gazed in wonder around the Great Ballroom. 'By gum-drops!' he cried. 'What a spliffling whoppsy room we is in! It is so gigantuous I is needing bicirculers and telescoops to see what is going on at the other end!'

Footmen arrived carrying silver trays with fried eggs, bacon, sausages and fried potatoes.

At this point, Mr Tibbs suddenly realized that in order

166

to serve the BFG at his twelve-foot-high-grandfather-clock table, he would have to climb to the top of one of the tall step-ladders. What's more, he must do it balancing a huge warm plate on the palm of one hand and holding a gigantic silver coffee-pot in the other. A normal man would have flinched at the thought of it. But good butlers never flinch. Up he went, up and up and up, while the Queen and Sophie watched him with great interest. It is possible they were both secretly hoping he would lose his balance and go crashing to the floor. But good butlers never crash.

At the top of the ladder, Mr Tibbs, balancing like an acrobat, poured the BFG's coffee and placed the enormous plate before him. On the plate there were eight eggs, twelve sausages, sixteen rashers of bacon and a heap of fried potatoes.

'What is this please, Your Majester?' the BFG asked, peering down at the Queen.

'He has never eaten anything except snozzcumbers

before in his life,' Sophie explained. 'They taste revolting.'

'They don't seem to have stunted his growth,' the Queen said.

The BFG grabbed the garden spade and scooped up all the eggs, sausages, bacon and potatoes in one go and shovelled them into his enormous mouth.

'By goggles!' he cried. 'This stuff is making snozzcumbers taste like swatchwallop!'

The Queen glanced up, frowning. Mr Tibbs looked down at his toes and his lips moved in silent prayer.

'That was only one titchy little bite,' the BFG said. 'Is you having any more of this delunctious grubble in your cupboard, Majester?'

'Tibbs,' the Queen said, showing true regal hospitality, 'fetch the gentleman another dozen fried eggs and a dozen sausages.'

Mr Tibbs swam out of the room muttering unspeakable words to himself and wiping his brow with a white handkerchief.

The BFG lifted the huge jug and took a swallow. 'Owch!' he cried, blowing a mouthful across the ballroom. 'Please, what is this horrible swigpill I is drinking, Majester?'

'It's coffee,' the Queen told him. 'Freshly roasted.'

'It's filthsome!' the BFG cried out. 'Where is the frobscottle?'

'The *what?*' the Queen asked.

'Delumptious fizzy frobscottle,' the BFG answered. 'Everyone must be drinking frobscottle with breakfast, Majester. Then we can all be whizzpopping happily together afterwards.'

170

before last. They was galloping off to Sweden for the Sweden sour taste.'

'Fetch me a telephone,' the Queen commanded.

Mr Tibbs placed the instrument on the table. The Queen lifted the receiver. 'Get me the King of Sweden,' she said.

'Good morning,' the Queen said. 'Is everything all right in Sweden?'

'Everything is terrible!' the King of Sweden answered. 'There is panic in the capital! Two nights ago, twenty-six of my loyal subjects disappeared! My whole country is in in a panic!'

'Your twenty-six loyal subjects were all eaten by giants,' the Queen said. 'Apparently they like the taste of Swedes.'

'Why do they like the taste of Swedes?' the King asked.

'Because the Swedes of Sweden have a sweet and sour taste. So says the BFG,' the Queen said.

'I don't know *what* you're talking about,' the King said, growing testy. 'It's hardly a joking matter when one's loyal subjects are being eaten like popcorn.'

'They've eaten mine as well,' the Queen said.

'Who's *they*, for heaven's sake?' the King asked.

'Giants,' the Queen said.

'Look here,' the King said, 'are you feeling all right?'

'It's been a rough morning,' the Queen said. 'First I had a horrid nightmare, then the maid dropped my breakfast and now I've got a giant on the piano.'

'You need a doctor quick!' cried the King.

'I'll be all right,' the Queen said. 'I must go now. Thanks for your help.' She replaced the receiver.

'Your BFG is right,' the Queen said to Sophie. 'Those nine man-eating brutes *did* go to Sweden.'

'It's horrible,' Sophie said. 'Please stop them, Your Majesty.'

'I'd like to make one more check before I call out the troops,' the Queen said. Once more, she looked up at the BFG. He was eating doughnuts now, popping them into his mouth ten at a time, like peas. 'Think hard, BFG,' she said. 'Where did those horrid giants say they were galloping off to *three* nights ago?'

The BFG thought long and hard.

'Ho-ho!' he cried at last. 'Yes, I is remembering!'

'Where?' asked the Queen.

'One was off to Baghdad,' the BFG said. 'As they is galloping past my cave, Fleshlumpeater is waving his arms and shouting at me, "I is off to Baghdad and I is going to Baghdad and mum and every one of their ten children as well!"'

Once more, the Queen lifted the receiver. 'Get me the Lord Mayor of Baghdad,' she said. 'If they don't have a Lord Mayor, get me the next best thing.'

In five seconds, a voice was on the line. 'Here is the Sultan of Baghdad speaking,' the voice said.

'Listen, Sultan,' the Queen said. 'Did anything unpleasant happen in your city three nights ago?'

'Every night unpleasant things are happening in Baghdad,' the Sultan said. 'We are chopping off people's heads like you are chopping parsley.'

'I've never chopped parsley in my life,' the Queen said. 'I want to know if anyone has *disappeared* recently in Baghdad?'

'Only my uncle, Caliph Haroun al Rashid,' the Sultan

said. 'He disappeared from his bed three nights ago together with his wife and ten children.'

'There you is!' cried the BFG, whose wonderful ears enabled him to hear what the Sultan was saying to the Queen on the telephone. 'Fleshlumpeater did that one! He went off to Baghdad to bag dad and mum and all the little kiddles!'

The Queen replaced the receiver. 'That proves it,' she said, looking up at the BFG. 'Your story is apparently quite true. Summon the Head of the Army and the Head of the Air Force immediately!'

The Plan

The Head of the Army and the Head of the Air Force
stood at attention beside the Queen's breakfast table.
Sophie was still in her seat and the BFG was still high up
on his crazy perch.

It took the Queen only five minutes to explain the
situation to the military men.

'I *knew* there was something like this going on, Your
Majesty,' the Head of the Army said. 'For the last
ten years we have been getting reports from nearly
every country in the world about people disappearing
mysteriously in the night. We had one only the other day
from Panama . . .'

'For the hatty taste!' cried the BFG.

'And one from Wellington, in New Zealand,' said the
Head of the Army.

'For the booty flavour!' cried the BFG.

'What *is* he talking about?' said the Head of the Air
Force.

'Work it out for yourself,' the Queen said. 'What time
is it? Ten a.m. In eight hours those nine blood-thirsty
brutes will be galloping off to gobble up another couple
of dozen unfortunate wretches. They have to be stopped.
We must act fast.'

'We'll bomb the blighters!' shouted the Head of the Air
Force.

'We'll mow them down with machine-guns!' cried the Head of the Army.

'I do not approve of murder,' the Queen said.

'But they are murderers themselves!' cried the Head of the Army.

'That is no reason why we should follow their example,' the Queen said. 'Two wrongs don't make a right.'

'And two rights don't make a left!' cried the BFG.

'We must bring them back alive,' the Queen said.

'How?' the two military men said together. 'They are all fifty feet high. They'd knock us down like ninepins!'

'Wait!' cried the BFG. 'Hold your horseflies! Keep your skirts on! I think I has the answer to the maiden's hair!'

'Let him speak,' the Queen said.

'Every afternoon,' the BFG said, 'all these giants is in the Land of Noddy.'

'I can't understand a word this feller says,' the Head of the Army snapped. 'Why doesn't he speak clearly?'

'He means the Land of Nod,' Sophie said. 'It's pretty obvious.'

'Exunckly!' cried the BFG. 'Every afternoon all these nine giants is lying on the ground snoozling away in a very deep sleep. They is always resting like that before they is galloping off to guzzle another helping of human beans.'

'Go on,' they said. 'So what?'

'So what you soldiers has to do is to creep up to the giants while they is still in the Land of Noddy and tie their arms and legs with mighty ropes and whunking chains.'

'Brilliant,' the Queen said.

'That's all very well,' said the Head of the Army. 'But how do we get the brutes back here? We can't load fifty-foot giants on to trucks! Shoot 'em on the spot, that's what I say!'

The BFG looked down from his lofty perch and said, this time to the Head of the Air Force, 'You is having bellypoppers, is you not?'

'Is he being rude?' the Head of the Air Force said.

'He means helicopters,' Sophie told him.

'Then why doesn't he say so? Of course we have helicopters.'

'Whoppsy big bellypoppers?' asked the BFG.

'Very big ones,' the Head of the Air Force said proudly. 'But no helicopter is big enough to get a giant like that inside it.'

'You do not put him inside,' the BFG said. 'You sling him underneath the belly of your bellypopper and carry him like a porteedo.'

'Like a *what*?' said the Head of the Air Force.

'Like a torpedo,' Sophie said.

'Could you do that, Air Marshal?' the Queen asked.

'Well, I suppose we *could*,' the Head of the Air Force admitted grudgingly.

'Then get cracking!' the Queen said, 'You'll need nine helicopters, one for each Giant.'

'Where is this place?' the Air Force man said to the BFG. 'I presume you can pinpoint it on the map?'

'*Pinpoint?*' said the BFG. '*Map?* I is never hearing these words before. Is this Air Force bean talking slushbungle?'

The Air Marshal's face turned the colour of a ripe plum. He was not used to being told he was talking slushbungle. The Queen, with her usual admirable tact and good sense, came to the rescue. 'BFG,' she said, 'can you tell us *more or less* where this Giant Country is?'

'No, Majester,' the BFG said. 'Not on my nelly.'

'Then we're jiggered!' cried the Army General.

'This is ridiculous!' cried the Air Marshal.

'You must not be giving up so easy,' the BFG said calmly. 'The first titchy bobsticle you meet and you begin shouting you is biffsquiggled.'

The Army General was no more used to being insulted than the Air Marshal. His face began to swell with fury and his cheeks blew out until they looked like two huge ripe tomatoes. 'Your Majesty!' he cried. 'We are dealing with a lunatic! I want nothing more to do with this ridiculous operation!'

The Queen, who was used to the tantrums of her senior officials, ignored him completely. 'BFG,' she said, 'Would you please tell these rather dim-witted characters exactly what to do.'

'A pleasure, Majester,' said the BFG. 'Now listen to me carefully, you two bootbogglers.'

The military men began to twitch, but they stayed put.

'I is not having the foggiest idea where Giant Country is in the world,' the BFG said, 'but I is always able to gallop there. I is galloping forthwards and backwards from Giant Country every night to blow my dreams into little chiddler's bedrooms. I is knowing the way very well. So all you is having to do is this. Put your nine big bellyhoppers up in the air and let them follow me as I is galloping along.'

'How long will the journey take?' the Queen asked.

'If we is leaving now,' the BFG said, 'we will be arriving just as the giants is having their afternoon snozzle.'

'Splendid,' said the Queen. Then turning to the two

military men, she said, 'Prepare to leave immediately.'

The Head of the Army, who was feeling pretty miffed by the whole business, said, 'That's all very well, Your Majesty, but what are we going to do with the blighters once we've got them back?'

'Don't you worry about that,' the Queen told him. 'We'll be ready for them. Hurry up, now! Off you go!'

'If it pleases Your Majesty,' Sophie said, 'I should like to ride with the BFG, to keep him company.'

'Where will you sit?' asked the Queen.

'In his ear,' Sophie said. 'Show them, BFG.'

The BFG got down from his high chair. He picked Sophie up in his fingers. He swivelled his huge right ear until it was parallel with the ground, then he placed Sophie gently inside it.

The Heads of the Army and the Air Force stood there goggling. The Queen smiled. 'You really are rather a wonderful giant,' she said.

'Majester,' the BFG said, 'I is wishing to ask a very special thing from you.'

'What is it?' the Queen said.

'Could I please bring back here in the bellypoppers all my collection of dreams? They is taking me years and years to collect and I is not wanting to lose them.'

'Why of course,' the Queen said. 'I wish you a safe journey.'

The BFG had made thousands of journeys to and from
Giant Country over the years, but he had never in his life
made one quite like this, with nine huge helicopters
roaring along just over his head. He had never before
travelled in broad daylight either. He hadn't dared to.

But this was different. Now he was doing it for the Queen of England herself and he was frightened of nobody.

As he galloped across the British Isles with the helicopters thundering above him, people stood and gaped and wondered what on earth was going on. They had never seen the likes of it before. And they never would again.

Every now and then, the pilots of the helicopters would catch a glimpse of a small girl wearing glasses crouching in the giant's right ear and waving to them. They always waved back. The pilots marvelled at the giant's speed and at the way he leapt across wide rivers and over huge houses.

But they hadn't seen anything yet.

'Be careful to hang on tight!' the BFG said. 'We is going fast as a fizzlecrump!' The BFG changed into his famous top gear and all at once he began to fly forward as though there were springs in his legs and rockets in his toes. He went skimming over the earth like some magical hop-skip-and-jumper with his feet hardly ever touching the ground. As usual, Sophie had to crouch low in the crevice of his ear to save herself from being swept clean away.

The nine pilots in their helicopters suddenly realized they were being left behind. The giant was streaking ahead. They opened their throttles to full speed, and even then they were only just able to keep up.

In the leading machine, the Head of the Air Force was sitting beside the pilot. He had a world atlas on his knees and he kept staring first at the atlas, then at the ground below, trying to figure out where they were going. Frantically he turned the pages of the atlas. 'Where the devil *are* we going?' he cried.

'I haven't the foggiest idea,' the pilot answered. 'The Queen's orders were to follow the giant and that's exactly what I'm doing.'

The pilot was a young Air Force officer with a bushy

moustache. He was very proud of his moustache. He was also quite fearless and he loved adventure. He thought this was a super adventure. 'It's fun going to new places,' he said.

'*New places!*' shouted the Head of the Air Force. 'What the blazes d'you mean *new places*?'

'This place we're flying over now isn't in the atlas, is it?' the pilot said, grinning.

'You're darn right it isn't in the atlas!' cried the Head of the Air Force. 'We've flown clear off the last page!'

'I expect that old giant knows where he's going,' the young pilot said.

'He's leading us to disaster!' cried the Head of the Air Force. He was shaking with fear. In the seat behind him sat the Head of the Army who was even more terrified.

'You don't mean to tell me we've gone right out of the atlas?' he cried, leaning forward to look.

'That's exactly what I *am* telling you!' cried the Air Force man. 'Look for yourself. Here's the very last map in the whole flaming atlas! We went off that over an hour ago!' He turned the page. As in all atlases, there were two completely blank pages at the very end. 'So now we must be somewhere here,' he said, putting a finger on one of the blank pages.

'Where's here?' cried the Head of the Army.

The young pilot was still grinning broadly. He said to them, 'That's why they always put two blank pages at the back of the atlas. They're for new countries. You're meant to fill them in yourself.'

The Head of the Air Force glanced down at the ground below. 'Just look at this godforsaken desert!' he cried. 'All the trees are dead and all the rocks are blue!'

'The giant has stopped,' the young pilot said. 'He's waving us down.'

The pilots throttled back the engines and all nine helicopters landed safely on the great yellow wasteland. Then each of them lowered a ramp from its belly. Nine jeeps, one from each helicopter, were driven down the ramps. Each jeep contained six soldiers and a vast quantity of thick rope and heavy chains.

'I don't see any giants,' the Head of the Army said.

'The giants is all just out of sight over there,' the BFG told him. 'But if you is taking these sloshbuckling noisy

186

bellypoppers any closer, all the giants is waking up at once and then pop goes the weasel.'

'So you want us to proceed by jeep?' the Head of the Army said.

'Yes,' the BFG said. 'But you must all be very very hushy quiet. No roaring of motors. No shouting. No mucking about. No piggery-jokery.'

The BFG, with Sophie still in his ear, trotted forward and the jeeps followed close behind.

Suddenly the most dreadful rumbling noise was heard by everyone. The Head of the Army went pea-green in the face. 'Those are guns!' he cried. 'There is a battle raging somewhere up ahead of us! Turn back, the lot of you! Let's get out of here!'

'Pigspiffle!' the BFG said. 'Those noises is not guns.'

'Of course they're guns!' shouted the Head of the Army. 'I am a military man and I know a gun when I hear one! Turn back!'

'Those is just the giants snortling in their sleep,' the BFG said. 'I is a giant myself and I know a giant's snortle when I is hearing one.'

'Are you quite sure?' the Army man said anxiously.

'Positive,' the BFG said.

'Proceed cautiously,' the Army man ordered.

They all moved on.

Then they saw them!

Even at a distance, they were enough to scare the daylights out of the soldiers. But when they got close and saw what the giants really looked like, they began to sweat with fear. Nine fearsome, ugly, half-naked, fifty-feet-long brutes lay sprawled over the ground in various

187

grotesque attitudes of sleep, and the sound of their snoring was indeed like gunfire in a battle.

The BFG raised a hand. The jeeps all stopped. The soldiers got out.

'What happens if one of them wakes up?' whispered the Head of the Army, his knees knocking together from fear.

'If any one of them is waking up, he will gobble you down before you can say knack jife,' the BFG answered, grinning hugely. 'Me is the only one what won't be gobbled up because giants is never eating giants. Me and Sophie is the only safe ones because I is hiding her if that happens.'

The Head of the Army took several paces to the rear. So did the Head of the Air Force. They climbed rather quickly back into their jeep, ready to make a fast getaway if necessary. 'Go forward, men!' the Head of the Army said. 'Go forward and do your duty bravely!'

The soldiers crept forward with their ropes and chains. All of them were trembling mightily. None dared speak a word.

The BFG, with Sophie now sitting on the palm of his hand, stood near by watching the operation.

To give the soldiers their due, they were extremely courageous. There were six well-trained efficient men working on each giant and within ten minutes eight out of the nine giants had been trussed up like chickens and were still snoring contentedly. The ninth, who happened to be the Fleshlumpeater, was causing trouble for the soldiers because he was lying with his right arm tucked underneath his enormous body. It was impossible to tie his wrists and arms together without first getting that arm out from underneath him.

Very very cautiously, the six soldiers who were working on the Fleshlumpeater began to pull at the huge arm, trying to release it. The Fleshlumpeater opened his tiny piggy black eyes.

'Which of you foulpesters is wiggling my arm?' he bellowed. 'Is that you, you rotsome Manhugger?'

Suddenly he saw the soldiers. In a flash, he was sitting up. He looked around him. He saw more soldiers. With a roar, he leapt to his feet. The soldiers, petrified with fear, froze where they were. They had no weapons with them. The Head of the Army put his jeep into reverse.

'Human beans!' the Flushlumpeater yelled. 'What is all you flushbunking rotsome half-baked beans doing in our country?' He made a grab at a soldier and swept him up in his hand.

'I is having early suppers today!' he shouted, holding the poor squirming soldier at arm's length and roaring with laughter.

Sophie, standing on the palm of the BFG's hand, was watching horrorstruck. 'Do something!' she cried.

'Quick, before he eats him!'

'Put that human bean down!' the BFG shouted.

The Fleshlumpeater turned and stared at the BFG. 'What is *you* doing here with all these grotty twiglets!' he bellowed. 'You is making me very suspichy!'

The BFG made a rush at the Fleshlumpeater, but the colossal fifty-four-foot-high giant simply knocked him over with a flick of his free arm. At the same time, Sophie fell off the BFG's palm on to the ground. Her mind was racing. She *must* do something! She *must!* She *must!* She remembered the sapphire brooch the Queen had pinned on to her chest. Quickly, she undid it.

'I is guzzling you nice and slow!' the Fleshlumpeater was saying to the soldier in his hand. 'Then I is guzzling ten or twenty more of you midgy little maggots down there! You is not getting away from me because I is galloping fifty times faster than you!'

Sophie ran up behind the Fleshlumpeater. She was holding the brooch between her fingers. When she was right up close to the great naked hairy legs, she rammed the three-inch long pin of the brooch as hard as she could into the Fleshlumpeater's right ankle. It went deep into the flesh and stayed there.

The giant gave a roar of pain and jumped high in the air. He dropped the soldier and made a grab for his ankle.

The B F G, knowing what a coward the Fleshlump-eater was, saw his chance. 'You is bitten by a snake!' he shouted. 'I seed it biting you! It was a frightsome poisnowse viper! It was a dreadly dungerous vindscreen viper!'

'Save our souls!' bellowed the Fleshlumpeater. 'Sound the crumpets! I is bitten by a septicous venomsome vindscreen viper!' He flopped to the ground and sat there howling his head off and clutching his ankle with both hands. His fingers felt the brooch. 'The teeth of the dreadly viper is still sticking into me!' he yelled. 'I is feeling the teeth sticking into my anklet!'

The B F G saw his second chance. 'We must be getting those viper's teeth out at once!' he cried. 'Otherwise you is deader than duck-soup! I is helping you!'

The B F G knelt down beside the Fleshlumpeater. 'You must grab your anklet very tight with both hands!' he ordered. 'That will stop the poisnowse juices from the venomsome viper going up your leg and into your heart!'

The Fleshlumpeater grabbed his ankle with both hands.

'Now close your eyes and grittle your teeth and look up to heaven and say your prayers while I is taking out the teeth of the venomsome viper,' the B F G said.

The terrified Fleshlumpeater did exactly as he was told.

The B F G signalled for some rope. A soldier rushed it over to him. With both the Fleshlumpeater's hands gripping his ankle, it was a simple matter for the B F G to tie the ankles and hands together with a tight knot.

193

'I is pulling out the frightsome viper's teeth!' the BFG
said as he pulled the knot tight.

'Do it quickly!' shouted the Fleshlumpeater, 'before I
is pizzened to death!'

'There we is,' said the BFG, standing up. 'You can
look now.'

When the Fleshlumpeater saw that he was trussed up
like a turkey, he gave a yell so loud that the heavens
trembled. He rolled and he wriggled, he fought and he
figgled, he squirmed and he squiggled. But there was not
a thing he could do.

'Well done you!' Sophie cried.

'Well done *you!*' said the BFG, smiling down at the
little girl. 'You is saving all of our lives!'

'Will you please get that brooch back for me,' Sophie
said. 'It belongs to the Queen.'

The BFG pulled the beautiful brooch out of the Fleshlumpeater's ankle. The Fleshlumpeater howled. The

BFG wiped the pin and handed it back to Sophie.

Curiously, not one of the other eight snoring giants had woken up during this shimozzle. 'When you is only sleeping one or two hours a day, you is sleeping extra doubly deep,' the BFG explained.

The Heads of the Army and the Air Force drove forward once again in their jeep. 'Her Majesty will be very pleased with me,' the Head of the Army said. 'I shall probably get a medal. What's the next move?'

'Now you is all driving over to my cave to load up my bottles of dreams,' the BFG said.

'We can't waste time with that rubbish,' the Army General said.

'It is the Queen's order,' Sophie said. She was now back on the BFG's hand.

So the nine jeeps drove across to the BFG's cave and the great dream-loading operation began. There were fifty-thousand jars in all to be loaded up, more than five thousand to each jeep, and it took over an hour to finish the job.

While the soldiers were loading the dreams, the BFG and Sophie disappeared over the mountains on a mysterious errand. When they came back, the BFG had a sack the size of a small house slung over his shoulder.

'What's that you've got in there?' the Head of the Army demanded to know.

'Curiosity is killing the rat,' the BFG said, and he turned away from the silly man.

When he was sure that all his precious dreams had been safely loaded on to the jeeps, the BFG said, 'Now we is driving back to the bellypoppers and picking up the frightsome giants.'

The jeeps drove back to the helicopters. The fifty thousand dreams were carried carefully, jar by jar, on to the helicopters. The soldiers climbed back on board, but the B F G and Sophie stayed on the ground. Then they all returned to where the nine giants were lying.

It was a fine sight to see them, these great air machines hovering over the trussed-up giants. It was an even finer sight to see the giants being woken up by the terrific thundering of the engines overhead, and the finest sight of all was to observe those nine hideous brutes squirming and twisting about on the ground like a mass of mighty snakes as they tried to free themselves from their ropes and chains.

'I is flushbunkled!' roared the Fleshlumpeater.
'I is splitzwiggled!' yelled the Childchewer.
'I is swogswalloped!' bellowed the Bonecruncher.
'I is goosegruggled!' howled the Manhugger.
'I is gunzleswiped!' shouted the Meatdripper.
'I is fluckgungled!' screamed the Maidmasher.
'I is slopgroggled!' squawked the Gizzardgulper.
'I is crodsquinkled!' yowled the Bloodbottler.
'I is bopmuggered!' screeched the Butcher Boy.

The nine giant-carrying helicopters each chose a separate giant and hovered directly over him. Very strong steel hawsers with hooks on the ends of them were lowered from the front and rear of each helicopter. The BFG quickly secured the hooks to the giants' chains, one hook near the legs and the other near the arms. Then very slowly, the giants were winched up into the air, parallel with the ground. The giants roared and bellowed, but there was nothing they could do.

The BFG, with Sophie once more resting comfortably in his ear, set off at a gallop for England. The helicopters all banked around and followed after him.

It was an amazing spectacle, those nine helicopters winging through the sky, each with a trussed-up fifty-foot-long giant slung underneath it. The giants themselves must have found it an interesting experience. They never stopped bellowing, but their howls were drowned by the noise of the engines.

When it began to get dark, the helicopters switched on powerful searchlights and trained them on to the galloping giant so as to keep him in sight. They flew right through the night and arrived in England just as dawn was breaking.

Feeding Time

While the giants were being captured, a tremendous
bustle and hustle was going on back home in England.
Every earth-digger and mechanical contrivance in the
country had been mobilized to dig the colossal hole
in which the nine giants were to be permanently
imprisoned.

Ten thousand men and ten thousand machines worked
ceaselessly through the night under powerful arc-lights,
and the massive task was completed only just in time.

The hole itself was about twice the size of a football
field and five hundred feet deep. The walls were
perpendicular and engineers had calculated that there
was no way a giant could escape once he was put in. Even
if all nine giants were to stand on each other's shoulders,
the topmost giant would still be some fifty feet from the
top of the hole.

The nine giant-carrying helicopters hovered over the
massive pit. The giants, one by one, were lowered to
the floor. But they were still trussed up and now came
the tricky business of releasing them from their bonds.
Nobody wanted to go down and do this because the
moment a giant was freed, he would be sure to turn on
the wretched person who had freed him and gobble him
up.

As usual, the BFG had the answer. 'I has told you

before,' he said, 'giants is never eating giants, so I is going down and I shall untie them myself before you can say rack jobinson.'

With thousands of fascinated spectators, including the Queen, peering down into the pit, the BFG was lowered on a rope. One by one, he released the giants. They stood up, stretched their stiffened limbs and started leaping about in fury.

'Why is they putting us down here in this grobsludging hole?' they shouted at the BFG.

'Because you is guzzling human beans,' the BFG answered. 'I is always warning you not to do it and you is never taking the titchiest bit of notice.'

'In that case,' the Fleshlumpeater bellowed, 'I think we is guzzling *you* instead!'

The BFG grabbed the dangling rope and was hoisted out of the pit just in time.

The great bulging sack he had brought back with him from Giant Country lay at the top of the pit.

'What's in there?' the Queen asked him.

The BFG put an arm into the sack and pulled out a gigantic black and white striped object the size of a man.

'Snozzcumbers!' he cried. 'This is the repulsant snozzcumber, Majester, and that is all we is going to give these disgustive giants from now on!'

'May I taste it?' the Queen asked.

'Don't, Majester, don't!' cried the BFG. 'It is tasting of trogfilth and pigsquibble!' With that he tossed the snozzcumber down to the giants below. 'There's your supper!' he shouted. 'Have a munch on that!' He fished out more snozzcumbers from the sack and threw them

down. The giants below howled and cursed. The BFG laughed. 'It serves them right left and centre!' he said.

'What will we feed them on when the snozzcumbers are all used up?' the Queen asked him.

'They is never being used up, Majester,' the BFG answered, smiling. 'I is also bringing in this sack a whole bungle of snozzcumber plants which I is giving, with your permission, to the royal gardener to put in the soil. Then we is having an everlasting supply of this repulsant food to feed these thirstbloody giants on.'

'What a clever fellow you are,' the Queen said. 'You are not very well educated but you are really nobody's fool, I can see that.'

The Author

Every country in the world that had in the past been visited by the foul man-eating giants sent telegrams of congratulations and thanks to the BFG and to Sophie. Kings and Presidents and Prime Ministers and Rulers of every kind showered the enormous giant and the little girl with compliments and thank-yous, as well as all sorts of medals and presents.

The Ruler of India sent the BFG a magnificent elephant, the very thing he had been wishing for all his life.

The King of Arabia sent them a camel each.

The Lama of Tibet sent them a llama each.

Wellington sent them one hundred pairs of wellies each.

Panama sent them beautiful hats.

The King of Sweden sent them a barrelful of sweet and sour pork.

Jersey sent them pullovers.

There was no end to the gratitude of the world.

The Queen herself gave orders that a special house with tremendous high ceilings and enormous doors should immediately be built in Windsor Great Park, next to her own castle, for the BFG to live in. And a pretty little cottage was put up next door for Sophie. The BFG's house was to have a special dream-storing room with hundreds of shelves in it where he could put his beloved bottles. What is more, he was given the title of The Royal Dream-Blower. He was allowed to go galloping off to any place in England on any night of the year to blow his splendid phizzwizards in through the windows to sleeping children. And letters poured into his house by the million from children begging him to pay them a visit.

Meanwhile, tourists from all over the globe came flocking to gaze down in wonder at the nine horrendous man-eating giants in the great pit. They came especially at feeding-time, when the snozzcumbers were being thrown down to them by the keeper, and it was a pleasure to listen to the howls and growls of horror coming up from the pit as the giants began to chew upon the filthiest-tasting vegetable on earth.

There was only one disaster. Three silly men who had drunk too much beer for lunch decided to climb over the high fence surrounding the pit, and of course they fell in. There were yells of delight from the giants below, followed by the crunching of bones. The head keeper immediately put up a big notice on the fence saying, IT IS FORBIDDEN TO FEED THE GIANTS. And after that, there were no more disasters.

The BFG expressed a wish to learn how to speak properly, and Sophie herself, who loved him as she would a father, volunteered to give him lessons every day. She even taught him how to spell and to write sentences, and he turned out to be a splendid intelligent pupil. In his spare time, he read books. He became a tremendous reader. He read all of Charles Dickens (whom he no longer called Dahl's Chickens), and all of Shakespeare and literally thousands of other books. He also started to write essays about his own past life. When Sophie read some of them, she said, 'These are very good. I think perhaps one day you could become a real writer.'

'Oh, I would love that!' cried the BFG. 'Do you think I could?'

'I know you could,' Sophie said. 'Why don't you start by writing a book about you and me?'

'Very well,' the BFG said. 'I'll give it a try.'

So he did. He worked hard on it and in the end he completed it. Rather shyly, he showed it to the Queen. The Queen read it aloud to her grandchildren. Then the Queen said, 'I think we ought to get this book printed properly and published so that other children can read it.' This was arranged, but because the BFG was a very modest giant, he wouldn't put his own name on it. He used somebody else's name instead.

But where, you might ask, is this book that the BFG wrote?

It's right here. You've just finished reading it.

CHARLIE AND THE CHOCOLATE FACTORY

'Greetings to you, the lucky finder of this Golden Ticket, from Mr Willy Wonka! I shake you warmly by the hand! Tremendous things are in store for you!'

The Golden Ticket allows Charlie to fulfil his dearest wish, to have a specially conducted tour of the mysterious chocolate factory, and who wouldn't want to wander in a place which made Whipple-Scrumptious Fudgemallow Delight or Cavity-filling Caramels or Strawberry-Juice Water Pistols or Lickable Wallpaper for nurseries? But there are dangers in store as well, especially for such unlovable characters as Veruca Salt, who disappears down the Great Rubbish Chute, or Augustus Gloop who is swept away in a river of hot melted chocolate, or Violet Beauregarde who ... but it's all here in this famous story, waiting 'to entrance, delight, intrigue, astonish and perplex you beyond measure' just as it has delighted and astonished nearly two million paperback readers already.

This sumptuous edition of *Charlie and the Chocolate Factory* has new illustrations by Michael Foreman. Its sequel, *Charlie and the Great Glass Elevator*, is also published in Puffin.

Ages unlimited, but guaranteed pleasure for anyone old or young enough to enjoy Hot Ice Cream, Eatable Marshmallow Pillows or Mr Wonka's Three Course Dinner chewing-gum.

ROALD DAHL

Charlie
and the
Chocolate Factory

Illustrated by Michael Foreman

Puffin Books

Puffin Books, Penguin Books Ltd, Harmondsworth, Middlesex, England
Viking Penguin Inc., 40 West 23rd Street, New York, New York 10010, U.S.A.
Penguin Books Australia Ltd, Ringwood, Victoria, Australia
Penguin Books Canada Limited, 2801 John Street, Markham, Ontario, Canada L3R 1B4
Penguin Books (N.Z.) Ltd, 182–190 Wairau Road, Auckland 10, New Zealand

First published in the U.S.A. 1964
Published in Great Britain
by George Allen & Unwin 1967
Published in Puffin Books 1973
Reprinted 1973 (four times), 1974 (three times), 1975 (three times),
1976 (twice), 1977 (twice), 1978 (twice), 1979 (twice),
1980, 1981 (twice), 1982 (twice), 1983 (twice), 1984
This edition published 1985
Reprinted 1985 (twice), 1986

Made and printed in Great Britain by
Richard Clay (The Chaucer Press) Ltd
Bungay, Suffolk
Filmset in Monophoto Photina by
Northumberland Press Ltd, Gateshead
Tyne and Wear

For Theo

Contents

There are five children in this book:

AUGUSTUS GLOOP
A greedy boy

VERUCA SALT
A girl who is spoiled by her parents

VIOLET BEAUREGARDE
A girl who chews gum all day long

MIKE TEAVEE
A boy who does nothing but watch television

and

CHARLIE BUCKET
The hero

I

Here Comes Charlie

These two very old people are the father and mother of Mr Bucket. Their names are Grandpa Joe and Grandma Josephine.

And *these* two very old people are the father and mother of
Mrs Bucket. Their names are Grandpa George and Grandma
Georgina.

This is Mr Bucket.   This is Mrs Bucket.

Mr and Mrs Bucket have a small boy whose name is Charlie Bucket.

This is Charlie.

How d'you do? And how d'you do? And how d'you do again?
He is pleased to meet you.

The whole of this family – the six grown-ups (count them) and little Charlie Bucket – live together in a small wooden house on the edge of a great town.

The house wasn't nearly large enough for so many people, and life was extremely uncomfortable for them all. There were only two rooms in the place altogether, and there was only one bed. The bed was given to the four old grandparents because they were so old and tired. They were so tired, they never got out of it.

Grandpa Joe and Grandma Josephine on this side, Grandpa George and Grandma Georgina on this side.

Mr and Mrs Bucket and little Charlie Bucket slept in the other room, upon mattresses on the floor.

In the summertime, this wasn't too bad, but in the winter, freezing cold draughts blew across the floor all night long, and it was awful.

There wasn't any question of them being able to buy a better house – or even one more bed to sleep in. They were far too poor for that.

Mr Bucket was the only person in the family with a job. He worked in a toothpaste factory, where he sat all day long at a bench and screwed the little caps on to the tops of the tubes of toothpaste after the tubes had been filled. But a toothpaste cap-screwer is never paid very much money, and poor Mr Bucket, however hard he worked, and however fast he screwed on the caps, was never able to make enough to buy one half of the things that so large a family needed. There wasn't even enough money to buy proper food for them all. The only meals they could afford were bread and margarine for breakfast, boiled potatoes and cabbage for lunch, and cabbage soup for supper. Sundays were a bit better. They all looked forward to Sundays because then, although they had exactly the same, everyone was allowed a second helping.

The Buckets, of course, didn't starve, but every one of them – the two old grandfathers, the two old grandmothers, Charlie's father, Charlie's mother, and especially little Charlie himself – went about from morning till night with a horrible empty feeling in their tummies.

Charlie felt it worst of all. And although his father and mother often went without their own share of lunch or supper so that they could give it to him, it still wasn't nearly enough for a growing boy. He desperately wanted something more filling and satisfying than cabbage and cabbage soup. The one thing he longed for more than anything else was ... CHOCO-LATE.

Walking to school in the mornings, Charlie could see great slabs of chocolate piled up high in the shop windows, and he would stop and stare and press his nose against the glass, his mouth watering like mad. Many times a day, he would see other children taking bars of creamy chocolate out of their pockets and munching them greedily, and *that*, of course, was *pure* torture.

Only once a year, on his birthday, did Charlie Bucket ever get to taste a bit of chocolate. The whole family saved up their money for that special occasion, and when the great day arrived, Charlie was always presented with one small chocolate bar to eat all by himself. And each time he received it, on those marvellous birthday mornings, he would place it carefully in a small wooden box that he owned, and treasure it as though it were a bar of solid gold; and for the next few days, he would allow himself only to look at it, but never to touch it. Then at last, when he could stand it no longer, he would peel back a *tiny* bit of the paper wrapping at one corner to expose a *tiny* bit of chocolate, and then he would take a *tiny* nibble – just enough to allow the lovely sweet taste to spread out slowly over his tongue. The next day, he would take another tiny nibble, and so on, and so on. And in this way, Charlie would make his sixpenny bar of birthday chocolate last him for more than a month.

But I haven't yet told you about the one awful thing that tortured little Charlie, the lover of chocolate, more than *anything* else. This thing, for him, was far, far worse than seeing slabs of chocolate in the shop windows or watching other children munching bars of creamy chocolate right in front of him. It was the most terrible torturing thing you could imagine, and it was this:

In the town itself, actually within *sight* of the house in which Charlie lived, there was an ENORMOUS CHOCOLATE FACTORY!

Just imagine that!

And it wasn't simply an ordinary enormous chocolate factory, either. It was the largest and most famous in the whole world! It was WONKA'S FACTORY, owned by a man called Mr Willy Wonka, the greatest inventor and maker of chocolates that there has ever been. And what a tremendous, marvellous place it was! It had huge iron gates leading into it, and a high wall surrounding it, and smoke belching from its chimneys, and strange whizzing sounds coming from deep inside it. And outside the walls, for half a mile around in every direction, the air was scented with the heavy rich smell of melting chocolate!

Twice a day, on his way to and from school, little Charlie Bucket had to walk right past the gates of the factory. And every time he went by, he would begin to walk very, very slowly, and he would hold his nose high in the air and take long deep sniffs of the gorgeous chocolatey smell all around him.

Oh, how he loved that smell!

And oh, how he wished he could go inside the factory and see what it was like!

2

Mr Willy Wonka's Factory

In the evenings, after he had finished his supper of watery cabbage soup, Charlie always went into the room of his four grandparents to listen to their stories, and then afterwards to say good night.

Every one of these old people was over ninety. They were as shrivelled as prunes, and as bony as skeletons, and throughout the day, until Charlie made his appearance, they lay huddled in their one bed, two at either end, with nightcaps on to keep their heads warm, dozing the time away with nothing to do. But as soon as they heard the door opening, and heard Charlie's voice saying, 'Good evening, Grandpa Joe and Grandma Josephine, and Grandpa George and Grandma Georgina,' then all four of them would suddenly sit up, and their old wrinkled faces would light up with smiles of pleasure – and the talking would begin. For they loved this little boy. He was the only bright thing in their lives, and his evening visits were something that they looked forward to all day long. Often, Charlie's mother and father would come in as well, and stand by the door, listening to the stories that the old people told; and thus, for perhaps half an hour every night, this room would become a happy place, and the whole family would forget that it was hungry and poor.

One evening, when Charlie went in to see his grandparents, he said to them, 'Is it *really* true that Wonka's Chocolate Factory is the biggest in the world?'

'*True?*' cried all four of them at once. 'Of course it's true! Good heavens, didn't you know *that*? It's about *fifty* times as big as any other!'

'And is Mr Willy Wonka *really* the cleverest chocolate maker in the world?'

'My *dear* boy,' said Grandpa Joe, raising himself up a little higher on his pillow, 'Mr Willy Wonka is the most *amazing*, the most *fantastic*, the most *extraordinary* chocolate maker the world has ever seen! I thought *everybody* knew that!'

'I knew he was famous, Grandpa Joe, and I knew he was very clever . . .'

'*Clever!*' cried the old man. 'He's more than that! He's a *magician* with chocolate! He can make *anything* – anything he wants! Isn't that a fact, my dears?'

The other three old people nodded their heads slowly up and down, and said, '*Absolutely* true. *Just* as true as can be.'

And Grandpa Joe said, 'You mean to say I've never *told* you about Mr Willy Wonka and his factory?'

'Never,' answered little Charlie.

'Good heavens above! I don't know what's the matter with me!'

'Will you tell me now, Grandpa Joe, please?'

'I certainly will. Sit down beside me on the bed, my dear, and listen carefully.'

Grandpa Joe was the oldest of the four grandparents. He was ninety-six and a half, and that is just about as old as anybody can be. Like all extremely old people, he was delicate and weak, and throughout the day he spoke very little. But in the evenings, when Charlie, his beloved grandson, was in the room, he seemed in some marvellous way to grow quite young again. All his tiredness fell away from him, and he became as eager and excited as a young boy.

'Oh, what a man he is, this Mr Willy Wonka!' cried Grandpa Joe. 'Did you know, for example, that he has himself invented more than two hundred new kinds of chocolate bars, each with a different centre, each far sweeter and creamier and more delicious than anything the other chocolate factories can make!'

'Perfectly true!' cried Grandma Josephine. 'And he sends them to *all* the four corners of the earth! Isn't that so, Grandpa Joe?'

'It is, my dear, it is. And to all the kings and presidents of the world as well. But it isn't only chocolate bars that he makes. Oh, dear me, no! He has some really *fantastic* inventions up his sleeve, Mr Willy Wonka has! Did you know that he's invented a way of making chocolate ice cream so that it stays cold for hours and hours without being in the refrigerator? You can even leave it lying in the sun all morning on a hot day and it won't go runny!'

'But that's *impossible!*' said little Charlie, staring at his grandfather.

'Of course it's impossible!' cried Grandpa Joe. 'It's completely *absurd!* But Mr Willy Wonka has done it!'

'Quite right!' the others agreed, nodding their heads. 'Mr Wonka has done it.'

'And then again,' Grandpa Joe went on speaking very slowly now so that Charlie wouldn't miss a word, 'Mr Willy Wonka can make marshmallows that taste of violets, and rich caramels that change colour every ten seconds as you suck them, and little feathery sweets that melt away deliciously the moment you put them between your lips. He can make chewing-gum that never loses its taste, and sugar balloons that you can blow up to enormous sizes before you pop them with a pin and gobble them up. And, by a most secret method, he can make lovely blue birds' eggs with black spots on them, and when you put one of these in your mouth, it gradually gets smaller and smaller until suddenly there is nothing left except a tiny little pink sugary baby bird sitting on the tip of your tongue.'

Grandpa Joe paused and ran the point of his tongue slowly over his lips. 'It makes my mouth water just *thinking* about it,' he said.

'Mine, too,' said little Charlie. 'But *please* go on.'

While they were talking, Mr and Mrs Bucket, Charlie's mother and father, had come quietly into the room, and now both were standing just inside the door, listening.

'Tell Charlie about that crazy Indian prince,' said Grandma Josephine. 'He'd like to hear that.'

'You mean Prince Pondicherry?' said Grandpa Joe, and he began chuckling with laughter.

'*Completely* dotty!' said Grandpa George.

'But *very* rich,' said Grandma Georgina.

'What did he do?' asked Charlie eagerly.

'Listen,' said Grandpa Joe, 'and I'll tell you.'

3

Mr Wonka and the Indian Prince

'Prince Pondicherry wrote a letter to Mr Willy Wonka,' said Grandpa Joe, 'and asked him to come all the way out to India and build him a colossal palace entirely out of chocolate.'

'Did Mr Wonka do it, Grandpa?'

'He did, indeed. And what a palace it was! It had one hundred rooms, and *everything* was made of either dark or light chocolate! The bricks were chocolate, and the cement holding them together was chocolate, and the windows were chocolate, and all the walls and ceilings were made of chocolate, so were the carpets and the pictures and the furniture and the beds; and when you turned on the taps in the bathroom, hot chocolate came pouring out.

'When it was all finished, Mr Wonka said to Prince Pondicherry, "I warn you, though, it won't last very long, so you'd better start eating it right away."

'"Nonsense!" shouted the Prince. "I'm not going to eat my palace! I'm not even going to nibble the staircase or lick the walls! I'm going to *live* in it!"

'But Mr Wonka was right, of course, because soon after this, there came a very hot day with a boiling sun, and the whole palace began to melt, and then it sank slowly to the ground,

24

and the crazy prince, who was dozing in the living room at the
time, woke up to find himself swimming around in a huge
brown sticky lake of chocolate.'

Little Charlie sat very still on the edge of the bed, staring at
his grandfather. Charlie's face was bright, and his eyes were
stretched so wide you could see the whites all around. 'Is all this
really true?' he asked. 'Or are you pulling my leg?'

'It's true!' cried all four of the old people at once. 'Of course
it's true! Ask anyone you like!'

'And I'll tell you something else that's true,' said Grandpa
Joe, and now he leaned closer to Charlie, and lowered his voice
to a soft, secret whisper. *'Nobody . . . ever . . . comes . . . out!'*

'Out of where?' asked Charlie.

'*And ... nobody ... ever ... goes ... in!*'

'In *where?*' cried Charlie.

'Wonka's factory, of course!'

'Grandpa, what *do* you mean?'

'I mean *workers*, Charlie.'

'Workers?'

'All factories,' said Grandpa Joe, 'have workers streaming in and out of the gates in the mornings and evenings – except Wonka's! Have *you* ever seen a single person going into that place – or coming out?'

Little Charlie looked slowly around at each of the four old faces, one after the other, and they all looked back at him. They were friendly smiling faces, but they were also quite serious. There was no sign of joking or leg-pulling on any of them.

'Well? Have *you?*' asked Grandpa Joe.

'I ... I really don't know, Grandpa,' Charlie stammered. 'Whenever *I* walk past the factory, the gates seem to be closed.'

'Exactly!' said Grandpa Joe.

'But there *must* be people working there ...'

'Not *people*, Charlie. Not *ordinary* people, anyway.'

'Then who?' cried Charlie.

'Ah-ha ... That's it, you see ... That's another of Mr Willy Wonka's clevernesses.'

'Charlie, dear,' Mrs Bucket called out from where she was standing by the door, 'it's time for bed. That's enough for tonight.'

'But mother, I *must* hear ...'

'Tomorrow, my darling ...'

'That's right,' said Grandpa Joe, 'I'll tell you the rest of it tomorrow evening.'

4

The Secret Workers

The next evening, Grandpa Joe went on with his story.

'You see, Charlie,' he said, 'not so very long ago there used to be thousands of people working in Mr Willy Wonka's factory. Then one day, all of a sudden, Mr Wonka had to ask *every single one of them* to leave, to go home, never to come back.'

'But why?' asked Charlie.

'Because of spies.'

'Spies?'

'Yes. All the other chocolate makers, you see, had begun to grow jealous of the wonderful sweets that Mr Wonka was making, and they started sending in spies to steal his secret recipes. The spies took jobs in the Wonka factory, pretending that they were ordinary workers, and while they were there, each one of them found out exactly how a certain special thing was made.'

'And did they go back to their own factories and tell?' asked Charlie.

'They must have,' answered Grandpa Joe, 'because soon after that, Fickelgruber's factory started making an ice cream that would never melt, even in the hottest sun. Then Mr Prodnose's factory came out with a chewing-gum that never lost its flavour however much you chewed it. And then Mr Slugworth's factory began making sugar balloons that you could blow up to huge sizes before you popped them with a pin and gobbled them up. And so on, and so on. And Mr Willy Wonka tore his beard and shouted, "This is terrible! I shall be ruined! There are spies everywhere! I shall have to close the factory!"'

'But he didn't do that!' Charlie said.

'Oh, yes he did. He told *all* the workers that he was sorry, but they would have to go home. Then, he shut the main gates and fastened them with a chain. And suddenly, Wonka's giant chocolate factory became silent and deserted. The chimneys stopped smoking, the machines stopped whirring, and from then on, not a single chocolate or sweet was made. Not a soul went in or out, and even Mr Willy Wonka himself disappeared completely.

'Months and months went by,' Grandpa Joe went on, 'but still the factory remained closed. And everybody said, "Poor Mr Wonka. He was so nice. And he made such marvellous things. But he's finished now. It's all over."

'Then something astonishing happened. One day, early in the morning, thin columns of white smoke were seen to be coming out of the tops of the tall chimneys of the factory! People in the town stopped and stared. "What's going on?" they cried. "Someone's lit the furnaces! Mr Wonka must be opening up again!" They ran to the gates, expecting to see them wide open and Mr Wonka standing there to welcome his workers back.

'But no! The great iron gates were still locked and chained as securely as ever, and Mr Wonka was nowhere to be seen.

'"But the factory *is* working!" the people shouted. "Listen! You can hear the machines! They're all whirring again! And you can smell the smell of melting chocolate in the air!"'

Grandpa Joe leaned forward and laid a long bony finger on Charlie's knee, and he said softly, 'But most mysterious of all, Charlie, were the shadows in the windows of the factory. The people standing on the street outside could see small dark shadows moving about behind the frosted glass windows.'

'Shadows of whom?' said Charlie quickly.

'That's exactly what everybody else wanted to know.

'"The place is full of workers!" the people shouted. "But nobody's gone in! The gates are locked! It's crazy! Nobody ever comes out, either!"

'But there was no question at all,' said Grandpa Joe, 'that the factory *was* running. And it's gone on running ever since, for these last ten years. What's more, the chocolates and sweets it's been turning out have become more fantastic and delicious all the time. And of course *now* when Mr Wonka invents some new and wonderful sweet, neither Mr Fickelgruber nor Mr Prodnose nor Mr Slugworth nor anybody else is able to copy it. No spies can go into the factory to find out how it is made.'

'But Grandpa, *who*,' cried Charlie, '*who* is Mr Wonka using to do all the work in the factory?'

'Nobody knows, Charlie.'

'But that's *absurd*! Hasn't someone asked Mr Wonka?'

'Nobody sees him any more. He never comes out. The only things that come out of that place are chocolates and sweets. They come out through a special trap door in the wall, all packed and addressed, and they are picked up every day by Post Office trucks.'

'But Grandpa, what *sort* of people are they that work in there?'

'My dear boy,' said Grandpa Joe, 'that is one of the great mysteries of the chocolate-making world. We know only one thing about them. They are very small. The faint shadows that sometimes appear behind the windows, especially late at night when the lights are on, are those of *tiny* people, people no taller than my knee . . .'

'There aren't any such people,' Charlie said.

Just then, Mr Bucket, Charlie's father, came into the room. He was home from the toothpaste factory, and he was waving an evening newspaper rather excitedly. 'Have you heard the news?' he cried. He held up the paper so that they could see the huge headline. The headline said:

WONKA FACTORY TO BE OPENED AT LAST TO LUCKY FEW

5

The Golden Tickets

'You mean people are actually going to be allowed to go inside the factory?' cried Grandpa Joe. 'Read us what it says – quickly!'

'All right,' said Mr Bucket, smoothing out the newspaper. 'Listen.'

Evening Bulletin

Mr Willy Wonka, the confectionary genius whom nobody has seen for the last ten years, sent out the following notice today:

I, Willy Wonka, have decided to allow five children – just *five*, mind you, and no more – to visit my factory this year. These lucky five will be shown around personally by me, and they will be allowed to see all the secrets and the magic of my factory. Then, at the end of the tour, as a special present, all of them will be given enough chocolates and Sweets to last them for the rest of their lives! So watch out for the Golden Tickets! Five Golden Tickets have been printed on golden paper, and these five Golden Tickets have been hidden underneath the ordinary wrapping paper of five ordinary bars of chocolate. These five chocolate bars may be anywhere – in any shop in any street in any town in any

country in the world – upon any counter where Wonka's Sweets are sold. And the five lucky finders of these five Golden Tickets are the *only* ones who will be allowed to visit my factory and see what it's like *now* inside! Good luck to you all, and happy hunting! (Signed Willy Wonka.)

'The man's dotty!' muttered Grandma Josephine.

'He's brilliant!' cried Grandpa Joe. 'He's a magician! Just imagine what will happen now! The whole world will be searching for those Golden Tickets! Everyone will be buying Wonka's chocolate bars in the hope of finding one! He'll sell more than ever before! Oh, how exciting it would be to find one!'

'And all the chocolate and sweets that you could eat for the rest of your life – *free!*' said Grandpa George. 'Just imagine that!'

'They'd have to deliver them in a truck!' said Grandma Georgina.

'It makes me quite ill to think of it,' said Grandma Josephine.

'Nonsense!' cried Grandpa Joe. 'Wouldn't it be *something*, Charlie, to open a bar of chocolate and see a Golden Ticket glistening inside!'

'It certainly would, Grandpa. But there isn't a hope,' Charlie said sadly. 'I only get one bar a year.'

'You never know, darling,' said Grandma Georgina. 'It's your birthday next week. You have as much chance as anybody else.'

'I'm afraid that simply isn't true,' said Grandpa George. 'The kids who are going to find the Golden Tickets are the ones who can afford to buy bars of chocolate every day. Our Charlie gets only one a year. There isn't a hope.'

6

The First Two Finders

The very next day, the first Golden Ticket was found. The finder was a boy called Augustus Gloop, and Mr Bucket's evening newspaper carried a large picture of him on the front page. The picture showed a nine-year-old boy who was so enormously fat he looked as though he had been blown up with a powerful pump. Great flabby folds of fat bulged out from every part of his body, and his face was like a monstrous ball of dough with two small greedy curranty eyes peering out upon the world. The town in which Augustus Gloop lived, the newspaper said, had gone wild with excitement over their hero. Flags were flying from all the windows, children had been given a holiday from school, and a parade was being organized in honour of the famous youth.

'I just *knew* Augustus would find a Golden Ticket,' his mother had told the newspapermen. 'He eats *so many* bars of chocolate a day that it was almost *impossible* for him *not* to find one. Eating is his hobby, you know. That's *all* he's interested in. But still, that's better than being a *hooligan* and shooting off *zip guns* and things like that in his spare time, isn't it? And what I always say is, he wouldn't go on eating like he does unless he *needed* nourishment, would he? It's all *vitamins*, anyway. What a *thrill* it will be for him to visit Mr Wonka's marvellous factory! We're just as *proud* as anything!'

'What a revolting woman,' said Grandma Josephine.

'And what a repulsive boy,' said Grandma Georgina.

'Only four Golden Tickets left,' said Grandpa George. 'I wonder who'll get *those*.'

And now the whole country, indeed, the whole world, seemed suddenly to be caught up in a mad chocolate-buying spree, everybody searching frantically for those precious remaining tickets. Fully grown women were seen going into sweet shops and buying ten Wonka bars at a time, then tearing off the wrappers on the spot and peering eagerly underneath for a glint of golden paper. Children were taking hammers and smashing their piggy banks and running out to the shops with handfuls of money. In one city, a famous gangster robbed a bank of a thousand pounds and spent the whole lot on Wonka bars that same afternoon. And when the police entered his house to arrest him, they found him sitting on the floor amidst mountains of chocolate, ripping off the wrappers with the blade of a long dagger. In far-off Russia, a woman called Charlotte Russe claimed to have found the second ticket, but it turned out to be a clever fake. The famous English scientist, Professor Foulbody, invented a machine which would tell you at once, without opening the wrapper of a bar of chocolate, whether or not there was a Golden Ticket hidden underneath it. The machine had a mechanical arm that shot out with tremendous force and grabbed hold of anything that had the slightest bit of gold inside it, and for a moment, it looked like the answer to everything. But unfortunately, while the Professor was showing off the machine to the public at the sweet counter of a large department store, the mechanical arm shot out and made a grab for the gold filling in the back tooth of a duchess who was standing near by. There was an ugly scene, and the machine was smashed by the crowd.

Suddenly, on the day before Charlie Bucket's birthday, the newspapers announced that the second Golden Ticket had been found. The lucky person was a small girl called Veruca Salt who lived with her rich parents in a great city far away. Once again Mr Bucket's evening newspaper carried a big picture of the finder. She was sitting between her beaming father and mother in the living room of their house, waving the Golden Ticket above her head, and grinning from ear to ear.

Veruca's father, Mr Salt, had eagerly explained to the news-papermen exactly how the ticket was found. 'You see, boys,' he had said, 'as soon as my little girl told me that she simply *had* to have one of those Golden Tickets, I went out into the town and started buying up all the Wonka bars I could lay my hands on. *Thousands* of them, I must have bought. *Hundreds* of thousands! Then I had them loaded on to trucks and sent directly to my *own* factory. I'm in the peanut business, you see, and I've got about a hundred women working for me over at my place, shelling peanuts for roasting and salting. That's what they do all day long, those women, they sit there shelling peanuts. So I says to them, "Okay, girls," I says, "from now on, you can stop shelling peanuts and start shelling the wrappers off these chocolate bars instead!" And they did. I had every worker in the place yanking the paper off those bars of chocolate full speed ahead from morning till night.

'But three days went by, and we had no luck. Oh, it was terrible! My little Veruca got more and more upset each day, and every time I went home she would scream at me. *"Where's my Golden Ticket! I want my Golden Ticket!"* And she would lie for hours on the floor, kicking and yelling in the most disturbing way. Well, I just hated to see my little girl feeling unhappy like that, so I vowed I would keep up the search until I'd got her what she wanted. Then suddenly ... on the evening of the fourth day, one of my women workers yelled, "I've got it! A Golden Ticket!" And I said, "Give it to me, quick!" and she did, and I rushed it home and gave it to my darling Veruca, and now she's all smiles, and we have a happy home once again.'

'That's even worse than the fat boy,' said Grandma Josephine.

'She needs a really good spanking,' said Grandma Georgina.

'I don't think the girl's father played it quite fair, Grandpa, do you?' Charlie murmured.

'He spoils her,' Grandpa Joe said. 'And no good can ever come from spoiling a child like that, Charlie, you mark my words.'

'Come to bed, my darling,' said Charlie's mother. 'Tomorrow's your birthday, don't forget that, so I expect you'll be up early to open your present.'

'A Wonka chocolate bar!' cried Charlie. 'It is a Wonka bar, isn't it?'

'Yes, my love,' his mother said. 'Of course it is.'

'Oh, wouldn't it be wonderful if I found the third Golden Ticket inside it?' Charlie said.

'Bring it in here when you get it,' Grandpa Joe said. 'Then we can all watch you taking off the wrapper.'

7

Charlie's Birthday

'Happy birthday!' cried the four old grandparents, as Charlie came into their room early the next morning.

Charlie smiled nervously and sat down on the edge of the bed. He was holding his present, his only present, very carefully in his two hands. WONKA'S WHIPPLE-SCRUMPTIOUS FUDGEMALLOW DELIGHT, it said on the wrapper.

The four old people, two at either end of the bed, propped themselves up on their pillows and stared with anxious eyes at the bar of chocolate in Charlie's hands.

Mr and Mrs Bucket came in and stood at the foot of the bed, watching Charlie.

The room became silent. Everybody was waiting now for Charlie to start opening his present. Charlie looked down at the bar of chocolate. He ran his fingers slowly back and forth along the length of it, stroking it lovingly, and the shiny paper wrapper made little sharp crackly noises in the quiet room.

Then Mrs Bucket said gently, 'You mustn't be too disappointed, my darling, if you don't find what you're looking for underneath that wrapper. You really can't expect to be as lucky as all that.'

'She's quite right,' Mr Bucket said.

Charlie didn't say anything.

'After all,' Grandma Josephine said, 'in the whole wide world there are only three tickets left to be found.'

'The thing to remember,' Grandma Georgina said, 'is that whatever happens, you'll still have the bar of chocolate.'

'Wonka's Whipple-Scrumptious Fudgemallow Delight!' cried Grandpa George. 'It's the best of them all! You'll just *love* it!'

'Yes,' Charlie whispered. 'I know.'

'Just forget all about those Golden Tickets and enjoy the chocolate,' Grandpa Joe said. 'Why don't you do that?'

They all knew it was ridiculous to expect this one poor little bar of chocolate to have a magic ticket inside it, and they were trying as gently and as kindly as they could to prepare Charlie for the disappointment. But there was one other thing that the grown-ups also knew, and it was this: that however *small* the chance might be of striking lucky, *the chance was there*.

The chance *had* to be there.

This particular bar of chocolate had as much chance as any other of having a Golden Ticket.

And that was why all the grandparents and parents in the room were actually just as tense and excited as Charlie was, although they were pretending to be very calm.

'You'd better go ahead and open it up, or you'll be late for school,' Grandpa Joe said.

'You might as well get it over with,' Grandpa George said.

'Open it, my dear,' Grandma Georgina said. 'Please open it. You're making me jumpy.'

Very slowly, Charlie's fingers began to tear open one small corner of the wrapping paper.

The old people in the bed all leaned forward, craning their scraggy necks.

Then suddenly, as though he couldn't bear the suspense any

longer, Charlie tore the wrapper right down the middle . . . and on to his lap, there fell . . . a light-brown creamy-coloured bar of chocolate.

There was no sign of a Golden Ticket anywhere.

'Well – that's *that*!' said Grandpa Joe brightly. 'It's just what we expected.'

Charlie looked up. Four kind old faces were watching him intently from the bed. He smiled at them, a small sad smile, and then he shrugged his shoulders and picked up the chocolate bar and held it out to his mother, and said, 'Here Mother, have a bit. We'll share it. I want everybody to taste it.'

'Certainly not!' his mother said.

And the others all cried, 'No, no! We wouldn't dream of it! It's *all* yours!'

'*Please*,' begged Charlie, turning round and offering it to Grandpa Joe.

But neither he nor anyone else would take even a tiny bit.

'It's time to go to school, my darling,' Mrs Bucket said, putting an arm around Charlie's skinny shoulders. 'Come on, or you'll be late.'

8

Two More Golden Tickets Found

That evening, Mr Bucket's newspaper announced the finding of not only the third Golden Ticket, but the fourth as well. TWO GOLDEN TICKETS FOUND TODAY, screamed the head-lines. ONLY ONE MORE LEFT.

'All right,' said Grandpa Joe, when the whole family was gathered in the old people's room after supper, 'let's hear who found them.'

'The third ticket,' read Mr Bucket, holding the newspaper up close to his face because his eyes were bad and he couldn't afford glasses, 'the third ticket was found by a Miss Violet Beauregarde. There was great excitement in the Beauregarde household when our reporter arrived to interview the lucky young lady – cameras were clicking and flashbulbs were flash-ing and people were pushing and jostling and trying to get a bit closer to the famous girl. And the famous girl was standing on a chair in the living room waving the Golden Ticket madly at arm's length as though she were flagging a taxi. She was talking very fast and very loudly to everyone, but it was not easy to hear all that she said because she was chewing so ferociously upon a piece of gum at the same time.

'"I'm a gum chewer, normally," she shouted, "but when I

heard about these ticket things of Mr Wonka's, I gave up gum and started on chocolate bars in the hope of striking lucky. *Now*, of course, I'm back on gum. I just *adore* gum. I can't do without it. I munch it all day long except for a few minutes at mealtimes when I take it out and stick it behind my ear for safekeeping. To tell you the truth, I simply wouldn't feel *comfortable* if I didn't have that little wedge of gum to chew on every moment of the day, I really wouldn't My mother says it's not ladylike and it looks ugly to see a girl's jaws going up and down like mine do all the time, but I don't agree. And who's she to criticize, anyway, because if you ask me, I'd say that *her* jaws are going up and down almost as much as mine are just from *yelling* at me every minute of the day."

42

'"Now, Violet," Mrs Beauregarde said from a far corner of the room where she was standing on the piano to avoid being trampled by the mob.

'"All right, Mother, keep your hair on!" Miss Beauregarde shouted. "And now," she went on, turning to the reporters again, "it may interest you to know that this piece of gum I'm chewing right at this moment is one I've been working on for over *three months solid*. That's a record, that is. It's beaten the record held by my best friend, Miss Cornelia Prinzmetel. And was she furious! It's my most treasured possession now, this piece of gum is. At night-time, I just stick it on the end of the bedpost, and it's as good as ever in the mornings – a bit hard at first, maybe, but it soon softens up again after I've given it a few good chews. Before I started chewing for the world record, I used to change my piece of gum once a day. I used to do it in our lift on the way home from school. Why the lift? Because I liked sticking the gooey piece that I'd just finished with on to one of the control buttons. Then the next person who came along and pressed the button got my old gum on the end of his or her finger. Ha-ha! And what a racket they kicked up, some of them. You get the best results with women who have expensive gloves on. Oh yes, I'm thrilled to be going to Mr Wonka's factory. And I understand that afterwards he's going to give me enough gum to last me for the rest of my whole life. Whoopee! Hooray!"'

'*Beastly* girl,' said Grandma Josephine.

'Despicable!' said Grandma Georgina. 'She'll come to a sticky end one day, chewing all that gum, you see if she doesn't.'

'And who got the fourth Golden Ticket?' Charlie asked.

'Now, let me see,' said Mr Bucket, peering at the newspaper again. 'Ah yes, here we are. The fourth Golden Ticket,' he read, 'was found by a boy called Mike Teavee.'

'Another bad lot, I'll be bound,' muttered Grandma Josephine.

'Don't interrupt, Grandma,' said Mrs Bucket.

'The Teavee household,' said Mr Bucket, going on with his reading, 'was crammed, like all the others, with excited visitors when our reporter arrived, but young Mike Teavee, the lucky winner, seemed extremely annoyed by the whole business. "Can't you fools see I'm watching television?" he said angrily, "I wish you wouldn't interrupt!"'

'The nine-year-old boy was seated before an enormous television set, with his eyes glued to the screen, and he was watching a film in which one bunch of gangsters was shooting up another bunch of gangsters with machine guns. Mike Teavee himself had no less than eighteen toy pistols of various sizes hanging from belts around his body, and every now and again he would leap up into the air and fire off half a dozen rounds from one or another of these weapons.

'"Quiet!" he shouted, when someone tried to ask him a question. "Didn't I *tell* you not to interrupt! This show's an absolute whiz-banger! It's terrific! I watch it every day. I watch all of them every day, even the rotten ones, where there's no shooting. I like the gangsters best. They're terrific, those gangsters! Especially when they start pumping each other full of lead, or flashing the old stilettos, or giving each other the one-two-three with their knuckledusters! Gosh, what wouldn't I give to be doing that myself! It's the *life*, I tell you! It's terrific!"'

'That's quite enough!' snapped Grandma Josephine. 'I can't *bear* to listen to it!'

'Nor me,' said Grandma Georgina. 'Do *all* children behave like this nowadays – like these brats we've been hearing about?'

'Of course not,' said Mr Bucket, smiling at the old lady in the bed. 'Some do, of course. In fact, quite a lot of them do. But not *all*.'

'And now there's only *one ticket left*!' said Grandpa George.

'Quite so,' sniffed Grandma Georgina. 'And just as sure as I'll be having cabbage soup for supper tomorrow, that ticket'll go to some nasty little beast who doesn't deserve it!'

9

Grandpa Joe Takes a Gamble

The next day, when Charlie came home from school and went in to see his grandparents, he found that only Grandpa Joe was awake. The other three were all snoring loudly.

'Ssshh!' whispered Grandpa Joe, and he beckoned Charlie to come closer. Charlie tiptoed over and stood beside the bed. The old man gave Charlie a sly grin, and then he started rummaging under his pillow with one hand; and when the hand came out again, there was an ancient leather purse clutched in the fingers. Under cover of the bedclothes, the old man opened the purse and tipped it upside down. Out fell a single silver sixpence. 'It's my secret hoard,' he whispered. 'The others don't know I've got it. And now, you and I are going to have one more fling at finding that last ticket. How about it, eh? But you'll have to help me.'

'Are you *sure* you want to spend your money on that, Grandpa?' Charlie whispered.

'Of course I'm sure!' spluttered the old man excitedly. 'Don't stand there arguing! I'm as keen as you are to find that ticket! Here – take the money and run down the street to the nearest shop and buy the first Wonka bar you see and bring it straight back to me, and we'll open it together.'

Charlie took the little silver coin, and slipped quickly out of the room. In five minutes, he was back.

'Have you got it?' whispered Grandpa Joe, his eyes shining with excitement.

Charlie nodded and held out the bar of chocolate. WONKA'S NUTTY CRUNCH SURPRISE, it said on the wrapper.

'Good!' the old man whispered, sitting up in the bed and rubbing his hands. 'Now – come over here and sit close to me and we'll open it together. Are you ready?'

'Yes,' Charlie said. 'I'm ready.'

'All right. You tear off the first bit.'

'No,' Charlie said, 'you paid for it. You do it all.'

The old man's fingers were trembling most terribly as they fumbled with the wrapper. 'We don't have a hope, really,' he whispered, giggling a bit. 'You do know we don't have a hope, don't you?'

'Yes,' Charlie said. 'I know that.'

They looked at each other, and both started giggling nervously.

'Mind you,' said Grandpa Joe, 'there is just that *tiny* chance that it *might* be the one, don't you agree?'

'Yes,' Charlie said. 'Of course. Why don't you open it Grandpa?'

'All in good time, my boy, all in good time. Which end do you think I ought to open first?'

'That corner. The one furthest from you. Just tear off a *tiny* bit, but not quite enough for us to see anything.'

'Like that?' said the old man.

'Yes. Now a little bit more.'

'You finish it,' said Grandpa Joe. 'I'm too nervous.'

'No, Grandpa. You must do it yourself.'

'Very well, then. Here goes.' He tore off the wrapper.

They both stared at what lay underneath.

It was a bar of chocolate – nothing more.

All at once, they both saw the funny side of the whole thing, and they burst into peals of laughter.

'What on earth's going on!' cried Grandma Josephine, waking up suddenly.

'Nothing,' said Grandpa Joe. 'You go on back to sleep.'

IO

The Family Begins to Starve

During the next two weeks, the weather turned very cold. First came the snow. It began very suddenly one morning just as Charlie Bucket was getting dressed for school. Standing by the window, he saw the huge flakes drifting slowly down out of an icy sky that was the colour of steel.

By evening, it lay four feet deep around the tiny house, and Mr Bucket had to dig a path from the front door to the road.

After the snow, there came a freezing gale that blew for days and days without stopping. And oh, how bitter cold it was! Everything that Charlie touched seemed to be made of ice, and each time he stepped outside the door, the wind was like a knife on his cheek.

Inside the house, little jets of freezing air came rushing in through the sides of the windows and under the doors, and there was no place to go to escape them. The four old ones lay silent and huddled in their bed, trying to keep the cold out of their bones. The excitement over the Golden Tickets had long since been forgotten. Nobody in the family gave a thought now to anything except the two vital problems of trying to keep warm and trying to get enough to eat.

There is something about very cold weather that gives one

49

an enormous appetite. Most of us find ourselves beginning to
crave rich steaming stews and hot apple pies and all kinds of
delicious warming dishes; and because we are all a great deal
luckier than we realize, we usually get what we want – or near
enough. But Charlie Bucket never got what he wanted because
the family couldn't afford it, and as the cold weather went on
and on, he became ravenously and desperately hungry. Both
bars of chocolate, the birthday one and the one Grandpa Joe
had bought, had long since been nibbled away, and all he got
now were those thin, cabbagy meals three times a day.

Then all at once, the meals became even thinner.

The reason for this was that the toothpaste factory, the place
where Mr Bucket worked, suddenly went bust and had to close
down. Quickly, Mr Bucket tried to get another job. But he had
no luck. In the end, the only way in which he managed to earn
a few pennies was by shovelling snow in the streets. But it
wasn't enough to buy even a quarter of the food that seven
people needed. The situation became desperate. Breakfast was
a single slice of bread for each person now, and lunch was
maybe half a boiled potato.

Slowly but surely, everybody in the house began to starve.

And every day, little Charlie Bucket, trudging through the
snow on his way to school, would have to pass Mr Willy
Wonka's giant chocolate factory. And every day, as he came
near to it, he would lift his small pointed nose high in the air
and sniff the wonderful sweet smell of melting chocolate. Sometimes, he would stand motionless outside the gates for several
minutes on end, taking deep swallowing breaths as though he
were trying to *eat* the smell itself.

'That child,' said Grandpa Joe, poking his head up from under
the blanket one icy morning, 'that child has *got* to have more
food. It doesn't matter about us. We're too old to bother with.

But a *growing boy*! He can't go on like this! He's beginning to look like a skeleton!'

'What can one *do?*' murmured Grandma Josephine miserably. 'He refuses to take any of ours. I hear his mother tried to slip her own piece of bread on to his plate at breakfast this morning, but he wouldn't touch it. He made her take it back.'

'He's a fine little fellow,' said Grandpa George. 'He deserves better than this.'

The cruel weather went on and on.

And every day, Charlie Bucket grew thinner and thinner. His face became frighteningly white and pinched. The skin was drawn so tightly over the cheeks that you could see the shapes of the bones underneath. It seemed doubtful whether he could go on much longer like this without becoming dangerously ill.

And now, very calmly, with that curious wisdom that seems to come so often to small children in times of hardship, he began to make little changes here and there in some of the things that he did, so as to save his strength. In the mornings, he left the house ten minutes earlier so that he could walk slowly to school, without ever having to run. He sat quietly in the classroom during break, resting himself, while the others rushed outdoors and threw snowballs and wrestled in the snow. Everything he did now, he did slowly and carefully, to prevent exhaustion.

Then one afternoon, walking back home with the icy wind in his face (and incidentally feeling hungrier than he had ever felt before), his eye was caught suddenly by something silvery lying in the gutter, in the snow. Charlie stepped off the kerb and bent down to examine it. Part of it was buried under the snow, but he saw at once what it was.

It was a fifty pence piece!

Quickly he looked around him.

Had somebody just dropped it?

No – that was impossible because of the way part of it was buried.

Several people went hurrying past him on the pavement, their chins sunk deep in the collars of their coats, their feet crunching in the snow. None of them was searching for any money; none of them was taking the slightest notice of the small boy crouching in the gutter.

Then was it *his*, this fifty pence?

Could he *have* it?

Carefully, Charlie pulled it out from under the snow. It was damp and dirty, but otherwise perfect.

A WHOLE fifty pence!

He held it tightly between his shivering fingers, gazing down at it. It meant one thing to him at that moment, only *one* thing. It meant FOOD.

Automatically, Charlie turned and began moving towards the nearest shop. It was only ten paces away ... it was a newspaper and stationery shop, the kind that sells almost everything, including sweets and cigars ... and what he would *do*, he whispered quickly to himself ... he would buy one luscious bar of chocolate and eat it *all* up, every bit of it, right then and there ... and the rest of the money he would take straight back home and give to his mother.

11

The Miracle

Charlie entered the shop and laid the damp fifty pence on the counter.

'One Wonka's Whipple-Scrumptious Fudgemallow Delight,' he said, remembering how much he had loved the one he had on his birthday.

The man behind the counter looked fat and well-fed. He had big lips and fat cheeks and a very fat neck. The fat around his neck bulged out all around the top of his collar like a rubber ring. He turned and reached behind him for the chocolate bar, then he turned back again and handed it to Charlie. Charlie grabbed it and quickly tore off the wrapper and took an enormous bite. Then he took another ... and another ... and oh, the joy of being able to cram large pieces of something sweet and solid into one's mouth! The sheer blissful joy of being able to fill one's mouth with rich solid food!

'You look like you wanted that one, sonny,' the shopkeeper said pleasantly.

Charlie nodded, his mouth bulging with chocolate.

The shopkeeper put Charlie's change on the counter. 'Take it easy,' he said. 'It'll give you a tummy-ache if you swallow it like that without chewing.'

Charlie went on wolfing the chocolate. He couldn't stop. And in less than half a minute, the whole thing had disappeared down his throat. He was quite out of breath, but he felt marvellously, extraordinarily happy. He reached out a hand to take the change. Then he paused. His eyes were just above the level of the counter. They were staring at the silver coins lying there. The coins were all five-penny pieces. There were nine of them altogether. Surely it wouldn't matter if he spent just one more . . .

'I think,' he said quietly, 'I think . . . I'll have just one more of those chocolate bars. The same kind as before, please.'

'Why not?' the fat shopkeeper said, reaching behind him again and taking another Whipple-Scrumptious Fudgemallow Delight from the shelf. He laid it on the counter.

Charlie picked it up and tore off the wrapper . . . and *suddenly* . . . from underneath the wrapper . . . there came a brilliant flash of gold.

Charlie's heart stood still.

'It's a Golden Ticket!' screamed the shopkeeper, leaping about a foot in the air. 'You've got a Golden Ticket! You've found the last Golden Ticket! Hey, would you believe it! Come and look at this, everybody! The kid's found Wonka's last Golden Ticket! There it is! It's right here in his hands!'

It seemed as though the shopkeeper might be going to have a fit. 'In my shop, too!' he yelled. 'He found it right here in my own little shop! Somebody call the newspapers quick and let them know! Watch out now, sonny! Don't tear it as you unwrap it! That thing's precious!'

In a few seconds, there was a crowd of about twenty people clustering around Charlie, and many more were pushing their way in from the street. Everybody wanted to get a look at the Golden Ticket and at the lucky finder.

'Where is it?' somebody shouted. 'Hold it up so all of us can see it!'

'There it is, there!' someone else shouted. 'He's holding it in his hands! See the gold shining!'

'How did *he* manage to find it, I'd like to know?' a large boy shouted angrily. '*Twenty* bars a day I've been buying for weeks and weeks!'

'Think of all the free stuff he'll be getting too!' another boy said enviously. 'A lifetime supply!'

'He'll need it, the skinny little shrimp!' a girl said, laughing.

Charlie hadn't moved. He hadn't even unwrapped the Golden Ticket from around the chocolate. He was standing very still, holding it tightly with both hands while the crowd pushed and shouted all around him. He felt quite dizzy. There was a peculiar floating sensation coming over him, as though he were floating up in the air like a balloon. His feet didn't seem to be touching the ground at all. He could hear his heart thumping away loudly somewhere in his throat.

At that point, he became aware of a hand resting lightly on his shoulder, and when he looked up, he saw a tall man standing over him. 'Listen,' the man whispered. 'I'll buy it from you. I'll give you fifty pounds. How about it, eh? And I'll give you a new bicycle as well. Okay?'

'Are you *crazy?*' shouted a woman who was standing equally close. 'Why, I'd give him *two hundred* pounds for that ticket! You want to sell that ticket for two hundred pounds, young man?'

'That's *quite* enough of that!' the fat shopkeeper shouted, pushing his way through the crowd and taking Charlie firmly by the arm. 'Leave the kid alone, will you! Make way there! Let him out!' And to Charlie, as he led him to the door, he whispered, 'Don't you let *anybody* have it! Take it straight home, quickly, before you lose it! Run all the way and don't stop till you get there, you understand?'

Charlie nodded.

'You know something,' the fat shopkeeper said, pausing a moment and smiling at Charlie, 'I have a feeling you needed a break like this. I'm awfully glad you got it. Good luck to you, sonny.'

'Thank you,' Charlie said, and off he went, running through the snow as fast as his legs would go. And as he flew past Mr Willy Wonka's factory, he turned and waved at it and sang out, 'I'll be seeing you! I'll be seeing you soon!' And five minutes later he arrived at his own home.

12

What It Said on the Golden Ticket

Charlie burst through the front door, shouting, *'Mother! Mother! Mother!'*

Mrs Bucket was in the old grandparents' room, serving them their evening soup.

'Mother!' yelled Charlie, rushing in on them like a hurricane. 'Look! I've got it! Look, Mother, look! The last Golden Ticket! It's mine! I found some money in the street and I bought two bars of chocolate and the second one had the Golden Ticket and there were *crowds* of people all around me wanting to see it and the shopkeeper rescued me and I ran all the way home and here I am! *IT'S THE FIFTH GOLDEN TICKET, MOTHER, AND I'VE FOUND IT!'*

Mrs Bucket simply stood and stared, while the four old grandparents, who were sitting up in bed balancing bowls of soup on their laps, all dropped their spoons with a clatter and froze against their pillows.

For about ten seconds there was absolute silence in the room. Nobody dared to speak or move. It was a magic moment.

Then, very softly, Grandpa Joe said, 'You're pulling our legs. Charlie, aren't you? You're having a little joke?'

'I am *not*!' cried Charlie, rushing up to the bed and holding out the large and beautiful Golden Ticket for him to see.

Grandpa Joe leaned forward and took a close look, his nose almost touching the ticket. The others watched him, waiting for the verdict.

Then very slowly, with a slow and marvellous grin spreading all over his face, Grandpa Joe lifted his head and looked straight at Charlie. The colour was rushing to his cheeks, and his eyes were wide open, shining with joy, and in the centre of each eye, right in the very centre, in the black pupil, a little spark of wild excitement was slowly dancing. Then the old man took a deep breath, and suddenly, with no warning whatsoever, an explosion seemed to take place inside him. He threw up his arms and yelled *'Yippeeeeeeee!'* And at the same time, his long bony body rose up out of the bed and his bowl of soup went flying into the face of Grandma Josephine, and in one fantastic leap, this old fellow of ninety-six and a half, who hadn't been out of bed these last twenty years, jumped on to the floor and started doing a dance of victory in his pyjamas.

'Yippeeeeeeeeee!' he shouted. 'Three cheers for Charlie! Hip, hip, hooray!'

At this point, the door opened, and Mr Bucket walked into the room. He was cold and tired, and he looked it. All day long, he had been shovelling snow in the streets.

'*Cripes!*' he cried. 'What's going on in here?'

It didn't take them long to tell him what had happened.

'I don't believe it!' he said. 'It's not possible.'

'Show him the ticket, Charlie!' shouted Grandpa Joe, who was still dancing around the floor like a dervish in his striped pyjamas. 'Show your father the fifth and last Golden Ticket in the world!'

'Let me see it, Charlie,' Mr Bucket said, collapsing into a chair and holding out his hand. Charlie came forward with the precious document.

It was a very beautiful thing, this Golden Ticket, having been made, so it seemed, from a sheet of pure gold hammered out almost to the thinness of paper. On one side of it, printed by some clever method in jet-black letters, was the invitation itself – from Mr Wonka.

'Read it aloud,' said Grandpa Joe, climbing back into bed again at last. 'Let's all hear exactly what it says.'

'Mr Bucket held the lovely Golden Ticket up close to his eyes. His hands were trembling slightly, and he seemed to be overcome by the whole business. He took several deep breaths. Then he cleared his throat, and said, 'All right, I'll read it. Here we go:

'*Greetings to you*, the lucky finder of this Golden Ticket, from Mr Willy Wonka! I shake you warmly by the hand! Tremendous things are in store for you! Many wonderful surprises await you! For now, I do invite you to come to my factory and be my guest for one whole day – you and all others who are lucky enough to find my Golden

Tickets. I, Willy Wonka, will conduct you around the factory myself, showing you everything that there is to see, and afterwards, when it is time to leave, you will be escorted home by a procession of large trucks. These trucks, I can promise you, will be loaded with enough delicious eatables to last you and your entire household for many years. If, at any time thereafter, you should run out of supplies, you have only to come back to the factory and show this Golden Ticket, and I shall be happy to refill your cupboard with whatever you want. In this way, you will be able to keep yourself supplied with tasty morsels for the rest of your life. But this is by no means the most exciting thing that will happen on the day of your visit. I am preparing other surprises that are even more marvellous and more fantastic for you and for all my beloved Golden Ticket holders – mystic and marvellous surprises that will entrance, delight, intrigue, astonish, and perplex you beyond measure. In your wildest dreams you could not imagine that such things could happen to you! Just wait and see! And now, here are your instructions: The day I have chosen for the visit is the first day in the month of February. On this day, and on no other, you must come to the factory gates at ten o'clock sharp in the morning. Don't be late! And you are allowed to bring with you either one or two members of your own family to look after you and to ensure that you don't get into mischief. One more thing – be certain to have this ticket with you, otherwise you will not be admitted.

(Signed) Willy Wonka.'

'The first day of *February*!' cried Mrs Bucket. 'But that's *tomorrow*! Today is the last day of January. *I know it is!*'

'Cripes!' said Mr Bucket. 'I think you're right!'

'You're just in time!' shouted Grandpa Joe. 'There's not a moment to lose. You must start making preparations at once! Wash your face, comb your hair, scrub your hands, brush your teeth, blow your nose, cut your nails, polish your shoes, iron your shirt, and for heaven's sake, get all that mud off your pants! You must get ready, my boy! You must get ready for the biggest day of your life!'

'Now don't over-excite yourself, Grandpa,' Mrs Bucket said. 'And don't fluster poor Charlie. We must all try to keep very calm. Now the first thing to decide is this – who is going to go with Charlie to the factory?'

'*I* will!' shouted Grandpa Joe, leaping out of bed once again. 'I'll take him! I'll look after him! You leave it to me!'

Mrs Bucket smiled at the old man, then she turned to her husband and said, 'How about you, dear? Don't you think *you* ought to go?'

'Well ...' Mr Bucket said, pausing to think about it, 'no ... I'm not so sure that I should.'

'But you *must*.'

'There's no *must* about it, my dear,' Mr Bucket said gently. 'Mind you, I'd *love* to go. It'll be tremendously exciting. But on the other hand ... I believe that the person who really *deserves* to go most of all is Grandpa Joe himself. He seems to know more about it than we do. Provided, of course, that he feels well enough ...'

'Yippeeeeee!' shouted Grandpa Joe, seizing Charlie by the hands and dancing round the room.

'He certainly *seems* well enough,' Mrs Bucket said, laughing. 'Yes ... perhaps you're right after all. Perhaps Grandpa Joe should be the one to go with him. I certainly can't go myself and leave the other three old people all alone in bed for a whole day.'

'Hallelujah!' yelled Grandpa Joe. 'Praise the Lord!'

At that point, there came a loud knock on the front door. Mr Bucket went to open it, and the next moment, swarms of newspapermen and photographers were pouring into the house. They had tracked down the finder of the fifth Golden

Ticket, and now they all wanted to get the full story for the front pages of the morning papers. For several hours, there was complete pandemonium in the little house, and it must have been nearly midnight before Mr Bucket was able to get rid of them so that Charlie could go to bed.

13

The Big Day Arrives

The sun was shining brightly on the morning of the big day, but the ground was still white with snow and the air was very cold.

Outside the gates of Wonka's factory, enormous crowds of people had gathered to watch the five lucky ticket holders going in. The excitement was tremendous. It was just before ten o'clock. The crowds were pushing and shouting, and policemen with arms linked were trying to hold them back from the gates.

Right beside the gates, in a small group that was carefully shielded from the crowds by the police, stood the five famous children, together with the grown-ups who had come with them.

The tall bony figure of Grandpa Joe could be seen standing quietly among them, and beside him, holding tightly on to his hand, was little Charlie Bucket himself.

All the children, except Charlie, had both their mothers and fathers with them, and it was a good thing that they had, otherwise the whole party might have got out of hand. They were so eager to get going that their parents were having to hold them back by force to prevent them from climbing over the gates. 'Be patient!' cried the fathers. 'Be still! It's not *time* yet! It's not ten o'clock!'

Behind him, Charlie Bucket could hear the shouts of the people in the crowd as they pushed and fought to get a glimpse of the famous children.

'There's Violet Beauregarde!' he heard someone shouting. 'That's her all right! I can remember her face from the newspapers!'

'And you know what?' somebody else shouted back. 'She's still chewing that dreadful old piece of gum she's had for three months! You look at her jaws! They're still working on it!'

'Who's the big fat boy?'

'That's Augustus Gloop!'

'So it is!'

'Enormous, isn't he!'

'Fantastic!'

'Who's the kid with a picture of The Lone Ranger stencilled on his windcheater?'

'That's Mike Teavee! He's the television fiend!'

'He must be crazy! Look at all those toy pistols he's got hanging all over him!'

'The one *I* want to see is Veruca Salt!' shouted another voice in the crowd. 'She's the girl whose father bought up half a million chocolate bars and then made the workers in his peanut factory unwrap every one of them until they found a Golden Ticket! He gives her anything she wants! Absolutely anything! She only has to start screaming for it and she gets it!'

'Dreadful, isn't it?'

'Shocking, I call it!'

'Which do you think is her?'

'That one ! Over there on the left! The little girl in the silver mink coat!'

'Which one is Charlie Bucket?'

'Charlie Bucket? He must be that skinny little shrimp standing beside the old fellow who looks like a skeleton. Very close to us. Just there! See him?'

'Why hasn't he got a coat on in this cold weather?'

'Don't ask me. Maybe he can't afford to buy one.'

'Goodness me! He must be freezing!'

Charlie, standing only a few paces away from the speaker, gave Grandpa Joe's hand a squeeze, and the old man looked down at Charlie and smiled.

Somewhere in the distance, a church clock began striking ten.

Very slowly, with a loud creaking of rusty hinges, the great iron gates of the factory began to swing open.

The crowd became suddenly silent. The children stopped jumping about. All eyes were fixed upon the gates.

'There he is!' somebody shouted. *'That's him!'*

And so it was!

14

Mr Willy Wonka

Mr Wonka was standing all alone just inside the open gates of the factory.

And what an extraordinary little man he was!

He had a black top hat on his head.

He wore a tail coat made of a beautiful plum-coloured velvet.

His trousers were bottle green.

His gloves were pearly grey.

And in one hand he carried a fine gold-topped walking cane.

Covering his chin, there was a small, neat, pointed black beard – a goatee. And his eyes – his eyes were most marvellously bright. They seemed to be sparkling and twinkling at you all the time. The whole face, in fact, was alight with fun and laughter.

And oh, how clever he looked! How quick and sharp and full of life! He kept making quick jerky little movements with his head, cocking it this way and that, and taking everything in with those bright twinkling eyes. He was like a squirrel in the quickness of his movements, like a quick clever old squirrel from the park.

Suddenly, he did a funny little skipping dance in the snow, and he spread his arms wide, and he smiled at the five children who were clustered near the gates, and he called out, 'Welcome, my little friends! Welcome to the factory!'

His voice was high and flutey. 'Will you come forward one at a time, please,' he called out, 'and bring your parents. Then show me your Golden Ticket and give me your name. Who's first?'

The big fat boy stepped up. 'I'm Augustus Gloop,' he said.

'Augustus!' cried Mr Wonka, seizing his hand and pumping it up and down with terrific force. 'My *dear* boy, how *good* to see you! Delighted! Charmed! Overjoyed to have you with us! And *these* are your parents? How *nice*! Come in! Come in! That's right! Step through the gates!'

Mr Wonka was clearly just as excited as everybody else.

'My name,' said the next child to go forward, 'is Veruca Salt.'

'My *dear* Veruca! How *do* you do? What a pleasure this is! You *do* have an interesting name, don't you? I always thought that a veruca was a sort of wart that you got on the sole of your foot! But I must be wrong, mustn't I? How pretty you look in that lovely mink coat! I'm so glad you could come! Dear me, this is going to be *such* an exciting day! I *do* hope you enjoy it! I'm sure you *will*! I *know* you will! Your father? How *are* you, Mr Salt? And Mrs Salt? Overjoyed to see you! Yes, the ticket is *quite* in order! Please go in!'

The next two children, Violet Beauregarde and Mike Teavee, came forward to have their tickets examined and then to have their arms practically pumped off their shoulders by the energetic Mr Wonka.

And last of all, a small nervous voice whispered, 'Charlie Bucket.'

'Charlie!' cried Mr Wonka. 'Well, well, well! So *there* you are! You're the one who found your ticket only yesterday, aren't you? Yes, yes. I read *all* about it in this morning's papers! *Just* in time, my dear boy! I'm so glad! So happy for you! And this? Your grandfather? Delighted to meet you, sir! Overjoyed! Enraptured! Enchanted! All right! Excellent! Is everybody in now? Five children? Yes! Good! Now will you please follow me! Our tour is about to begin! But *do* keep together! *Please* don't wander off by yourselves! I shouldn't like to lose any of you at *this* stage of the proceedings! Oh, dear me, no!'

Charlie glanced back over his shoulder and saw the great iron entrance gates slowly closing behind him. The crowds on the outside were still pushing and shouting. Charlie took a last look at them. Then, as the gates closed with a clang, all sight of the outside world disappeared.

'Here we are!' cried Mr Wonka, trotting along in front of the group. 'Through this big red door, please! *That's* right! It's nice and warm inside! I have to keep it warm inside the factory because of the workers! My workers are used to an *extremely* hot climate! They can't stand the cold! They'd perish if they went outdoors in this weather! They'd freeze to death!'

'But who *are* these workers?' asked Augustus Gloop.

'All in good time, my dear boy!' said Mr Wonka, smiling at Augustus. 'Be patient! You shall see everything as we go along! Are all of you inside? Good! Would you mind closing the door? Thank you!'

Charlie Bucket found himself standing in a long corridor that stretched away in front of him as far as he could see. The corridor was so wide that a car could easily have been driven along it. The walls were pale pink, the lighting was soft and pleasant.

'How lovely and warm!' whispered Charlie.

'I know. And what a marvellous smell!' answered Grandpa Joe, taking a long deep sniff. All the most wonderful smells in the world seemed to be mixed up in the air around them – the smell of roasting coffee and burnt sugar and melting chocolate and mint and violets and crushed hazelnuts and apple blossom and caramel and lemon peel . . .

And far away in the distance, from the heart of the great factory, came a muffled roar of energy as though some monstrous gigantic machine were spinning its wheels at breakneck speed.

'Now *this*, my dear children,' said Mr Wonka, raising his voice above the noise, 'this is the main corridor. Will you please hang your coats and hats on those pegs over there, and then follow me. *That's* the way! Good! Everyone ready! Come on, then! Here we go!' He trotted off rapidly down the corridor with the tails of his plum-coloured velvet coat flapping behind him, and the visitors all hurried after him.

It was quite a large party of people, when you came to think of it. There were nine grown-ups and five children, fourteen in all. So you can imagine that there was a good deal of pushing and shoving as they hustled and bustled down the passage, trying to keep up with the swift little figure in front of them. 'Come *on*!' cried Mr Wonka. 'Get a move on, please! We'll *never* get round today if you dawdle like this!'

Soon, he turned right off the main corridor into another slightly narrower passage.

Then he turned left.

Then left again.

Then right.

Then left.

Then right.

Then right.

Then left.

The place was like a gigantic rabbit warren, with passages leading this way and that in every direction.

'Don't you let go my hand, Charlie,' whispered Grandpa Joe.

'Notice how all these passages are sloping downwards!' called out Mr Wonka. 'We are now going underground! *All* the most important rooms in my factory are deep down below the surface!'

'Why is that?' somebody asked.

'There wouldn't be *nearly* enough space for them up on top!' answered Mr Wonka. 'These rooms we are going to see are *enormous*! They're larger than football fields! No building in the *world* would be big enough to house them! But down here, underneath the ground, I've got *all* the space I want. There's no limit – so long as I hollow it out.'

Mr Wonka turned right.

He turned left.

He turned right again.

The passages were sloping steeper and steeper downhill now.

Then suddenly, Mr Wonka stopped. In front of him, there was a shiny metal door. The party crowded round. On the door, in large letters, it said:

THE CHOCOLATE ROOM

15

The Chocolate Room

'An important room, this!' cried Mr Wonka, taking a bunch of keys from his pocket and slipping one into the keyhole of the door. '*This* is the nerve centre of the whole factory, the heart of the whole business! And so *beautiful*! I *insist* upon my rooms being beautiful! I can't *abide* ugliness in factories! *In* we go, then! But *do* be careful, my dear children! Don't lose your heads! Don't get over-excited! Keep very calm!'

Mr Wonka opened the door. Five children and nine grown-ups pushed their ways in – and *oh*, what an amazing sight it was that now met their eyes!

They were looking down upon a lovely valley. There were green meadows on either side of the valley, and along the bottom of it there flowed a great brown river.

What is more, there was a tremendous waterfall halfway along the river – a steep cliff over which the water curled and rolled in a solid sheet, and then went crashing down into a boiling churning whirlpool of froth and spray.

Below the waterfall (and this was the most astonishing sight of all), a whole mass of enormous glass pipes were dangling down into the river from somewhere high up in the ceiling! They really were *enormous*, those pipes. There must have been a dozen of them at least, and they were sucking up the brownish muddy water from the river and carrying it away to goodness knows where. And because they were made of glass, you could see the liquid flowing and bubbling along inside them, and above the noise of the waterfall, you could hear the never-ending suck-suck-sucking sound of the pipes as they did their work.

Graceful trees and bushes were growing along the riverbanks – weeping willows and alders and tall clumps of rhododendrons with their pink and red and mauve blossoms. In the meadows there were thousands of buttercups.

'There!' cried Mr Wonka, dancing up and down and pointing his gold-topped cane at the great brown river. 'It's *all* chocolate! Every drop of that river is hot melted chocolate of the finest quality. The *very* finest quality. There's enough chocolate in there to fill *every* bathtub in the *entire* country! *And* all the swimming pools as well! Isn't it *terrific?* And just look at my pipes! They suck up the chocolate and carry it away to all the other rooms in the factory where it is needed! Thousands of gallons an hour, my dear children! Thousands and thousands of gallons!'

The children and their parents were too flabbergasted to speak. They were staggered. They were dumbfounded. They were bewildered and dazzled. They were completely bowled over by the hugeness of the whole thing. They simply stood and stared.

'The waterfall is *most* important!' Mr Wonka went on. 'It mixes the chocolate! It churns it up! It pounds it and beats it! It makes it light and frothy! No other factory in the world mixes its chocolate by waterfall! But it's the *only* way to do it properly! The *only* way! And do you like my trees?' he cried, pointing with his stick. 'And my lovely bushes? Don't you think they look pretty? I told you I hated ugliness! And of course they are *all* eatable! All made of something different and delicious! And do you like my meadows? Do you like my grass and my buttercups? The grass you are standing on, my dear little ones, is made of a new kind of soft, minty sugar that I've just invented! I call it swudge! Try a blade! Please do! It's delectable!'

Automatically, everybody bent down and picked one blade of grass – everybody, that is, except Augustus Gloop, who took a big handful.

And Violet Beauregarde, before tasting her blade of grass, took the piece of world-record-breaking chewing-gum out of her mouth and stuck it carefully behind her ear.

'Isn't it *wonderful*!' whispered Charlie. 'Hasn't it got a wonderful taste, Grandpa?'

'I could eat the whole *field*!' said Grandpa Joe, grinning with delight. 'I could go around on all fours like a cow and eat every blade of grass in the field!'

'Try a buttercup!' cried Mr Wonka. 'They're even *nicer*!'

Suddenly, the air was filled with screams of excitement. The screams came from Veruca Salt. She was pointing frantically to the other side of the river. '*Look*! Look over there!' she screamed. 'What *is* it? He's moving! He's walking! It's a little *person*! It's a little *man*! Down there below the waterfall!'

Everybody stopped picking buttercups and stared across the river.

'*She's right, Grandpa!*' cried Charlie. 'It *is* a little man! Can you *see* him?'

'I see him, Charlie!' said Grandpa Joe excitedly.

And now everybody started shouting at once.

'There's *two* of them!'

75

'My gosh, so there is!'

'There's more than two! There's one, two, three, four, five!'

'What are they *doing*?'

'Where do they *come* from?'

'Who *are* they?'

Children and parents alike rushed down to the edge of the river to get a closer look.

'Aren't they *fantastic*!'

'No higher than my knee!'

'Look at their funny long hair!'

The tiny men – they were no larger than medium-sized dolls – had stopped what they were doing, and now they were staring back across the river at the visitors. One of them pointed towards the children, and then he whispered something to the other four, and all five of them burst into peals of laughter.

'But they can't be *real* people,' Charlie said.

'Of course they're real people,' Mr Wonka answered. 'They're Oompa-Loompas.'

16

The Oompa-Loompas

'Oompa-Loompas!' everyone said at once. *'Oompa-Loompas!'*
'Imported direct from Loompaland,' said Mr Wonka proudly.
'There's no such place,' said Mrs Salt.
'Excuse me, dear lady, but ...'
'Mr Wonka,' cried Mrs Salt. 'I'm a teacher of geography ...'
'Then you'll know all about it,' said Mr Wonka. 'And oh,
what a terrible country it is! Nothing but thick jungles infested
by the most dangerous beasts in the world – hornswogglers and
snozzwangers and those terrible wicked whangdoodles. A
whangdoodle would eat ten Oompa-Loompas for breakfast and
come galloping back for a second helping. When I went out
there, I found the little Oompa-Loompas living in tree houses.
They *had* to live in tree houses to escape from the whangdoodles
and the hornswogglers and the snozzwangers. And they were
living on green caterpillars, and the caterpillars tasted revolting, and the Oompa-Loompas spent every moment of their days
climbing through the treetops looking for other things to mash
up with the caterpillars to make them taste better – red beetles,
for instance, and eucalyptus leaves, and the bark of the bong-
bong tree, all of them beastly, but not quite so beastly as the
caterpillars. Poor little Oompa-Loompas! The one food that they

longed for more than any other was the cacao bean. But they couldn't get it. An Oompa-Loompa was lucky if he found three or four cacao beans a year. But oh, how they craved them. They used to dream about cacao beans all night and talk about them all day. You had only to *mention* the word "cacao" to an Oompa-Loompa and he would start dribbling at the mouth. The cacao bean,' Mr Wonka continued, 'which grows on the cacao tree, happens to be *the thing* from which all chocolate is made. You cannot make chocolate without the cacao bean. The cacao bean *is* chocolate. I myself use billions of cacao beans every week in this factory. And so, my dear children, as soon as I discovered that the Oompa-Loompas were crazy about this particular food, I climbed up to their tree-house village and poked my head in through the door of the tree house belonging to the leader of the tribe. The poor little fellow, looking thin and starved, was sitting there trying to eat a bowl full of mashed-up green caterpillars without being sick. "Look here," I said (speaking not in English, of course, but in Oompa-Loompish), "look here, if you and all your people will come back to my country and live in my factory, you can have *all* the cacao beans you want! I've got mountains of them in my storehouses! You can have cacao beans for every meal! You can gorge yourselves silly on them! I'll even pay your wages in cacao beans if you wish!"

'"You really mean it?" asked the Oompa-Loompa leader, leaping up from his chair.

'"Of course I mean it," I said. "And you can have chocolate as well. Chocolate tastes even better than cacao beans because it's got milk and sugar added."

'The little man gave a great whoop of joy and threw his bowl of mashed caterpillars right out of the tree-house window. "It's a deal!" he cried. "Come on! Let's go!"

'So I shipped them all over here, every man, woman, and child in the Oompa-Loompa tribe. It was easy. I smuggled them over in large packing cases with holes in them, and they all got here safely. They are wonderful workers. They all speak English now. They love dancing and music. They are always making up songs. I expect you will hear a good deal of singing today from time to time. I must warn you, though, that they are rather mischievous. They like jokes. They still wear the same kind of clothes they wore in the jungle. They insist upon that. The men, as you can see for yourselves across the river, wear only deerskins. The women wear leaves, and the children wear nothing at all. The women use fresh leaves every day ...'

'*Daddy!*' shouted Veruca Salt (the girl who got everything she wanted). '*Daddy!* I want an Oompa-Loompa! I want you to get me an Oompa-Loompa! I want an Oompa-Loompa right away! I want to take it home with me! Go on, Daddy! Get me an Oompa-Loompa!'

'Now, now, my pet!' her father said to her, 'we mustn't interrupt Mr Wonka.'

'*But I want an Oompa-Loompa!*' screamed Veruca.

'All *right*, Veruca, all *right*. But I can't get it for you this second. Please be patient. I'll see you have one before the day is out.'

'Augustus!' shouted Mrs Gloop. 'Augustus, sweetheart, I don't think you had better do *that*.' Augustus Gloop, as you might have guessed, had quietly sneaked down to the edge of the river, and he was now kneeling on the riverbank, scooping hot melted chocolate into his mouth as fast as he could.

17

Augustus Gloop Goes up the Pipe

When Mr Wonka turned round and saw what Augustus Gloop was doing, he cried out, 'Oh, no! *Please*, Augustus, *please*! I beg of you not to do that. My chocolate must be untouched by human hands!'

'Augustus!' called out Mrs Gloop. 'Didn't you hear what the man said? Come away from that river at once!'

'This stuff is fabulous!' said Augustus, taking not the slightest notice of his mother or Mr Wonka. 'Gosh, I need a bucket to drink it properly!'

'Augustus,' cried Mr Wonka, hopping up and down and waggling his stick in the air, 'you *must* come away. You are dirtying my chocolate!'

'Augustus!' cried Mrs Gloop.

'Augustus!' cried Mr Gloop.

But Augustus was deaf to everything except the call of his enormous stomach. He was now lying full length on the ground with his head far out over the river, lapping up the chocolate like a dog.

'Augustus!' shouted Mrs Gloop. 'You'll be giving that nasty cold of yours to about a million people all over the country!'

'Be careful, Augustus!' shouted Mr Gloop. 'You're leaning too far out!'

Mr Gloop was absolutely right. For suddenly there was a shriek, and then a splash, and into the river went Augustus Gloop, and in one second he had disappeared under the brown surface.

'Save him!' screamed Mrs Gloop, going white in the face, and waving her umbrella about. 'He'll drown! He can't swim a yard! Save him! Save him!'

'Good heavens, woman,' said Mr Gloop, 'I'm not diving in there! I've got my best suit on!'

Augustus Gloop's face came up again to the surface, painted brown with chocolate. 'Help! Help! Help!' he yelled. 'Fish me out!'

'Don't just *stand* there!' Mrs Gloop screamed at Mr Gloop. '*Do* something!'

'I *am* doing something!' said Mr Gloop, who was now taking off his jacket and getting ready to dive into the chocolate. But while he was doing this, the wretched boy was being sucked closer and closer towards the mouth of one of the great pipes that was dangling down into the river. Then all at once, the powerful suction took hold of him completely, and he was pulled under the surface and then into the mouth of the pipe.

The crowd on the riverbank waited breathlessly to see where he would come out.

'*There he goes!*' somebody shouted, pointing upwards.

And sure enough, because the pipe was made of glass, Augustus Gloop could be clearly seen shooting up inside it, head first, like a torpedo.

'Help! Murder! Police!' screamed Mrs Gloop. 'Augustus, come back at once! Where are you going?'

'It's a wonder to me,' said Mr Gloop, 'how that pipe is big enough for him to go through it.'

'It *isn't* big enough!' said Charlie Bucket. 'Oh dear, look! He's slowing down!'

'So he is!' said Grandpa Joe.

'He's going to stick!' said Charlie.

'I think he is!' said Grandpa Joe.

'By golly, he *has* stuck!' said Charlie.

'It's his stomach that's done it!' said Mr Gloop.

'He's blocked the whole pipe!' said Grandpa Joe.

'Smash the pipe!' yelled Mrs Gloop, still waving her umbrella. 'Augustus, come out of there at once!'

The watchers below could see the chocolate swishing around the boy in the pipe, and they could see it building up behind him in a solid mass, pushing against the blockage. The pressure was terrific. Something had to give. Something did give, and that something was Augustus. *WHOOF!* Up he shot again like a bullet in the barrel of a gun.

'He's disappeared!' yelled Mrs Gloop. 'Where does that pipe go to? Quick! Call the fire brigade!'

'Keep calm!' cried Mr Wonka. 'Keep calm, my dear lady, keep calm. There is no danger! No danger whatsoever! Augustus has gone on a little journey, that's all. A most interesting little journey. But he'll come out of it just fine, you wait and see.'

'How can he possibly come out just fine!' snapped Mrs Gloop. 'He'll be made into marshmallows in five seconds!'

'Impossible!' cried Mr Wonka. 'Unthinkable! Inconceivable! Absurd! He could never be made into marshmallows!'

'And why not, may I ask?' shouted Mrs Gloop.

'Because that pipe doesn't go anywhere near it! That pipe – the one Augustus went up – happens to lead directly to the room where I make a most delicious kind of strawberry-flavoured chocolate-coated fudge ...'

'Then he'll be made into strawberry-flavoured chocolate-coated fudge!' screamed Mrs Gloop. 'My poor Augustus! They'll be selling him by the pound all over the country tomorrow morning!'

'Quite right,' said Mr Gloop.

'I *know* I'm right,' said Mrs Gloop.

'It's beyond a joke,' said Mr Gloop.

'Mr Wonka doesn't seem to think so!' cried Mrs Gloop. 'Just look at him! He's laughing his head off! How *dare* you laugh like that when my boy's just gone up the pipe! You monster!' she shrieked, pointing her umbrella at Mr Wonka as though she were going to run him through. 'You think it's a joke, do you? You think that sucking my boy up into your Fudge Room like that is just one great big colossal joke?'

'He'll be perfectly safe,' said Mr Wonka, giggling slightly.

'He'll be chocolate fudge!' shrieked Mrs Gloop.

'Never!' cried Mr Wonka.

'Of course he will!' shrieked Mrs Gloop.

'I wouldn't allow it!' cried Mr Wonka.

'And why not?' shrieked Mrs Gloop.

'Because the taste would be terrible,' said Mr Wonka. 'Just imagine it! Augustus-flavoured chocolate-coated Gloop! No one would buy it.'

'They most certainly would!' cried Mr Gloop indignantly.

'I don't want to think about it!' shrieked Mrs Gloop.

'Nor do I,' said Mr Wonka. 'And I do promise you, madam, that your darling boy is perfectly safe.'

'If he's perfectly safe, then where is he?' snapped Mrs Gloop. 'Lead me to him this instant!'

Mr Wonka turned around and clicked his fingers sharply, *click, click, click,* three times. Immediately, an Oompa-Loompa appeared, as if from nowhere, and stood beside him.

The Oompa-Loompa bowed and smiled, showing beautiful white teeth. His skin was rosy-white, his long hair was golden-brown, and the top of his head came just above the height of Mr Wonka's knee. He wore the usual deerskin slung over his shoulder.

'Now listen to me!' said Mr Wonka, looking down at the tiny man, 'I want you to take Mr and Mrs Gloop up to the Fudge Room and help them to find their son, Augustus. He's just gone up the pipe.'

The Oompa-Loompa took one look at Mrs Gloop and exploded into peals of laughter.

'Oh, do be quiet!' said Mr Wonka. 'Control yourself! Pull yourself together! Mrs Gloop doesn't think it's at all funny!'

'You can say that again!' said Mrs Gloop.

'Go straight to the Fudge Room,' Mr Wonka said to the Oompa-Loompa, 'and when you get there, take a long stick and start poking around inside the big chocolate-mixing barrel. I'm almost certain you'll find him in there. But you'd better look sharp! You'll have to hurry! If you leave him in the chocolate-mixing barrel too long, he's liable to get poured out into the fudge boiler, and that really *would* be a disaster, wouldn't it? My fudge would become *quite* uneatable!'

Mrs Gloop let out a shriek of fury.

'I'm joking,' said Mr Wonka, giggling madly behind his beard. 'I didn't mean it. Forgive me. I'm so sorry. Good-bye, Mrs Gloop! And Mr Gloop! Good-bye! I'll see you later . . .'

As Mr and Mrs Gloop and their tiny escort hurried away, the five Oompa-Loompas on the far side of the river suddenly began hopping and dancing about and beating wildly upon a number of very small drums. 'Augustus Gloop!' they chanted. 'Augustus Gloop! Augustus Gloop! Augustus Gloop!'

'Grandpa!' cried Charlie. 'Listen to them, Grandpa! What *are* they doing?'

'Ssshh!' whispered Grandpa Joe. 'I think they're going to sing us a song!'

> '*Augustus Gloop!*' chanted the Oompa-Loompas.
> '*Augustus Gloop! Augustus Gloop!*
> *The great big greedy nincompoop!*
> *How long could we allow this beast*
> *To gorge and guzzle, feed and feast*
> *On everything he wanted to?*
> *Great Scott! It simply wouldn't do!*
> *However long this pig might live.*
> *We're positive he'd never give*
> *Even the smallest bit of fun*

Or happiness to anyone.
So what we do in cases such
As this, we use the gentle touch,
And carefully we take the brat
And turn him into something that
Will give great pleasure to us all –
A doll, for instance, or a ball,
Or marbles or a rocking horse.
But this revolting boy, of course,
Was so unutterably vile,
So greedy, foul, and infantile,
He left a most disgusting taste
Inside our mouths, and so in haste
We chose a thing that, come what may,
Would take the nasty taste away.
"Come on!" we cried. "The time is ripe
To send him shooting up the pipe!
He has to go! It has to be!"
And very soon, he's going to see
Inside the room to which he's gone
Some funny things are going on.
But don't, dear children, be alarmed;
Augustus Gloop will not be harmed,
Although, of course, we must admit
He will be altered quite a bit.
He'll be quite *changed from what he's been*,
When he goes through the fudge machine:
Slowly, the wheels go round and round,
The cogs begin to grind and pound;
A hundred knives go slice, slice, slice;
We add some sugar, cream, and spice;
We boil him for a minute more,

Until we're absolutely sure
That all the greed and all the gall
Is boiled away for once and all.
Then out he comes! And now! By grace!
A miracle has taken place!
This boy, who only just before
Was loathed by men from shore to shore,
This greedy brute, this louse's ear,
Is loved by people everywhere!
For who could hate or bear a grudge
Against a luscious bit of fudge?'

'I *told* you they loved singing!' cried Mr Wonka. 'Aren't they delightful? Aren't they charming? But you mustn't believe a word they said. It's all nonsense, every bit of it!'

'Are the Oompa-Loompas really joking, Grandpa?' asked Charlie.

'Of course they're joking,' answered Grandpa Joe. 'They *must* be joking. At least, I hope they're joking. Don't you?'

18

Down the Chocolate River

'Off we go!' cried Mr Wonka. 'Hurry up, everybody! Follow me to the next room! And please don't worry about Augustus Gloop. He's bound to come out in the wash. They always do. We shall have to make the next part of the journey by boat! Here she comes! Look!'

A steamy mist was rising up now from the great warm chocolate river, and out of the mist there appeared suddenly a most fantastic pink boat. It was a large open row boat with a tall front and a tall back (like a Viking boat of old), and it was of such a shining sparkling glistening pink colour that the whole thing looked as though it were made of bright, pink glass. There were many oars on either side of it, and as the boat came closer, the watchers on the riverbank could see that the oars were being pulled by masses of Oompa-Loompas – at least ten of them to each oar.

'This is my private yacht!' cried Mr Wonka, beaming with pleasure. 'I made her by hollowing out an enormous boiled sweet! Isn't she beautiful! See how she comes cutting through the river!'

The gleaming pink boiled-sweet boat glided up to the river-bank. One hundred Oompa-Loompas rested on their oars and stared up at the visitors. Then suddenly, for some reason best known to themselves, they all burst into shrieks of laughter.

'What's so funny?' asked Violet Beauregarde.

'Oh, don't worry about *them*!' cried Mr Wonka. 'They're always laughing! They think everything's a colossal joke! Jump into the boat, all of you! Come on! Hurry up!'

As soon as everyone was safely in, the Oompa-Loompas pushed the boat away from the bank and began to row swiftly down river.

'Hey, there! Mike Teavee!' shouted Mr Wonka. 'Please do not lick the boat with your tongue! It'll only make it sticky!'

'Daddy,' said Veruca Salt, 'I want a boat like this! I want you to buy me a big pink boiled-sweet boat exactly like Mr Wonka's! And I want lots of Oompa-Loompas to row me about, and I want a chocolate river and I want ... I want ...'

'She wants a good kick in the pants,' whispered Grandpa Joe to Charlie. The old man was sitting in the back of the boat and little Charlie Bucket was right beside him. Charlie was holding tightly on to his grandfather's bony old hand. He was in a whirl of excitement. Everything that he had seen so far – the great chocolate river, the waterfall, the huge sucking pipes, the minty sugar meadows, the Oompa-Loompas, the beautiful pink boat, and most of all, Mr Willy Wonka himself – had been so astonishing that he began to wonder whether there could possibly be any more astonishments left. Where were they going now? What were they going to see? And what in the world was going to happen in the next room?

'Isn't it marvellous?' said Grandpa Joe, grinning at Charlie.

Charlie nodded and smiled up at the old man.

Suddenly, Mr Wonka, who was sitting on Charlie's other side, reached down into the bottom of the boat, picked up a large mug, dipped it into the river, filled it with chocolate, and handed it to Charlie. 'Drink this,' he said. 'It'll do you good! You look starved to death!'

Then Mr Wonka filled a second mug and gave it to Grandpa Joe. 'You, too,' he said. 'You look like a skeleton! What's the matter? Hasn't there been anything to eat in your house lately?'

'Not much,' said Grandpa Joe.

Charlie put the mug to his lips, and as the rich warm creamy chocolate ran down his throat into his empty tummy, his whole body from head to toe began to tingle with pleasure, and a feeling of intense happiness spread over him.

'You like it?' asked Mr Wonka.

'Oh, it's wonderful!' Charlie said.

'The creamiest loveliest chocolate I've ever tasted!' said Grandpa Joe, smacking his lips.

'That's because it's been mixed by waterfall,' Mr Wonka told him.

The boat sped on down the river. The river was getting narrower. There was some kind of a dark tunnel ahead – a great round tunnel that looked like an enormous pipe – and the river was running right into the tunnel. And so was the boat! 'Row on!' shouted Mr Wonka, jumping up and waving his stick in the air. 'Full speed ahead!' And with the Oompa-Loompas rowing faster than ever, the boat shot into the pitch-dark tunnel, and all the passengers screamed with excitement.

'How can they see where they're going?' shrieked Violet Beauregarde in the darkness.

'There's no knowing where they're going!' cried Mr Wonka, hooting with laughter.

> *'There's no earthly way of knowing*
> *Which direction they are going!*
> *There's no knowing where they're rowing,*
> *Or which way the river's flowing!*
> *Not a speck of light is showing,*
> *So the danger must be growing,*
> *For the rowers keep on rowing,*
> *And they're certainly not showing*
> *Any signs that they are slowing ...'*

'He's gone off his rocker!' shouted one of the fathers, aghast, and the other parents joined in the chorus of frightened shouting. 'He's crazy!' they shouted.

'He's balmy!'

'He's nutty!'

'He's screwy!'

'He's batty!'

'He's dippy!'

'He's dotty!'

'He's daffy!'

'He's goofy!'

'He's beany!'

'He's buggy!'

'He's wacky!'

'He's loony!'

'No, he is *not*!' said Grandpa Joe.

'Switch on the lights!' shouted Mr Wonka. And suddenly, on came the lights and the whole tunnel was brilliantly lit up, and Charlie could see that they were indeed inside a gigantic pipe, and the great upward-curving walls of the pipe were pure white and spotlessly clean. The river of chocolate was flowing very fast inside the pipe, and the Oompa-Loompas were all rowing like mad, and the boat was rocketing along at a furious pace. Mr Wonka was jumping up and down in the back of the boat and calling to the rowers to row faster and faster still. He seemed to love the sensation of whizzing through a white tunnel in a pink boat on a chocolate river, and he clapped his hands and laughed and kept glancing at his passengers to see if they were enjoying it as much as he.

'Look, Grandpa!' cried Charlie. 'There's a door in the wall!' It was a green door and it was set into the wall of the tunnel just above the level of the river. As they flashed past it there was just enough time to read the writing on the door: STORE-ROOM NUMBER 54, it said. ALL THE CREAMS – DAIRY CREAM, WHIPPED CREAM, VIOLET CREAM, COFFEE CREAM, PINEAPPLE CREAM, VANILLA CREAM, AND HAIR CREAM.

'Hair cream?' cried Mike Teavee. 'You don't use *hair cream*?'

'Row on!' shouted Mr Wonka. 'There's no time to answer silly questions!'

They streaked past a black door. STOREROOM NUMBER 71, it said on it. WHIPS – ALL SHAPES AND SIZES.

'*Whips!*' cried Veruca Salt. 'What on earth do you use whips for?'

'For whipping cream, of course,' said Mr Wonka. 'How can you whip cream without whips? Whipped cream isn't whipped cream at all unless it's been whipped with whips. Just as a poached egg isn't a poached egg unless it's been stolen from the woods in the dead of night! Row on, please!'

They passed a yellow door on which it said: STOREROOM NUMBER 77 – ALL THE BEANS, CACAO BEANS, COFFEE BEANS, JELLY BEANS, AND HAS BEANS.

'Has beans?' cried Violet Beauregarde.

'You're one yourself!' said Mr Wonka. 'There's no time for arguing! Press on, press on!' But five seconds later, when a bright red door came into sight ahead, he suddenly waved his gold-topped cane in the air and shouted, 'Stop the boat!'

19

The Inventing Room – Everlasting Gobstoppers and Hair Toffee

When Mr Wonka shouted 'Stop the boat!' the Oompa-Loompas jammed their oars into the river and backed water furiously. The boat stopped.

The Oompa-Loompas guided the boat alongside the red door. On the door it said, INVENTING ROOM – PRIVATE – KEEP OUT. Mr Wonka took a key from his pocket, leaned over the side of the boat, and put the key in the keyhole.

'*This* is the most important room in the entire factory!' he said. 'All my most secret new inventions are cooking and simmering in here! Old Fickelgruber would give his front teeth to be allowed inside just for three minutes! So would Prodnose and Slugworth and all the other rotten chocolate makers! But now, listen to me! I want no messing about when you go in! No touching, no meddling, and no tasting! Is that agreed?'

'Yes, yes!' the children cried. 'We won't touch a thing!'

'Up to now,' Mr Wonka said, 'nobody else, not even an Oompa-Loompa, has ever been allowed in here!' He opened the door and stepped out of the boat into the room. The four children and their parents all scrambled after him.

'Don't touch!' shouted Mr Wonka. 'And don't knock anything over!'

Charlie Bucket stared around the gigantic room in which he now found himself. The place was like a witch's kitchen! All about him black metal pots were boiling and bubbling on huge stoves, and kettles were hissing and pans were sizzling, and strange iron machines were clanking and spluttering, and there were pipes running all over the ceiling and walls, and the whole place was filled with smoke and steam and delicious rich smells.

Mr Wonka himself had suddenly become even more excited than usual, and anyone could see that this was the room he loved best of all. He was hopping about among the saucepans and the machines like a child among his Christmas presents, not knowing which thing to look at first. He lifted the lid from a huge pot and took a sniff; then he rushed over and dipped a finger into a barrel of sticky yellow stuff and had a taste; then he skipped across to one of the machines and turned half a dozen knobs this way and that; then he peered anxiously through the glass door of a gigantic oven, rubbing his hands and cackling with delight at what he saw inside. Then he ran over to another machine, a small shiny affair that kept going *phut-phut-phut-phut-phut*, and every time it went *phut*, a large green marble dropped out of it into a basket on the floor. At least it looked like a marble.

'Everlasting Gobstoppers!' cried Mr Wonka proudly. 'They're completely new! I am inventing them for children who are given very little pocket money. You can put an Everlasting Gobstopper in your mouth and you can suck it and suck it and suck it and suck it and it will *never* get any smaller!'

'It's like gum!' cried Violet Beauregarde.

'It is *not* like gum,' Mr Wonka said. 'Gum is for chewing, and if you tried chewing one of these Gobstoppers here you'd break your teeth off! And they *never* get any smaller! They *never* disappear! *NEVER!* At least I don't think they do. There's one of them being tested this very moment in the Testing Room next door. An Oompa-Loompa is sucking it. He's been sucking it for very nearly a year now without stopping, and it's still just as good as ever!

'Now, over here,' Mr Wonka went on, skipping excitedly across the room to the opposite wall, 'over here I am inventing a completely new line in toffees!' He stopped beside a large saucepan. The saucepan was full of a thick gooey purplish treacle, boiling and bubbling. By standing on his toes, little Charlie could just see inside it.

'That's Hair Toffee!' cried Mr Wonka. 'You eat just one tiny bit of that, and in exactly half an hour a brand-new luscious thick silky beautiful crop of hair will start growing out all over the top of your head! And a moustache! And a beard!'

'A beard!' cried Veruca Salt. 'Who wants a beard, for heaven's sake?'

'It would suit you very well,' said Mr Wonka, 'but unfortunately the mixture is not quite right yet. I've got it too strong. It works too well. I tried it on an Oompa-Loompa yesterday in the

Testing Room and immediately a huge black beard started shooting out of his chin, and the beard grew so fast that soon it was trailing all over the floor in a thick hairy carpet. It was growing faster than we could cut it! In the end we had to use a lawn mower to keep it in check! But I'll get the mixture right soon! And when I do, then there'll be no excuse any more for little boys and girls going about with bald heads!'

'But Mr Wonka,' said Mike Teavee, 'little boys and girls never *do* go about with . . .'

'Don't argue, my dear child, *please* don't argue!' cried Mr Wonka. 'It's such a waste of precious time! Now, over *here*, if you will all step this way, I will show you something that I am terrifically proud of. Oh, do be careful! Don't knock anything over! Stand back!'

20

The Great Gum Machine

Mr Wonka led the party over to a gigantic machine that stood in the very centre of the Inventing Room. It was a mountain of gleaming metal that towered high above the children and their parents. Out of the very top of it there sprouted hundreds and hundreds of thin glass tubes, and the glass tubes all curled downwards and came together in a bunch and hung suspended over an enormous round tub as big as a bath.

'Here we go!' cried Mr Wonka, and he pressed three different buttons on the side of the machine. A second later, a mighty rumbling sound came from inside it, and the whole machine began to shake most frighteningly, and steam began hissing out of it all over, and then suddenly the watchers noticed that runny stuff was pouring down the insides of all the hundreds of little glass tubes and squirting out into the great tub below. And in every single tube the runny stuff was of a different colour, so that all the colours of the rainbow (and many others as well) came sloshing and splashing into the tub. It was a lovely sight. And when the tub was nearly full, Mr Wonka pressed another button, and immediately the runny stuff disappeared, and a whizzing whirring noise took its place; and then a giant whizzer started whizzing round inside the enormous tub, mixing up all the

different coloured liquids like an ice-cream soda. Gradually, the
mixture began to froth. It became frothier and frothier, and it
turned from blue to white to green to brown to yellow, then back
to blue again.

'Watch!' said Mr Wonka.

Click went the machine, and the whizzer stopped whizzing.
And now there came a sort of sucking noise, and very quickly
all the blue frothy mixture in the huge basin was sucked back
into the stomach of the machine. There was a moment of silence.

Then a few queer rumblings were heard. Then silence again. Then suddenly, the machine let out a monstrous mighty groan, and at the same moment a tiny drawer (no bigger than the drawer in a slot machine) popped out of the side of the machine, and in the drawer there lay something so small and thin and grey that everyone thought it must be a mistake. The thing looked like a little strip of grey cardboard.

The children and their parents stared at the little grey strip lying in the drawer.

'You mean that's *all?*' said Mike Teavee, disgusted.

'That's all,' answered Mr Wonka, gazing proudly at the result. 'Don't you know what it is?'

There was a pause. Then suddenly, Violet Beauregarde, the silly gum-chewing girl, let out a yell of excitement. 'By gum, it's *gum!*' she shrieked. 'It's a stick of chewing-gum!'

'Right you are!' cried Mr Wonka, slapping Violet hard on the back. 'It's a stick of gum! It's a stick of the most *amazing* and *fabulous* and *sensational* gum in the world!'

21

Good-bye Violet

'This gum,' Mr Wonka went on, 'is my latest, my greatest, my most fascinating invention! It's a chewing-gum meal! It's ... it's ... it's ... that tiny little strip of gum lying there is a whole three-course dinner all by itself!'

'What sort of nonsense is this?' said one of the fathers.

'My dear sir!' cried Mr Wonka, 'when I start selling this gum in the shops it will change *everything*! It will be the end of all kitchens and all cooking! There will be no more shopping to do! No more buying of meat and groceries! There'll be no knives and forks at mealtimes! No plates! No washing up! No rubbish! No mess! Just a little strip of Wonka's magic chewing-gum – and that's all you'll ever need at breakfast, lunch, and supper! This piece of gum I've just made happens to be tomato soup, roast beef, and blueberry pie, but you can have almost anything you want!'

'What *do* you mean, it's tomato soup, roast beef, and blueberry pie?' said Violet Beauregarde.

'If you were to start chewing it,' said Mr Wonka, 'then that is exactly what you would get on the menu. It's absolutely amazing! You can actually *feel* the food going down your throat and into your tummy! And you can taste it perfectly! And it fills you up! It satisfies you! It's terrific!'

'It's utterly impossible,' said Veruca Salt.

'Just so long as it's gum,' shouted Violet Beauregarde, 'just so long as it's a piece of gum and I can chew it, then *that's* for me!' And quickly she took her own world-record piece of chewing-gum out of her mouth and stuck it behind her left ear. 'Come on, Mr Wonka,' she said, 'hand over this magic gum of yours and we'll see if the thing works.'

'Now, Violet,' said Mrs Beauregarde, her mother; 'don't let's do anything silly, Violet.'

'I want the gum!' Violet said obstinately. 'What's so silly?'

'I would rather you didn't take it,' Mr Wonka told her gently. 'You see, I haven't got it *quite right* yet. There are still one or two things ...'

'Oh, to blazes with that!' said Violet, and suddenly, before Mr Wonka could stop her, she shot out a fat hand and grabbed the stick of gum out of the little drawer and popped it into her mouth. At once, her huge, well-trained jaws started chewing away on it like a pair of tongs.

'Don't!' said Mr Wonka.

'Fabulous!' shouted Violet. 'It's tomato soup! It's hot and creamy and delicious! I can feel it running down my throat!'

'Stop!' said Mr Wonka. 'The gum isn't ready yet! It's not right!'

'Of course it's right!' said Violet. 'It's working beautifully! Oh my, what lovely soup this is!'

'Spit it out!' said Mr Wonka.

'It's changing!' shouted Violet, chewing and grinning both at the same time. 'The second course is coming up! It's roast beef! It's tender and juicy! Oh boy, what a flavour! The baked potato is marvellous, too! It's got a crispy skin and it's all filled with butter inside!'

'But how *in*-teresting, Violet,' said Mrs Beauregarde. 'You are a clever girl.'

'Keep chewing, baby!' said Mr Beauregarde. 'Keep right on chewing! This is a great day for the Beauregardes! Our little girl is the first person in the world to have a chewing-gum meal!'

Everybody was watching Violet Beauregarde as she stood there chewing this extraordinary gum. Little Charlie Bucket was staring at her absolutely spellbound, watching her huge rubbery lips as they pressed and unpressed with the chewing, and Grandpa Joe stood beside him, gaping at the girl. Mr Wonka was wringing his hands and saying, 'No, no, no, no, no! It isn't ready for eating! It isn't right! You mustn't do it!'

'Blueberry pie and cream!' shouted Violet. 'Here it comes! Oh my, it's perfect! It's beautiful! It's ... it's exactly as though I'm swallowing it! It's as though I'm chewing and swallowing great big spoonfuls of the most marvellous blueberry pie in the world!'

'Good heavens, girl!' shrieked Mrs Beauregarde suddenly, staring at Violet, 'what's happening to your nose!'

'Oh, be quiet, mother, and let me finish!' said Violet.

'It's turning blue!' screamed Mrs Beauregarde. 'Your nose is turning blue as a blueberry!'

'Your mother is right!' shouted Mr Beauregarde. 'Your whole nose has gone purple!'

'What *do* you mean?' said Violet, still chewing away.

'Your cheeks!' screamed Mrs Beauregarde. 'They're turning blue as well! So is your chin! Your whole face is turning blue!'

'Spit that gum out at once!' ordered Mr Beauregarde.

'Mercy! Save us!' yelled Mrs Beauregarde. 'The girl's going blue and purple all over! Even her hair is changing colour! Violet, you're turning violet, Violet! What *is* happening to you?'

'I *told* you I hadn't got it quite right,' sighed Mr Wonka, shaking his head sadly.

'I'll say you haven't!' cried Mrs Beauregarde. 'Just look at the girl now!'

Everybody was staring at Violet. And what a terrible, peculiar sight she was! Her face and hands and legs and neck, in fact the skin all over her body, as well as her great big mop of curly hair, had turned a brilliant, purplish-blue, the colour of blueberry juice!

'It *always* goes wrong when we come to the dessert,' sighed Mr Wonka. 'It's the blueberry pie that does it. But I'll get it right one day, you wait and see.'

'Violet,' screamed Mrs Beauregarde, 'you're swelling up!'

'I feel sick,' Violet said.

'You're swelling up!' screamed Mrs Beauregarde again.

'I feel most peculiar!' gasped Violet.

'I'm not surprised!' said Mr Beauregarde.

'Great heavens, girl!' screeched Mrs Beauregarde. 'You're blowing up like a balloon!'

'Like a blueberry,' said Mr Wonka.

'Call a doctor!' shouted Mr Beauregarde.

'Prick her with a pin!' said one of the other fathers.

'Save her!' cried Mrs Beauregarde, wringing her hands.

But there was no saving her now. Her body was swelling up and changing shape at such a rate that within a minute it had turned into nothing less than an enormous round blue ball – a gigantic blueberry, in fact – and all that remained of Violet Beauregarde herself was a tiny pair of legs and a tiny pair of arms sticking out of the great round fruit and little head on top.

'It *always* happens like that,' sighed Mr Wonka. 'I've tried it twenty times in the Testing Room on twenty Oompa-Loompas, and every one of them finished up as a blueberry. It's most annoying. I just can't understand it.'

'But I don't want a blueberry for a daughter!' yelled Mrs Beauregarde. 'Put her back to what she was this instant!'

Mr Wonka clicked his fingers, and ten Oompa-Loompas appeared immediately at his side.

'Roll Miss Beauregarde into the boat,' he said to them, 'and take her along to the Juicing Room at once.'

'The *Juicing Room?*' cried Mrs Beauregarde. 'What are they going to do to her there?'

'Squeeze her,' said Mr Wonka. 'We've got to squeeze the juice out of her immediately. After that, we'll just have to see how she comes out. But don't worry, my dear Mrs Beauregarde. We'll get her repaired if it's the last thing we do. I *am* sorry about it all, I really am . . .'

Already the ten Oompa-Loompas were rolling the enormous blueberry across the floor of the Inventing Room towards the door that led to the chocolate river where the boat was waiting. Mr and Mrs Beauregarde hurried after them. The rest of the party, including little Charlie Bucket and Grandpa Joe, stood absolutely still and watched them go.

'Listen!' whispered Charlie. 'Listen, Grandpa! The Oompa-Loompas in the boat outside are starting to sing!'

The voices, one hundred of them singing together, came loud and clear into the room:

> '*Dear friends, we surely all agree*
> *There's almost nothing worse to see*
> *Than some repulsive little bum*
> *Who's always chewing chewing-gum.*
> *(It's very near as bad as those*
> *Who sit around and pick the nose.)*

So please believe us when we say
That chewing gum will never pay;
This sticky habit's bound to send
The chewer to a sticky end.
Did any of you ever know
A person called Miss Bigelow?
This dreadful woman saw no wrong
In chewing, chewing all day long.
She chewed while bathing in the tub,
She chewed while dancing at her club,
She chewed in church and on the bus;
it really was quite ludicrous!
And when she couldn't find her gum,
She'd chew up the linoleum,
Or anything that happened near –

A pair of boots, the postman's ear,
Or other people's underclothes,
And once she chewed her boy friend's nose.
She went on chewing till, at last,
Her chewing muscles grew so vast
That from her face her giant chin
Stuck out just like a violin.
For years and years she chewed away,
Consuming fifty bits a day,
Until one summer's eve, alas,
A horrid business came to pass.
Miss Bigelow went late to bed,
For half an hour she lay and read,
Chewing and chewing all the while
Like some great clockwork crocodile.
At last, she put her gum away
Upon a special little tray,
And settled back and went to sleep –
(She managed this by counting sheep).
But now, how strange! Although she slept,
Those massive jaws of hers still kept
On chewing, chewing through the night,
Even with nothing there to bite.
They were, you see, in such a groove
They positively had to move.
And very grim it was to hear
In pitchy darkness, loud and clear,
This sleeping woman's great big trap
Opening and shutting, snap-snap-snap!
Faster and faster, chop-chop-chop,
The noise went on, it wouldn't stop.
Until at last her jaws decide

To pause and open extra wide,
And with the most tremendous chew
They bit the lady's tongue in two.
Thereafter, just from chewing gum,
Miss Bigelow was always dumb,
And spent her life shut up in some
Disgusting sanatorium.
And that is why we'll try so hard
To save Miss Violet Beauregarde
From suffering an equal fate.
She's still quite young. It's not too late,
Provided she survives the cure.
We hope she does. We can't be sure.'

22

Along the Corridor

'Well, well, well,' sighed Mr Willy Wonka, 'two naughty little children gone. Three good little children left. I think we'd better get out of this room quickly before we lose anyone else!'

'But Mr Wonka,' said Charlie Bucket anxiously, 'will Violet Beauregarde *ever* be all right again or will she always be a blueberry?'

'They'll de-juice her in no time flat!' declared Mr Wonka. 'They'll roll her into the de-juicing machine, and she'll come out just as thin as a whistle!'

'But will she still be blue all over?' asked Charlie.

'She'll be *purple*!' cried Mr Wonka. 'A fine rich purple from head to toe! But there you are! That's what comes from chewing disgusting gum all day long!'

'If you think gum is so disgusting,' said Mike Teavee, 'then why do you make it in your factory?'

'I do wish you wouldn't mumble,' said Mr Wonka, 'I can't hear a word you're saying. Come on! Off we go! Hurry up! Follow me! We're going into the corridors again!' And so saying, Mr Wonka scuttled across to the far end of the Inventing Room and went out through a small secret door hidden behind a lot of pipes and stoves. The three remaining children – Veruca Salt, Mike

Teavee, and Charlie Bucket – together with the five remaining grown-ups, followed after him.

Charlie Bucket saw that they were now back in one of those long pink corridors with many other pink corridors leading out of it. Mr Wonka was rushing along in front, turning left and right and right and left, and Grandpa Joe was saying, 'Keep a good hold of my hand, Charlie. It would be terrible to get lost in here.'

Mr Wonka was saying, 'No time for any more messing about! We'll never get *anywhere* at the rate we've been going!' And on he rushed, down the endless pink corridors, with his black top hat perched on the top of his head and his plum-coloured velvet coat-tails flying out behind him like a flag in the wind.

They passed a door in the wall. 'No time to go in!' shouted Mr Wonka. 'Press on! Press on!'

They passed another door, then another and another. There were doors every twenty paces or so along the corridor now, and they all had something written on them, and strange clanking noises were coming from behind several of them, and delicious smells came wafting through the keyholes, and sometimes little jets of coloured steam shot out from the cracks underneath.

Grandpa Joe and Charlie were half running and half walking to keep up with Mr Wonka, but they were able to read what it said on quite a few of the doors as they hurried by. EATABLE MARSHMALLOW PILLOWS, it said on one.

'Marshmallow pillows are terrific!' shouted Mr Wonka as he dashed by. 'They'll be all the rage when I get them into the shops! No time to go in, though! No time to go in!'

LICKABLE WALLPAPER FOR NURSERIES, it said on the next door.

'Lovely stuff, lickable wallpaper!' cried Mr Wonka, rushing past. 'It has pictures of fruits on it – bananas, apples, oranges, grapes, pineapples, strawberries, and snozzberries ...'

'*Snozzberries?*' said Mike Teavee.

'Don't interrupt!' said Mr Wonka. 'The wallpaper has pictures of all these fruits printed on it, and when you lick the picture of a banana, it tastes of banana. When you lick a strawberry, it tastes of strawberry. And when you lick a snozzberry, it tastes just exactly like a snozzberry ...'

'But what *does* a snozzberry taste like?'

'You're mumbling again,' said Mr Wonka. 'Speak louder next time. On we go! Hurry up!'

HOT ICE CREAMS FOR COLD DAYS, it said on the next door.

'*Extremely* useful in the winter,' said Mr Wonka, rushing on. 'Hot ice cream warms you up no end in freezing weather. I also make hot ice cubes for putting in hot drinks. Hot ice cubes make hot drinks hotter.'

COWS THAT GIVE CHOCOLATE MILK, it said on the next door.

'Ah, my pretty little cows!' cried Mr Wonka. 'How I love those cows!'

'But why can't we *see* them?' asked Veruca Salt. 'Why do we have to go rushing on past all these lovely rooms?'

'We shall stop in time!' called out Mr Wonka. 'Don't be so madly impatient!'

FIZZY LIFTING DRINKS, it said on the next door.

'Oh, those are fabulous!' cried Mr Wonka. 'They fill you with bubbles, and the bubbles are full of a special kind of gas, and this gas is so terrifically *lifting* that it lifts you right off the ground just like a balloon, and up you go until your head hits the ceiling – and there you stay.'

'But how do you come down again?' asked little Charlie.

'You do a burp, of course,' said Mr Wonka. 'You do a great big long rude burp, and *up* comes the gas and *down* comes you!

But don't drink it outdoors! There's no knowing how high up you'll be carried if you do that. I gave some to an old Oompa-Loompa once out in the back yard and he went up and up and disappeared out of sight! It was very sad. I never saw him again.'

'He should have burped,' Charlie said.

'Of course he should have burped,' said Mr Wonka. 'I stood there shouting, "Burp, you silly ass, burp, or you'll never come down again!" But he didn't or couldn't or wouldn't, I don't know which. Maybe he was too polite. He must be on the moon by now.'

On the next door, it said, SQUARE SWEETS THAT LOOK ROUND.

'Wait!' cried Mr Wonka, skidding suddenly to a halt. 'I am very proud of my square sweets that look round. Let's take a peek.'

23

Square Sweets That Look Round

Everybody stopped and crowded to the door. The top half of the door was made of glass. Grandpa Joe lifted Charlie up so that he could get a better view, and looking in, Charlie saw a long table, and on the table there were rows and rows of small white square-shaped sweets. The sweets looked very much like square sugar lumps – except that each of them had a funny little pink face painted on one side. At the end of the table, a number of Oompa-Loompas were busily painting more faces on more sweets.

'There you are!' cried Mr Wonka. 'Square sweets that look round!'

'They don't look round to me,' said Mike Teavee.

'They look square,' said Veruca Salt. 'They look completely square.'

'But they *are* square,' said Mr Wonka. 'I never said they weren't.'

'You said they were *round*!' said Veruca Salt.

'I never said anything of the sort,' said Mr Wonka. 'I said they *looked* round.'

'But they *don't* look round!' said Veruca Salt. 'They look square!'

'They look round,' insisted Mr Wonka.

'They most certainly do not look round!' cried Veruca Salt.

'Veruca, darling,' said Mrs Salt, 'pay no attention to Mr Wonka! He's lying to you!'

'My dear old fish,' said Mr Wonka, 'go and boil your head!'

'How dare you speak to me like that!' shouted Mrs Salt.

'Oh, do shut up,' said Mr Wonka. 'Now watch this!'

He took a key from his pocket, and unlocked the door, and flung it open ... and suddenly ... at the sound of the door opening, all the rows of little square sweets looked quickly round to see who was coming in. The tiny faces actually turned towards the door and stared at Mr Wonka.

'There you are!' he cried triumphantly. 'They're looking round! There's no argument about it! They are square sweets that look round!'

'By golly, he's right!' said Grandpa Joe.

'Come on!' said Mr Wonka, starting off down the corridor again. 'On we go! We mustn't dawdle!'

BUTTERSCOTCH AND BUTTERGIN, it said on the next door they passed.

'Now *that* sounds a bit more interesting,' said Mr Salt, Veruca's father.

'Glorious stuff!' said Mr Wonka. 'The Oompa-Loompas all adore it. It makes them tiddly. Listen! You can hear them in there now, whooping it up.'

Shrieks of laughter and snatches of singing could be heard coming through the closed door.

'They're drunk as lords,' said Mr Wonka. 'They're drinking butterscotch and soda. They like that best of all. Buttergin and tonic is also very popular. Follow me, please! We really mustn't keep stopping like this.' He turned left. He turned right. They came to a long flight of stairs. Mr Wonka slid down the bannisters. The three children did the same. Mrs Salt and Mrs Teavee, the only women now left in the party, were getting very out of breath. Mrs Salt was a great fat creature with short legs, and she was blowing like a rhinoceros. 'This way!' cried Mr Wonka, turning left at the bottom of the stairs.

'Go *slower*!' panted Mrs Salt.

'Impossible,' said Mr Wonka. 'We should never get there in time if I did.'

'Get where?' asked Veruca Salt.

'Never you mind,' said Mr Wonka. 'You just wait and see.'

24

Veruca in the Nut Room

Mr Wonka rushed on down the corridor. THE NUT ROOM, it said on the next door they came to.

'All right,' said Mr Wonka, 'stop here for a moment and catch your breath, and take a peek through the glass panel of this door. But don't go in! Whatever you do, don't go into THE NUT ROOM! If you go in, you'll disturb the squirrels!'

Everyone crowded around the door.

'Oh look, Grandpa, look!' cried Charlie.

'Squirrels!' shouted Veruca Salt.

'Crikey!' said Mike Teavee.

It was an amazing sight. One hundred squirrels were seated upon high stools around a large table. On the table, there were mounds and mounds of walnuts, and the squirrels were all working away like mad, shelling the walnuts at a tremendous speed.

'These squirrels are specially trained for getting the nuts out of walnuts,' Mr Wonka explained.

'Why use squirrels?' Mike Teavee asked. 'Why not use Oompa-Loompas?'

'Because,' said Mr Wonka, 'Oompa-Loompas can't get walnuts out of walnut shells in one piece. They always break

them in two. Nobody except squirrels can get walnuts *whole* out
of walnut shells every time. It is extremely difficult. But in my
factory, I insist upon only whole walnuts. Therefore I have to
have squirrels to do the job. Aren't they wonderful, the way they
get those nuts out! And see how they first tap each walnut with
their knuckles to be sure it's not a bad one! If it's bad, it makes
a hollow sound, and they don't bother to open it. They just throw
it down the rubbish chute. There! Look! Watch that squirrel
nearest to us! I think he's got a bad one now!'

They watched the little squirrel as he tapped the walnut shell
with his knuckles. He cocked his head to one side, listening
intently, then suddenly he threw the nut over his shoulder into
a large hole in the floor.

'Hey, Mummy!' shouted Veruca Salt suddenly, 'I've decided I
want a squirrel! Get me one of those squirrels!'

'Don't be silly, sweetheart,' said Mrs Salt. 'These all belong to
Mr Wonka.'

'I don't care about that!' shouted Veruca. 'I want one. All I've
got at home is two dogs and four cats and six bunny rabbits and
two parakeets and three canaries and a green parrot and a turtle
and a bowl of goldfish and a cage of white mice and a silly old
hamster! I want a *squirrel*!'

'All right, my pet,' Mrs Salt said soothingly. 'Mummy'll get
you a squirrel just as soon as she possibly can.'

'But I don't want *any* old squirrel!' Veruca shouted. 'I want
a *trained* squirrel!'

At this point, Mr Salt, Veruca's father, stepped forward. 'Very
well, Wonka,' he said importantly, taking out a wallet full of
money, 'how much d'you want for one of these squirrels? Name
your price.'

'They're not for sale,' Mr Wonka answered. 'She can't have
one.'

'Who says I can't!' shouted Veruca. 'I'm going in to get myself one this very minute!'

'Don't!' said Mr Wonka quickly, but he was too late. The girl had already thrown open the door and rushed in.

The moment she entered the room, one hundred squirrels stopped what they were doing and turned their heads and stared at her with small black beady eyes.

Veruca Salt stopped also, and stared back at them. Then her gaze fell upon a pretty little squirrel sitting nearest to her at the end of the table. The squirrel was holding a walnut in its paws.

'All right,' Veruca said, 'I'll have *you*!'

She reached out her hands to grab the squirrel ... but as she did so ... in that first split second when her hands started to go forward, there was a sudden flash of movement in the room, like a flash of brown lightning, and every single squirrel around the table took a flying leap towards her and landed on her body.

Twenty-five of them caught hold of her right arm, and pinned it down.

Twenty-five more caught hold of her left arm, and pinned that down.

Twenty-five caught hold of her right leg and anchored it to the ground.

Twenty-*four* caught hold of her left leg.

And the one remaining squirrel (obviously the leader of them all) climbed up on to her shoulder and started tap-tap-tapping the wretched girl's head with its knuckles.

'Save her!' screamed Mrs Salt. 'Veruca! Come back! What are they *doing* to her?'

'They're testing her to see if she's a bad nut,' said Mr Wonka. 'You watch.'

Veruca struggled furiously, but the squirrels held her tight and she couldn't move. The squirrel on her shoulder went tap-tap-tapping the side of her head with his knuckles.

Then all at once, the squirrels pulled Veruca to the ground and started carrying her across the floor.

'My goodness, she *is* a bad nut after all,' said Mr Wonka. 'Her head must have sounded quite hollow.'

Veruca kicked and screamed, but it was no use. The tiny strong paws held her tightly and she couldn't escape.

'Where are they taking her?' shrieked Mrs Salt.

'She's going where all the other bad nuts go,' said Mr Willy Wonka. 'Down the rubbish chute.'

'By golly, she *is* going down the chute!' said Mr Salt, staring
through the glass door at his daughter.

'Then save her!' cried Mrs Salt.

'Too late,' said Mr Wonka. 'She's gone!'

And indeed she had.

'But where?'' shrieked Mrs Salt, flapping her arms. 'What
happens to the bad nuts? Where does the chute go to?'

'That *particular* chute,' Mr Wonka told her, 'runs directly into
the great big main rubbish pipe which carries away all the
rubbish from every part of the factory – all the floor sweepings
and potato peelings and rotten cabbages and fish heads and stuff
like that.'

'Who eats fish and cabbage and potatoes in *this* factory, I'd like
to know?' said Mike Teavee.

'I do, of course,' answered Mr Wonka. 'You don't think *I* live on cacao beans, do you?'

'But . . . but . . . but . . .' shrieked Mrs Salt, 'where does the great big pipe go to in the end?'

'Why, to the furnace, of course,' Mr Wonka said calmly. 'To the incinerator.'

Mrs Salt opened her huge red mouth and started to scream.

'Don't worry,' said Mr Wonka, 'there's always a chance that they've decided not to light it today.'

'A *chance*!' yelled Mrs Salt. 'My darling Veruca! She'll . . . she'll . . . she'll be sizzled like a sausage!'

'Quite right, my dear,' said Mr Salt. 'Now see here, Wonka,' he added, 'I think you've gone *just* a shade too far this time, I do indeed. My daughter may be a bit of a frump – I don't mind admitting it – but that doesn't mean you can roast her to a crisp. I'll have you know I'm extremely cross about this, I really am.'

'On, don't be cross, my dear sir!' said Mr Wonka. 'I expect she'll turn up again sooner or later. She may not even have gone down at all. She may be stuck in the chute just below the entrance hole, and if *that's* the case, all you'll have to do is go in and pull her up again.'

Hearing this, both Mr and Mrs Salt dashed into the Nut Room and ran over to the hole in the floor and peered in.

'Veruca!' shouted Mrs Salt. 'Are you down there!'

There was no answer.

Mrs Salt bent further forward to get a closer look. She was now kneeling right on the edge of the hole with her head down and her enormous behind sticking up in the air like a giant mushroom. It was a dangerous position to be in. She needed only one tiny little push . . . one gentle nudge in the right place . . . and *that* is exactly what the squirrels gave her!

Over she toppled, into the hole head first, screeching like a parrot.

'Good gracious me!' said Mr Salt, as he watched his fat wife go tumbling down the hole, '*what* a lot of rubbish there's going to be today!' He saw her disappearing into the darkness. 'What's it like down there, Angina?' he called out. He leaned further forward.

The squirrels rushed up behind him ...

'Help!' he shouted.

But he was already toppling forward, and down the chute he went, just as his wife had done before him – and his daughter.

'Oh *dear!*' cried Charlie, who was watching with the others through the door, 'what on earth's going to happen to them now?'

'I expect someone will catch them at the bottom of the chute,' said Mr Wonka.

'But what about the great fiery incinerator?' asked Charlie.

'They only light it every other day,' said Mr Wonka. 'Perhaps this is one of the days when they let it go out. You never know ... they might be lucky ...'

'Ssshh!' said Grandpa Joe. 'Listen! Here comes another song!'

From far away down the corridor came the beating of drums. Then the singing began.

> '*Veruca Salt!*' sang the Oompa-Loompas.
> '*Veruca Salt, the little brute,*
> *Has just gone down the rubbish chute,*
> (*And as we very rightly thought*
> *That in a case like this we ought*
> *To see the thing completely through,*
> *We've polished off her parents, too).*
> *Down goes Veruca! Down the drain!*

And here, perhaps, we should explain
That she will meet, as she descends,
A rather different set of friends
To those that she has left behind –
These won't be nearly so refined.
A fish head, for example, cut
This morning from a halibut.
"Hello! Good morning! How d'you do?
How nice to meet you! How are you?"
And then a little further down
A mass of others gather round:
A bacon rind, some rancid lard,
A loaf of bread gone stale and hard,
A steak that nobody could chew,
An oyster from an oyster stew,
Some liverwurst so old and grey
One smelled it from a mile away,
A rotten nut, a reeky pear,
A thing the cat left on the stair,
And lots of other things as well,
Each with a rather horrid smell.
These are Veruca's new found friends
That she will meet as she descends,
And this is the price she has to pay
For going so very far astray.
But now, my dears, we think you might
Be wondering – Is it really right
That every single bit of blame
And all the scolding and the shame
Should fall upon Veruca Salt?
Is she the only one at fault?

For though she's spoiled, and dreadfully so,
A girl can't spoil herself, you know.
Who spoiled her, then? Ah, who indeed?
Who pandered to her every need?
Who turned her into such a brat?
Who are the culprits? Who did that?
Alas! You needn't look so far
To find out who these sinners are.
They are (and this is very sad)
Her loving parents, MUM and DAD.
And that is why we're glad they fell
Into the rubbish chute as well.'

25

The Great Glass Lift

'I've never seen anything like it!' cried Mr Wonka. 'The children are disappearing like rabbits! But you mustn't worry about it! They'll *all* come out in the wash!'

Mr Wonka looked at the little group that stood beside him in the corridor. There were only two children left now – Mike Teavee and Charlie Bucket. And there were three grown-ups, Mr and Mrs Teavee and Grandpa Joe. 'Shall we move on?' Mr Wonka asked.

'Oh, yes!' cried Charlie and Grandpa Joe, both together.

'My feet are getting tired,' said Mike Teavee. 'I want to watch television.'

'If you're tired then we'd better take the lift,' said Mr Wonka. 'It's over here. Come on! In we go!' He skipped across the passage to a pair of double doors. The doors slid open. The two children and the grown-ups went in.

'Now then,' cried Mr Wonka, 'which button shall we press first? Take your pick!'

Charlie Bucket stared around him in astonishment. This was the craziest lift he had ever seen. There were buttons everywhere! The walls, and even the *ceiling*, were covered all over with rows and rows and rows of small, black push buttons! There must have been a thousand of them on each wall, and another thousand on the ceiling! And now Charlie noticed that every single button had a tiny printed label beside it telling you which room you would be taken to if you pressed it.

'This isn't just an ordinary up-and-down lift!' announced Mr Wonka proudly. 'This lift can go sideways and longways and slantways and any other way you can think of! It can visit any single room in the whole factory, no matter where it is! You simply press the button ... and *zing*! ... you're off!'

'*Fantastic!*' murmured Grandpa Joe. His eyes were shining with excitement as he stared at the rows of buttons.

'The whole lift is made of thick, clear glass!' Mr Wonka declared. 'Walls, doors, ceiling, floor, everything is made of glass so that you can see out!'

'But there's nothing to see,' said Mike Teavee.

'Choose a button!' said Mr Wonka. 'The two children may press one button each. So take your pick! Hurry up! In every room, something delicious and wonderful is being made.'

Quickly, Charlie started reading some of the labels alongside the buttons.

THE ROCK-CANDY MINE – 10,000 FEET DEEP, it said on one.

COKERNUT-ICE SKATING RINKS, it said on another.

Then ... STRAWBERRY-JUICE WATER PISTOLS.

TOFFEE-APPLE TREES FOR PLANTING OUT IN YOUR GARDEN – ALL SIZES.

EXPLODING SWEETS FOR YOUR ENEMIES.

LUMINOUS LOLLIES FOR EATING IN BED AT NIGHT.

MINT JUJUBES FOR THE BOY NEXT DOOR – THEY'LL GIVE HIM GREEN TEETH FOR A MONTH.

CAVITY-FILLING CARAMELS – NO MORE DEN-
TISTS.

STICKJAW FOR TALKATIVE PARENTS.

WRIGGLE-SWEETS THAT WRIGGLE DELIGHT-
FULLY IN YOUR TUMMY AFTER SWALLOWING.

INVISIBLE CHOCOLATE BARS FOR EATING IN
CLASS.

SUGAR-COATED PENCILS FOR SUCKING.

FIZZY LEMONADE SWIMMING POOLS.

MAGIC HAND-FUDGE – WHEN YOU HOLD IT IN
YOUR HAND, YOU TASTE IT IN YOUR MOUTH.

RAINBOW DROPS – SUCK THEM AND YOU CAN
SPIT IN SIX DIFFERENT COLOURS.

'Come on, come on!' cried Mr Wonka. 'We can't wait all day!'

'Isn't there a *Television Room* in all this lot?' asked Mike
Teavee.

'Certainly there's a television room,' Mr Wonka said. 'That
button over there.' He pointed with his finger. Everybody
looked. TELEVISION CHOCOLATE, it said on the tiny label
beside the button.

'*Whoopee!*' shouted Mike Teavee. 'That's for me!' He stuck out
his thumb and pressed the button. Instantly, there was a
tremendous whizzing noise. The doors clanged shut and the lift
leaped away as though it had been stung by a wasp. But it leapt
sideways! And all the passengers (except Mr Wonka, who was
holding on to a strap from the ceiling) were flung off their feet
on to the floor.

'Get up, get up!' cried Mr Wonka, roaring with laughter. But
just as they were staggering to their feet, the lift changed
direction and swerved violently round a corner. And over they
went once more.

'Help!' shouted Mrs Teavee.

'Take my hand, madam,' said Mr Wonka gallantly. 'There you are! Now grab this strap! Everybody grab a strap. The journey's not over yet!'

Old Grandpa Joe staggered to his feet and caught hold of a strap. Little Charlie, who couldn't possibly reach as high as that, put his arms around Grandpa Joe's legs and hung on tight.

The lift rushed on at the speed of a rocket. Now it was beginning to climb. It was shooting up and up and up on a steep slanty course as if it were climbing a very steep hill. Then suddenly, as though it had come to the top of the hill and gone over a precipice, it dropped like a stone and Charlie felt his tummy coming right up into his throat, and Grandpa Joe shouted, 'Yippee! Here we go!' and Mrs Teavee cried out, 'The rope has broken! We're going to crash!' And Mr Wonka said, 'Calm yourself, my dear lady,' and patted her comfortingly on the arm. And then Grandpa Joe looked down at Charlie who was clinging to his legs, and he said, 'Are you all right, Charlie?' Charlie shouted, 'I love it! It's like being on a roller coaster!' And through the glass walls of the lift, as it rushed along, they caught sudden glimpses of strange and wonderful things going on in some of the other rooms:

An enormous spout with brown sticky stuff oozing out of it on to the floor ...

A great, craggy mountain made entirely of fudge, with Oompa-Loompas (all roped together for safety) hacking huge hunks of fudge out of its sides ...

A machine with white powder spraying out of it like a snowstorm ...

A lake of hot caramel with steam coming off it ...

A village of Oompa-Loompas, with tiny houses and streets and hundreds of Oompa-Loompa children no more than four inches high playing in the streets ...

And now the lift began flattening out again, but it seemed to be going faster than ever, and Charlie could hear the scream of the wind outside as it hurtled forward ... and it twisted ... and it turned ... and it went up ... and it went down ... and ...

'I'm going to be sick!' yelled Mrs Teavee, turning green in the face.

'Please don't be sick,' said Mr Wonka.

'Try and stop me!' said Mrs Teavee.

'Then you'd better take this,' said Mr Wonka, and he swept his magnificent black top hat off his head, and held it out, upside down, in front of Mrs Teavee's mouth.

'Make this awful thing stop!' ordered Mr Teavee.

'Can't do that,' said Mr Wonka. 'It won't stop till we get there. I only hope no one's using the *other* lift at this moment.'

'What other lift?' screamed Mrs Teavee.

'The one that goes the opposite way on the same track as this one,' said Mr Wonka.

'Holy mackerel!' cried Mr Teavee. 'You mean we might have a collision?'

'I've always been lucky so far,' said Mr Wonka.

'Now I *am* going to be sick!' yelled Mrs Teavee.

'No, no!' said Mr Wonka. 'Not now! We're nearly there! Don't spoil my hat!'

The next moment, there was a screaming of brakes, and the lift began to slow down. Then it stopped altogether.

'Some ride!' said Mr Teavee, wiping his great sweaty face with a handkerchief.

'Never again!' gasped Mrs Teavee. And then the doors of the lift slid open and Mr Wonka said, 'Just a minute now! Listen to me! I want everybody to be very careful in this room. There is dangerous stuff around in here and you *must not* tamper with it.'

26

The Television-Chocolate Room

The Teavee family, together with Charlie and Grandpa Joe, stepped out of the lift into a room so dazzlingly bright and dazzlingly white that they screwed up their eyes in pain and stopped walking. Mr Wonka handed each of them a pair of dark glasses and said, 'Put these on quick! And don't take them off in here whatever you do! This light could blind you!'

As soon as Charlie had his dark glasses on, he was able to

look around him in comfort. He saw a long narrow room. The room was painted white all over. Even the floor was white, and there wasn't a speck of dust anywhere. From the ceiling, huge lamps hung down and bathed the room in a brilliant blue-white light. The room was completely bare except at the far ends. At one of these ends there was an enormous camera on wheels, and a whole army of Oompa-Loompas was clustering around it, oiling its joints and adjusting its knobs and polishing its great glass lens. The Oompa-Loompas were all dressed in the most extraordinary way. They were wearing bright-red space suits, complete with helmets and goggles – at least they looked like space suits – and they were working in complete silence. Watching them, Charlie experienced a queer sense of danger. There was something dangerous about this whole business, and the Oompa-Loompas knew it. There was no chattering or singing among them here, and they moved about over the huge black camera slowly and carefully in their scarlet space suits.

At the other end of the room, about fifty paces away from the camera, a single Oompa-Loompa (also wearing a space suit) was sitting at a black table gazing at the screen of a very large television set.

'Here we go!' cried Mr Wonka, hopping up and down with excitement. 'This is the Testing Room for my very latest and greatest invention – Television Chocolate!'

'But what *is* Television Chocolate?' asked Mike Teavee.

'Good heavens, child, stop interrupting me!' said Mr Wonka. 'It works by television. I don't like television myself. I suppose it's all right in small doses, but children never seem to be able to take it in small doses. They want to sit there all day long staring and staring at the screen ...'

'That's me!' said Mike Teavee.

'Shut up!' said Mr Teavee.

'Thank you,' said Mr Wonka. 'I shall now tell you how this amazing television set of mine works. But first of all, do you know how ordinary television works? It is very simple. At one end, where the picture is being taken, you have a large ciné camera and you start photographing something. The photographs are then split up into millions of tiny little pieces which are so small that you can't see them, and these little pieces are shot out into the sky by electricity. In the sky, they go whizzing around all over the place until suddenly they hit the antenna on the roof of somebody's house. They then go flashing down the wire that leads right into the back of the television set, and in there they get jiggled and joggled around until at last every single one of those millions of tiny pieces is fitted back into its right place (just like a jigsaw puzzle), and presto! – the photograph appears on the screen ...'

'That isn't *exactly* how it works,' Mike Teavee said.

'I am a little deaf in my left ear,' Mr Wonka said. 'You must forgive me if I don't hear everything you say.'

'I said, that isn't *exactly* how it works!' shouted Mike Teavee.

'You're a nice boy,' Mr Wonka said, 'but you talk too much. Now then! The very first time I saw ordinary television working, I was struck by a tremendous idea. "Look here!" I shouted, "if these people can break up a *photograph* into millions of pieces and send the pieces whizzing through the air and then put them together again at the other end, why can't *I* do the same thing with a bar of chocolate? Why can't *I* send a real bar of chocolate whizzing through the air in tiny pieces and then put the pieces together at the other end, all ready to be eaten?"'

'Impossible!' said Mike Teavee.

'You think so?' cried Mr Wonka. 'Well, watch this! I shall now send a bar of my very best chocolate from one end of this room to the other – by television! Get ready, there! Bring in the chocolate!'

Immediately, six Oompa-Loompas marched forward carrying on their shoulders the most enormous bar of chocolate Charlie had ever seen. It was about the size of the mattress he slept on at home.

'It has to be big,' Mr Wonka explained, 'because whenever you send something by television, it always comes out much smaller than it was when it went in. Even with *ordinary* television, when you photograph a big man, he never comes out on your screen any taller than a pencil, does he? Here we go, then! Get ready! *No, no! Stop! Hold everything!* You there! Mike Teavee! Stand back! You're too close to the camera! There are dangerous rays coming out of that thing! They could break you up into a million tiny pieces in one second! That's why the Oompa-Loompas are wearing space suits! The suits protect them! All right! That's better! Now, then! *Switch on!*'

One of the Oompa-Loompas caught hold of a large switch and pulled it down.

There was a blinding flash.

'The chocolate's gone!' shouted Grandpa Joe, waving his arms.

He was quite right! The whole enormous bar of chocolate had disappeared completely into thin air!

'It's on its way!' cried Mr Wonka. 'It is now rushing through the air above our heads in a million tiny pieces. Quick! Come over here!' He dashed over to the other end of the room where the large television set was standing, and the others followed him. 'Watch the screen!' he cried. 'Here it comes! Look!'

The screen flickered and lit up. Then suddenly, a small bar of chocolate appeared in the middle of the screen.

'Take it!' shouted Mr Wonka, growing more and more excited.

'How can you take it?' asked Mike Teavee, laughing. 'It's just a picture on a television screen!'

'Charlie Bucket!' cried Mr Wonka. '*You* take it! Reach out and grab it!'

Charlie put out his hand and touched the screen, and suddenly, miraculously, the bar of chocolate came away in his fingers. He was so surprised he nearly dropped it.

'Eat it!' shouted Mr Wonka. 'Go on and eat it! It'll be delicious! It's the same bar! It's got smaller on the journey, that's all!'

'It's absolutely fantastic!' gasped Grandpa Joe. 'It's ... it's ... it's a miracle!'

'Just imagine,' cried Mr Wonka, 'when I start using this across the country ... you'll be sitting at home watching television and suddenly a commercial will flash on to the screen and a voice will say, "EAT WONKA'S CHOCOLATES! THEY'RE THE BEST IN THE WORLD! IF YOU DON'T BELIEVE US, TRY ONE FOR YOURSELF – *NOW*!" And you simply reach out and take one! How about that, eh?'

'Terrific!' cried Grandpa Joe. 'It will change the world!'

27

Mike Teavee is Sent by Television

Mike Teavee was even more excited than Grandpa Joe at seeing a bar of chocolate being sent by television. 'But Mr Wonka,' he shouted, 'can you send *other things* through the air in the same way? Breakfast cereal, for instance?'

'Oh, my sainted aunt!' cried Mr Wonka. 'Don't mention that disgusting stuff in front of me! Do you *know* what breakfast cereal is made of? It's made of all those little curly wooden shavings you find in pencil sharpeners!'

'But could you send it by television if you wanted to, as you do chocolate?' asked Mike Teavee.

'Of course I could!'

'And what about people?' asked Mike Teavee. 'Could you send a real live person from one place to another in the same way?'

'A *person*!' cried Mr Wonka. 'Are you off your rocker?'

'But *could* it be done?'

'Good heavens, child, I really don't know ... I suppose it *could* ... yes. I'm pretty sure it could ... of course it could ... I wouldn't like to risk it, though ... it might have some very nasty results ...'

But Mike Teavee was already off and running. The moment he heard Mr Wonka saying, 'I'm pretty sure it could ... of course it could,' he turned away and started running as fast as he could towards the other end of the room where the great camera was standing. 'Look at me!' he shouted as he ran. 'I'm going to be the first person in the world to be sent by television!'

'No, no, no, no!' cried Mr Wonka.

'Mike!' screamed Mrs Teavee. 'Stop! Come back! You'll be turned into a million tiny pieces!'

But there was no stopping Mike Teavee now. The crazy boy rushed on, and when he reached the enormous camera, he jumped straight for the switch, scattering Oompa-Loompas right and left as he went.

'See you later, alligator!' he shouted, and he pulled down the switch, and as he did so, he leaped out into the full glare of the mighty lens.

There was a blinding flash.

Then there was silence.

Then Mrs Teavee ran forward ... but she stopped dead in the middle of the room ... and she stood there ... she stood staring at the place where her son had been . . . and her great red mouth opened wide and she screamed, 'He's gone! He's gone!'

'Great heavens, he *has* gone!' shouted Mr Teavee.

Mr Wonka hurried forward and placed a hand gently on Mrs Teavee's shoulder. 'We shall have to hope for the best,' he said. 'We must pray that your little boy will come out unharmed at the other end.'

'Mike!' screamed Mrs Teavee, clasping her head in her hands. 'Where are you?'

'I'll tell you where he is,' said Mr Teavee, 'he's whizzing around above our heads in a million tiny pieces!'

'Don't talk about it!' wailed Mrs Teavee.

'We must watch the television set,' said Mr Wonka. 'He may come through any moment.'

Mr and Mrs Teavee and Grandpa Joe and little Charlie and Mr Wonka all gathered round the television and stared tensely at the screen. The screen was quite blank.

'He's taking a heck of a long time to come across,' said Mr Teavee, wiping his brow.

'Oh dear, oh dear,' said Mr Wonka, 'I do hope that no part of him gets left behind.'

'What on earth do you mean?' asked Mr Teavee sharply.

'I don't wish to alarm you,' said Mr Wonka, 'but it does sometimes happen that only about half the little pieces find their way into the television set. It happened last week. I don't know why, but the result was that only half a bar of chocolate came through.'

Mrs Teavee let out a scream of horror. 'You mean only a half of Mike is coming back to us?' she cried.

'Let's hope it's the top half,' said Mr Teavee.

'Hold everything!' said Mr Wonka. 'Watch the screen! Something's happening!'

The screen had suddenly begun to flicker.

Then some wavy lines appeared.

Mr Wonka adjusted one of the knobs and the wavy lines went away.

And now, very slowly, the screen began to get brighter and brighter.

'Here he comes!' yelled Mr Wonka. 'Yes, that's him all right!'

'Is he all in one piece?' cried Mrs Teavee.

'I'm not sure,' said Mr Wonka. 'It's too early to tell.'

Faintly at first, but becoming clearer and clearer every second, the picture of Mike Teavee appeared on the screen. He was standing up and waving at the audience and grinning from ear to ear.

'But he's a midget!' shouted Mr Teavee.

'Mike,' cried Mrs Teavee, 'are you all right? Are there any bits of you missing?'

'Isn't he going to get any bigger?' shouted Mr Teavee.

'Talk to me, Mike!' cried Mrs Teavee. 'Say something! Tell me you're all right!'

A tiny little voice, no louder than the squeaking of a mouse, came out of the television set. 'Hi, Mum!' it said. 'Hi, Pop! Look at *me*! I'm the first person ever to be sent by television!'

'Grab him!' ordered Mr Wonka. 'Quick!'

Mrs Teavee shot out a hand and picked the tiny figure of Mike Teavee out of the screen.

'Hooray!' cried Mr Wonka. 'He's all in one piece! He's completely unharmed!'

'You call *that* unharmed?' snapped Mrs Teavee, peering at the little speck of a boy who was now running to and fro across the palm of her hand, waving his pistols in the air.

He was certainly not more than an inch tall.

'He's *shrunk*!' said Mr Teavee.

'Of course he's shrunk,' said Mr Wonka. 'What did you expect?'

'This is terrible!' wailed Mrs Teavee. 'What *are* we going to do?'

And Mr Teavee said, 'We can't send him back to school like this! He'll get trodden on! He'll get squashed!'

'He won't be able to do *anything*!' cried Mrs Teavee.

'Oh, yes I will!' squeaked the tiny voice of Mike Teavee. 'I'll still be able to watch television!'

'*Never again!*' shouted Mr Teavee. 'I'm throwing the television set right out the window the moment we get home. I've had enough of television!'

When he heard this, Mike Teavee flew into a terrible tantrum. He started jumping up and down on the palm of his mother's hand, screaming and yelling and trying to bite her fingers. 'I want to watch television!' he squeaked. 'I want to watch television! I want to watch television! I want to watch television!'

'Here! Give him to me!' said Mr Teavee, and he took the tiny boy and shoved him into the breast pocket of his jacket and stuffed a handkerchief on top. Squeals and yells came from inside the pocket, and the pocket shook as the furious little prisoner fought to get out.

'Oh, Mr Wonka,' wailed Mrs Teavee, 'how can we make him grow?'

'Well,' said Mr Wonka, stroking his beard and gazing thoughtfully at the ceiling, 'I must say that's a wee bit tricky. But small boys are extremely springy and elastic. They stretch like mad. So what we'll do, we'll put him in a special machine I have for testing the stretchiness of chewing-gum! Maybe that will bring him back to what he was.'

'Oh, thank you!' said Mrs Teavee.

'Don't mention it, dear lady.'

'How far d'you think he'll stretch?' asked Mr Teavee.

'Maybe miles,' said Mr Wonka. 'Who knows? But he's going to be awfully thin. Everything gets thinner when you stretch it.'

'You mean like chewing-gum?' asked Mr Teavee.

'Exactly.'

'How thin will he be?' asked Mrs Teavee anxiously.

'I haven't the foggiest idea,' said Mr Wonka. 'And it doesn't really matter, anyway, because we'll soon fatten him up again. All we'll have to do is give him a triple overdose of my wonderful Supervitamin Chocolate. Supervitamin Chocolate contains huge amounts of vitamin A and vitamin B. It also contains vitamin C, vitamin D, vitamin E, vitamin F, vitamin G, vitamin I, vitamin J, vitamin K, vitamin L, vitamin M, vitamin N, vitamin O, vitamin P, vitamin Q, vitamin R, vitamin T, vitamin U, vitamin V, vitamin W, vitamin X, vitamin Y, *and*, believe it or not, vitamin Z! The only two vitamins it doesn't have in it are vitamin S, because it makes you sick, and vitamin H, because it makes you grow horns on the top of your head, like a bull. But it *does* have in it a very small amount of the rarest and most magical vitamin of them all – vitamin Wonka.'

'And what will *that* do to him?' asked Mr Teavee anxiously.

'It'll make his toes grow out until they're as long as his fingers ...'

'Oh, no!' cried Mrs Teavee.

'Don't be silly,' said Mr Wonka. 'It's most useful. He'll be able to play the piano with his feet.'

'But Mr Wonka ...'

'No arguments, *please!*' said Mr Wonka. He turned away and clicked his fingers three times in the air. An Oompa-Loompa appeared immediately and stood beside him. 'Follow these orders,' said Mr Wonka, handing the Oompa-Loompa a piece of paper on which he had written full instructions. 'And you'll find the boy in his father's pocket. Off you go! Good-bye, Mr Teavee! Good-bye, Mrs Teavee! And please don't look so worried! They all come out in the wash, you know; every one of them ...'

At the end of the room, the Oompa-Loompas around the giant camera were already beating their tiny drums and beginning to jog up and down to the rhythm.

'There they go again!' said Mr Wonka. 'I'm afraid you can't stop them singing.'

Little Charlie caught Grandpa Joe's hand, and the two of them stood beside Mr Wonka in the middle of the long bright room, listening to the Oompa-Loompas. And this is what they sang:

> *'The most important thing we've learned,*
> *So far as children are concerned,*

Is never, NEVER, NEVER *let*
Them near your television set –
Or better still, just don't install
The idiotic thing at all.
In almost every house we've been,
We've watched them gaping at the screen.
They loll and slop and lounge about,
And stare until their eyes pop out.
(Last week in someone's place we saw
A dozen eyeballs on the floor.)
They sit and stare and stare and sit
Until they're hypnotized by it,
Until they're absolutely drunk
With all that shocking ghastly junk.
Oh yes, we know it keeps them still,
They don't climb out the window sill,
They never fight or kick or punch,
They leave you free to cook the lunch
And wash the dishes in the sink –
But did you ever stop to think,
To wonder just exactly what
This does to your beloved tot?
IT ROTS THE SENSES IN THE HEAD!
IT KILLS IMAGINATION DEAD!
IT CLOGS AND CLUTTERS UP THE MIND!
IT MAKES A CHILD SO DULL AND BLIND
HE CAN NO LONGER UNDERSTAND
A FANTASY, A FAIRYLAND!
HIS BRAIN BECOMES AS SOFT AS CHEESE!
HIS POWERS OF THINKING RUST AND FREEZE!
HE CANNOT THINK – HE ONLY SEES!
"All right!" you'll cry. "All right!" you'll say,

"But if we take the set away,
What shall we do to entertain
Our darling children! Please explain!"
We'll answer this by asking you,
"What used the darling ones to do?
How used they keep themselves contented
Before this monster was invented?"
Have you forgotten? Don't you know?
We'll say it very loud and slow:
THEY ... USED ... TO ... READ! They'd READ and READ,
AND READ and READ, and then proceed
TO READ some more. Great Scott! Gadzooks!
One half their lives was reading books!
The nursery shelves held books galore!
Books cluttered up the nursery floor!
And in the bedroom, by the bed,
More books were waiting to be read!
Such wondrous, fine, fantastic tales
Of dragons, gypsies, queens, and whales
And treasure isles, and distant shores
Where smugglers rowed with muffled oars,
And pirates wearing purple pants,
And sailing ships and elephants,
And cannibals crouching round the pot,
Stirring away at something hot.
(It smells so good, what can it be?
Good gracious, it's Penelope.)
The younger ones had Beatrix Potter
With Mr Tod, the dirty rotter,
And Squirrel Nutkin, Pigling Bland,
And Mrs Tiggy-Winkle and –
Just How The Camel Got His Hump,

And How The Monkey Lost His Rump,
And Mr Toad, and bless my soul,
There's Mr Rat and Mr Mole –
Oh, books, what books they used to know,
Those children living long ago!
So please, oh please, we beg, we pray,
Go throw your TV set away,
And in its place you can install
A lovely bookshelf on the wall.
Then fill the shelves with lots of books,
Ignoring all the dirty looks,
The screams and yells, the bites and kicks,
And children hitting you with sticks –
Fear not, because we promise you
That, in about a week or two
Of having nothing else to do,
They'll now begin to feel the need
Of having something good to read.
And once they start – oh boy, oh boy!
You watch the slowly growing joy
That fills their hearts. They'll grow so keen
They'll wonder what they'd ever seen
In that ridiculous machine,
That nauseating, foul, unclean,
Repulsive television screen!
And later, each and every kid
Will love you more for what you did.
P.S. Regarding Mike Teavee,
We very much regret that we
Shall simply have to wait and see
If we can get him back his height.
But if we can't – it serves him right.'

28

Only Charlie Left

'Which room shall it be next?' said Mr Wonka as he turned away and darted into the lift. 'Come on! Hurry up! We *must* get going! And how many children are there left now?'

Little Charlie looked at Grandpa Joe, and Grandpa Joe looked back at little Charlie.

'But Mr Wonka,' Grandpa Joe called after him, 'there's ... there's only Charlie left now.'

Mr Wonka swung round and stared at Charlie.

There was a silence. Charlie stood there holding tightly on to Grandpa Joe's hand.

'You mean you're the *only* one left?' Mr Wonka said, pretending to be surprised.

'Why yes,' whispered Charlie. 'Yes.'

Mr Wonka suddenly exploded with excitement. 'But my *dear boy*,' he cried out, '*that means you've won!*' He rushed out of the lift and started shaking Charlie's hand so furiously it nearly came off. 'Oh, I do congratulate you!' he cried. 'I really do! I'm absolutely delighted! It couldn't be better! How wonderful this is! I had a hunch, you know, right from the beginning, that it was going to be you! Well *done*, Charlie, well *done*! This is terrific! Now the fun is really going to start! But we mustn't dilly! We mustn't dally! There's even less time to lose now than there was before! We have an *enormous* number of things to do before the day is out! Just think of the *arrangements* that have to be made! And the people we have to fetch! But luckily for us, we have the great glass lift to speed things up! Jump in, my dear Charlie, jump in! You too, Grandpa Joe, sir! No, no, *after* you! That's the way! Now then! This time *I* shall choose the button we are going to press!' Mr Wonka's bright twinkling blue eyes rested for a moment on Charlie's face.

Something crazy is going to happen now, Charlie thought. But he wasn't frightened. He wasn't even nervous. He was just terrifically excited. And so was Grandpa Joe. The old man's face was shining with excitement as he watched every move that Mr Wonka made. Mr Wonka was reaching for a button high up on the glass ceiling of the lift. Charlie and Grandpa Joe both craned their necks to read what it said on the little label beside the button.

It said . . . UP AND OUT.

'*Up* and *out*,' thought Charlie. 'What sort of a room is that?'

Mr Wonka pressed the button.

The glass doors closed.

'Hold on!' cried Mr Wonka.

Then *WHAM!* The lift shot straight up like a rocket! 'Yippee!' shouted Grandpa Joe. Charlie was clinging to Grandpa Joe's legs and Mr Wonka was holding on to a strap from the ceiling, and up they went, up, up, up, straight up this time, with no twistings or turnings, and Charlie could hear the whistling of the air outside as the lift went faster and faster. 'Yippee!' shouted Grandpa Joe again. 'Yippee! Here we go!'

'Faster!' cried Mr Wonka, banging the wall of the lift with his hand. 'Faster! Faster! If we don't go any faster than this, we shall never get through!'

'Through what?' shouted Grandpa Joe. 'What have we got to get through?'

'Ah-ha!' cried Mr Wonka, 'you wait and see! I've been *longing* to press this button for years! But I've never done it until now! I was tempted many times! Oh, yes, I was tempted! But I couldn't bear the thought of making a great big hole in the roof of the factory! Here we go, boys! Up and out!'

'But you don't mean . . .' shouted Grandpa Joe, '. . . you don't *really* mean that this lift . . .'

'Oh yes, I do!' answered Mr Wonka. 'You wait and see! Up and out!'

'But . . . but . . . but . . . it's made of glass!' shouted Grandpa Joe. 'It'll break into a million pieces!'

'I suppose it might,' said Mr Wonka, cheerful as ever, 'but it's pretty thick glass, all the same.'

The lift rushed on, going up and up and up, faster and faster and faster . . .

Then suddenly, *CRASH!* – and the most tremendous noise of splintering wood and broken tiles came from directly above their heads, and Grandpa Joe shouted, 'Help! It's the end! We're done for!' and Mr Wonka said, 'No, we're not! We're through!

We're out!' Sure enough, the lift had shot right up through the roof of the factory and was now rising into the sky like a rocket, and the sunshine was pouring in through the glass roof. In five seconds they were a thousand feet up in the sky.

'The lift's gone mad!' shouted Grandpa Joe.

'Have no fear, my dear sir,' said Mr Wonka calmly, and he pressed another button. The lift stopped. It stopped and hung in mid-air, hovering like a helicopter, hovering over the factory and over the very town itself which lay spread out below them like a picture postcard! Looking down through the glass floor on which he was standing, Charlie could see the small far-away houses and the streets and the snow that lay thickly over everything. It was an eerie and frightening feeling to be standing on clear glass high up in the sky. It made you feel that you weren't standing on anything at all.

'Are we all right?' cried Grandpa Joe. 'How does this thing stay up?'

'Sugar power!' said Mr Wonka. 'One million sugar power! Oh, look,' he cried, pointing down, 'there go the other children! They're returning home!'

29

The Other Children Go Home

'We *must* go down and take a look at our little friends before we do anything else,' said Mr Wonka. He pressed a different button, and the lift dropped lower, and soon it was hovering just above the entrance gates to the factory.

Looking down now, Charlie could see the children and their parents standing in a little group just inside the gates.

'I can only see three,' he said. 'Who's missing?'

'I expect it's Mike Teavee,' Mr Wonka said. 'But he'll be coming along soon. Do you see the trucks?' Mr Wonka pointed to a line of gigantic covered vans parked in a line near by.

'Yes,' Charlie said. 'What are *they* for?'

'Don't you remember what it said on the Golden Tickets? Every child goes home with a lifetime's supply of sweets. There's one truckload for each of them, loaded to the brim. Ah-ha,' Mr Wonka went on, 'there goes our friend Augustus Gloop! D'you see him? He's getting into the first truck with his mother and father!'

'You mean he's *really* all right?' asked Charlie, astonished. 'Even after going up that awful pipe?'

'He's very much all right,' said Mr Wonka.

'He's changed!' said Grandpa Joe, peering down through the glass wall of the elevator. 'He used to be fat! Now he's thin as a straw!'

'Of course he's changed,' said Mr Wonka, laughing. 'He got

154

squeezed in the pipe. Don't you remember? And look! There goes Miss Violet Beauregarde, the great gum-chewer! It seems as though they managed to de-juice her after all. I'm so glad. And how healthy she looks! Much better than before!'

'But she's purple in the face!' cried Grandpa Joe.

'So she is,' said Mr Wonka. 'Ah, well, there's nothing we can do about that.'

'Good gracious!' cried Charlie. 'Look at poor Veruca Salt and Mr Salt and Mrs Salt! They're simply *covered* with rubbish!'

'And here comes Mike Teavee!' said Grandpa Joe. 'Good heavens! What *have* they done to him? He's about ten feet tall and thin as a wire!'

'They've overstretched him on the gum-stretching machine,' said Mr Wonka. 'How very careless.'

'But how dreadful for him!' cried Charlie.

'Nonsense,' said Mr Wonka, 'he's very lucky. Every basket-ball team in the country will be trying to get him. But now,' he added, 'it is time we left these four silly children. I have something very important to talk to you about, my dear Charlie.' Mr Wonka pressed another button, and the lift swung upwards into the sky.

30

Charlie's Chocolate Factory

The great glass lift was now hovering high over the town. Inside the lift stood Mr Wonka, Grandpa Joe, and little Charlie.

'How I love my chocolate factory,' said Mr Wonka, gazing down. Then he paused, and he turned around and looked at Charlie with a most serious expression on his face. 'Do *you* love it too, Charlie?' he asked.

'Oh, yes,' cried Charlie, 'I think it's the most wonderful place in the whole world!'

'I am very pleased to hear you say that,' said Mr Wonka, looking more serious than ever. He went on staring at Charlie. 'Yes,' he said, 'I am very pleased indeed to hear you say that. And now I shall tell you why.' Mr Wonka cocked his head to one side and all at once the tiny twinkling wrinkles of a smile appeared around the corners of his eyes, and he said, 'You see, my dear boy, I have decided to make you a present of the whole place. As soon as you are old enough to run it, the entire factory will become yours.'

Charlie stared at Mr Wonka. Grandpa Joe opened his mouth to speak, but no words came out.

'It's quite true,' Mr Wonka said, smiling broadly now. 'I really am giving it to you. That's all right, isn't it?'

'*Giving* it to him?' gasped Grandpa Joe. 'You must be joking.'

'I'm not joking, sir. I'm deadly serious.'

'But ... but ... why should you want to give your factory to little Charlie?'

'Listen,' Mr Wonka said, 'I'm an old man. I'm much older than you think. I can't go on for ever. I've got no children of my own, no family at all. So who is going to run the factory when I get too old to do it myself? *Someone's* got to keep it going – if only for the sake of the Oompa-Loompas. Mind you, there are thousands of clever men who would give anything for the chance to come in and take over from me, but I don't *want* that sort of person. I don't want a grown-up person at all. A grown-up won't listen to me; he won't learn. He will try to do things his own way and not mine. So I have to have a child. I want a good sensible loving child, one to whom I can tell all my most precious sweet-making secrets – while I am still alive.'

'So *that* is why you sent out the Golden Tickets!' cried Charlie.

'Exactly!' said Mr Wonka. 'I decided to invite five children to the factory, and the one I liked best at the end of the day would be the winner!'

'But Mr Wonka,' stammered Grandpa Joe, 'do you really and truly mean that you are giving the whole of this enormous factory to little Charlie? After all ...'

'There's no time for arguments!' cried Mr Wonka. 'We must go at once and fetch the rest of the family – Charlie's father and his mother and anyone else that's around! They can all live in the factory from now on! They can all help to run it until Charlie is old enough to do it by himself! Where do you live, Charlie?'

Charlie peered down through the glass floor at the snow-covered houses that lay below. 'It's over there,' he said, pointing. 'It's that little cottage right on the edge of the town, the tiny little one ...'

'I see it!' cried Mr Wonka, and he pressed some more buttons and the lift shot down towards Charlie's house.

'I'm afraid my mother won't come with us,' Charlie said sadly.

'Why ever not?'

'Because she won't leave Grandma Josephine and Grandma Georgina and Grandpa George.'

'But they must come too.'

'They can't,' Charlie said. 'They're very old and they haven't been out of bed for twenty years.'

'Then we'll take the bed along as well, with them in it,' said Mr Wonka. 'There's plenty of room in this lift for a bed.'

'You couldn't get the bed out of the house,' said Grandpa Joe. 'It won't go through the door.'

'You mustn't despair!' cried Mr Wonka. 'Nothing is impossible! You watch!'

The lift was now hovering over the roof of the Buckets' little house.

'What are you going to do?' cried Charlie.

'I'm going right on in to fetch them,' said Mr Wonka.

'How?' asked Grandpa Joe.

'Through the roof,' said Mr Wonka, pressing another button.

'No!' shouted Charlie.

'Stop!' shouted Grandpa Joe.

CRASH went the lift, right down through the roof of the house into the old people's bedroom. Showers of dust and broken tiles and bits of wood and cockroaches and spiders and bricks and cement went raining down on the three old ones who were lying in bed, and each of them thought that the end of the world was come. Grandma Georgina fainted, Grandma Josephine dropped her false teeth, Grandpa George put his head under the blanket, and Mr and Mrs Bucket came rushing in from the next room.

'Save us!' cried Grandma Josephine.

'Calm yourself, my darling wife,' said Grandpa Joe, stepping out of the lift. 'It's only us.'

'Mother!' cried Charlie, rushing into Mrs Bucket's arms. 'Mother! Mother! Listen to what's happened! We're all going back to live in Mr Wonka's factory and we're going to help him to run it and he's given it *all* to me and ... and ... and ... and ...'

'What *are* you talking about?' said Mrs Bucket.

'Just look at our house!' cried poor Mr Bucket. 'It's in ruins!'

'My dear sir,' said Mr Wonka, jumping forward and shaking Mr Bucket warmly by the hand, 'I'm so very glad to meet you. You mustn't worry about your house. From now on, you're never going to need it again, anyway.'

'Who *is* this crazy man?' screamed Grandma Josephine. 'He could have killed us all.'

'This,' said Grandpa Joe, 'is Mr Willy Wonka himself.'

It took quite a time for Grandpa Joe and Charlie to explain to everyone exactly what had been happening to them all day. And even then they all refused to ride back to the factory in the lift.

'I'd rather die in my bed!' shouted Grandma Josephine.

'So would I!' cried Grandma Georgina.

'I refuse to go!' announced Grandpa George.

So Mr Wonka and Grandpa Joe and Charlie, taking no notice of their screams, simply pushed the bed into the lift. They pushed Mr and Mrs Bucket in after it. Then they got in themselves. Mr Wonka pressed a button. The doors closed. Grandma Georgina screamed. And the lift rose up off the floor and shot through the hole in the roof, out into the open sky.

Charlie climbed on to the bed and tried to calm the three old people who were still petrified with fear. 'Please don't be frightened,' he said. 'It's quite safe. And we're going to the most wonderful place in the world!'

'Charlie's right,' said Grandpa Joe.

'Will there be anything to eat when we get there?' asked Grandma Josephine. 'I'm starving! The whole family is starving!'

'Anything to *eat?*' cried Charlie laughing. 'Oh, you just wait and see!'

PUFFIN BOOKS

CHARLIE AND THE GREAT GLASS ELEVATOR

Charlie had won! Willy Wonka's famous chocolate factory (see *Charlie and the Chocolate Factory*) was his now, and his parents Mr and Mrs Bucket, his three bed-ridden grandparents and sprightly Grandfather Joe were on their way to take over the factory. Rich and joyful, they were travelling in yet another of Willy Wonka's marvels, the Great Glass Lift – or Elevator, as he preferred to call it.

But all was not going quite according to plan, for the Elevator had left the building and was zooming higher and higher into the sky. The grandparents were getting nervous, and Willy Wonka himself was obviously not very happy about things. Zoom, zoom, went the Elevator, faster and faster, higher and higher, until it gave a ghastly groan, turned over, and left them bobbing like balloons inside it.

'Did we go too far?' inquired Charlie, to break the eerie silence. 'Too *far*?' cried Mr Wonka. 'Of course we went too far. You know where we've gone, my friends? We've gone into orbit!'

They weren't the only ones. Nearby was a spacecraft with three all-American astronauts and the staff of a luxury hotel aboard, and also in orbit a terrifying and intelligent breed of space monsters, the Vermicious Knids, which didn't think much of these human invaders . . . What was Charlie to do to put things right?

Roald Dahl was born in Wales of Norwegian parents. He spent his childhood in England and was educated at Repton. At eighteen he went to work for the Shell Oil Company in Africa and when World War II broke out he joined the RAF, became a fighter pilot, and saw service in Greece and Syria. In 1942 he went to Washington as Assistant Air Attaché and it was there he started to write short stories. He now lives in Buckinghamshire.

ROALD DAHL

Charlie
and the
Great Glass Elevator

Illustrated by Michael Foreman

Puffin Books

Puffin Books, Penguin Books Ltd, Harmondsworth, Middlesex, England
Viking Penguin Inc., 40 West 23rd Street, New York, New York 10010, U.S.A.
Penguin Books Australia Ltd, Ringwood, Victoria, Australia
Penguin Books Canada Limited, 2801 John Street, Markham, Ontario, Canada L3R 1B4
Penguin Books (N.Z.) Ltd, 182–190 Wairau Road, Auckland 10, New Zealand

First published by George Allen & Unwin 1973
Published in Puffin Books 1975
Reprinted 1975 (twice), 1976 (twice), 1977, 1978 (twice),
1979, 1980 (twice), 1981, 1982, 1983, 1984 (twice), 1985
This edition published 1986

Made and printed in Great Britain by
Richard Clay (The Chaucer Press) Ltd, Bungay, Suffolk
Set in Monophoto Photina

For my daughters
Tessa   Ophelia   Lucy

and for my godson
Edmund Pollinger

Contents

I

Mr Wonka Goes Too Far

The last time we saw Charlie, he was riding high above his home town in the Great Glass Lift. Only a short while before, Mr Wonka had told him that the whole gigantic fabulous Chocolate Factory was his, and now our small friend was returning in triumph with his entire family to take over. The passengers in the Lift (just to remind you) were:

Charlie Bucket, our hero.

Mr Willy Wonka, chocolate-maker extraordinary.

Mr and Mrs Bucket, Charlie's father and mother.

Grandpa Joe and Grandma Josephine, Mr Bucket's father and mother.

Grandpa George and Grandma Georgina, Mrs Bucket's father and mother.

Grandma Josephine, Grandma Georgina and Grandpa George were still in bed, the bed having been pushed on board just before take-off. Grandpa Joe, as you remember, had got out of bed to go around the Chocolate Factory with Charlie.

The Great Glass Lift was a thousand feet up and cruising nicely. The sky was brilliant blue. Everybody on board was wildly excited at the thought of going to live in the famous

Chocolate Factory. Grandpa Joe was singing. Charlie was jumping up and down. Mr and Mrs Bucket were smiling for the first time in years, and the three old ones in the bed were grinning at one another with pink toothless gums.

'What in the world keeps this crazy thing up in the air?' croaked Grandma Josephine.

'Madam,' said Mr Wonka, 'it is not a lift any longer. Lifts only go up and down *inside* buildings. But now that it has taken us up into the sky, it has become an ELEVATOR. It is THE GREAT GLASS ELEVATOR.'

'And what keeps it up?' said Grandma Josephine.

'Skyhooks,' said Mr Wonka.

'You amaze me,' said Grandma Josephine.

'Dear lady,' said Mr Wonka, 'you are new to the scene. When you have been with us a little longer, nothing will amaze you.'

'These skyhooks,' said Grandma Josephine. 'I assume one end is hooked on to this contraption we're riding in. Right?'

'Right,' said Mr Wonka.

'What's the other end hooked on to?' said Grandma Josephine.

'Every day,' said Mr Wonka, 'I get deafer and deafer. Remind me, please, to call up my ear doctor the moment we get back.'

'Charlie,' said Grandma Josephine. 'I don't think I trust this gentleman very much.'

'Nor do I,' said Grandma Georgina. 'He footles around.'

Charlie leaned over the bed and whispered to the two old women. 'Please,' he said, 'don't spoil everything. Mr Wonka is a fantastic man. He's my friend. I love him.'

'Charlie's right,' whispered Grandpa Joe, joining the group. 'Now you be quiet, Josie, and don't make trouble.'

'We must hurry!' said Mr Wonka. 'We have so much time and so little to do! No! Wait! Cross that out! Reverse it! Thank you! Now back to the factory!' he cried, clapping his hands once and springing two feet in the air with two feet. 'Back we fly to the factory! But we must go *up* before we can come down. We must go *higher and higher*!'

'What did I tell you,' said Grandma Josephine. 'The man's cracked!'

'Be quiet, Josie,' said Grandpa Joe. 'Mr Wonka knows exactly what he's doing.'

'He's cracked as a crab!' said Grandma Georgina.

'We must go higher!' said Mr Wonka. 'We must go tremendously high! Hold on to your stomach!' He pressed a brown button. The Elevator shuddered, and then with a fearful whooshing noise it shot vertically upward like a rocket. Everybody clutched hold of everybody else and as the great machine gathered speed, the rushing whooshing sound of the wind outside grew louder and louder and shriller and shriller until it became a piercing shriek and you had to yell to make yourself heard.

'Stop!' yelled Grandma Josephine. 'Joe, you make him stop! I want to get off!'

'Save us!' yelled Grandma Georgina.

'Go down!' yelled Grandpa George.

'No, no!' Mr Wonka yelled back. 'We've got to go up!'

'But why?' they all shouted at once. 'Why up and not down?'

'Because the higher we are when we start coming down, the faster we'll all be going when we hit,' said Mr Wonka. 'We've got to be going at an absolutely sizzling speed when we hit.'

'When we hit *what?*' they cried.

'The factory, of course,' answered Mr Wonka.

'You must be whackers,' said Grandma Josephine. 'We'll all be pulpified!'

'We'll be scrambled like eggs!' said Grandma Georgina.

'That,' said Mr Wonka, 'is a chance we shall have to take.'

'You're joking,' said Grandma Josephine. 'Tell us you're joking.'

'Madam,' said Mr Wonka, 'I never joke.'

'Oh, my dears!' cried Grandma Georgina. 'We'll be *lixivated*, every one of us!'

'More than likely,' said Mr Wonka.

Grandma Josephine screamed and disappeared under the bedclothes, Grandma Georgina clutched Grandpa George so tight he changed shape. Mr and Mrs Bucket stood hugging each other, speechless with fright. Only Charlie and Grandpa Joe kept moderately cool. They had travelled a long way with Mr Wonka and had grown accustomed to surprises. But as the Great Elevator continued to streak upward further and further away from the earth, even Charlie began to feel a trifle nervous. 'Mr Wonka!' he yelled above the noise, 'what I don't understand is *why* we've got to come down at such a terrific speed.'

'My dear boy,' Mr Wonka answered, 'if we don't come down at a terrific speed, we'll never burst our way back in through the roof of the factory. It's not easy to punch a hole in a roof as strong as that.'

'But there's a hole in it already,' said Charlie. 'We made it when we came out.'

'Then we shall make another,' said Mr Wonka. 'Two holes are better than one. Any mouse will tell you that.'

Higher and higher rushed the Great Glass Elevator until soon they could see the countries and oceans of the Earth spread out below them like a map. It was all very beautiful, but when you are standing on a glass floor looking down, it gives you a nasty feeling. Even Charlie was beginning to feel frightened now. He hung on tightly to Grandpa Joe's hand and looked up anxiously into the old man's face. 'I'm scared, Grandpa,' he said.

Grandpa Joe put an arm around Charlie's shoulders and held him close. 'So am I, Charlie,' he said.

'Mr Wonka!' Charlie shouted. 'Don't you think this is about high enough?'

'Very nearly,' Mr Wonka answered. 'But not quite. Don't talk to me now, please. Don't disturb me. I must watch things very carefully at this stage. Split-second timing, my boy, that's what it's got to be. You see this green button. I must press it at exactly the right instant. If I'm just half a second late, then we'll go *too high!*'

'What happens if we go too high?' asked Grandpa Joe.

'Do please stop talking and let me concentrate!' Mr Wonka said.

At that precise moment, Grandma Josephine poked her head out from under the sheets and peered over the edge of the bed. Through the glass floor she saw the entire continent of North America nearly two hundred miles below and looking no bigger than a bar of chocolate. '*Someone*'s got to stop this maniac!' she screeched and she shot out a wrinkled old hand and grabbed Mr Wonka by the coat-tails and yanked him backwards on to the bed.

14

'No, no!' cried Mr Wonka, struggling to free himself. 'Let me go! I have things to see to! Don't disturb the pilot!'

'You madman!' shrieked Grandma Josephine, shaking Mr Wonka so fast his head became a blur. 'You get us back home this instant!'

'Let me go!' cried Mr Wonka, 'I've got to press that button or we'll go too high! Let me go! Let me go!' But Grandma Josephine hung on. 'Charlie!' shouted Mr Wonka. 'Press the button! The green one! Quick, quick, quick!'

Charlie leaped across the Elevator and banged his thumb down on the green button. But as he did so, the Elevator gave a mighty groan and rolled over on to its side and the rushing whooshing noise stopped altogether. There was an eerie silence.

'Too late!' cried Mr Wonka. 'Oh, my goodness me, we're cooked!' As he spoke, the bed with the three old ones in it and Mr Wonka on top lifted gently off the floor and hung suspended in mid-air. Charlie and Grandpa Joe and Mr and Mrs Bucket also floated upwards so that in a twink the entire company, as well as the bed, were floating around like balloons inside the Great Glass Elevator.

'*Now* look what you've done!' said Mr Wonka, floating about.

'What happened?' Grandma Josephine called out. She

had floated clear of the bed and was hovering near the ceiling in her nightshirt.

'Did we go too far?' Charlie asked.

'Too *far?*' cried Mr Wonka. 'Of course we went too far! You know where we've gone, my friends? We've gone into orbit!'

They gaped, they gasped, they stared. They were too flabbergasted to speak.

'We are now rushing around the Earth at seventeen thousand miles an hour,' Mr Wonka said. 'How does that grab you?'

'I'm choking!' gasped Grandma Georgina. 'I can't breathe!'

'Of course you can't,' said Mr Wonka. 'There's no air up here.' He sort of swam across under the ceiling to a button marked OXYGEN. He pressed it. 'You'll be all right now,' he said. 'Breathe away.'

'This is the queerest feeling,' Charlie said, swimming about. 'I feel like a bubble.'

'It's great,' said Grandpa Joe. 'It feels as though I don't weigh anything at all.'

'You don't,' said Mr Wonka. 'None of us weighs anything – not even one ounce.'

'What piffle!' said Grandma Georgina. 'I weigh one hundred and thirty-seven pounds exactly.'

'Not now you don't,' said Mr Wonka. 'You are completely weightless.'

The three old ones, Grandpa George, Grandma Georgina and Grandma Josephine, were trying frantically to get back into bed, but without success. The bed was floating about in mid-air. They, of course, were also floating, and every time they got above the bed and tried to lie down, they simply floated up out of it. Charlie and Grandpa Joe were hooting with laughter. 'What's so funny?' said Grandma Josephine.

'We've got you out of bed at last,' said Grandpa Joe.

'Shut up and help us back!' snapped Grandma Josephine.

'Forget it,' said Mr Wonka. 'You'll never stay down. Just keep floating around and be happy.'

'The man's a madman!' cried Grandma Georgina. 'Watch out, I say, or he'll lixivate the lot of us!'

2

Space Hotel 'U.S.A.'

Mr Wonka's Great Glass Elevator was not the only thing orbiting the Earth at that particular time. Two days before, the United States of America had successfully launched its first Space Hotel, a gigantic sausage-shaped capsule no less than one thousand feet long. It was called Space Hotel

'U.S.A.' and it was the marvel of the space age. It had inside it a tennis-court, a swimming pool, a gymnasium, a children's playroom and five hundred luxury bedrooms, each with a private bath. It was fully air-conditioned. It was also equipped with a gravity-making machine so that you didn't float about inside it. You walked normally.

This extraordinary object was now speeding round and round the earth at a height of 240 miles. Guests were to be taken up and down by a taxi-service of small capsules blasting off from Cape Kennedy every hour on the hour, Mondays to Fridays. But as yet there was nobody on board at all, not even an astronaut. The reason for this was that no one had really believed such an enormous thing would ever get off the ground without blowing up.

But the launching had been a great success and now that the Space Hotel was safely in orbit, there was a tremendous hustle and bustle to send up the first guests. It was rumoured that the President of the United States himself was going to be among the first to stay in the hotel, and of course there was a mad rush by all sorts of other people across the world to book rooms. Several kings and queens had cabled the White House in Washington for reservations, and a Texas millionaire called Orson Cart, who was about to marry a Hollywood starlet called Helen Highwater, was offering one hundred thousand dollars a day for the honeymoon suite.

But you cannot send guests to an hotel unless there are lots of people there to look after them, and that explains why there was yet another interesting object orbiting the earth at that moment. This was the large Transport Capsule containing the entire staff for Space Hotel 'U.S.A.' There were managers, assistant managers, desk-clerks, waitresses, bell boys, chambermaids, pastry chefs and hall porters. The capsule they were travelling in was manned by the three famous astronauts, Shuckworth, Shanks and Showler, all of them handsome, clever and brave.

'In exactly one hour,' said Shuckworth, speaking to the passengers over the loudspeaker, 'we shall link up with

Space Hotel "U.S.A.", your happy home for the next ten years. And any moment now, if you look straight ahead, you should catch your first glimpse of this magnificent space-ship. Ah-ha! I see something there! That must be it, folks! There's definitely something up there ahead of us!'

Shuckworth, Shanks and Showler, as well as the managers, assistant managers, desk-clerks, waitresses, bell-boys, chambermaids, pastry chefs and hall porters, all stared excitedly through the windows. Shuckworth fired a couple of small rockets to make the capsule go faster, and they began to catch up very quickly.

'Hey!' yelled Showler. 'That isn't our space hotel!'

'Holy rats!' cried Shanks. 'What in the name of Nebuchadnezzar is it!'

'Quick! Give me the telescope!' yelled Shuckworth. With one hand he focused the telescope and with the other he flipped the switch connecting him to Ground Control.

'Hello, Houston!' he cried into the mike. 'There's something crazy going on up here! There's a thing orbiting ahead of us and it's not like any space-ship I've ever seen, that's for sure!'

'Describe it at once,' ordered Ground Control in Houston.

'It's . . . it's all made of glass and it's kind of square and it's got lots of people inside it! They're all floating about like fish in a tank!'

'How many astronauts on board?'

'None,' said Shuckworth. 'They can't possibly be astronauts.'

'What makes you say that?'

'Because at least three of them are in nightshirts!'

'Don't be a fool, Shuckworth!' snapped Ground Control. 'Pull yourself together, man! This is serious!'

'I swear it!' cried poor Shuckworth. 'There's three of them in nightshirts! Two old women and one old man! I can see them clearly! I can even see their faces! Jeepers, they're older than Moses! They're about ninety years old!'

'You've gone mad, Shuckworth!' shouted Ground Control. 'You're fired! Give me Shanks!'

'Shanks speaking,' said Shanks. 'Now listen here, Houston. There's these three old birds in nightshirts floating around in this crazy glass box and there's a funny little guy with a pointed beard wearing a black top-hat and a plum-coloured velvet tail-coat and bottle-green trousers . . .'

'Stop!' screamed Ground Control.

'That's not all,' said Shanks. 'There's also a little boy about ten years old . . .'

'That's no boy, you idiot!' shouted Ground Control. 'That's an astronaut in disguise! It's a midget astronaut dressed up as a little boy! Those old people are astronauts too! They're all in disguise!'

'But who *are* they?' cried Shanks.

22

'How the heck would I know?' said Ground Control. 'Are they heading for our Space Hotel?'

'That's exactly where they are heading!' cried Shanks. 'I can see the Space Hotel now about a mile ahead.'

'They're going to blow it up!' yelled Ground Control. 'This is desperate! This is . . .' Suddenly his voice was cut off and Shanks heard another quite different voice in his earphones. It was deep and rasping.

'I'll take charge of this,' said the deep rasping voice. 'Are you there, Shanks?'

'Of course I'm here,' said Shanks. 'But how dare you butt in. Keep your big nose out of this. Who are you anyway?'

'This is the President of the United States,' said the voice.

'And this is the Wizard of Oz,' said Shanks. 'Who are you kidding?'

'Cut the piffle, Shanks,' snapped the President. 'This is a national emergency!'

'Good grief!' said Shanks, turning to Shuckworth and Showler. 'It really *is* the President. It's President Gilligrass himself . . . Well, *hello there*, Mr President, sir. How are *you* today?'

'How many people are there in that glass capsule?' rasped the President.

'Eight,' said Shanks. 'All floating.'

'Floating?'

'We're outside the pull of gravity up here, Mr President. Everything floats. We'd be floating ourselves if we weren't strapped down. Didn't you know that?'

'Of course I knew it,' said the President. 'What else can you tell me about that glass capsule?'

'There's a bed in it,' said Shanks. 'A big double bed and that's floating too.'

'A bed!' barked the President. 'Whoever heard of a bed in a spacecraft!'

'I swear it's a bed,' said Shanks.

'You must be loopy, Shanks,' declared the President. 'You're dotty as a doughnut! Let me talk to Showler!'

'Showler here, Mr President,' said Showler, taking the mike from Shanks. 'It is a great honour to talk to you Mr President, sir.'

'Oh, shut up!' said the President. 'Just tell me what you see.'

'It's a bed all right, Mr President. I can see it through my telescope. It's got sheets and blankets and a mattress . . .'

'That's not a bed, you drivelling thickwit!' yelled the President. 'Can't you understand it's a trick! It's a bomb. It's a bomb disguised as a bed! They're going to blow up our magnificent Space Hotel!'

'Who's *they*, Mr President, sir?' said Showler.

'Don't talk so much and let me think,' said the President.

There were a few moments of silence. Showler waited tensely. So did Shanks and Shuckworth. So did the managers and assistant managers and desk-clerks and waitresses and bell-boys and chambermaids and pastry chefs and hall porters. And down in the huge Control Room at Houston, one hundred controllers sat motionless in front of their dials and monitors, waiting to see what orders the President would give next to the astronauts.

'I've just thought of something,' said the President. 'Don't you have a television camera up there on the front of your spacecraft, Showler?'

'Sure do, Mr President.'

'Then switch it on, you nit, and let all of us down here get a look at this object!'

24

'I never thought of that,' said Showler. 'No *wonder* you're the President. Here goes . . .' He reached out and switched on the TV camera in the nose of the spacecraft, and at that moment, five hundred million people all over the world who had been listening in on their radios rushed to their television sets.

On their screens they saw exactly what Shuckworth and Shanks and Showler were seeing – a weird glass box in splendid orbit around the earth, and inside the box, seen not too clearly but seen nonetheless, were seven grown-ups and one small boy and a big double bed, all floating. Three of the grown-ups were barelegged and wearing nightshirts. And far off in the distance, beyond the glass box, the TV watchers could see the enormous, glistening, silvery shape of Space Hotel 'U.S.A.'

But it was the sinister glass box itself that everyone was staring at, and the cargo of sinister creatures inside it – eight astronauts so tough and strong they didn't even bother to wear space-suits. Who were these people and where did they come from? And what in heaven's name was that big evil-looking thing disguised as a double bed? The President had said it was a bomb and he was probably right. But what were they going to do with it? All across America and Canada and Russia and Japan and India and China and Africa and England and France and Germany and everywhere else in the world a kind of panic began to take hold of the television watchers.

'Keep well clear of them, Showler!' ordered the President over the radio link.

'Sure will, Mr President!' Showler answered. 'I *sure will!*'

3

The Link-Up

Inside the Great Glass Elevator there was also a good deal of excitement. Charlie and Mr Wonka and all the others could see clearly the huge silvery shape of Space Hotel 'U.S.A.' about a mile ahead of them. And behind them was the smaller (but still pretty enormous) Transport Capsule. The Great Glass Elevator (not looking at all great now beside these two monsters) was in the middle. And of course everybody, even Grandma Josephine, knew very well what was going on. They even knew that the three astronauts in charge of the Transport Capsule were called Shuckworth, Shanks and Showler. The whole world knew about these things. Newspapers and television had been shouting about almost nothing else for the past six months. Operation Space Hotel was the event of the century.

'What a load of luck!' cried Mr Wonka. 'We've landed ourselves slap in the middle of the biggest space operation of all time!'

'We've landed ourselves in the middle of a nasty mess,' said Grandma Josephine. 'Turn back at once!'

'No, Grandma,' said Charlie. 'We've *got* to watch it now. We *must* see the Transport Capsule linking up with the Space Hotel.'

Mr Wonka floated right up close to Charlie. 'Let's beat them to it, Charlie,' he whispered. 'Let's get there first and go aboard the Space Hotel ourselves!'

Charlie gaped. Then he gulped. Then he said softly, 'It's impossible. You've got to have all sorts of special gadgets to link up with another spacecraft, Mr Wonka.'

'My Elevator could link up with a crocodile if it had to,' said Mr Wonka. 'Just leave it to me, my boy!'

'Grandpa Joe!' cried Charlie. 'Did you hear that? We're going to link up with the Space Hotel and go on board!'

'Yippeeeeee!' shouted Grandpa Joe. 'What a brilliant thought, sir! What a staggering idea!' He grabbed Mr Wonka's hand and started shaking it like a thermometer.

'Be quiet, you balmy old bat!' said Grandma Josephine. 'We're in a hot enough stew already. I want to go home.'

'Me, too!' said Grandma Georgina.

'What if they come after us?' said Mr Bucket, speaking for the first time.

'What if they capture us?' said Mrs Bucket.

'What if they shoot us?' said Grandma Georgina.

'What if my beard were made of green spinach?' cried Mr Wonka. 'Bunkum and tummyrot! You'll never get anywhere if you go about what-iffing like that. Would Columbus have discovered America if he'd said "What if I sink on the way over? What if I meet pirates? What if I never come back?" He wouldn't even have started. We want no what-iffers around here, right Charlie? Off we go, then. But wait . . . this is a very tricky manoeuvre and I'm going to need help. There are three lots of buttons we have to press all in different parts of the Elevator. I shall take those two over there, the white and the black.' Mr Wonka made a funny blowing noise with his mouth and glided effortlessly, like a huge bird, across the Elevator to the white and black buttons, and there he hovered. 'Grandpa Joe, sir, kindly station yourself beside that silver button there . . . yes, that's the one . . . And you, Charlie, go up and stay floating beside that little golden button near the ceiling. I must tell you that each of these buttons fires booster rockets from different places outside the Elevator. That's how we change direction. Grandpa Joe's rockets turn us to starboard, to the right. Charlie's turn us to port, to the left. Mine make us go higher or lower or faster or slower. All ready?'

'No! Wait!' cried Charlie, who was floating exactly midway between the floor and the ceiling. 'How do I get up? I can't get up to the ceiling!' He was thrashing his arms and legs violently, like a drowning swimmer, but getting nowhere.

'My dear boy,' said Mr Wonka. 'You can't *swim* in this stuff. It isn't water, you know. It's air and very thin air at that. There's nothing to push against. So you have to use jet propulsion. Watch me. First, you take a deep breath, then you make a small round hole with your mouth and you blow as hard as you can. If you blow downward, you jet-propel yourself up. If you blow to the left, you shoot off to the right and so on. You manoeuvre yourself like a spacecraft, but using your mouth as a booster rocket.'

Suddenly everyone began practising this business of flying about, and the whole Elevator was filled with the blowings and snortings of the passengers. Grandma Georgina, in her red flannel nightgown with two skinny bare legs sticking out of the bottom, was trumpeting and spitting like a rhinoceros and flying from one side of the Elevator to the other, shouting 'Out of my way! Out of my way!' and crashing into poor Mr and Mrs Bucket with terrible speed.

Grandpa George and Grandma Josephine were doing the same. And well may you wonder what the millions of people down on earth were thinking as they watched these crazy happenings on their television screens. You must realize they couldn't see things very clearly. The Great Glass Elevator was only about the size of a grapefruit on their screens, and the people inside, slightly blurred through the glass, were no bigger than the pips of the grapefruit. Even so, the watchers below could see them buzzing about wildly like insects in a glass box.

'What in the world are they doing?' shouted the President of the United States, staring at the screen.

'Looks like some kind of a war-dance, Mr President,' answered astronaut Showler over the radio.

'You mean they're Red Indians!' said the President.

'I didn't say that, sir.'

'Oh, yes you did, Showler.'

'Oh, no I didn't, Mr President.'

'Silence!' said the President. 'You're muddling me up.'

Back in the Elevator, Mr Wonka was saying, '*Please! Please!* Do stop flying about! Keep still everybody so we can get on with the docking!'

'You miserable old mackerel!' said Grandma Georgina, sailing past him. 'Just when we start having a bit of fun, you want to stop it!'

'Look at me, everybody!' shouted Grandma Josephine. 'I'm flying! I'm a golden eagle!'

'I can fly faster than any of you!' cried Grandpa George, whizzing round and round, his nightgown billowing out behind him like the tail of a parrot.

'Grandpa George!' cried Charlie. 'Do please calm down. If we don't hurry, those astronauts will get there before us.

Don't you want to see inside the Space Hotel, any of you?'

'Out of my way!' shouted Grandma Georgina, blowing herself back and forth. 'I'm a jumbo jet!'

'You're a balmy old bat!' said Mr Wonka.

In the end, the old people grew tired and out of breath, and everyone settled quietly into a floating position.

'All set, Charlie and Grandpa Joe, sir?' said Mr Wonka.

'All set, Mr Wonka,' Charlie answered, hovering near the ceiling.

'I'll give the orders,' said Mr Wonka. 'I'm the pilot. Don't fire your rockets until I tell you. And don't forget who is who. Charlie, you're port. Grandpa Joe, you're starboard.' Mr Wonka pressed one of his own two buttons and immediately booster rockets began firing underneath the Great Glass Elevator. The Elevator leaped forward, but swerved violently to the right. 'Hard a-port!' yelled Mr Wonka.

Charlie pressed his button. His rockets fired. The Elevator swung back into line. 'Steady as you go!' cried Mr Wonka. 'Starboard ten degrees! . . . Steady! . . . Steady! . . . Keep her there! . . .'

Soon they were hovering directly underneath the tail of the enormous silvery Space Hotel. 'You see that little square door with the bolts on it?' said Mr Wonka. 'That's the docking entrance. It won't be long now . . . Port a fraction! . . . Steady! . . . Starboard a bit! . . . Good . . . Good . . . Easy does it . . . we're nearly there . . .'

To Charlie, it felt rather as though he were in a tiny rowboat underneath the stern of the biggest ship in the world. The Space Hotel towered over them. It was enormous. 'I can't wait,' thought Charlie, 'to get inside and see what it's like.'

4

The President

Half a mile back, Shuckworth, Shanks and Showler were keeping the television camera aimed all the time at the Glass Elevator. And across the world, millions and millions of people were clustered around their TV screens, watching tensely the drama being acted out two hundred and forty miles above the earth. In his study in the White House sat Lancelot R. Gilligrass, President of the United States of America, the most powerful man on Earth. In this moment of crisis, all his most important advisers had been summoned urgently to his presence, and there they all were now, following closely on the giant television screen every move made by this dangerous-looking glass capsule and its eight desperate-looking astronauts. The entire Cabinet was present. The Chief of the Army was there, together with four other generals. There was the Chief of the Navy and the Chief of the Air Force and a sword-swallower from Afghanistan, who was the President's best friend. There was the President's Chief Financial Adviser, who was standing in the middle of the room trying to balance the budget on top of his head, but it kept falling off. Standing nearest of all to the President was the Vice-President, a huge lady of eighty-nine with a whiskery chin. She had been the President's nurse when he was a baby and her name was Miss Tibbs. Miss Tibbs was the power behind the throne. She stood no nonsense from anyone. Some people said she was as strict with the President now as when he was a little boy. She was the terror of the White House and even the Head of the Secret Service broke into a sweat when summoned to her presence. Only the President was allowed to call her Nanny. The President's famous cat, Mrs Taubsypuss, was also in the room.

There was absolute silence now in the Presidential study. All eyes were riveted on the TV screen as the small glass object, with its booster-rockets firing, slid smoothly up behind the giant Space Hotel.

'They're going to link up!' shouted the President. 'They're going on board our Space Hotel!'

'They're going to blow it up!' cried the Chief of the Army. 'Let's blow *them* up first, crash bang wallop bang-bang-

33

bang-bang.' The Chief of the Army was wearing so many medal-ribbons they covered the entire front of his tunic on both sides and spread down on to his trousers as well. 'Come on, Mr P.,' he said. 'Let's have some really super-duper explosions!'

'Silence, you silly boy!' said Miss Tibbs, and the Chief of the Army slunk into a corner.

'Listen,' said the President. 'The point is this. *Who are they? And where do they come from?* Where's my Chief Spy?'

'Here, sir, Mr President, sir!' said the Chief Spy.

He had a false moustache, a false beard, false eyelashes, false teeth and a falsetto voice.

'Knock-Knock,' said the President.

'Who's there?' said the Chief Spy.

'Courteney.'

'Courteney who?'

'Courteney one yet?' said the President.

There was a brief silence. 'The President asked you a question,' said Miss Tibbs in an icy voice. 'Have you Courteney one yet?'

'No, ma'am, not yet,' said the Chief Spy, beginning to twitch.

'Well, here's your chance,' snarled Miss Tibbs.

'Quite right,' said the President. 'Tell me immediately who those people are in that glass capsule!'

'Ah-ha,' said the Chief Spy, twirling his false moustache. 'That is a very difficult question.'

'You mean you don't know?'

'I mean I do know, Mr President. At least I think I know. Listen. We have just launched the finest hotel in the world. Right?'

'Right!'

34

'And who is so madly jealous of this wonderful hotel of ours that he wants to blow it up?'

'Miss Tibbs,' said the President.

'Wrong,' said the Chief Spy. 'Try again.'

'Well,' said the President, thinking deeply. 'In that case, could it not perhaps be some other hotel owner who is envious of our lovely hotel?'

'Brilliant!' cried the Chief Spy. 'Go on, sir! You're getting warm!'

'It's Mr Savoy!' said the President.

'Warmer and warmer, Mr President!'

'Mr Ritz!'

'You're hot, sir! You're boiling hot! Go on!'

'I've got it!' cried the President. 'It's Mr Hilton!'

'Well done, sir!' said the Chief Spy.

'Are you sure it's him?'

'Not sure, but it's certainly a warm possibility, Mr President. After all, Mr Hilton's got hotels in just about every country in the world but he hasn't got one in space. And we have. He must be madder than a maggot!'

'By gum, we'll soon fix this!' snapped the President, grabbing one of the eleven telephones on his desk. 'Hello!' he said into the phone. 'Hello hello hello! Where's the operator?' He jiggled furiously on the little thing you jiggle when you want the operator. 'Operator, where are you?'

'They won't answer you now,' said Miss Tibbs. 'They're all watching television.'

'Well, *this* one'll answer!' said the President, snatching up a bright red telephone. This was the hot line direct to the Premier of Soviet Russia in Moscow. It was always open and only used in terrible emergencies. 'It's just as likely to be the Russians as Mr Hilton,' the President went on. 'Don't you agree, Nanny?'

'It's bound to be the Russians,' said Miss Tibbs.

'Premier Yugetoff speaking,' said the voice from Moscow. 'What's on your mind, Mr President?'

'Knock-Knock,' said the President.

'Who's there?' said the Soviet Premier.

'Warren.'

'Warren who?'

'Warren Peace by Leo Tolstoy,' said the President. 'Now see here, Yugetoff! You get those astronauts of yours off that Space Hotel of ours this instant! Otherwise, I'm afraid we're going to have to show you just where you get off, Yugetoff!'

'Those astronauts are not Russians, Mr President.'

'He's lying,' said Miss Tibbs.

'You're lying,' said the President.

'Not lying, sir,' said Premier Yugetoff. 'Have you looked closely at those astronauts in the glass box? I myself cannot see them too clearly on my TV screen, but one of them, the little one with the pointed beard and the top hat, has a distinctly Chinese look about him. In fact, he reminds me very much of my friend the Prime Minister of China . . .'

'Great garbage!' cried the President, slamming down the red phone and picking up a porcelain one. The porcelain phone went direct to the Head of the Chinese Republic in Peking.

'Hello hello hello!' said the President.

'Wing's Fish and Vegetable Store in Shanghai,' said a small distant voice. 'Mr Wing speaking.'

'Nanny!' cried the President, banging down the phone. 'I thought this was a direct line to the Premier!'

'It is,' said Miss Tibbs. 'Try again.'

The President picked up the receiver. 'Hello!' he yelled.

'Mr Wong speaking,' said a voice at the other end.

'*Mister Who?*' screamed the President.

'Mr Wong, assistant stationmaster, Chungking, and if you asking about ten o'clock tlain, ten o'clock tlain no lunning today. Boiler burst.'

The President threw the phone across the room at the Postmaster General. It hit him in the stomach. 'What's the matter with this thing?' shouted the President.

'It is very difficult to phone people in China, Mr President,' said the Postmaster General. 'The country's so full of Wings and Wongs, every time you wing you get the wong number.'

'You're not kidding,' said the President.

The Postmaster General replaced the telephone on the desk. 'Try it just once more, Mr President, please,' he said. 'I've tightened the screws underneath.'

The President again picked up the receiver.

'Gleetings, honourable Mr Plesident,' said a soft faraway voice. 'Here is Assistant-Plemier Chu-On-Dat speaking. How can I do for you?'

'Knock-Knock,' said the President.

'Who der?'

'Ginger.'

'Ginger who?'

'Ginger yourself much when you fell off the Great Wall of China?' said the President. 'Okay, Chu-On-Dat. Let me speak to Premier How-Yu-Bin.'

'Much regret Plemier How-Yu-Bin not here just this second, Mr Plesident.'

'Where is he?'

'He outside mending a puncture on his bicycle.'

'Oh no he isn't,' said the President. 'You can't fool me, you crafty old mandarin! At this very minute he's boarding our magnificent Space Hotel with seven other rascals to blow it up!'

'Excuse pleese, Mr Plesident. You make big mistake . . .'

'No mistake!' barked the President. 'And if you don't call them off right away I'm going to tell my Chief of the Army to blow them all sky high! So chew on that, Chu-On-Dat!'

'Hooray!' said the Chief of the Army. 'Let's blow everyone up! Bang-bang! Bang-bang!'

'Silence!' barked Miss Tibbs.

'I've done it!' cried the Chief Financial Adviser. 'Look at me, everybody! I've balanced the budget!' And indeed he had. He stood proudly in the middle of the room with the enormous 200 billion dollar budget balanced beautifully on the top of his bald head. Everyone clapped. Then suddenly the voice of astronaut Shuckworth cut in urgently on the radio loudspeaker in the President's study. 'They've linked

up and gone on board!' shouted Shuckworth. 'And they've
taken in the bed . . . I mean the bomb!'

The President sucked in his breath sharply. He also sucked
in a big fly that happened to be passing at the time. He
choked. Miss Tibbs thumped him on the back. He swallowed
the fly and felt better. But he was very angry. He seized
pencil and paper and began to draw a picture. As he drew,
he kept muttering, 'I won't have flies in my office! I won't
put up with them!' His advisers waited eagerly. They knew
that the great man was about to give the world yet another
of his brilliant inventions. The last had been the Gilligrass
Left-handed Corkscrew which had been hailed by left-
handers across the nation as one of the greatest blessings of
the century.

'There you are!' said the President, holding up the paper.

39

'This is the Gilligrass Patent Fly-Trap!' They all crowded round to look.

'The fly climbs up the ladder on the left,' said the President. 'He walks along the plank. He stops. He sniffs. He smells something good. He peers over the edge and sees the sugar-lump. "Ah-ha!" he cries. "Sugar!" He is just about to climb down the string to reach it when he sees the basin of water below. "Ho-ho!" he says. "It's a trap! They want me to fall in!" So he walks on, thinking what a clever fly he is. But as you see, I have left out one of the rungs in the ladder he goes down by, so he falls and breaks his neck.'

'Tremendous, Mr President!' they all exclaimed. 'Fantastic! A stroke of genius!'

'I wish to order one hundred thousand for the Army immediately,' said the Chief of the Army.

'Thank you,' said the President, making a careful note of the order.

'I repeat,' said the frantic voice of Shuckworth over the loudspeaker. 'They've gone on board and taken the bomb with them!'

'Stay well clear of them, Shuckworth,' ordered the President. 'There's no point in getting your boys blown up as well.'

And now, all over the world, the millions of watchers waited more tensely than ever in front of their television sets. The picture on their screens, in vivid colour, showed the sinister little glass box securely linked up to the under-belly of the gigantic Space Hotel. It looked like some tiny baby animal clinging to its mother. And when the camera zoomed closer, it was clear for all to see that the glass box was completely empty. All eight of the desperadoes had climbed into the Space Hotel and they had taken their bomb with them.

5

Men from Mars

There was no floating inside the Space Hotel. The gravity-making machine saw to that. So once the docking had been triumphantly achieved, Mr Wonka, Charlie, Grandpa Joe and Mr and Mrs Bucket were able to walk out of the Great Glass Elevator into the lobby of the Hotel. As for Grandpa George, Grandma Georgina and Grandma Josephine, none of them had had their feet on the ground for over twenty years and they certainly weren't going to change their habits now. So when the floating stopped, they all three plopped right back into bed again and insisted that the bed, with them in it, be pushed into the Space Hotel.

Charlie gazed around the huge lobby. On the floor there was a thick green carpet. Twenty tremendous chandeliers hung shimmering from the ceiling. The walls were covered with valuable pictures and there were big soft armchairs all over the place. At the far end of the room there were the doors of five lifts. The group stared in silence at all this luxury. Nobody dared speak. Mr Wonka had warned them that every word they uttered would be picked up by Space Control in Houston, so they had better be careful. A faint humming noise came from somewhere below the floor, but that only made the silence more spooky. Charlie took hold of Grandpa Joe's hand and held it tight. He wasn't sure he liked this very much. They had broken into the greatest machine ever built by man, the property of the United States Government, and if they were discovered and captured as they surely must be in the end, what would happen to them then? Jail for life? Yes, or something worse.

Mr Wonka was writing on a little pad. He held up the pad. It said: ANYBODY HUNGRY?

The three old ones in the bed began waving their arms and nodding and opening and shutting their mouths. Mr Wonka turned the paper over. On the other side it said: THE KITCHENS OF THIS HOTEL ARE LOADED

WITH LUSCIOUS FOOD, LOBSTERS, STEAKS,
ICE-CREAM. WE SHALL HAVE A FEAST TO END
ALL FEASTS.

Suddenly, a tremendous booming voice came out of a
loudspeaker hidden somewhere in the room. '*ATTEN-
TION!*' boomed the voice and Charlie jumped. So did
Grandpa Joe. Everybody jumped, even Mr Wonka. 'ATTEN-
TION THE EIGHT FOREIGN ASTRONAUTS! THIS
IS SPACE CONTROL IN HOUSTON, TEXAS, U.S.A.!
YOU ARE TRESPASSING ON AMERICAN PROP-
ERTY! YOU ARE ORDERED TO IDENTIFY YOUR-
SELVES IMMEDIATELY! SPEAK NOW!'

'Ssshhh!' whispered Mr Wonka, finger to lips.

There followed a few seconds of awful silence. Nobody moved except Mr Wonka who kept saying 'Ssshhh! Ssshhh!'

'WHO ... ARE ... YOU?' boomed the voice from Houston, and the whole world heard it. 'I REPEAT ... WHO ... ARE ... YOU?' shouted the urgent angry voice, and five hundred million people crouched in front of their television sets waiting for an answer to come from the mysterious strangers inside the Space Hotel. The television was not able to show a picture of these mysterious strangers. There was no camera in there to record the scene. Only the words came through. The TV watchers saw nothing but the outside of the giant hotel in orbit, photographed of course by Shuckworth, Shanks and Showler who were following behind. For half a minute the world waited for a reply.

But no reply came.

'SPEAK!' boomed the voice, getting louder and louder and ending in a fearful frightening shout that rattled Charlie's eardrums. *'SPEAK! SPEAK! SPEAK!'* Grandma Georgina shot under the sheet. Grandma Josephine stuck her fingers in her ears. Grandpa George buried his head in the pillow. Mr and Mrs Bucket, both petrified, were once again in each other's arms. Charlie was clutching Grandpa Joe's hand, and the two of them were staring at Mr Wonka and begging him with their eyes to do something. Mr Wonka stood very still, and although his face looked calm, you can be quite sure his clever inventive brain was spinning like a dynamo.

'THIS IS YOUR LAST CHANCE!' boomed the voice. 'WE ARE ASKING YOU ONCE MORE ... WHO ... ARE ... YOU? REPLY IMMEDIATELY! IF YOU DO NOT REPLY WE SHALL BE FORCED TO REGARD

YOU AS DANGEROUS ENEMIES. WE SHALL THEN PRESS THE EMERGENCY FREEZER SWITCH AND THE TEMPERATURE IN THE SPACE HOTEL WILL DROP TO MINUS ONE HUNDRED DEGREES CENTIGRADE. ALL OF YOU WILL BE INSTANTLY DEEP FROZEN. YOU HAVE FIFTEEN SECONDS TO SPEAK. AFTER THAT YOU WILL TURN INTO ICICLES ... ONE ... TWO ... THREE ...'

'Grandpa!' whispered Charlie as the counting continued, 'we *must do* something! We *must*! Quick!'—

'SIX!' said the voice. 'SEVEN! ... EIGHT! ... NINE! ...'

Mr Wonka had not moved. He was still gazing straight ahead, still quite cool, perfectly expressionless. Charlie and Grandpa Joe were staring at him in horror. Then, all at once, they saw the tiny twinkling wrinkles of a smile appear around the corners of his eyes. He sprang to life. He spun round on his toes, skipped a few paces across the floor and then, in a frenzied unearthly sort of scream he cried, *'FIMBO FEEZ!'*

The loudspeaker stopped counting. There was silence. All over the world there was silence.

Charlie's eyes were riveted on Mr Wonka. He was going to speak again. He was taking a deep breath. *'BUNGO BUNI!'* he screamed. He put so much force into his voice that the effort lifted him right up on to the tips of his toes.

'BUNGO BUNI
DAFU DUNI
YUBEE LUNI!'

Again the silence.

The next time Mr Wonka spoke, the words came out

so fast and sharp and loud they were like bullets from a machine-gun. 'ZOONK-ZOONK-ZOONK-*ZOONK*-*ZOONK!*' he barked. The noise echoed around and around the lobby of the Space Hotel. It echoed around the world.

Mr Wonka now turned and faced the far end of the lobby where the loudspeaker voice had come from. He walked a few paces forward as a man would, perhaps, who wanted a more intimate conversation with his audience. And this time, the tone was much quieter, the words came more slowly, but there was a touch of steel in every syllable:

'KIRASUKU MALIBUKU,
WEEBEE WIZE UN YUBEE KUKU!

ALIPENDA KAKAMENDA,
PANTZ FORLDUN IFNO SUSPENDA!

FUIKIKA KANDERIKA,
WEEBE STRONGA YUBEE WEEKA!

POPOKOTA BORUMOKA
VERI RISKI YU PROVOKA!

KATIKATI MOONS UN STARS
FANFANISHA VENUS MARS!'

Mr Wonka paused dramatically for a few seconds. Then he took an enormous deep breath and in a wild and fearsome voice, he yelled out:

'KITIMBIBI *ZOONK!*
FUMBOLEEZI *ZOONK!*
GUGUMIZA *ZOONK!*
FUMIKAKA *ZOONK!*
ANAPOLALA *ZOONK ZOONK ZOONK!*'

The effect of all this on the world below was electric. In the Control Room in Houston, in the White House in Washington, in palaces and city buildings and mountain shacks from America to China to Peru, the five hundred million people who heard that wild and fearsome voice yelling out these strange and mystic words all shivered with fear before their television sets. Everybody began turning to everybody else and saying, 'Who are they? What language was that? Where do they come from?'

In the President's study in the White House, Vice-President Tibbs, the members of the Cabinet, the Chiefs of the Army and the Navy and the Air Force, the sword-swallower from Afghanistan, the Chief Financial Adviser and Mrs Taubsypuss the cat, all stood tense and rigid. They were very much afraid. But the President himself kept a cool head and a clear brain. 'Nanny!' he cried. 'Oh, Nanny, what on earth do we do now?'

'I'll get you a nice warm glass of milk,' said Miss Tibbs.

'I hate the stuff,' said the President. 'Please don't make me drink it!'

'Summon the Chief Interpreter,' said Miss Tibbs.

'Summon the Chief Interpreter!' said the President. 'Where is he?'

'Right here, Mr President,' said the Chief Interpreter.

'What language was that creature spouting up there in the Space Hotel? Be quick! Was it Eskimo?'

'Not Eskimo, Mr President.'

'Ha! Then it was Tagalog! Either Tagalog or Ugro!'

'Not Tagalog, Mr President. Not Ugro, either.'

'Was it Tulu, then? Or Tungus or Tupi?'

'Definitely not Tulu, Mr President. And I'm quite sure it wasn't Tungus or Tupi.'

'Don't stand there telling him what it *wasn't*, you idiot!' said Miss Tibbs. 'Tell him what it *was*!'

'Yes, ma'am, Miss Vice-President, ma'am,' said the Chief Interpreter, beginning to shake. 'Believe me, Mr President,' he went on, 'it was not a language I have ever heard before.'

'But I thought you knew every language in the world?'

'I do, Mr President.'

'Don't lie to me, Chief Interpreter. How can you possibly know every language in the world when you don't know this one?'

'It is not a language of this world, Mr President.'

'Nonsense, man!' barked Miss Tibbs. 'I understood some of it myself!'

'These people, Miss Vice-President, ma'am, have obviously tried to learn just a few of our easier words, but the rest of it is a language that has never been heard before on this Earth!'

48

'Screaming scorpions!' cried the President. 'You mean to tell me they could be coming from . . . from . . . from *somewhere else?*'

'Precisely, Mr President.'

'Like where?' said the President.

'Who knows?' said the Chief Interpreter. 'But did you not notice, Mr President, how they used the words Venus and Mars?'

'Of course I noticed it,' said the President. 'But what's that got to do with it? . . . Ah-ha! I see what you're driving at! Good gracious me! Men from Mars!'

'And Venus,' said the Chief Interpreter.

'That,' said the President, 'could make for trouble.'

'I'll say it could!' said the Chief Interpreter.

'He wasn't talking to you,' said Miss Tibbs.

'What do we do now, General?' said the President.

'Blow 'em up!' cried the General.

'You're always wanting to blow things up,' said the President crossly. 'Can't you think of something *else?*'

'I like blowing things up,' said the General. 'It makes such a lovely noise. *Woomph-woomph!*'

'Don't be a fool!' said Miss Tibbs. 'If you blow these people up, Mars will declare war on us! So will Venus!'

'Quite right, Nanny,' said the President. 'We'd be troculated like turkeys, every one of us! We'd be mashed like potatoes!'

'I'll take 'em on!' shouted the Chief of the Army.

'Shut up!' snapped Miss Tibbs. 'You're fired!'

'Hooray!' said all the other generals. 'Well done, Miss Vice-President, ma'am!'

Miss Tibbs said, 'We've *got* to treat these fellows gently. The one who spoke just now sounded extremely cross.

49

We've got to be polite to them, butter them up, make them happy. The last thing we want is to be invaded by men from Mars! You've got to talk to them, Mr President. Tell Houston we want another direct radio link with the Space Hotel. And hurry!'

6

Invitation to the White House

'The President of the United States will now address you!' announced the loudspeaker voice in the lobby of the Space Hotel.

Grandma Georgina's head peeped cautiously out from under the sheets. Grandma Josephine took her fingers out of her ears and Grandpa George lifted his face out of the pillow.

'You mean he's actually going to speak to us?' whispered Charlie.

'Ssshhh!' said Mr Wonka. 'Listen!'

'Dear friends!' said the well-known Presidential voice over the loudspeaker. 'Dear, *dear* friends! Welcome to Space Hotel "U.S.A." Greetings to the brave astronauts from Mars and Venus . . .'

'Mars and Venus!' whispered Charlie. 'You mean he thinks we're from . . .'

'Ssshh-ssshh-ssshh!' said Mr Wonka. He was doubled up with silent laughter, shaking all over and hopping from one foot to the other.

'You have come a long way,' the President continued, 'so why don't you come just a tiny bit farther and pay *us* a visit down here on our humble little Earth? I invite all eight of you to stay with me here in Washington as my honoured guests. You could land that wonderful glass air-machine of yours on the lawn in back of the White House. We shall have the red carpet out and ready. I do hope you know enough of our language to understand me. I shall wait most anxiously for your reply . . .'

There was a click and the President went off the air.

'What a fantastic thing!' whispered Grandpa Joe. 'The White House, Charlie! We're invited to the White House as honoured guests!'

Charlie caught hold of Grandpa Joe's hands and the two of them started dancing round and round the lobby of the hotel. Mr Wonka, still shaking with laughter, went and sat down on the bed and signalled everyone to gather round close so they could whisper without being heard by the hidden microphones.

'They're scared to death,' he whispered. 'They won't bother us any more now. So let's have that feast we were talking about and afterward we can explore the hotel.'

'Aren't we going to the White House?' whispered Grandma Josephine. 'I want to go to the White House and stay with the President.'

'My dear old dotty dumpling,' said Mr Wonka. 'You look as much like a man from Mars as a bedbug! They'd know at once they'd been fooled. We'd be arrested before we could say how d'you do.'

Mr Wonka was right. There could be no question of accepting the President's invitation and they all knew it.

'But we've got to say *something* to him,' Charlie whispered. 'He must be sitting down there in the White House this very minute waiting for an answer.'

'Make an excuse,' said Mr Bucket.

'Tell him we're otherwise engaged,' said Mrs Bucket.

'You are right,' whispered Mr Wonka. 'It is rude to ignore an invitation.' He stood up and walked a few paces from the group. For a moment or two he remained quite still, gathering his thoughts. Then once again Charlie saw those tiny twinkling smiling wrinkles around the corners of the eyes, and when he began to speak, his voice this time was like the voice of a giant, deep and devilish, very loud and very slow:

> *'In the quelchy quaggy sogmire,*
> *In the mashy mideous harshland,*
> *At the witchy hour of gloomness,*
> *All the grobes come oozing home.*
>
> *You can hear them softly slimeing,*
> *Glissing hissing o'er the slubber,*
> *All those oily boily bodies*
> *Oozing onward in the gloam.*
>
> *So start to run! Oh, skid and daddle*
> *Through the slubber slush and sossel!*
> *Skip jump hop and try to skaddle!*
> *All the grobes are on the roam!'*

In his study two hundred and forty miles below, the President turned white as the White House, 'Jumping jackrabbits!' he cried. 'I think they're after us!'

'Oh, *please* let me blow them up!' said the Ex-Chief of the Army.

'Silence!' said Miss Tibbs. 'Go stand in the corner!'

In the lobby of the Space Hotel, Mr Wonka had merely

paused in order to think up another verse, and he was just about to start off again when a frightful piercing scream stopped him cold. The screamer was Grandma Josephine. She was sitting up in bed and pointing with shaking finger at the lifts at the far end of the lobby. She screamed a second time, still pointing, and all eyes turned toward the lifts. The door of the one on the left was sliding slowly open and the watchers could clearly see that there was something ... something thick ... something brown ... something not exactly brown, but greenish-brown ... something with slimy skin and large eyes ... squatting inside the lift!

7

Something Nasty in the Lifts

Grandma Josephine had stopped screaming now. She had
gone rigid with shock. The rest of the group by the bed,
including Charlie and Grandpa Joe, had become as still as
stone. They dared not move. They dared hardly breathe.
And Mr Wonka, who had swung quickly around to look
when the first scream came, was as dumbstruck as the rest.
He stood motionless, gaping at the thing in the lift, his
mouth slightly open, his eyes stretched wide as two wheels.
What he saw, what they all saw, was this:

It looked more than anything like an enormous egg balanced on its pointed end. It was as tall as a big boy and wider than the fattest man. The greenish-brown skin had a shiny wettish appearance and there were wrinkles in it. About three-quarters of the way up, in the widest part, there were two large round eyes as big as tea-cups. The eyes were white, but each had a brilliant red pupil in the centre. The red pupils were resting on Mr Wonka. But now they began travelling slowly across to Charlie and Grandpa Joe and the others by the bed, settling upon them and gazing at them with a cold malevolent stare. The eyes were everything. There were no other features, no nose or mouth or ears, but the entire egg-shaped body was itself moving very very slightly, pulsing and bulging gently here and there as though the skin were filled with some thick fluid.

At this point, Charlie suddenly noticed that the next lift was coming down. The indicator numbers above the door were flashing ... 6 ... 5 ... 4 ... 3 ... 2 ... 1 ... L (for lobby). There was a slight pause. The door slid open and there, inside the second lift, was another enormous slimy wrinkled greenish-brown egg with eyes!

Now the numbers were flashing above all three of the remaining lifts. Down they came ... down ... down ... down ... And soon, at precisely the same time, they reached the lobby floor and the doors slid open ... five open doors now ... one creature in each ... five in all ... and five pairs of eyes with brilliant red centres all watching Mr Wonka and watching Charlie and Grandpa Joe and the others.

There were slight differences in size and shape between the five, but all had the same greenish-brown wrinkled skin and the skin was rippling and pulsing.

For about thirty seconds nothing happened. Nobody

stirred, nobody made a sound. The silence was terrible. So was the suspense. Charlie was so frightened he felt himself shrinking inside his skin. Then he saw the creature in the left-hand lift suddenly starting to change shape! Its body was slowly becoming longer and longer, and thinner and thinner, going up and up towards the roof of the lift, not straight up, but curving a little to the left, making a snake-like curve that was curiously graceful, up to the left and then curling over the top to the right and coming down again in a half-circle . . . and then the bottom end began to grow out as well, like a tail . . . creeping along the floor . . . creeping along the floor to the left . . . until at last the creature, which had originally looked like a huge egg, now looked like a long curvy serpent standing up on its tail.

Then the one in the next lift began stretching itself in much the same way, and what a weird and oozy thing it was to watch! It was twisting itself into a shape that was a bit different from the first, balancing itself almost but not quite on the tip of its tail.

Then the three remaining creatures began stretching themselves all at the same time, each one elongating itself slowly upward, growing taller and taller, thinner and thinner, curving and twisting, stretching and stretching, curling and bending, balancing either on the tail or the head or both, and turned sideways now so that only one eye was visible. When they had all stopped stretching and bending, this was how they finished up:

'*Scram!*' shouted Mr Wonka. 'Get out quick!'

People have never moved faster than Grandpa Joe and Charlie and Mr and Mrs Bucket at that moment. They all got behind the bed and started pushing like crazy. Mr Wonka ran in front of them shouting 'Scram! Scram! Scram!' and in ten seconds flat all of them were out of the lobby and back inside the Great Glass Elevator. Frantically, Mr Wonka began undoing bolts and pressing buttons. The door of the Great Glass Elevator snapped shut and the whole thing leaped sideways. They were away! And of course all of them, including the three old ones in the bed, floated up again into the air.

8

The Vermicious Knids

'Oh, my goodness me!' gasped Mr Wonka. 'Oh, my sainted
pants! Oh, my painted ants! Oh, my crawling cats! I hope
never to see anything like *that* again!' He floated over to
the white button and pressed it. The booster-rockets fired.
The Elevator shot forward at such a speed that soon the
Space Hotel was out of sight far behind.

'But who *were* those awful creatures?' Charlie asked.

'You mean you didn't *know?*' cried Mr Wonka. 'Well, it's
a good thing you didn't! If you'd had even the faintest idea
of what horrors you were up against, the marrow would
have run out of your bones! You'd have been fossilized with
fear and glued to the ground! Then they'd have got you!
You'd have been a cooked cucumber! You'd have been
rasped into a thousand tiny bits, grated like cheese and
flocculated alive! They'd have made necklaces from your
knucklebones and bracelets from your teeth! Because those
creatures, my dear ignorant boy, are the most brutal, vin-
dictive, venomous, murderous beasts in the entire universe!'
Here Mr Wonka paused and ran the tip of a pink tongue
all the way around his lips. 'VERMICIOUS KNIDS!' he
cried. 'That's what they were!' He sounded the K . . .
K'NIDS, like that.

'I thought they were grobes,' Charlie said. 'Those oozy-woozy grobes you were telling the President about.'

'Oh, no, I just made those up to scare the White House,' Mr Wonka answered. 'But there is nothing made-up about Vermicious Knids, believe you me. They live, as everybody knows, on the planet Vermes, which is eighteen thousand four hundred and twenty-seven million miles away and they are very, very clever brutes indeed. The Vermicious Knid can turn itself into any shape it wants. It has no bones. Its body is really one huge muscle, enormously strong, but very stretchy and squishy, like a mixture of rubber and putty with steel wires inside. Normally it is egg-shaped, but it can just as easily give itself two legs like a human or four legs like a horse. It can become as round as a ball or as long as a kite-string. From fifty yards away, a fully-grown Vermicious Knid could stretch out its neck and bite your head off without even getting up!'

'Bite off your head with what?' said Grandma Georgina. 'I didn't see any mouth.'

'They have other things to bite with,' said Mr Wonka darkly.

'Such as what?' said Grandma Georgina.

'Ring off,' said Mr Wonka. 'Your time's up. But listen, everybody. I've just had a funny thought. There I was fooling around with the President and pretending we were creatures from some other planet and, by golly, there actually *were* creatures from some other planet on board!'

'Do you think there were many?' Charlie asked. 'More than the five we saw?'

'Thousands!' said Mr Wonka. 'There are five hundred rooms in that Space Hotel and there's probably a family of them in every room!'

'Somebody's going to get a nasty shock when they go on board!' said Grandpa Joe.

'They'll be eaten like peanuts,' said Mr Wonka. 'Every one of them.'

'You don't really mean that, do you, Mr Wonka?' Charlie said.

'Of course I mean it,' said Mr Wonka. 'These Vermicious Knids are the terror of the Universe. They travel through space in great swarms, landing on other stars and planets and destroying everything they find. There used to be some rather nice creatures living on the moon a long time ago. They were called Poozas. But the Vermicious Knids ate the lot. They did the same on Venus and Mars and any other planets.'

'Why haven't they come down to our Earth and eaten us?' Charlie asked.

'They've tried to, Charlie, many times, but they've never made it. You see, all around our Earth there is a vast envelope of air and gas, and anything hitting *that* at high speed gets red hot. Space capsules are made of special heat-proof metal, and when they make a re-entry, their speeds are reduced right down to about 2,000 miles an hour, first by retro-rockets and then by something called "friction". But even so, they get badly scorched. Knids, which are not heat-proof at all, and don't have any retro-rockets, get sizzled up completely before they're half-way through. Have you ever seen a shooting star?'

'Lots of them,' Charlie said.

'Actually, they're not shooting stars at all,' said Mr Wonka. 'They're Shooting Knids. They're Knids trying to enter the Earth's atmosphere at high speed and going up in flames.'

'What rubbish,' said Grandma Georgina.

'You wait,' said Mr Wonka. 'You may see it happening before the day is done.'

'But if they're so fierce and dangerous,' Charlie said, 'why didn't they eat us up right away in the Space Hotel? Why did they waste time twisting their bodies into letters and writing SCRAM?'

'Because they're show-offs,' Mr Wonka replied. 'They're tremendously proud of being able to write like that.'

'But why say *scram* when they wanted to catch us and eat us?'

'It's the only word they know,' Mr Wonka said.

'*Look!*' screamed Grandma Josephine, pointing through the glass. 'Over there!'

Before he even looked, Charlie knew exactly what he was going to see. So did the others. They could tell by the high hysterical note in the old lady's voice.

And there it was, cruising effortlessly alongside them, a simply colossal Vermicious Knid, as thick as a whale, as long as a lorry, with the most brutal vermicious look in its eye! It was no more than a dozen yards away, egg-shaped, slimy, greenish-brown, with one malevolent red eye (the only one visible) fixed intently upon the people floating inside the Great Glass Elevator!

'The end has come!' screamed Grandma Georgina.

'He'll eat us all!' cried Mrs Bucket.

'In one gulp!' said Mr Bucket.

'We're done for, Charlie,' said Grandpa Joe. Charlie nodded. He couldn't speak or make a sound. His throat was seized up with fright.

But this time Mr Wonka didn't panic. He remained perfectly calm. 'We'll soon get rid of *that*!' he said and he

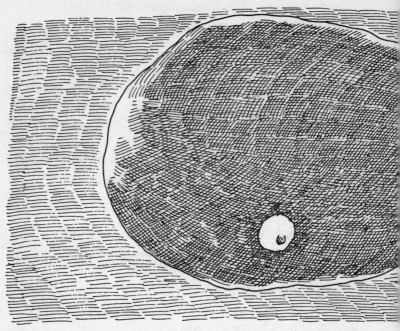

pressed six buttons all at once and six booster-rockets went off simultaneously under the Elevator. The Elevator leaped forward like a stung horse, faster and faster, but the great green greasy Knid kept pace alongside it with no trouble at all.

'Make it go away!' yelled Grandma Georgina. 'I can't stand it looking at me!'

'Dear lady,' said Mr Wonka, 'it can't possibly get in here. I don't mind admitting I was a trifle alarmed back there in the Space Hotel. And with good reason. But here we have nothing to fear. The Great Glass Elevator is shockproof, waterproof, bombproof, bulletproof and Knidproof! So just relax and enjoy it.'

'Oh you Knid, you are vile and vermicious!'

cried Mr Wonka.

> *'You are slimy and soggy and squishous!*
> *But what do we care*
> *'Cause you can't get in here,*
> *So hop it and don't get ambitious!'*

At this point, the massive Knid outside turned and started cruising away from the Elevator. 'There you are,' cried Mr Wonka, triumphant. 'It heard me! It's going home!' But Mr Wonka was wrong. When the creature was about a hundred yards off, it stopped, hovered for a moment, then went smoothly into reverse, coming back toward the Elevator with its rear-end (which was the pointed end of the egg) now in front. Even going backwards, its acceleration was unbelievable. It was like some monstrous bullet coming at them and it came so fast nobody had time even to cry out.

CRASH! It struck the Glass Elevator with the most enormous bang and the whole thing shivered and shook but the glass held and the Knid bounced off like a rubber ball.

'What did I tell you!' shouted Mr Wonka, triumphant. 'We're safe as sausages in here!'

'He'll have a nasty headache after that,' said Grandpa Joe.

'It's not his head, it's his bottom!' said Charlie. 'Look Grandpa, there's a big bump coming up on the pointed end where he hit! It's going black and blue!'

And so it was. A purple bruisy bump the size of a small car was appearing on the pointed rear-end of the giant Knid. 'Hello, you dirty great beast!' cried Mr Wonka.

'*Hello, you great Knid! Tell us, how do you do?*
You're a rather strange colour today.
Your bottom is purple and lavender blue.
Should it really be looking that way?

Are you not feeling well? Are you going to faint?
Is it something we cannot discuss?
It must be a very unpleasant complaint,
For your backside's as big us a bus!

Let me get you a doctor. I know just the man
For a Knid with a nasty disease.
He's a butcher by trade which is not a bad plan,
And he charges quite reasonable fees.

The Vermicious Knids

Ah, here he is now! "Doc, you really are kind
To travel so far into space.
There's your patient, the Knid with the purple behind!
Do you think it's a desperate case?"

"Great heavens above! It's no wonder he's pale!"
Said the doc with a horrible grin.
"There's a sort of balloon on the end of his tail!
I must prick it at once with a pin!"

So he got out a thing like an Indian spear,
With feathers all over the top,
And he lunged and he caught the Knid smack in the rear,
But alas, the balloon didn't pop!

Cried the Knid, "What on earth am I going to do
With this painful preposterous lump?
I can't remain standing the whole summer through!
And I cannot sit down on my rump!"

"It's a bad case of rear-ache," the medico said,
"And it's something I cannot repair.
If you want to sit down, you must sit on your head,
With your bottom high up in the air!" '

9

Gobbled Up

On the day when all this was happening, no factories opened anywhere in the world. All offices and schools were closed. Nobody moved away from the television screens, not even for a couple of minutes to get a Coke or to feed the baby. The tension was unbearable. Everybody heard the American President's invitation to the men from Mars to visit him in the White House. And they heard the weird rhyming reply, which sounded rather threatening. They also heard a piercing scream (Grandma Josephine), and a little later on, they heard someone shouting, 'Scram! Scram! Scram!' (Mr Wonka). Nobody could make head or tail of the shouting. They took it to be some kind of Martian language. But when the eight mysterious astronauts suddenly rushed back into their glass capsule and broke away from the Space Hotel, you could almost hear the great sigh of relief that rose up from the peoples of the earth. Telegrams and messages poured into the White House congratulating the President upon his brilliant handling of a frightening situation.

The President himself remained calm and thoughtful. He sat at his desk rolling a small piece of wet chewing-gum between his finger and thumb. He was waiting for the moment when he could flick it at Miss Tibbs without her seeing him. He flicked it and missed Miss Tibbs but hit the Chief of the Air Force on the tip of his nose.

'Do you think the men from Mars have accepted my invitation to the White House?' the President asked.

'Of course they have,' said the Foreign Secretary. 'It was a brilliant speech, sir.'

'They're probably on their way down here right now,' said Miss Tibbs. 'Go and wash that nasty sticky chewing-gum off your fingers quickly. They could be here any minute.'

'Let's have a song first,' said the President. 'Sing another one about me, Nanny . . . please.'

THE NURSE'S SONG

This mighty man of whom I sing,
The greatest of them all,
Was once a teeny little thing,
Just eighteen inches tall.

I knew him as a tiny tot.
I nursed him on my knee.
I used to sit him on the pot
And wait for him to wee.

I always washed between his toes,
And cut his little nails.
I brushed his hair and wiped his nose
And weighed him on the scales.

Through happy childhood days he strayed,
As all nice children should.
I smacked him when he disobeyed,
And stopped when he was good.

It soon began to dawn on me
He wasn't very bright,
Because when he was twenty-three
He couldn't read or write.

'What shall we do?' his parents sob.
'The boy has got the vapours!
He couldn't even get a job
Delivering the papers!'

'Ah-ha,' I said. 'This little clot
Could be a politician.'
'Nanny,' he cried. 'Oh Nanny, what
A super proposition!'

'Okay,' I said. 'Let's learn and note
The art of politics.
Let's teach you how to miss the boat
And how to drop some bricks,
And how to win the people's vote
And lots of other tricks.

Let's learn to make a speech a day
Upon the TV screen,
In which you never never say
Exactly what you mean.

And most important, by the way,
Is not to let your teeth decay,
And keep your fingers clean.'

And now that I am eighty-nine,
It's too late to repent.
The fault was mine the little swine
Became the President.

'Bravo Nanny!' cried the President, clapping his hands. 'Hooray!' shouted the others. 'Well done, Miss Vice-President, ma'am! Brilliant! Tremendous!'

'My goodness!' said the President. 'Those men from Mars will be here any moment! What on earth are we going to give them for lunch? Where's my Chief Cook?'

The Chief Cook was a Frenchman. He was also a French spy and at this moment he was listening at the keyhole of the President's study. 'Ici, Monsieur le President!' he said, bursting in.

'Chief Cook,' said the President. 'What do men from Mars eat for lunch?'

'Mars Bars,' said the Chief Cook.

'Baked or boiled?' asked the President.

'Oh, *baked*, of course, Monsieur le President. You will ruin a Mars Bar by boiling!'

The voice of astronaut Shuckworth cut in over the loudspeaker in the President's study. 'Request permission to link up and go aboard Space Hotel?' he said.

'Permission granted,' said the President. 'Go right ahead, Shuckworth. It's all clear now . . . Thanks to me.'

And so the large Transport Capsule, piloted by Shuckworth, Shanks and Showler, with all the hotel managers and assistant managers and hall porters and pastry chefs and bell-boys and waitresses and chambermaids on board, moved in smoothly and linked up with the giant Space Hotel.

'Hey there! We've lost our television picture,' called the President.

'I'm afraid the camera got smashed against the side of the Space Hotel, Mr President,' Shuckworth replied. The President said a very rude word into the microphone and ten million children across the nation began repeating it gleefully and got smacked by their parents.

'All astronauts and one hundred and fifty hotel staff safely aboard Space Hotel!' Shuckworth reported over the radio. 'We are now standing in the lobby!'

'And what do you think of it all?' asked the President. He knew the whole world was listening in and he wanted Shuckworth to say how wonderful it was. Shuckworth didn't let him down.

'Gee, Mr President, it's just *great!*' he said. 'It's *unbelievable!* It's so *enormous!* And so . . . it's kind of hard to find words to describe it, it's so truly grand, especially the chandeliers and the carpets and all! I have the Chief Hotel Manager, Mr Walter W. Wall, beside me now. He would like the honour of a word with you, sir.'

'Put him on,' said the President.

'Mr President, sir, this is Walter Wall. What a sumptuous hotel this is! The decorations are superb!'

'Have you noticed that all the carpets are wall-to-wall, Mr Walter Wall?' said the President.

'I have indeed, Mr President.'

'All the wallpaper is all wall-to-wall, too, Mr Walter Wall.'

72

'Yes, sir, Mr President! Isn't that something! It's going to be a real pleasure running a beautiful hotel like this! ... *Hey! What's going on over there? Something's coming out of the lifts! Help!*' Suddenly the loudspeaker in the President's study gave out a series of the most ghastly screams and yells. *'Ayeeeee! Owwwww! Ayeeeee! Hel-l-l-lp! Hel-l-l-l-l-lp! Hel-l-l-l-l-l-l-l-lp!'*

'What on earth's going on?' said the President. *'Shuckworth! Are you there, Shuckworth? ... Shanks! Showler! Mr Walter Wall! Where are you all! What's happening?'*

The screams continued. They were so loud the President had to put his fingers in his ears. Every house in the world that had a television or radio receiver heard those awful screams. There were other noises, too. Loud grunts and snortings and crunching sounds. Then there was silence.

Frantically the President called the Space Hotel on the radio. Houston called the Space Hotel. The President called Houston. Houston called the President. Then both of them called the Space Hotel again. But answer came there none. Up there in space all was silent.

'Something nasty's happened,' said the President.

'It's those men from Mars,' said the Ex-Chief of the Army. 'I *told* you to let me blow them up.'

'Silence!' snapped the President. 'I've got to think.'

The loudspeaker began to crackle. 'Hello!' it said. 'Hello hello hello! Are you receiving me, Space Control in Houston?'

The President grabbed the mike on his desk. 'Leave this to me, Houston!' he shouted, 'President Gilligrass here receiving you loud and clear! Go ahead!'

'Astronaut Shuckworth here, Mr President, back aboard the Transport Capsule ... *thank heavens!*'

'What happened, Shuckworth? Who's with you?'

'We're most of us here, Mr President, I'm glad to say. Shanks and Showler are with me, and a whole bunch of other folks. I guess we lost maybe a couple of dozen people altogether, pastry chefs, hall porters, that sort of thing. It sure was a scramble getting out of that place alive!'

'What do you mean you *lost* two dozen people?' shouted the President. 'How did you lose them?'

'Gobbled up!' replied Shuckworth. 'One gulp and that was it! I saw a big six-foot-tall assistant-manager being swallowed up just like you'd swallow a lump of ice-cream, Mr President! No chewing – nothing! Just down the hatch!'

'But *who?*' yelled the President. 'Who are you talking about? Who did the swallowing?'

'*Hold it!*' cried Shuckworth. 'Oh, my lord, here they all come now! They're coming after us! They're swarming out of the Space Hotel! They're coming out in swarms! You'll have to excuse me a moment, Mr President. No time to talk right now!'

10

Transport Capsule in Trouble — Attack No. 1

While Shuckworth, Shanks and Showler were being chased out of the Space Hotel by the Knids, Mr Wonka's Great Glass Elevator was orbiting the Earth at tremendous speed. Mr Wonka had all his booster-rockets firing and the Elevator was reaching speeds of thirty-four thousand miles an hour instead of the normal seventeen thousand. They were trying, you see, to get away from that huge angry Vermicious Knid with the purple behind. Mr Wonka wasn't afraid of it, but Grandma Josephine was petrified. Every time she looked at it, she let out a piercing scream and clapped her hands over her eyes. But of course thirty-four thousand miles an hour is dawdling to a Knid. Healthy young Knids think nothing of travelling a million miles between lunch and supper, and then another million before breakfast the next day. How else could they travel between the planet Vermes and other stars? Mr Wonka should have known this and saved his rocket-power, but he kept right on going and the giant Knid kept right on cruising effortlessly alongside, glaring into the Elevator with its wicked red eye. 'You people have bruised my backside,' the Knid seemed to be saying, 'and in the end I'm going to *get* you for that.'

They had been streaking around the Earth like this for about forty-five minutes when Charlie, who was floating comfortably beside Grandpa Joe near the ceiling, said suddenly, 'There's something ahead! Can you see it, Grandpa? Straight in front of us!'

'I can, Charlie, I can ... Good heavens, it's the Space Hotel!'

'It can't be, Grandpa. We left it miles behind us long ago.'

'Ah-ha,' said Mr Wonka. 'We've been going so fast we've gone all the way around the Earth and caught up with it again! A splendid effort!'

'And there's the Transport Capsule! Can you see it, Grandpa? It's just behind the Space Hotel!'

'There's something else there, too, Charlie, if I'm not mistaken!'

'*I know what those are!*' screamed Grandma Josephine. 'They're Vermicious Knids! Turn back at once!'

'Reverse!' yelled Grandma Georgina. 'Go the other way!'

'Dear lady,' said Mr Wonka. 'This isn't a car on the motorway. When you are in orbit, you cannot stop and you cannot go backwards.'

'I don't care about that!' shouted Grandma Josephine. 'Put on the brakes! Stop! Back-pedal! The Knids'll get us!'

'Now let's for heaven's sake *stop* this nonsense once and for all,' Mr Wonka said sternly. 'You know very well my Elevator is completely Knidproof. You have nothing to fear.'

They were closer now and they could see the Knids pouring out from the tail of the Space Hotel and swarming like wasps around the Transport Capsule.

'They're attacking it!' cried Charlie. 'They're after the Transport Capsule!'

It was a fearsome sight. The huge green egg-shaped Knids were grouping themselves into squadrons with about twenty Knids to a squadron. Then each squadron formed itself into a line abreast, with one yard between Knids. Then, one after another, the squadrons began attacking the Transport Capsule. They attacked in reverse with their pointed rear-ends in front and they came in at a fantastic speed.

WHAM! One squadron attacked, bounced off and wheeled away.

CRASH! Another squadron smashed against the side of the Transport Capsule.

'Get us out of here, you madman!' screamed Grandma Josephine. 'What are you waiting for?'

'They'll be coming after *us* next!' yelled Grandma Georgina. 'For heaven's sake, man, turn back!'

'I doubt very much if that capsule of theirs is Knidproof,' said Mr Wonka.

'Then we must help them!' cried Charlie. 'We've got to do something! There are a hundred and fifty people inside that thing!'

Down on the Earth, in the White House study, the President and his advisers were listening in horror to the voices of the astronauts over the radio.

'They're coming at us in droves!' Shuckworth was shouting. 'They're bashing us to bits!'

'But *who?*' yelled the President. 'You haven't even told us who's attacking you!'

'These dirty great greenish-brown brutes with red eyes!' shouted Shanks, butting in. 'They're shaped like enormous eggs and they're coming at us backwards!'

'Backwards?' cried the President. 'Why backwards?'

'Because their bottoms are even more pointy than their tops!' shouted Shuckworth. 'Look out! Here comes another lot!' *BANG!* 'We won't be able to stand this much longer, Mr President! The waitresses are screaming and the chambermaids are all hysterical and the bell-boys are being sick and the hall porters are saying their prayers so what shall we do, Mr President, sir, what on earth shall we do?'

'Fire your rockets, you idiot, and make a re-entry!' shouted the President. 'Come back to Earth immediately!'

'That's impossible!' cried Showler. 'They've busted our rockets! They've smashed them to smithereens!'

'We're cooked, Mr President!' shouted Shanks. 'We're done for! Because even if they don't succeed in destroying the capsule, we'll have to stay up here in orbit for the rest of our lives! We can't make a re-entry without rockets!'

The President was sweating and the sweat ran all the way down the back of his neck and inside his collar.

'Any moment now, Mr President,' Shanks went on, 'we're going to lose contact with you altogether! There's another lot coming at us from the left and they're aiming straight for our radio aerial! Here they come! I don't think we'll be able to . . .' The voice cut. The radio went dead.

'Shanks!' cried the President. 'Where are you, Shanks? . . . Shuckworth! Shanks! Showler! . . . Showlworth! Shucks! Shankler! . . . Shankworth! Show! Shuckler! Why don't you answer me?!'

Up in the Great Glass Elevator where they had no radio and could hear nothing of these conversations, Charlie was saying, 'Surely their only hope is to make a re-entry and dive back to Earth quickly!'

'Yes,' said Mr Wonka. 'But in order to re-enter the Earth's atmosphere they've got to kick themselves out of orbit. They've got to change course and head downwards and to do that they need rockets! But their rocket tubes are all dented and bent! You can see that from here! They're crippled!'

'Why can't we tow them down?' Charlie asked.

Mr Wonka jumped. Even though he was floating, he somehow jumped. He was so excited he shot upwards and hit his head on the ceiling. Then he spun round three times in the air and cried, 'Charlie! You've got it! That's it! We'll tow them out of orbit! To the buttons, quick!'

'What do we tow them with?' asked Grandpa Joe. 'Our neckties?'

'Don't you worry about a little thing like that!' cried Mr Wonka. 'My Great Glass Elevator is ready for anything! In we go! Into the breach, dear friends, into the breach!'

'Stop him!' screamed Grandma Josephine.

'You be quiet, Josie,' said Grandpa Joe. 'There's someone over there needs a helping hand and it's our job to give it. If you're frightened, you'd better just close your eyes tight and stick your fingers in your ears.'

11

The Battle of the Knids

'Grandpa Joe, sir!' shouted Mr Wonka. 'Kindly jet yourself over to the far corner of the Elevator there and turn that handle! It lowers the rope!'

'A rope's no good, Mr Wonka! The Knids will bite through a rope in one second!'

'It's a steel rope,' said Mr Wonka. 'It's made of re-inscorched steel. If they try to bite through *that* their teeth will splinter like spillikins! To your buttons, Charlie! You've got to help me manoeuvre! We're going right over the top of the Transport Capsule and then we'll try to hook on to it somewhere and get a firm hold!'

Like a battleship going into action, the Great Glass Elevator with booster rockets firing moved smoothly in over the top of the enormous Transport Capsule. The Knids immediately stopped attacking the Capsule and went for the Elevator. Squadron after squadron of giant Vermicious Knids flung themselves furiously against Mr Wonka's marvellous machine! WHAM! CRASH! BANG! The noise was thunderous and terrible. The Elevator was tossed about the sky like a leaf, and inside it, Grandma Josephine, Grandma Georgina and Grandpa George, floating in their nightshirts, were all yowling and screeching and flapping their arms and calling for help. Mrs Bucket had wrapped her arms around Mr Bucket and was clasping him so tightly that one of his shirt buttons punctured his skin. Charlie and Mr Wonka, as cool as two cubes of ice, were up near the ceiling working the booster-rocket controls, and Grandpa Joe, shouting war-cries and throwing curses at the Knids, was down below turning the handle that unwound the steel rope. At the same time, he was watching the rope through the glass floor of the Elevator.

'Starboard a bit, Charlie!' shouted Grandpa Joe. 'We're right on top of her now! . . . Forward a couple of yards, Mr Wonka! . . . I'm trying to get the hook hooked around that stumpy thing sticking out in front there! . . . Hold it! . . . I've got it . . . That's it! . . . Forward a little now and see if it holds! . . . More! . . . More! . . .' The big steel rope tightened. It held! And now, wonder of wonders, with her booster-rockets blazing, the Elevator began to tow the huge Transport Capsule forward and away!

'Full speed ahead!' shouted Grandpa Joe. 'She's going to hold! She's holding! She's holding fine!'

'All boosters firing!' cried Mr Wonka, and the Elevator leaped ahead. Still the rope held. Mr Wonka jetted himself down to Grandpa Joe and shook him warmly by the hand. 'Well done, sir,' he said. 'You did a brilliant job under heavy fire!'

Charlie looked back at the Transport Capsule some thirty yards behind them on the end of the tow-line. It had little windows up front, and in the windows he could clearly see the flabbergasted faces of Shuckworth, Shanks and Showler. Charlie waved to them and gave them the thumbs up signal. They didn't wave back. They simply gaped. They couldn't believe what was happening.

Grandpa Joe blew himself upward and hovered beside Charlie, bubbling with excitement. 'Charlie, my boy,' he said. 'We've been through a few funny things together lately, but never anything like this!'

'Grandpa, where are the Knids? They've suddenly vanished!'

Everyone looked round. The only Knid in sight was their old friend with the purple behind, still cruising alongside in its usual place, still glaring into the Elevator.

'*Just* a minute!' cried Grandma Josephine. 'What's *that* I see over there?' Again they looked, and this time, sure enough, away in the distance, in the deep blue sky of outer space, they saw a massive cloud of Vermicious Knids wheeling and circling like a fleet of bombers.

'If you think we're out of the woods yet, you're crazy!' shouted Grandma Georgina.

'I fear no Knids!' said Mr Wonka. 'We've got them beaten now!'

'Poppyrot and pigwash!' said Grandma Josephine. 'Any moment now they'll be at us again! Look at them! They're coming in! They're coming closer!'

This was true. The huge fleet of Knids had moved in at incredible speed and was now flying level with the Great Glass Elevator, a couple of hundred yards away on the right hand side. The one with the bump on its rear-end was much closer, only twenty yards away on the same side.

'It's changing shape!' cried Charlie. 'That nearest one! What's it going to do? It's getting longer and longer!' And indeed it was. The mammoth egg-shaped body was slowly stretching itself out like chewing-gum, becoming longer and longer and thinner and thinner, until in the end it looked exactly like a long slimy-green serpent as thick as a thick tree and as long as a football pitch. At the front end were the eyes, big and white with red centres, at the back a kind of tapering tail and at the very end of the tail was the enormous round swollen bump it had got when it crashed against the glass.

The people floating inside the Elevator watched and waited. Then they saw the long rope-like Knid turning and coming straight but quite slowly toward the Great Glass Elevator. Now it began actually wrapping its ropy body around the Elevator itself. Once around it went . . . then twice around, and very horrifying it was to be inside and to see the soft green body squishing against the outside of the glass no more than a few inches away.

'It's tying us up like a parcel!' yelled Grandma Josephine.

'Bunkum!' said Mr Wonka.

'It's going to crush us in its coils!' wailed Grandma Georgina.

'Never!' said Mr Wonka.

Charlie glanced quickly back at the Transport Capsule. The sheet-white faces of Shuckworth, Shanks and Showler were pressed against the glass of the little windows, terror-struck, stupefied, stunned, their mouths open, their expressions frozen like fishfingers. Once again, Charlie gave them the thumbs up signal. Showler acknowledged it with a sickly grin, but that was all.

'Oh, oh, oh!' screamed Grandma Josephine. 'Get that beastly squishy thing away from here!'

Having curled its body twice around the Elevator, the Knid now proceeded to tie a knot with its two ends, a good strong knot, left over right, then right over left. When it had pulled the knot tight, there remained about five yards of one end hanging loose. This was the end with the eyes on it. But it didn't hang loose for long. It quickly curled itself into the shape of a huge hook and the hook stuck straight out sideways from the Elevator as though waiting for something else to hook itself on to it.

While all this was going on, nobody had noticed what the other Knids were up to. 'Mr Wonka!' Charlie cried. 'Look at the others! What *are* they doing?'

What indeed?

These, too, had all changed shape and had become longer, but not nearly so long or so thin as the first one. Each of them had turned itself into a kind of thick rod and the rod was curled around at both ends – at the tail end and at the head end – so that it made a double-ended hook. And now all the hooks were linking up into one long chain . . . one thousand Knids . . . all joining together and curving around in the sky to make a chain of Knids half a mile long or more! And the Knid at the very front of the chain (whose front hook was not, of course, hooked up to anything) was leading them in a wide circle and sweeping in toward the Great Glass Elevator.

'Hey!' shouted Grandpa Joe. 'They're going to hook up with this brute who's tied himself around us!'

'And tow us away!' cried Charlie.

'To the planet Vermes,' gasped Grandma Josephine. 'Eighteen thousand four hundred and twenty-seven million miles from here!'

'They can't do that!' cried Mr Wonka. '*We're* doing the towing around here!'

'They're going to link up, Mr Wonka!' Charlie said. 'They really are! Can't we stop them? They're going to tow us away and they're going to tow the people we're towing away as well!'

'Do something, you old fool!' shrieked Grandma Georgina. 'Don't just float about looking at them!'

'I must admit,' said Mr Wonka, 'that for the first time in my life I find myself at a bit of a loss.'

They all stared in horror through the glass at the long chain of Vermicious Knids. The leader of the chain was coming closer and closer. The hook, with two big angry eyes on it, was out and ready. In thirty seconds it would link up with the hook of the Knid wrapped around the Elevator.

'I want to go home!' wailed Grandma Josephine. 'Why can't we all go home?'

'Great thundering tomcats!' cried Mr Wonka. '*Home* is right! What on earth am I thinking of! Come on, Charlie! Quick! *Re-entry!* You take the yellow button! Press it for all you're worth! I'll handle this lot!' Charlie and Mr Wonka literally flew to the buttons. 'Hold your hats!' shouted Mr Wonka. 'Grab your gizzards! We're going down!'

Rockets started firing out of the Elevator from all sides. It tilted and gave a sickening lurch and then plunged downward into the Earth's atmosphere at a simply colossal speed. '*Retro-rockets!*' bellowed Mr Wonka. 'I mustn't forget to fire the retro-rockets!' He flew over to another series of buttons and started playing on them like a piano.

The Elevator was now streaking downward head first, upside down, and all the passengers found themselves floating upside down as well. 'Help!' screamed Grandma Georgina. 'All the blood's going to my head!'

'Then turn yourself the other way up,' said Mr Wonka. 'That's easy enough, isn't it?'

Everyone blew and puffed and turned somersaults in the air until at last they were all the right way up. 'How's the tow-rope holding, Grandpa?' Mr Wonka called out.

'They're still with us, Mr Wonka, sir! The rope's holding fine!'

It was an amazing sight – the Glass Elevator streaking down toward the Earth with the huge Transport Capsule in tow behind it. But the long chain of Knids was coming after them, following them down, keeping pace with them easily, and now the hook of the leading Knid in the chain was actually reaching out and grasping for the hook made by the Knid on the Elevator!

'We're too late!' screamed Grandma Georgina. 'They're going to link up and haul us back!'

'I think not,' said Mr Wonka. 'Don't you remember what happens when a Knid enters the Earth's atmosphere at high speed? He gets red-hot. He burns away in a long fiery trail. He becomes a shooting Knid. Soon these dirty beasts will start popping like popcorn!'

As they streaked on downward, sparks began to fly off the sides of the Elevator. The glass glowed pink, then red, then scarlet. Sparks also began to fly on the long chain of Knids, and the leading Knid in the chain started to shine like a red-hot poker. So did all the others. So did the great slimy brute coiled around the Elevator itself. This one, in fact, was trying frantically to uncoil itself and get away, but it was having trouble untying the knot, and in another ten seconds it began to sizzle. Inside the Elevator they could actually hear it sizzling. It made a noise like bacon frying. And exactly the same sort of thing was happening to the other one thousand Knids in the chain. The tremendous heat was simply sizzling them up. They were red-hot, every one of them. Then suddenly, they became white-hot and they gave out a dazzling white light.

'They're shooting Knids!' cried Charlie.

'What a splendid sight,' said Mr Wonka. 'It's better than fireworks.'

In a few seconds more, the Knids had blown away in a

cloud of ashes and it was all over. 'We've done it!' cried Mr Wonka. 'They've been roasted to a crisp! They've been frizzled to a fritter! We're saved!'

'What do you mean saved?' said Grandma Josephine. 'We'll all be frizzled ourselves if this goes on any longer! We'll be barbecued like beefsteaks! Look at that glass! It's hotter than a fizzgig!'

'Have no fears, dear lady,' answered Mr Wonka. 'My Elevator is air-conditioned, ventilated, aerated and automated in every possible way. We're going to be all right now.'

'I haven't the faintest idea what's been going on,' said Mrs Bucket, making one of her rare speeches. 'But whatever it is, I don't like it.'

'Aren't you enjoying it, mother?' Charlie asked her.

'No,' she said. 'I'm not. Nor is your father.'

'What a great sight it is!' said Mr Wonka. 'Just look at the Earth down there, Charlie, getting bigger and bigger!'

'And us going to meet it at two thousand miles an hour!' groaned Grandma Georgina. 'How are you going to slow down, for heaven's sake? You didn't think of that, did you!'

'He's got parachutes,' Charlie told her. 'I'll bet he's got great big parachutes that open just before we hit.'

'*Parachutes!*' said Mr Wonka with contempt. 'Parachutes are only for astronauts and sissies! And anyway, we don't want to *slow down*. We want to *speed up*. I've told you already we've got to be going at an absolutely tremendous speed when we hit. Otherwise we'll never punch our way in through the roof of the Chocolate Factory.'

'How about the Transport Capsule?' Charlie asked anxiously.

'We'll be letting them go in a few seconds now,' Mr

Wonka answered. 'They *do* have parachutes, three of them, to slow them down on the last bit.'

'How do you know we won't land in the Pacific Ocean?' said Grandma Josephine.

'I don't,' said Mr Wonka. 'But we all know how to swim, do we not?'

'This man,' shouted Grandma Josephine, 'is crazy as a crumpet!'

'He's cracked as a crayfish!' cried Grandma Georgina.

Down and down plunged the Great Glass Elevator. Nearer and nearer came the Earth below. Oceans and continents rushed up to meet them, getting bigger every second . . .

'Grandpa Joe, sir! Throw out the rope! Let it go!' ordered Mr Wonka. 'They'll be all right now so long as their parachutes are working.'

'Rope gone!' called out Grandpa Joe, and the huge Transport Capsule, on its own now, began to swing away to one side. Charlie waved to the three astronauts in the front window. None of them waved back. They were still sitting there in a kind of shocked daze, gaping at the old ladies and the old men and the small boy floating about in the Glass Elevator.

'It won't be long now,' said Mr Wonka, reaching for a row of tiny pale blue buttons in one corner. 'We shall soon know whether we are alive or dead. Keep very quiet please for this final bit. I have to concentrate awfully hard, otherwise we'll come down in the wrong place.'

They plunged into a thick bank of cloud and for ten seconds they could see nothing. When they came out of the cloud, the Transport Capsule had disappeared, and the Earth was very close, and there was only a great spread of land

beneath them with mountains and forests ... then fields
and trees ... then a small town.

'There it is!' shouted Mr Wonka. 'My Chocolate Factory!
My beloved Chocolate Factory!'

'You mean *Charlie's* Chocolate Factory,' said Grandpa
Joe.

'That's *right*!' said Mr Wonka, addressing Charlie. 'I'd
clean forgotten! I do apologize to you, my dear boy! Of
course it's yours! And here we go!'

Through the glass floor of the Elevator, Charlie caught a
quick glimpse of the huge red roof and the tall chimneys of
the giant factory. They were plunging straight down on to
it.

'Hold your breath!' shouted Mr Wonka. 'Hold your nose!
Fasten your seat-belts and say your prayers! We're going
through the roof!'

Back to the Chocolate Factory

And then the noise of splintering wood and broken glass
and absolute darkness and the most awful crunching
sounds as the Elevator rushed on and on, smashing
everything before it.

All at once, the crashing noises stopped and the ride
became smoother and the Elevator seemed to be travelling
on guides or rails, twisting and turning like a roller-coaster.
And when the lights came on, Charlie suddenly realized
that for the last few seconds he hadn't been floating at all.
He had been standing normally on the floor. Mr Wonka
was on the floor, too, and so was Grandpa Joe and Mr and
Mrs Bucket and also the big bed. As for Grandma Josephine,
Grandma Georgina and Grandpa George, they must have
fallen right back on to the bed because they were now all
three on top of it and scrabbling to get under the blanket.

'We're through!' yelled Mr Wonka. 'We've done it! We're
in!' Grandpa Joe grabbed him by the hand and said, 'Well
done, sir! How splendid! What a magnificent job!'

'Where in the world are we now?' said Mrs Bucket.

'We're back, mother!' Charlie cried. 'We're in the Chocolate Factory!'

'I'm very glad to hear it,' said Mrs Bucket. 'But didn't we come rather a long way round?'

'We had to,' said Mr Wonka, 'to avoid the traffic.'

'I have never met a man,' said Grandma Georgina, 'who talks so much absolute nonsense!'

'A little nonsense now and then, is relished by the wisest men,' Mr Wonka said.

'Why don't you pay some attention to where this crazy Elevator's going!' shouted Grandma Josephine. 'And stop footling about!'

'A little footling round about, will stop you going up the spout,' said Mr Wonka.

'What did I tell you!' cried Grandma Georgina. 'He's round the twist! He's bogged as a beetle! He's dotty as a dingbat! He's got rats in the roof! I want to go home!'

'Too late,' said Mr Wonka. 'We're there!' The Elevator stopped. The doors opened and Charlie found himself looking out once again at the great Chocolate Room with the chocolate river and the chcocolate waterfall, where everything was eatable – the trees, the leaves, the grass, the pebbles and even the rocks. And there to meet them were hundreds and hundreds of tiny Oompa-Loompas, all waving and cheering. It was a sight that took one's breath away. Even Grandma Georgina was stunned into silence for a few seconds. But not for long. 'Who in the world are all those peculiar little men?' she said.

'They're Oompa-Loompas,' Charlie told her. 'They're wonderful. You'll love them.'

'Ssshh!' said Grandpa Joe. 'Listen, Charlie! The drums are starting up! They're going to sing.'

> *'Alleluia!'* sang the Oompa-Loompas.
> *'Oh alleluia and hooray!*
> *Our Willy Wonka's back today!*
> *We thought you'd never make it home!*
> *We thought you'd left us all alone!*
> *We knew that you would have to face*
> *Some frightful creatures up in space.*
> *We even thought we heard the crunch*
> *Of someone eating you for lunch . . .'*

'All right!' shouted Mr Wonka, laughing and raising both hands. 'Thank you for your welcome! Will some of you please help to get this bed out of here!'

Fifty Oompa-Loompas ran forward and pushed the bed with the three old ones in it out of the Elevator. Mr and Mrs Bucket, both looking completely overwhelmed by it all, followed the bed out. Then came Grandpa Joe, Charlie and Mr Wonka.

'Now,' said Mr Wonka, addressing Grandpa George, Grandma Georgina and Grandma Josephine. 'Up you hop out of that bed and let's get cracking. I'm sure you'll all want to lend a hand running the factory.'

'Who, us?' said Grandma Josephine.

'Yes, you,' said Mr Wonka.

'You must be joking,' said Grandma Georgina.

'I never joke,' said Mr Wonka.

'Now just you listen to me, sir!' said old Grandpa George,

sitting up straight in bed. 'You've got us into quite enough
tubbles and trumbles for one day!'

'I've got you out of them, too,' said Mr Wonka proudly.
'And I'm going to get you out of that bed as well, you see if I
don't!'

13

How Wonka-Vite Was Invented

'I haven't been out of this bed in twenty years and I'm not getting out now for anybody!' said Grandma Josephine firmly.

'Nor me,' said Grandma Georgina.

'You were out of it just now, every one of you,' said Mr Wonka.

'That was floating,' said Grandpa George. 'We couldn't help it.'

'We never put our feet on the floor,' said Grandma Josephine.

'Try it,' said Mr Wonka. 'You might surprise yourself.'

'Go on, Josie,' said Grandpa Joe. 'Give it a try. I did. It was easy.'

'We're perfectly comfortable where we are, thank you very much,' said Grandma Josephine.

Mr Wonka sighed and shook his head very slowly and very sadly. 'Oh well,' he said, 'so that's that.' He laid his head on one side and gazed thoughtfully at the three old people in the bed, and Charlie, watching him closely, saw those bright little eyes of his beginning to spark and twinkle once again.

Ha-ha, thought Charlie. What's coming now?

'I suppose,' said Mr Wonka, placing the tip of one finger on the point of his nose and pressing gently, 'I suppose ... because this is a very special case ... I suppose I *could* spare you just a tiny little bit of ...' He stopped and shook his head.

'A tiny little bit of what?' said Grandma Josephine sharply.

'No,' said Mr Wonka. 'It's pointless. You seem to have decided to stay in that bed whatever happens. And anyway, the stuff is much too precious to waste. I'm sorry I mentioned it.' He started to walk away.

'Hey!' shouted Grandma Georgina. 'You can't begin something and not go on with it! *What* is too precious to waste?'

Mr Wonka stopped. Slowly he turned around. He looked long and hard at the three old people in the bed. They looked back at him, waiting. He kept silent a little longer, allowing their curiosity to grow. The Oompa-Loompas stood absolutely still behind him, watching.

'What is this thing you're talking about?' said Grandma Georgina.

'Get on with it, for heaven's sake!' said Grandma Josephine.

'Very well,' Mr Wonka said at last. 'I'll tell you. And listen carefully because this could change your whole lives. It could even change *you*.'

'I don't want to be *changed*!' shouted Grandma Georgina.

'May I go on, madam? Thank you. Not long ago, I was fooling about in my Inventing Room, stirring stuff around and mixing things up the way I do every afternoon at four o'clock, when suddenly I found I had made something that seemed very unusual. This thing I had made kept changing colour as I looked at it, and now and again it gave a little jump, it actually jumped up in the air, as though it were alive. *"What have we here?"* I cried, and I rushed it quickly to the Testing Room and gave some to the Oompa-Loompa who was on duty there at the time. The result was immediate! It was flabbergasting! It was unbelievable! It was also rather unfortunate.'

'What happened?' said Grandma Georgina, sitting up.

'What indeed,' said Mr Wonka.

'Answer her question,' said Grandma Josephine. 'What happened to the Oompa-Loompa?'

'Ah,' said Mr Wonka, 'yes ... well ... there's no point in crying over spilled milk, is there? I realized, you see, that I had stumbled upon a new and tremendously powerful vitamin, and I also knew that if only I could make it safe, if only I could stop it doing to others what it did to that Oompa-Loompa ...'

'What *did* it do to that Oompa-Loompa?' said Grandma Georgina sternly.

'The older I get, the deafer I become,' said Mr Wonka. 'Do please raise your voice a trifle next time. Thank you so much. Now then. I simply *had* to find a way of making this stuff safe, so that people could take it without ... er ...'

'Without *what?*' snapped Grandma Georgina.

'Without a leg to stand on,' said Mr Wonka. 'So I rolled up my sleeves and set to work once more in the Inventing Room. I mixed and I mixed. I must have tried just about every mixture under the moon. By the way, there is a little hole in one wall of the Inventing Room which connects directly with the Testing Room next door, so I was able all the time to keep passing stuff through for testing to whichever brave volunteer happened to be on duty. Well, the first few weeks were pretty depressing and we won't talk about them. Let me tell you instead what happened on the one hundred and thirty-second day of my labours. That morning, I had changed the mixture drastically, and this time the little pill I produced at the end of it all was not nearly so active or alive as the others had been. It kept changing colour, yes, but only from lemon-yellow to blue, then back to yellow again. And when I placed it on the palm of my hand, it didn't jump about like a grasshopper. It only quivered, and then ever so slightly.

'I ran to the hole in the wall that led to the Testing Room. A very old Oompa-Loompa was on duty there that morning. He was a bald, wrinkled, toothless old fellow. He was in a wheel-chair. He had been in the wheel-chair for at least fifteen years.

'"This is test number one hundred and thirty-two!" I said, chalking it up on the board.

'I handed him the pill. He looked at it nervously. I couldn't blame him for being a bit jittery after what had happened to the other one hundred and thirty-one volunteers.'

'What *had* happened to them?' shouted Grandma Georgina. 'Why don't you answer the question instead of skidding around it on two wheels?'

'Who knows the way out of a rose?' said Mr Wonka. 'So this brave old Oompa-Loompa took the pill and, with the help of a little water, he gulped it down. And then, suddenly, the most amazing thing happened. Before my very eyes, queer little changes began taking place in the way he looked. A moment earlier, he had been practically bald, with just a fringe of snowy white hair around the sides and the back of his head. But now the fringe of white hair was turning gold and all over the top of his head new gold hair was beginning to sprout, like grass. In less than half a minute, he had grown a splendid new crop of long golden hair. At the same time, many of the wrinkles started disappearing from his face, not all of them, but about half, enough to make him look a good deal younger, and all of this must have given him a nice tickly feeling because he started grinning at me, then laughing, and as soon as he opened his mouth, I saw the strangest sight of all. Teeth were growing up out from those old toothless gums, good white teeth, and they were coming up so fast I could actually see them getting bigger and bigger.

'I was too flabbergasted to speak. I just stood there with my head poking through the hole in the wall, staring at the little Oompa-Loompa. I saw him slowly lifting himself out of his wheel-chair. He tested his legs on the ground. He stood up. He walked a few paces. Then he looked up at me and his face was bright. His eyes were huge and bright as two stars.

'"Look at me," he said softly. "I'm walking! It's a miracle!"

'"It's Wonka-Vite!" I said. "The great rejuvenator. It makes you young again. How old do you feel now?"

'He thought carefully about this question, then he said, "I feel almost exactly how I felt when I was fifty years old."

'"How old were you just now, before you took the Wonka-Vite?" I asked him.

'"Seventy last birthday," he answered.

' "That means," I said, "it has made you twenty years younger."

'"It has, it has!" he cried, delighted. "I feel as frisky as a froghopper!"

'"Not frisky enough," I told him. "Fifty is still pretty old. Let us see if I can't help you a bit more. Stay right where you are. I'll be back in a twink."

'I ran to my work-bench and began to make one more pill of Wonka-Vite, using exactly the same mixture as before.

'"Swallow this," I said, passing the second pill through the hatch. There was no hesitating this time. Eagerly, he popped it into his mouth and chased it down with a drink of water. And behold, within half a minute, another twenty years had fallen away from his face and body and he was now a slim and sprightly young Oompa-Loompa of thirty. He gave a whoop of joy and started dancing around the room, leaping high in the air and coming down on his toes. "Are you happy?" I asked him.

'"I'm ecstatic!" he cried, jumping up and down. "I'm

happy as a horse in a hay-field!" He ran out of the Testing Room to show himself off to his family and friends.

'Thus was Wonka-Vite invented!' said Mr Wonka. 'And thus was it made safe for all to use!'

'Why don't you use it yourself, then?' said Grandma Georgina. 'You told Charlie you were getting too old to run the factory, so why don't you just take a couple of pills and get forty years younger? Tell me that?'

'Anyone can ask questions,' said Mr Wonka. 'It's the answers that count. Now then, if the three of you in the bed would care to try a dose . . .'

'Just one minute!' said Grandma Josephine, sitting up straight. 'First I'd like to take a look at this seventy-year-old Oompa-Loompa who is now back to thirty!'

Mr Wonka flicked his fingers. A tiny Oompa-Loompa, looking young and perky, ran forward out of the crowd and did a marvellous little dance in front of the three old people in the big bed. 'Two weeks ago, he was seventy years old and in a wheel-chair!' Mr Wonka said proudly. 'And look at him now!'

'The drums, Charlie!' said Grandpa Joe. 'Listen! They're starting up again!'

Far away down on the bank of the chocolate river, Charlie could see the Oompa-Loompa band striking up once more. There were twenty Oompa-Loompas in the band, each with an enormous drum twice as tall as himself, and they were beating a slow mysterious rhythm that soon had all the other hundreds of Oompa-Loompas swinging and swaying from side to side in a kind of trance. They then began to chant:

How Wonka-Vite Was Invented

'If you are old and have the shakes,
If all your bones are full of aches,
If you can hardly walk at all,
If living drives you up the wall,
If you're a grump and full of spite,
If you're a human parasite,
THEN WHAT YOU NEED IS WONKA-VITE!
Your eyes will shine, your hair will grow,
Your face and skin will start to glow,
Your rotten teeth will all drop out
And in their place new teeth will sprout.
Those rolls of fat around your hips
Will vanish, and your wrinkled lips
Will get so soft and rosy-pink
That all the boys will smile and wink
And whisper secretly that this
Is just the girl they want to kiss!
But wait! For that is not the most
Important thing of which to boast.
Good looks you'll have, we've told you so,
But looks aren't everything, you know.
Each pill, as well, to you will give
AN EXTRA TWENTY YEARS TO LIVE!
So come, old friends, and do what's right!
Let's make your lives as bright as bright!
Let's take a dose of this delight!
This heavenly magic dynamite!
You can't go wrong, you must go right!
IT'S WILLY WONKA'S WONKA-VITE!'

14

Recipe for Wonka-Vite

'Here it is!' cried Mr Wonka, standing at the end of the bed and holding high in one hand a little bottle. 'The most valuable bottle of pills in the world! And that, by the way,' he said, giving Grandma Georgina a saucy glance, 'is why I haven't taken any myself. They are far too valuable to waste on me.'

He held the bottle out over the bed. The three old ones sat up and stretched their scrawny necks, trying to catch a glimpse of the pills inside. Charlie and Grandpa Joe also came forward to look. So did Mr and Mrs Bucket. The label said:

WONKA-VITE

Each pill will make you *younger* by exactly 20 years

CAUTION!

Do not take more than the amount recommended by Mr. Wonka

They could all see the pills through the glass. They were brilliant yellow, shimmering and quivering inside the bottle. Vibrating is perhaps a better word. They were vibrating so rapidly that each pill became a blur and you couldn't see its shape. You could only see its colour. You got the impression that there was something very small but incredibly powerful, something not quite of this world, locked up inside them and fighting to get out.

'They're wriggling,' said Grandma Georgina. 'I don't like things that wriggle. How do we know they won't go on wriggling inside us after we've swallowed them? Like those Mexican jumping beans of Charlie's I swallowed a couple of years back. You remember that, Charlie?'

'I told you not to eat them, Grandma.'

'They went on jumping about inside me for a month,' said Grandma Georgina. 'I couldn't sit still!'

'If I'm going to eat one of those pills, I jolly well want to know what's in it first,' said Grandma Josephine.

'I don't blame you,' said Mr Wonka. 'But the recipe is extremely complicated. Wait a minute . . . I've got it written down somewhere . . .' He started digging around in the pockets of his coat-tails. 'I know it's here somewhere,' he said. 'I can't have lost it. I keep all my most valuable and important things in these pockets. The trouble is, there's such a lot of them . . .' He started emptying the pockets and placing the contents on the bed – a homemade catapult . . . a yo-yo . . . a trick fried-egg made of rubber . . . a slice of salami . . . a tooth with a filling in it . . . a stinkbomb . . . a packet of itching-powder . . . 'It must be here, it *must* be, it must,' he kept muttering. 'I put it away so carefully . . . Ah! *Here* it is!' He unfolded a crumpled piece of paper, smoothed it out, held it up and began to read as follows:

RECIPE FOR MAKING WONKA-VITE

Take a block of finest chocolate weighing one ton (or twenty sackfuls of broken chocolate, whichever is the easier). Place chocolate in very large cauldron and melt over red-hot furnace. When melted, lower the heat slightly so as not to burn the chocolate, but keep it boiling. Now add the following, in precisely the order given, stirring well all the time and allowing each item to dissolve before adding the next:

> THE HOOF OF A MANTICORE
> THE TRUNK (AND THE SUITCASE) OF AN
> ELEPHANT
> THE YOLKS OF THREE EGGS FROM A
> WHIFFLE-BIRD
> A WART FROM A WART-HOG
> THE HORN OF A COW (IT MUST BE A LOUD
> HORN)
> THE FRONT TAIL OF A COCKATRICE
> SIX OUNCES OF SPRUNGE FROM A YOUNG
> SLIMESCRAPER
> TWO HAIRS (AND ONE RABBIT) FROM THE
> HEAD OF A HIPPOCAMPUS
> THE BEAK OF A RED-BREASTED
> WILBATROSS
> A CORN FROM THE TOE OF A UNICORN
> THE FOUR TENTACLES OF A QUADROPUS
> THE HIP (AND THE PO AND THE POT) OF A
> HIPPOPOTAMUS
> THE SNOUT OF A PROGHOPPER
> A MOLE FROM A MOLE
> THE HIDE (AND THE SEEK) OF A
> SPOTTED WHANGDOODLE

THE WHITES OF TWELVE EGGS FROM A
    TREE-SQUEAK
THE THREE FEET OF A SNOZZWANGER (IF
    YOU CAN'T GET THREE FEET, ONE YARD
    WILL DO)
THE SQUARE-ROOT OF A SOUTH AMERICAN
    ABACUS
THE FANGS OF A VIPER (IT MUST BE A
    VINDSCREEN VIPER)
THE CHEST (AND THE DRAWERS) OF A
    WILD GROUT

When all the above are thoroughly dissolved, boil for a further twenty-seven days but do not stir. At the end of this time, all liquid will have evaporated and there will be left in the bottom of the cauldron only a hard brown lump about the size of a football. Break this open with a hammer and in the very centre of it you will find a small round pill. This pill is WONKA-VITE.

15

Good-bye Georgina

When Mr Wonka had finished reading the recipe, he carefully folded the paper and put it back into his pocket. 'A very, *very* complicated mixture,' he said. 'So can you wonder it took me so long to get it just right?' He held the bottle up high and gave it a little shake and the pills rattled loudly inside it, like glass beads. 'Now, sir,' he said, offering the bottle first to Grandpa George. 'Will you take one pill or two?'

'Will you solemnly swear,' said Grandpa George, 'that it will do what you say it will and nothing else?'

Mr Wonka placed his free hand on his heart. 'I swear it,' he said.

Charlie edged forward. Grandpa Joe came with him. The two of them always stayed close together. 'Please excuse me for asking,' Charlie said, 'but are you really absolutely sure you've got it *quite right?*'

'Whatever makes you ask a funny question like that?' said Mr Wonka.

'I was thinking of the gum you gave to Violet Beauregarde,' Charlie said.

'So *that's* what's bothering you!' cried Mr Wonka. 'But

don't you understand, my dear boy, that I never did give that gum to Violet? She snatched it without permission. And I shouted, "Stop! Don't! Spit it out!" But the silly girl took no notice of me. Now Wonka-Vite is altogether different. I am *offering* these pills to your grandparents. I am *recommending* them. And when taken according to my instructions, they are as safe as sugar-candy!'

'Of course they are!' cried Mr Bucket. 'What are you waiting for, all of you!' An extraordinary change had come over Mr Bucket since he had entered the Chocolate Room. Normally he was a pretty timid sort of person. A lifetime devoted to screwing caps on to the tops of toothpaste tubes in a toothpaste factory had turned him into a rather shy and quiet man. But the sight of the marvellous Chocolate Factory had made his spirits soar. What is more, this business of the pills seemed to have given him a terrific kick. 'Listen!' he cried, going up to the edge of the bed. 'Mr Wonka's offering you a new life! Grab it while you can!'

'It's a delicious sensation,' Mr Wonka said. 'And it's very quick. You lose a year a second. Exactly one year falls away from you every second that goes by!' He stepped forward and placed the bottle of pills gently in the middle of the bed. 'So here you are, my dears,' he said. 'Help yourselves!'

'*Come on!*' cried all the Oompa-Loompas together.

> '*Come on, old friends, and do what's right!*
> *Come make your lives as bright as bright!*
> *Just take a dose of this delight!*
> *This heavenly magic dynamite!*
> *You can't go wrong, you must go right!*
> *IT'S WILLY WONKA'S WONKA-VITE!'*

This was too much for the old people in the bed. All three

of them made a dive for the bottle. Six scrawny hands shot out and started scrabbling to get hold of it. Grandma Georgina got it. She gave a grunt of triumph and unscrewed the cap and tipped all the little brilliant yellow pills on to the blanket on her lap. She cupped her hands around them so the others couldn't reach out and snatch them. 'All right!' she shouted excitedly, counting them quickly. 'There's twelve pills here! That's six for me and three each for you!'

'Hey! That's not fair!' shrilled Grandma Josephine. 'It's four for each of us!'

'Four each is right!' cried Grandpa George. 'Come on, Georgina! Hand over my share!'

Mr Wonka shrugged his shoulders and turned his back on them. He hated squabbles. He hated it when people got grabby and selfish. Let them fight it out among themselves, he thought, and he walked away. He walked slowly down toward the chocolate waterfall. It was an unhappy truth, he told himself, that nearly all people in the world behave badly when there is something really big at stake. Money is the thing they fight over most. But these pills were bigger than money. They could do things for you no amount of money could ever do. They were worth at least a million dollars a pill. He knew plenty of very rich men who would gladly pay that much in order to become twenty years younger. He reached the river-bank below the waterfall and he stood there gazing at the great gush and splash of melted chocolate pouring down. He had hoped the noise of the waterfall would drown the arguing voices of the old grandparents in the bed, but it didn't. Even with his back to them, he still couldn't help hearing most of what they were saying.

'I got them first!' Grandma Georgina was shouting. 'So they're mine to share out!'

'Oh no they're not!' shrilled Grandma Josephine. 'He didn't give them to you! He gave them to all three of us!'

'I want my share and no one's going to stop me getting it!' yelled Grandpa George. 'Come on, woman! Hand them over!'

Then came the voice of Grandpa Joe, cutting in sternly through the rabble. 'Stop this at once!' he ordered. 'All three of you! You're behaving like savages!'

'You keep out of this, Joe, and mind your own business!' said Grandma Josephine.

'Now you be careful, Josie,' Grandpa Joe went on. 'Four is too many for one person anyway.'

'That's right,' Charlie said. '*Please* Grandma, why don't you just take one or two each like Mr Wonka said, and that'll leave some for Grandpa Joe and mother and father.'

'Yes!' cried Mr Bucket. 'I'd love one!'

'Oh, wouldn't it be wonderful,' said Mrs Bucket, 'to be twenty years younger and not have aching feet any more! Couldn't you spare just one for each of us, mother?'

'I'm afraid not,' said Grandma Georgina. 'These pills are specially reserved for us three in the bed. Mr Wonka said so!'

'I want my share!' shouted Grandpa George. 'Come on, Georgina! Dish them out!'

'Hey, let me go, you brute!' cried Grandma Georgina. 'You're hurting me! Ow! ... ALL RIGHT! *All right! I'll* share them out if you'll stop twisting my arm ... That's better ... Here's four for Josephine ... and four for George ... and four for me.'

'Good,' said Grandpa George. 'Now who's got some water?'

Without looking around, Mr Wonka knew that three Oompa-Loompas would be running to the bed with three glasses of water. Oompa-Loompas were always ready to help. There was a brief pause, and then:

'Well, here goes!' cried Grandpa George.

'Young and beautiful, that's what I'll be!' shouted Grandma Josephine.

'Farewell, old age!' cried Grandma Georgina. 'All together now! Down the hatch!'

Then there was silence. Mr Wonka was itching to turn around and look, but he forced himself to wait. Out of the corner of one eye he could see a group of Oompa-Loompas, all motionless, their eyes fixed intently in the direction of the big bed over by the Elevator. Then Charlie's voice broke the silence. '*Wow!*' he was shouting. 'Just look at *that*! It's . . . it's incredible!'

'I can't believe it!' Grandpa Joe was yelling. 'They're getting younger and younger! They really are! Just *look* at Grandpa George's hair!'

'And his teeth!' cried Charlie. 'Hey, Grandpa! You're getting lovely white teeth all over again!'

'Mother!' shouted Mrs Bucket to Grandma Georgina. 'Oh, mother! You're beautiful! You're so young! And just *look* at dad!' she went on, pointing at Grandpa George. 'Isn't he handsome!'

'What's it feel like, Josie?' asked Grandpa Joe excitedly. 'Tell us what it feels like to be back to thirty again! . . . Wait a minute! You look younger than thirty! You can't be a day more than twenty now! . . . But that's enough, isn't it! . . . I should stop there if I were you! Twenty's quite young enough! . . .'

Mr Wonka shook his head sadly and passed a hand over his eyes. Had you been standing very close to him you would have heard him murmuring softly under his breath, 'Oh, deary deary me, here we go again . . .'

'*Mother!*' cried Mrs Bucket, and now there was a shrill note of alarm in her voice. 'Why don't you stop, mother! You're going too far! You're way under twenty! You can't be more than fifteen! . . . You're . . . you're . . . you're ten . . . *you're getting smaller, mother!*'

'Josie!' shouted Grandpa Joe. 'Hey Josie! Don't do it, Josie! You're shrinking! You're a little girl! Stop her, somebody! Quick!'

'They're *all* going too far!' cried Charlie.

'They took too much,' said Mr Bucket.

'Mother's shrinking faster than any of them!' wailed Mrs Bucket. '*Mother! Can't you hear me, mother? Can't you stop?*'

'My heavens, isn't it quick!' said Mr Bucket, who seemed to be the only one enjoying it. 'It really is a year a second!'

'But they've hardly got any more years left!' wailed Grandpa Joe.

'Mother's no more than four now!' Mrs Bucket cried out. 'She's three . . . two . . . one . . . *Gracious me!* What's happening to her! Where's she gone? Mother? Georgina! Where are you? Mr Wonka! Come quickly! Come here, Mr Wonka! Something frightful's happened! Something's gone wrong! My old mother's disappeared!'

Mr Wonka sighed and turned around and walked slowly and quite calmly back toward the bed.

'*Where's my mother?*' bawled Mrs Bucket.

Look at Josephine!' cried Grandpa Joe. 'Just look at her! I ask you!'

Mr Wonka looked first at Grandma Josephine. She was sitting in the middle of the huge bed, bawling her head off 'Wa! Wa! Wa!' she said. 'Wa! Wa! Wa! Wa! Wa!'

'She's a screaming baby!' cried Grandpa Joe. 'I've got a screaming baby for a wife!'

'The other one's Grandpa George!' Mr Bucket said, smiling happily. 'The slightly bigger one there crawling around. He's my wife's father.'

'That's right! He's my father!' wailed Mrs Bucket. 'And where's Georgina, my old mother? She's vanished! She's nowhere Mr Wonka! She's absolutely nowhere! I saw her getting smaller and smaller and in the end she got so small she just disappeared into thin air! What I want to know is where's she *gone* to! And how in the world are we going to get her back!'

'Ladies and gentlemen!' said Mr Wonka, coming up close and raising both hands for silence. '*Please*, I beg you, do not ruffle yourselves! There's nothing to worry about . . .'

'You call it nothing!' cried poor Mrs Bucket. 'When my old mother's gone down the drain and my father's a howling baby . . .'

116

'A lovely baby,' said Mr Wonka.

'I quite agree,' said Mr Bucket.

'What about my Josie?' cried Grandpa Joe.

'What *about* her?' said Mr Wonka.

'Well . . .'

'A great improvement, sir,' said Mr Wonka, 'don't you agree?'

'Oh, yes!' said Grandpa Joe. 'I mean *NO!* What am I saying. She's a howling baby!'

'But in perfect health,' said Mr Wonka. 'May I ask you, sir, how many pills she took?'

'Four,' said Grandpa Joe glumly. 'They all took four.'

Mr Wonka made a wheezing noise in his throat and a look of great sorrow came over his face. 'Why oh why can't people be more sensible?' he said sadly. 'Why don't they *listen* to me when I tell them something? I explained very carefully beforehand that each pill makes the taker exactly twenty years younger. So if Grandma Josephine took four of them, she automatically became younger by four times twenty, which is . . . wait a minute now . . . four twos are eight . . . add a nought . . . that's eighty . . . so she automatically became younger by eighty years. How old, sir, was your wife, if I may ask, before this happened?'

'She was eighty last birthday,' Grandpa Joe answered. 'She was eighty and three months.'

'There you are, then!' cried Mr Wonka, flashing a happy smile. 'The Wonka-Vite worked perfectly! She is now precisely three months old! And a plumper rosier infant I've never set eyes on!'

'Nor me,' said Mr Bucket. 'She'd win a prize in any baby competition.'

'*First* prize,' said Mr Wonka.

'Cheer up, Grandpa,' said Charlie, taking the old man's hand in his. 'Don't be sad. She's a beautiful baby.'

'Madam,' said Mr Wonka, turning to Mrs Bucket. 'How old, may I ask, was Grandpa George, your father?'

'Eighty-one,' wailed Mrs Bucket. 'He was eighty-one exactly.'

'Which makes him a great big bouncing one-year-old boy now,' said Mr Wonka happily.

'How splendid!' said Mr Bucket to his wife. 'You'll be the first person in the world to change her father's nappies!'

'He can change his own rotten nappies!' said Mrs Bucket. 'What I want to know is *where's my mother? Where's* Grandma *Georgina?*'

'Ah-ha,' said Mr Wonka. 'Oh-ho... Yes, indeed... Where oh where has Georgina gone? How old, please, was the lady in question?'

'Seventy-eight,' Mrs Bucket told him.

'Well, of *course!*' laughed Mr Wonka. 'That explains it!'

'What explains what?' snapped Mrs Bucket.

'My dear madam,' said Mr Wonka. 'If she was only seventy-eight and she took enough Wonka-Vite to make her eighty years younger, then naturally she's vanished. She's bitten off more than she could chew! She's taken off more years than she had!'

'Explain yourself,' said Mrs Bucket.

'Simple arithmetic,' said Mr Wonka. 'Subtract eighty from seventy-eight and what do you get?'

'Minus two!' said Charlie.

'Hooray!' said Mr Bucket. 'My mother-in-law's minus two years old!'

'Impossible!' said Mrs Bucket.

'It's true,' said Mr Wonka.

'And where is she now, may I ask?' said Mrs Bucket.

'That's a good question,' said Mr Wonka. 'A very good question. Yes, indeed. Where is she now?'

'You don't have the foggiest idea, do you?'

'Of course I do,' said Mr Wonka. 'I know exactly where she is.'

'Then tell me!'

'You must try to understand,' said Mr Wonka, 'that if she is now minus two, she's got to add two more years before she can start again from nought. She's got to wait it out.'

'Where does she wait?' said Mrs Bucket.

'In the Waiting Room, of course,' said Mr Wonka.

BOOM!-BOOM! said the drums of the Oompa-Loompa band. *BOOM-BOOM! BOOM-BOOM!* And all the Oompa-Loompas, all the hundreds of them standing there in the Chocolate Room began to sway and hop and dance to the rhythm of the music. 'Attention, please!' they sang.

> *'Attention, please! Attention, please!*
> *Don't dare to talk! Don't dare to sneeze!*
> *Don't doze or daydream! Stay awake!*
> *Your health, your very life's at stake!*
> *Ho-ho, you say, they can't mean me.*
> *Ha-ha, we answer, wait and see.*
>
> *Did any of you ever meet*
> *A child called Goldie Pinklesweet?*
> *Who on her seventh birthday went*
> *To stay with Granny down in Kent.*
> *At lunchtime on the second day*
> *Of dearest little Goldie's stay,*

Granny announced, "I'm going down
To do some shopping in the town."
(D'you know why Granny didn't tell
The child to come along as well?
She's going to the nearest inn
To buy herself a double gin.)

So out she creeps. She shuts the door.
And Goldie, after making sure
That she is really by herself,
Goes quickly to the medicine shelf,
And there, her little greedy eyes
See pills of every shape and size,
Such fascinating colours too –
Some green, some pink, some brown, some blue.
'All right,' she says, 'let's try the brown.'
She takes one pill and gulps it down.
'Yum-yum!' she cries. 'Hooray! What fun!
They're chocolate-coated, every one!'
She gobbles five, she gobbles ten,
She stops her gobbling only when
The last pill's gone. There are no more.
Slowly she rises from the floor.
She stops. She hiccups. Dear, oh dear,
She starts to feel a trifle queer.

You see, how could young Goldie know,
For nobody had told her so,
That Grandmama, her old relation,
Suffered from frightful constipation.
This meant that every night she'd give
Herself a powerful laxative,

And all the medicines that she'd bought
Were naturally of this sort.
The pink and red and blue and green
Were all extremely strong and mean.
But far more fierce and meaner still,
Was Granny's little chocolate pill.
Its blast effect was quite uncanny.
It used to shake up even Granny.
In point of fact she did not dare
To use them more than twice a year.
So can you wonder little Goldie
Began to feel a wee bit mouldy?

Inside her tummy, something stirred.
A funny gurgling sound was heard,
And then, oh dear, from deep within,
The ghastly rumbling sounds begin!
They rumbilate and roar and boom!
They bounce and echo round the room!
The floorboards shake and from the wall
Some bits of paint and plaster fall.
Explosions, whistles, awful bangs
Were followed by the loudest clangs.
(A man next door was heard to say,
'A thunderstorm is on the way.')
But on and on the rumbling goes.
A window cracks, a lamp-bulb blows.
Young Goldie clutched herself and cried,
'There's something wrong with my inside!'
This was, we very greatly fear,
The understatement of the year.
For wouldn't any child feel crummy,
With loud explosions in her tummy?

Granny, at half past two, came in,
Weaving a little from the gin,
But even so she quickly saw
The empty bottle on the floor.
'My precious laxatives!' she cried.
'I don't feel well,' the girl replied.
Angrily Grandma shook her head.
'I'm really not surprised,' she said.
'Why can't you leave my pills alone?'
With that, she grabbed the telephone
And shouted, 'Listen, send us quick
An ambulance! A child is sick!
It's number fifty, Fontwell Road!
Come fast! I think she might explode!'

We're sure you do not wish to hear
About the hospital and where
They did a lot of horrid things
With stomach-pumps and rubber rings.
Let's answer what you want to know;
Did Goldie live or did she go?
The doctors gathered round her bed,
'There's really not much hope' they said.
'She's going, going, gone!' they cried.
'She's had her chips! She's dead! She's dead!'
'I'm not so sure,' the child replied.
And all at once she opened wide
Her great big bluish eyes and sighed,
And gave the anxious docs a wink,
And said, 'I'll be okay, I think.'

So Goldie lived and back she went
At first to Granny's place in Kent.
Her father came the second day
And fetched her in a Chevrolet,
And drove her to their home in Dover.
But Goldie's troubles were not over.
You see, if someone takes enough
Of any highly dangerous stuff,
One will invariably find
Some traces of it left behind.
It pains us greatly to relate
That Goldie suffered from this fate.
She'd taken such a massive fill
Of this unpleasant kind of pill,
It got into her blood and bones,
It messed up all her chromosomes,
It made her constantly upset,
And she could never really get
The beastly stuff to go away.
And so the girl was forced to stay
For seven hours every day
Within the everlasting gloom
Of what we call The Ladies Room.
And after all, the W.C.
Is not the gayest place to be.
So now, before it is too late,
Take heed of Goldie's dreadful fate.
And seriously, all jokes apart,
Do promise us across your heart
That you will never help yourself
To medicine from the medicine shelf.'

16

Vita-Wonk and Minusland

'It's up to you, Charlie my boy,' said Mr Wonka. 'It's your factory. Shall we let your Grandma Georgina wait it out for the next two years or shall we try to bring her back right now?'

'You don't really mean you might be able to bring her back?' cried Charlie.

'There's no harm in trying, is there ... if that's the way you want it?'

'Oh yes! Of course I do! For mother's sake especially! Can't you see how sad she is!'

Mrs Bucket was sitting on the edge of the big bed, dabbing her eyes with a hanky. 'My poor old mum,' she kept saying. 'She's minus two and I won't see her again for months and months and months – if ever at all!' Behind her, Grandpa Joe, with the help of an Oompa-Loompa, was feeding his three-months-old wife, Grandma Josephine, from a bottle. Alongside them, Mr Bucket was spooning something called 'Wonka's Squdgemallow Baby Food' into one-year-old Grandpa George's mouth but mostly all over his chin and chest. 'Big deal!' he was muttering angrily. 'What a lousy rotten rotten this is! They tell me I'm going to the Chocolate

Factory to have a good time and I finish up being a mother to my father-in-law.'

'Everything's under control, Charlie,' said Mr Wonka, surveying the scene, 'They're doing fine. They don't need us here. Come along! We're off to hunt for Grandma!' He caught Charlie by the arm and went dancing towards the open door of the Great Glass Elevator. 'Hurry up, my dear boy, hurry up!' he cried. 'We've got to hustle if we're going to get there before!'

'Before *what*, Mr Wonka?'

'Before she gets subtracted of course! All Minuses are subtracted! Don't you know any arithmetic at all?'

They were in the Elevator now and Mr Wonka was searching among the hundreds of buttons for the one he wanted. '*Here* we are!' he said, placing his finger delicately upon a tiny ivory button on which it said 'MINUSLAND'.

The doors slid shut. And then, with a fearful whistling whirring sound the great machine leaped away to the right. Charlie grabbed Mr Wonka's legs and held on for dear life. Mr Wonka pulled a jump-seat out of the wall and said, 'Sit down Charlie, quick, and strap yourself in tight! This journey's going to be rough and choppy!' There were straps on either side of the seat and Charlie buckled himself firmly in. Mr Wonka pulled out a second seat for himself and did the same.

'We are going a long way down,' he said. 'Oh, such a long way down we are going.'

The Elevator was gathering speed. It twisted and swerved. It swung sharply to the left, then it went right, then left again, and it was heading downward all the time – down and down and down. 'I only hope,' said Mr Wonka, 'the Oompa-Loompas aren't using the other Elevator today.'

'What other Elevator?' asked Charlie.

'The one that goes the opposite way on the same track as this.'

'Holy snakes, Mr Wonka! You mean we might have a collision?'

'I've always been lucky so far, my boy . . . Hey! Take a look out there! Quick!'

Through the window, Charlie caught a glimpse of what seemed like an enormous quarry with a steep craggy-brown rock-face, and all over the rock-face there were hundreds of Oompa-Loompas working with picks and pneumatic drills.

'Rock-candy,' said Mr Wonka. 'That's the richest deposit of rock-candy in the world.'

The Elevator sped on. 'We're going deeper, Charlie. Deeper and deeper. We're about two hundred thousand feet down already.' Strange sights were flashing by outside, but the Elevator was travelling at such a terrific speed that only occasionally was Charlie able to recognize anything at all. Once, he thought he saw in the distance a cluster of tiny houses shaped like upside-down cups, and there were streets in between the houses and Oompa-Loompas walking in the streets. Another time, as they were passing some sort of a vast red plain dotted with things that looked like oil derricks, he saw a great spout of brown liquid spurting out of the ground high into the air. 'A gusher!' cried Mr Wonka, clapping his hands. 'A whacking great gusher! How splendid! Just when we needed it!'

'A what?' said Charlie.

'We've struck chocolate again, my boy. That'll be a rich new field. Oh, what a beautiful gusher! Just look at it go!'

On they roared, heading downward more steeply than ever now, and hundreds, literally hundreds of astonishing sights kept flashing by outside. There were giant cog-wheels turning and mixers mixing and bubbles bubbling and vast orchards of toffee-apple trees and lakes the size of football grounds filled with blue and gold and green liquid, and everywhere there were Oompa-Loompas!

'You realize,' said Mr Wonka, 'that what you saw earlier on when you went round the factory with all those naughty little children was only a tiny corner of the establishment. It goes down for miles and miles. And as soon as possible I shall show you all the way around slowly and properly. But that will take three weeks. Right now we have other things to think about and I have important things to tell you. Listen carefully to me, Charlie. I must talk fast, for we'll be there in a couple of minutes.

'I suppose you guessed,' Mr Wonka went on, 'what happened to all those Oompa-Loompas in the Testing Room when I was experimenting with Wonka-Vite. Of course you did. They disappeared and became Minuses just like your Grandma Georgina. The recipe was miles too strong. One of them actually became Minus eighty-seven! Imagine that!'

'You mean he's got to wait eighty-seven years before he can come back?' Charlie asked.

'That's what kept bugging me, my boy. After all, one can't allow one's best friends to wait around as miserable Minuses for eighty-seven years . . .'

'And get subtracted as well,' said Charlie. 'That would be frightful.'

'Of course it would, Charlie. So what did I do? "Willy Wonka," I said to myself, "if you can invent Wonka-Vite to make people younger, then surely to goodness you can also invent something else to make people older!"'

'Ah-ha!' cried Charlie. 'I see what you're getting at. Then you could turn the Minuses quickly back into Pluses and bring them home again.'

'Precisely, my dear boy, precisely – always supposing, of course, that I could *find out* where the Minuses had gone to!'

The Elevator plunged on, diving steeply toward the centre of the Earth. All was blackness outside now. There was nothing to be seen.

'So once again,' Mr Wonka went on, 'I rolled up my sleeves and set to work. Once again I squeezed my brain, searching for the new recipe . . . I had to create *age* . . . to make people *old . . . old, older, oldest . . .* "Ha-ha!" I cried, for now the ideas were beginning to come. "What is the oldest living thing in the world? What lives longer than anything else?" '

'A tree,' Charlie said.

'Right you are, Charlie! But what kind of a tree? Not the Douglas Fir. Not the Oak. Not the Cedar. No no, my boy. It is a tree called the Bristlecone Pine that grows upon the slopes of Wheeler Peak in Nevada, U.S.A. You can find Bristlecone Pines on Wheeler Peak today that are over 4000 years old! This is fact, Charlie. Ask any dendrochronologist you like (and look that word up in the dictionary when you get home, will you please?). So that started me off. I jumped into the Great Glass Elevator and rushed all over the world collecting special items from the oldest living things . . .

A PINT OF SAP FROM A 4000 YEAR OLD
  BRISTLECONE PINE

THE TOE-NAIL CLIPPINGS FROM A 168 YEAR
  OLD RUSSIAN FARMER CALLED PETRO-
  VITCH GREGOROVITCH

AN EGG LAID BY A 200 YEAR OLD TORTOISE
  BELONGING TO THE KING OF TONGA

THE TAIL OF A 51 YEAR OLD HORSE IN
  ARABIA

THE WHISKERS OF A 36 YEAR OLD CAT
  CALLED CRUMPETS

AN OLD FLEA WHICH HAD LIVED ON CRUM-
  PETS FOR 36 YEARS

THE TAIL OF A 207 YEAR OLD GIANT RAT
  FROM TIBET

THE BLACK TEETH OF A 9 7 YEAR OLD GRIM-
ALKIN LIVING IN A CAVE ON MOUNT
POPOCATEPETL
THE KNUCKLEBONES OF A 700 YEAR OLD
CATTALOO FROM PERU...

... All over the world, Charlie, I tracked down very old and ancient animals and took an important little bit of something from each one of them – a hair or an eyebrow or sometimes it was no more than an ounce or two of the jam scraped from between its toes while it was sleeping. I tracked down THE WHISTLE-PIG, THE BOBOLINK, THE SKROCK, THE POLLYFROG, THE GIANT CURLICUE, THE STINGING SLUG AND THE VENOMOUS SQUERKLE who can spit poison right into your eye from fifty yards away. But there's no time to tell you about them all now, Charlie. Let me just say quickly that in the end, after lots of boiling and bubbling and mixing and testing in my Inventing Room, I produced one tiny cupful of oily black liquid and gave four drops of it to a brave twenty-year-old Oompa-Loompa volunteer to see what happened.'

'What did happen?' Charlie asked.

'It was fantastic!' cried Mr Wonka. 'The moment he swallowed it, he began wrinkling and shrivelling up all over and his hair started dropping off and his teeth started falling out and, before I knew it, he had suddenly become an old fellow of seventy-five! And thus, my dear Charlie, was Vita-Wonk invented!'

'Did you rescue all the Oompa-Loompa Minuses, Mr Wonka?'

'Every single one of them, my boy! One hundred and

thirty-one all told! Mind you, it wasn't quite as easy as all that. There were lots of snags and complications along the way ... Good heavens! We're nearly there! I *must* stop talking now and watch where we're going.'

Charlie realized that the Elevator was no longer rushing and roaring. It was hardly moving at all now. It seemed to be drifting. 'Undo your straps,' Mr Wonka said. 'We must get ready for action.' Charlie undid his straps and stood up and peered out. It was an eerie sight. They were drifting in a heavy grey mist and the mist was swirling and swishing around them as though driven by winds from many sides. In the distance, the mist was darker and almost black and it seemed to be swirling more fiercely than ever over there. Mr Wonka slid open the doors. 'Stand back!' he said. 'Don't fall out, Charlie, whatever you do!'

The mist came into the Elevator. It had the fusty reeky smell of an old underground dungeon. The silence was overpowering. There was no sound at all, no whisper of wind, no voice of creature or insect, and it gave Charlie a queer frightening feeling to be standing there in the middle of this grey inhuman nothingness – as though he were in another world altogether, in some place where man should never be.

'Minusland!' whispered Mr Wonka. 'This is it, Charlie! The problem now is to find her. We may be lucky ... and there again, we may not!'

17

Rescue in Minusland

'I don't like it here at all,' Charlie whispered. 'It gives me the willies.'

'Me, too,' Mr Wonka whispered back. 'But we've got a job to do, Charlie, and we must go through with it.'

The mist was condensing now on the glass walls of the Elevator making it difficult to see out except through the open doors.

'Do any other creatures live here, Mr Wonka?'

'Plenty of Gnoolies.'

'Are they dangerous?'

'If they bite you, they are. You're a gonner, my boy, if you're bitten by a Gnooly.'

The Elevator drifted on, rocking gently from side to side. The grey-black oily fog swirled around them.

'What does a Gnooly look like, Mr Wonka?'

'They don't *look* like anything, Charlie. They can't.'

'You mean you've never seen one?'

'You can't *see* Gnoolies, my boy. You can't even feel them . . . until they puncture your skin . . . then it's too late. They've got you.'

'You mean . . . There might be swarms of them all around us this very moment?' Charlie asked.

'There might,' said Mr Wonka.

Charlie felt his skin beginning to creep. 'Do you die at once?' he asked.

'First you become subtracted . . . a little later you are divided . . . but very slowly . . . it takes a long time . . . it's long division and it's very painful. After that, you become one of them.'

'Couldn't we shut the door?' Charlie asked.

'I'm afraid not, my boy. We'd never see her through the glass. There's too much mist and moisture. She's not going to be easy to pick out anyway.'

Charlie stood at the open door of the Elevator and stared into the swirling vapours. This, he thought, is what hell must be like . . . hell without heat . . . there was something unholy about it all, something unbelievably diabolical . . . It was all so deathly quiet, so desolate and empty . . . At the same time, the constant movement, the twisting and swirling of the misty vapours, gave one the feeling that some very powerful force, evil and malignant, was at work all around . . . Charlie felt a jab on his arm! He jumped! He almost jumped out of the Elevator! 'Sorry,' said Mr Wonka. 'It's only me.'

'Oh-h-h!' Charlie gasped. 'For a second, I thought . . .'

'I know what you thought, Charlie . . . And by the way, I'm awfully glad you're with me. How would you like to come here alone . . . as I did . . . as I had to . . . many times?'

'I wouldn't,' said Charlie.

'There she is!' said Mr Wonka, pointing. 'No, she isn't! . . . Oh, dear! I could have sworn I saw her for a moment right over there on the edge of that dark patch. Keep watching, Charlie.'

'*There!*' said Charlie. '*Over there. Look!*'

'Where?' said Mr Wonka. 'Point to her, Charlie!'

'She's ... she's gone again. She sort of faded away,' Charlie said.

They stood at the open door of the Elevator, peering into the swirly grey vapours.

'*There! Quick! Right there!*' Charlie cried. '*Can't you see her?*'

'*Yes, Charlie! I see her!*' I'm moving up close now!'

Mr Wonka reached behind him and began touching a number of buttons.

'Grandma!' Charlie cried out. 'We've come to get you, Grandma!'

They could see her faintly through the mist, but oh so

faintly. And they could see the mist through *her* as well.
She was transparent. She was hardly there at all. She was
no more than a shadow. They could see her face and just
the faintest outline of her body swathed in a sort of gown.
But she wasn't upright. She was floating lengthwise in the
swirling vapour.

'Why is she lying down?' Charlie whispered.

'Because she's a Minus, Charlie. Surely you know what a
minus sign looks like . . . Like that . . .' Mr Wonka drew a
horizontal line in the air with his finger.

The Elevator glided close. The ghostly shadow of Grandma Georgina's face was no more than a yard away now.
Charlie reached out through the door to touch her but
there was nothing there to touch. His hand went right
through her skin. 'Grandma!' he gasped. She began to drift
away.

'*Stand back!*' ordered Mr Wonka, and suddenly, from some secret place inside his coat-tails he whisked out a spray-gun. It was one of those old-fashioned things people used to use for spraying fly-spray around the room before aerosols came along. He aimed the spray-gun straight at the shadow of Grandma Georgina and he pumped the handle hard *ONCE . . . TWICE . . . THREE TIMES!* Each time, a fine black spray spurted out from the nozzle of the gun. Instantly, Grandma Georgina disappeared.

'A bull's eye!' cried Mr Wonka, jumping up and down with excitement. 'I got her with both barrels! I plussed her good and proper! That's Vita-Wonk for you!'

'Where's she gone?' Charlie asked.

'Back where she came from, of course! To the factory! She's a Minus no longer, my boy! She's a one hundred per cent red-blooded Plus! Come along now! Let's get out of here quickly before the Gnoolies find us!' Mr Wonka jabbed a button. The doors closed and the Great Glass Elevator shot upwards for home.

'Sit down and strap yourself in again, Charlie!' said Mr Wonka. 'We're going flat out this time!'

The Elevator roared and rocketed up toward the surface of the Earth. Mr Wonka and Charlie sat side by side on their little jump-seats, strapped in tight. Mr Wonka started tucking the spray-gun back into that enormous pocket somewhere in his coat-tails. 'It's such a pity one has to use a clumsy old thing like this,' he said. 'But there's simply no other way of doing it. Ideally, of course, one would measure out exactly the right number of drops into a teaspoon and feed it carefully into the mouth. But it's impossible to feed anything into a Minus. It's like trying to feed one's own

136

shadow. That's why I've got to use a spray-gun. Spray 'em all over, my boy! That's the only way!'

'It worked fine, though, didn't it?' Charlie said.

'Oh, it worked all right, Charlie! It worked beautifully! All I'm saying is that there's bound to be a slight overdose . . .'

'I don't quite know what you mean, Mr Wonka.'

'My dear boy, if it only takes *four drops* of Vita-Wonk to turn a young Oompa-Loompa into an old man . . .' Mr Wonka lifted his hands and let them fall limply on to his lap.

'You mean Grandma may have got too much?' asked Charlie, turning slightly pale.

'I'm afraid that's putting it rather mildly,' said Mr Wonka.

'But . . . but why did you give her such a lot of it, then?' said Charlie, getting more and more worried. 'Why did you spray her *three times?* She must have got pints and pints of it!'

'*Gallons!*' cried Mr Wonka, slapping his thighs. 'Gallons and gallons! But don't let a little thing like that bother you, my dear Charlie! The important part of it is we've got her back! She's a Minus no longer! She's a lovely Plus!'

> '*She's as plussy as plussy can be!*
> *She's more plussy than you or than me!*
> *The question is how,*
> *Just how old is she now?*
> *Is she more than a hundred and three?*'

18

The Oldest Person in the World

'We return in triumph, Charlie!' cried Mr Wonka as the Great Glass Elevator began to slow down. 'Once more your dear family will all be together again!'

The Elevator stopped. The doors slid open. And there was the Chocolate Room and the chocolate river and the Oompa-Loompas and in the middle of it all the great bed belonging to the old grandparents. 'Charlie!' said Grandpa Joe, rushing forward. 'Thank heavens you're back!' Charlie hugged him. Then he hugged his mother and his father. 'Is she here?' he said. 'Grandma Georgina?'

Nobody answered. Nobody did anything except Grandpa Joe, who pointed to the bed. He pointed but he didn't look where he was pointing. None of them looked at the bed – except Charlie. He walked past them all to get a better view, and he saw at one end the two babies, Grandma Josephine and Grandpa George, both tucked in and sleeping peacefully. At the other end . . .

'Don't be alarmed,' said Mr Wonka, running up and placing a hand on Charlie's arm. 'She's bound to be just a teeny bit over-plussed. I warned you about that.'

'*What have you done to her?*' cried Mrs Bucket. 'My poor old mother!'

Propped up against the pillows at the other end of the bed was the most extraordinary-looking thing Charlie had ever seen! Was it some ancient fossil? It couldn't be that because it was moving slightly! And now it was making sounds! Croaking sounds – the kind of sounds a very old frog might make if it knew a few words. 'Well well well,' it croaked. 'If it isn't dear Charlie.'

'*Grandma!*' cried Charlie. '*Grandma Georgina! Oh . . . Oh . . . Oh!*'

Her tiny face was like a pickled walnut. There were such masses of creases and wrinkles that the mouth and eyes and even the nose were sunken almost out of sight. Her hair was pure white and her hands, which were resting on top of the blanket, were just little lumps of wrinkly skin.

The presence of this ancient creature seemed to have terrified not only Mr and Mrs Bucket, but Grandpa Joe as well. They stood well back, away from the bed. Mr Wonka, on the other hand, was as happy as ever. 'My dear lady!' he cried, advancing to the edge of the bed and clasping one of those tiny wrinkled hands in both of his. 'Welcome home! And how are you feeling on this bright and glorious day?'

'Not too bad,' croaked Grandma Georgina. 'Not too bad at all . . . considering my age.'

'Good for you!' said Mr Wonka. 'Atta girl! All we've got to do now is find out exactly how old you are! Then we shall be able to take further action!'

'You're taking no further action around here,' said Mrs Bucket, tight-lipped. 'You've done enough damage already!'

'But my dear old muddleheaded mugwump,' said Mr Wonka, turning to Mrs Bucket. 'What does it matter that the old girl has become a trifle too old? We can put that right in a jiffy! Have you forgotten Wonka-Vite and how every tablet makes you twenty years younger? We shall bring her back! We shall transform her into a blossoming blushing maiden in the twink of an eye!'

'What good is that when her husband's not even out of his nappies yet?' wailed Mrs Bucket, pointing a finger at the one-year-old Grandpa George. so peacefully sleeping.

'Madam,' said Mr Wonka, 'let us do one thing at a time . . .'

'I forbid you to give her that beastly Wonka-Vite!' said Mrs Bucket. 'You'll turn her into a Minus again just as sure as I'm standing here!'

'I don't want to be a Minus!' croaked Grandma Georgina. 'If I ever have to go back to that beastly Minusland again, the Gnoolies will knickle me!'

'Fear not!' said Mr Wonka. 'This time I *myself* will supervise the giving of the medicine. I shall personally see to it that you get the correct dosage. But listen very carefully now! I cannot work out how many pills to give you until I know exactly how old you are! That's obvious, isn't it?'

'It is not obvious at all,' said Mrs Bucket. 'Why can't you give her one pill at a time and play it safe?'

'Impossible, madam. In very serious cases such as this one, Wonka-Vite doesn't work at all when given in small doses. You've got to throw everything at her in one go. You've got to hit her with it hard. A single pill wouldn't even begin to shift her. She's too far gone for that. It's all or nothing.'

'No,' said Mrs Bucket firmly.

'Yes,' said Mr Wonka. 'Dear lady, please listen to me. If you have a very severe headache and you need *three* aspirins to cure it, it's no good taking only one at a time and waiting four hours between each. You'll never cure yourself that way. You've got to gulp them all down in one go. It's the same with Wonka-Vite. May I proceed?'

'Oh, all *right*, I suppose you'll have to,' said Mrs Bucket.

'Good,' said Mr Wonka, giving a little jump and twirling his feet in the air. 'Now then, how old are you, my dear Grandma Georgina?'

'I don't know,' she croaked. 'I lost count of that years and years ago.'

'Don't you have *any* idea?' said Mr Wonka.

'Of course I don't,' gibbered the old woman. 'Nor would you if you were as old as I am.'

'*Think!*' said Mr Wonka. 'You've *got* to think!'

The tiny old wrinkled brown walnut face wrinkled itself up more than ever. The others stood waiting. The Oompa-Loompas, enthralled by the sight of this ancient object, were all edging closer and closer to the bed. The two babies slept on.

'Are you, for example, a hundred?' said Mr Wonka. 'Or a hundred and ten? Or a hundred and twenty?'

'It's no good,' she croaked. 'I never did have a head for numbers.'

'This is a *catastrophe*!' cried Mr Wonka. 'If you can't tell me how old you are, I can't help you! I dare not risk an overdose!'

Gloom settled upon the entire company, including for once Mr Wonka himself. 'You've messed it up good and proper this time, haven't you?' said Mrs Bucket.

'Grandma,' Charlie said, moving forward to the bed. 'Listen, Grandma. Don't worry about exactly how old you might be. Try to think of a *happening* instead . . . think of something that *happened* to you . . . anything you like . . . as far back as you can . . . it may help us . . .'

'Lots of things happened to me, Charlie . . . so many many things happened to me . . .'

'But can you *remember* any of them, Grandma?'

'Oh, I don't know, my darling . . . I suppose I could remember one or two if I thought hard enough . . .'

'Good, Grandma, good!' said Charlie eagerly. 'Now what is the very earliest thing you can remember in your whole life?'

'Oh, my dear boy, that really would be going back a few years, wouldn't it?'

'When you were little, Grandma, like me. Can't you remember anything you did when you were little?'

The tiny sunken black eyes glimmered faintly and a sort of smile touched the corners of the almost invisible little slit of a mouth. 'There was a ship,' she said. 'I can remember a ship . . . I couldn't ever forget that ship . . .'

'Go on, Grandma! A ship! What sort of a ship? Did you sail on her?'

'Of course I sailed on her, my darling . . . we all sailed on her . . .'

'Where from? Where to?' Charlie went on eagerly.

'Oh no, I couldn't tell you that . . . I was just a tiny little girl . . .' She lay back on the pillow and closed her eyes. Charlie watched her, waiting for something more. Everybody waited. No one moved.

'. . . It had a lovely name, that ship . . . there was something beautiful . . . something so beautiful about that name . . . but of course I couldn't possibly remember it . . .'

Charlie, who had been sitting on the edge of the bed, suddenly jumped up. His face was shining with excitement. 'If I said the name, Grandma, would you remember it then?'

'I might, Charlie . . . yes . . . I think I might . . .'

'*THE MAYFLOWER!*' cried Charlie.

The old woman's head jerked up off the pillow. '*That's it!*' she croaked. 'You've *got* it, Charlie! The *Mayflower* . . . Such a lovely name . . .'

'Grandpa!' Charlie called out, dancing with excitement. 'What year did the *Mayflower* sail for America?'

'The *Mayflower* sailed out of Plymouth Harbour on September the sixth, sixteen hundred and twenty,' said Grandpa Joe.

'Plymouth . . .' croaked the old woman. 'That rings a bell, too . . . Yes, it might easily have been Plymouth . . .'

'Sixteen hundred and twenty!' cried Charlie. 'Oh, my heavens above! That means you're . . . you do it, Grandpa!'

'Well now,' said Grandpa Joe. 'Take sixteen hundred and twenty away from nineteen hundred and seventy-two . . . that leaves . . . don't rush me now, Charlie . . . That leaves three hundred . . . and . . . and fifty-two.'

'Jumping jackrabbits!' yelled Mr Bucket. 'She's three hundred and fifty-two years old!'

'She's more,' said Charlie. 'How old did you say you were, Grandma, when you sailed on the *Mayflower*? Were you about eight?'

'I think I was even younger than that, my darling . . . I was only a bitty little girl . . . probably no more than six . . .'

'Then she's *three hundred and fifty-eight!*' gasped Charlie.

'That's Vita-Wonk for you,' said Mr Wonka proudly. 'I told you it was powerful stuff.'

'Three hundred and fifty-eight!' said Mr Bucket. 'It's unbelievable!'

'Just imagine the things she must have seen in her lifetime!' said Grandpa Joe.

'My poor old mother!' wailed Mrs Bucket. 'What on earth . . .'

'Patience, dear lady,' said Mr Wonka. 'Now comes the interesting part. Bring on the Wonka-Vite!'

An Oompa-Loompa ran forward with a large bottle and gave it to Mr Wonka. He put it on the bed. 'How young does she want to be?' he asked.

'Seventy-eight,' said Mrs Bucket firmly. 'Exactly where she was before all this nonsense started!'

'Surely she'd like to be a bit younger than that?' said Mr Wonka.

'Certainly not!' said Mrs Bucket. 'It's too risky!'

'Too risky, too risky!' croaked Grandma Georgina. 'You'll only Minus me again if you try to be clever!'

'Have it your own way,' said Mr Wonka. 'Now then, I've got to do a few sums.' Another Oompa-Loompa trotted forward, holding up a blackboard. Mr Wonka took a piece of chalk from his pocket and wrote:

Present age of person... 358
Age she wants to be
(subtract this) — 78
Number of years younger = 280
she must become
If each pill of Wonka-Vite makes
you 20 years younger we must
divide 280 by 20 to find out
how many pills to give: 14
20)280

'Fourteen pills of Wonka-Vite exactly,' said Mr Wonka. The Oompa-Loompa took the blackboard away. Mr Wonka picked up the bottle from the bed and opened it and counted out fourteen of the little brilliant yellow pills. 'Water!' he said. Yet another Oompa-Loompa ran forward with a glass of water. Mr Wonka tipped all fourteen pills into the glass. The water bubbled and frothed. 'Drink it while it's fizzing,' he said, holding the glass up to Grandma Georgina's lips. 'All in one gulp!'

She drank it.

Mr Wonka sprang back and took a large brass clock from his pocket. 'Don't forget,' he cried, 'it's a year a second! She's got two hundred and eighty years to lose! That'll take her four minutes and forty seconds! Watch the centuries fall away!'

The room was so silent they could hear the ticking of Mr Wonka's clock. At first nothing much happened to the ancient person lying on the bed. She closed her eyes and lay back. Now and again, the puckered skin of her face gave a twitch and her little hands jerked up and down, but that was all . . .

'One minute gone!' called Mr Wonka. 'She's sixty years younger.'

'She looks just the same to me,' said Mr Bucket.

'Of course she does,' said Mr Wonka. 'What's a mere sixty years when you're over three hundred to start with!'

'Are you all right, mother?' said Mrs Bucket anxiously. 'Talk to me, mother!'

'Two minutes gone!' called Mr Wonka. 'She's one hundred and twenty years younger!'

And now definite changes were beginning to show in the old woman's face. The skin was quivering all over and some of the deepest wrinkles were becoming less and less deep, the mouth less sunken, the nose more prominent.

'Mother!' cried Mrs Bucket. 'Are you all right? Speak to me, mother, please!'

Suddenly, with a suddenness that made everyone jump, the old woman sat bolt upright in bed and shouted, *'Did you hear the news! Admiral Nelson has beaten the French at Trafalgar!'*

'She's going crazy!' said Mr Bucket.

'Not at all,' said Mr Wonka. 'She's going through the nineteenth century.'

'Three minutes gone!' said Mr Wonka.

Every second now she was growing slightly less and less shrivelled, becoming more and more lively. It was a marvellous thing to watch.

'Gettysburg!' she cried. *'General Lee is on the run!'*

146

And a few seconds later she let out a great wail of anguish and said, 'He's dead, he's dead, he's dead!'

'Who's dead?' said Mr Bucket, craning forward.

'Lincoln!' she wailed. *'There goes the train . . .'*

'She must have seen it!' said Charlie. 'She must have been there!'

'She *is* there,' said Mr Wonka. 'At least she was a few seconds ago.'

'Will someone please explain to me,' said Mrs Bucket, 'what on earth . . .'

'Four minutes gone!' said Mr Wonka. 'Only forty seconds left! Only forty more years to lose!'

'Grandma!' cried Charlie, running forward. 'You're looking almost exactly like you used to! Oh, I'm so glad!'

'Just as long as it all stops when it's meant to,' said Mrs Bucket.

'I'll bet it doesn't,' said Mr Bucket. 'Something always goes wrong.'

'Not when *I'm* in charge of it, sir,' said Mr Wonka. 'Time's up! She is now seventy-eight years old! How do you feel, dear lady? Is everything all right?'

'I feel tolerable,' she said. 'Just tolerable. But that's no thanks to you, you meddling old mackerel!'

There she was again, the same cantankerous grumbling old Grandma Georgina that Charlie had known so well before it all started. Mrs Bucket flung her arms around her and began weeping with joy. The old woman pushed her aside and said, 'What, may I ask, are those two silly babies doing at the other end of the bed?'

'One of them's your husband,' said Mr Bucket.

'Rubbish!' she said. 'Where *is* George?'

'I'm afraid it's true, mother,' said Mrs Bucket. 'That's him on the left. The other one's Josephine . . .'

'You . . . you chiselling old cheeseburger!' she shouted, pointing a fierce finger at Mr Wonka. 'What in the name of . . .'

'Now now now now now!' said Mr Wonka. 'Let us not for mercy's sake have another row so late in the day. If everyone will keep their hair on and leave this to Charlie and me, we shall have them exactly where they used to be in the flick of a fly's wing!'

19

The Babies Grow Up

'Bring on the Vita-Wonk!' said Mr Wonka. 'We'll soon fix these two babies.'

An Oompa-Loompa ran forward with a small bottle and a couple of silver teaspoons.

'Wait just one minute!' snapped Grandma Georgina. 'What sort of devilish dumpery are you up to now?'

'It's all right, Grandma,' said Charlie. 'I promise you it's all right. Vita-Wonk does the opposite to Wonka-Vite. It makes you older. It's what we gave *you* when you were a Minus. It saved you!'

'You gave me too much!' snapped the old woman.

'We had to, Grandma.'

'And now you want to do the same to Grandpa George!'

'Of course we don't,' said Charlie.

'I finished up three hundred and fifty-eight years old!' she went on. 'What's to stop you making another little mistake and giving him *fifty times more than you gave me?* Then I'd suddenly have a twenty-thousand-year-old caveman in bed beside me! *Imagine that*, and him with a big knobby club in one hand and dragging me around by my hair with the other! No, thank you!'

'Grandma,' Charlie said patiently. 'With you we had to use a spray because you were a Minus. You were a ghost. But here Mr Wonka can . . .'

'Don't talk to me about that man!' she cried. 'He's batty as a bullfrog!'

'No, Grandma, he is *not*. And here he can measure it out exactly right, drop by drop, and feed it into their mouths. That's true isn't it, Mr Wonka?'

'Charlie,' said Mr Wonka. 'I can see that the factory is going to be in good hands when I retire. You learn very fast. I am so pleased I chose you, my dear boy, so very pleased. Now then, what's the verdict? Do we leave them as babies or do we grow them up with Vita-Wonk?'

'You go ahead, Mr Wonka,' said Grandpa Joe. 'I'd like you to grow my Josie up so she's just the same as before – eighty years old.'

'Thank you, sir,' said Mr Wonka. 'I appreciate the confidence you place in me. But what about the other one, Grandpa George?'

'Oh, all *right*, then,' said Grandma Georgina. 'But if he ends up a caveman I don't want him in *this* bed any more!'

'That's settled then!' said Mr Wonka. 'Come along, Charlie! We'll do them both together. You hold one spoon and I'll hold the other. I shall measure out four drops and four drops only into each spoon and we'll wake them up and pop it into their mouths.'

'Which one shall I do, Mr Wonka?'

'You do Grandma Josephine, the tiny one. I'll do Grandpa George, the one-year-old. Here's your spoon.'

Charlie took the spoon and held it out. Mr Wonka opened the bottle and dripped four drops of oily black liquid into

Charlie's spoon. Then he did the same to his own. He handed
the bottle back to the Oompa-Loompa.

'Shouldn't someone hold the babies while you give it?'
said Grandpa Joe. 'I'll hold Grandma Josephine.'

'Are you mad!' said Mr Wonka. 'Don't you realize that
Vita-Wonk acts instantly? It's not one year a second like
Wonka-Vite. Vita-Wonk is as quick as lightning! The
moment the medicine is swallowed – ping! – and it all
happens! The getting bigger and the growing older and
everything else *all happens in one second!* So don't you see,
my dear sir,' he said to Grandpa Joe, 'that one moment
you'd be holding a tiny baby in your arms and just one
second later you'd find yourself staggering about with an
eighty-year-old woman and you'd drop her like a ton of
bricks on the floor!'

'I see what you mean,' said Grandpa Joe.

'All set, Charlie?'

'All set, Mr Wonka.' Charlie moved around the bed to where the tiny sleeping baby lay. He placed one hand behind her head and lifted it. The baby awoke and started yelling. Mr Wonka was on the other side of the bed doing the same to the one-year-old George. 'Both together now, Charlie!' said Mr Wonka. 'Ready, steady, *go*! Pop it in!' Charlie pushed his spoon into the open mouth of the baby and tipped the drops down her throat.

'Make sure she swallows it!' cried Mr Wonka. 'It won't work until it gets into their tummies!'

It is difficult to explain what happened next, and whatever it was, it only lasted for one second. A second is about as long as it takes you to say aloud and quickly, 'one-two-three-four-five'. And that is how long it took, with Charlie watching closely, for the tiny baby to grow and swell and wrinkle into the eighty-year-old Grandma Josephine. It was a frightening thing to see. It was like an explosion. A small baby suddenly exploded into an old woman, and Charlie all at once found himself staring straight into the well-known and much-loved wrinkly old face of his Grandma Josephine. '*Hello*, my darling,' she said. 'Where have *you* come from?'

'Josie!' cried Grandpa Joe, rushing forward. 'How marvellous! You're back!'

'I didn't know I'd been away,' she said.

Grandpa George had also made a successful comeback. 'You were better-looking as a baby,' Grandma Georgina said to him. 'But I'm glad you've grown up again, George . . . for one reason.'

'What's that?' asked Grandpa George.

'You won't wet the bed any more.'

20

How to Get Someone out of Bed

'I am sure,' said Mr Wonka, addressing Grandpa George, Grandma Georgina and Grandma Josephine, 'I am quite sure the three of you, after all *that*, will now want to jump out of bed and lend a hand in running the Chocolate Factory.'

'Who, us?' said Grandma Josephine.

'Yes, you,' said Mr Wonka.

'Are you crazy?' said Grandma Georgina. 'I'm staying right here where I am in this nice comfortable bed, thank you very much!'

'Me, too!' said Grandpa George.

At that moment, there was a sudden commotion among the Oompa-Loompas at the far end of the Chocolate Room. There was a buzz of excited chatter and a lot of running about and waving of arms, and out of all this a single Oompa-Loompa emerged and came rushing toward Mr Wonka, carrying a huge envelope in his hands. He came up close to Mr Wonka. He started whispering. Mr Wonka bent down low to listen.

'*Outside the factory gates?*' cried Mr Wonka. '*Men! . . . What sort of men? . . . Yes, but do they look dangerous? . . . Are they*

*ACTING dangerously? ... And a what? ... A HELICOP-
TER! ... And these men came out of it? ... They gave you
this? ...'*

Mr Wonka grabbed the huge envelope and quickly slit it
open and pulled out the folded letter inside. There was absolute silence as he skimmed swiftly over what was written
on the paper. Nobody moved. Charlie began to feel cold. He
knew something dreadful was going to happen. There was
a very definite smell of danger in the air. The men outside
the gates, the helicopter, the nervousness of the Oompa-
Loompas ... He was watching Mr Wonka's face, searching
for a clue, for some change in expression that would tell
him how bad the news was.

'*Great whistling whangdoodles!*' cried Mr Wonka, leaping
so high in the air that when he landed his legs gave way
and he crashed on to his backside.

'*Snorting snozzwangers!*' he yelled, picking himself up and
waving the letter about as though he were swatting

mosquitoes. 'Listen to this, all of you! Just you listen to this!'
He began to read aloud:

THE WHITE HOUSE
WASHINGTON D.C.

TO MR WILLY WONKA.

SIR

    TODAY THE ENTIRE NATION, INDEED THE WHOLE WORLD IS REJOICING AT THE SAFE RETURN OF OUR TRANSPORT CAPSULE FROM SPACE WITH 136 SOULS ON BOARD. HAD IT NOT BEEN FOR THE HELP THEY RECEIVED FROM AN UNKNOWN SPACESHIP, THESE 136 PEOPLE WOULD NEVER HAVE COME BACK. IT HAS BEEN REPORTED TO ME THAT THE COURAGE SHOWN BY THE EIGHT ASTRONAUTS ABOARD THIS UNKNOWN SPACESHIP WAS EXTRAORDINARY. OUR RADAR STATIONS, BY TRACKING THIS SPACESHIP ON ITS RETURN TO EARTH, HAVE DISCOVERED THAT IT SPLASHED DOWN IN A PLACE KNOWN AS WONKA'S CHOCOLATE FACTORY. THAT, SIR, IS WHY THIS LETTER IS BEING DELIVERED TO YOU.

    I WISH NOW TO SHOW THE GRATITUDE OF THE NATION BY INVITING ALL EIGHT OF THOSE INCREDIBLY BRAVE ASTRONAUTS TO COME AND STAY IN THE WHITE HOUSE FOR A FEW DAYS AS MY HONOURED GUESTS.

    I AM ARRANGING A SPECIAL CELEBRA-TION PARTY IN THE BLUE ROOM THIS EVEN-

ING AT WHICH I MYSELF WILL PIN MEDALS FOR BRAVERY UPON ALL EIGHT OF THESE GALLANT FLIERS. THE MOST IMPORTANT PERSONS IN THE LAND WILL BE PRESENT AT THIS GATHERING TO SALUTE THE HEROES WHOSE DAZZLING DEEDS WILL BE WRITTEN FOR EVER IN THE HISTORY OF OUR NATION. AMONG THOSE ATTENDING WILL BE THE VICE-PRESIDENT (MISS ELVIRA TIBBS), ALL THE MEMBERS OF MY CABINET, THE CHIEFS OF THE ARMY, THE NAVY AND THE AIR FORCE, ALL MEMBERS OF THE CONGRESS. A FAMOUS SWORD-SWALLOWER FROM AFGHANISTAN WHO IS NOW TEACHING ME TO EAT MY WORDS (WHAT YOU DO IS YOU TAKE THE S OFF THE BEGINNING OF THE SWORD AND PUT IT ON THE END BEFORE YOU SWALLOW IT). AND WHO ELSE IS COMING? OH YES, MY CHIEF INTERPRETER, AND THE GOVERNORS OF EVERY STATE IN THE UNION, AND OF COURSE MY CAT, MRS TAUBSYPUSS.

A HELICOPTER AWAITS ALL EIGHT OF YOU OUTSIDE THE FACTORY GATES. I MYSELF AWAIT YOUR ARRIVAL AT THE WHITE HOUSE WITH THE VERY GREATEST PLEASURE AND IMPATIENCE.

I BEG TO REMAIN, SIR,

MOST SINCERELY YOURS

Lancelot R. Gilligrass.

LANCELOT R. GILLIGRASS
President of the United States

P.S. COULD YOU PLEASE BRING ME A FEW
WONKA FUDGEMALLOW DELIGHTS. I LOVE
THEM SO MUCH BUT EVERYBODY AROUND
HERE KEEPS STEALING MINE OUT OF THE
DRAWER IN MY DESK. AND DON'T TELL
NANNY.

Mr Wonka stopped reading. And in the stillness that
followed Charlie could hear people breathing. He could hear
them breathing in and out much faster than usual. And
there were other things, too. There were so many feelings
and passions and there was so much sudden happiness
swirling around in the air it made his head spin. Grandpa
Joe was the first to say something ... *'Yippeeeeeeeeeee!'* he
yelled out, and he flew across the room and caught Charlie
by the hands and the two of them started dancing away
along the bank of the chocolate river. 'We're going, Charlie!'
sang Grandpa Joe. 'We're going to the White House after
all!' Mr and Mrs Bucket were also dancing and laughing
and singing, and Mr Wonka ran all over the room proudly
showing the President's letter to the Oompa-Loompas. After
a minute or so, Mr Wonka clapped his hands for attention.
'Come along, come along!' he called out. 'We mustn't dilly!
We mustn't dally! Come on, Charlie! And you, sir, Grandpa
Joe! And Mr and Mrs Bucket! The helicopter is outside the
gates! We can't keep it waiting!' He began hustling the four
of them toward the door.

'*Hey!*' screamed Grandma Georgina from the bed. 'What
about us? We were invited too, don't you forget that!'

'It said *all eight of us* were invited!' cried Grandma Josephine.

'And that includes *me*!' said Grandpa George.

Mr Wonka turned and looked at them. 'Of course it includes you,' he said. 'But we can't possibly get that bed into a helicopter. It won't go through the door.'

'You mean . . . you mean if we don't get out of bed we can't come?' said Grandma Georgina.

'That's exactly what I mean,' said Mr Wonka. 'Keep going, Charlie,' he whispered, giving Charlie a little nudge. 'Keep walking toward the door.'

Suddenly, behind them, there was a great *SWOOSH* of blankets and sheets and a pinging of bedsprings as the three old people all exploded out of the bed together. They came sprinting after Mr Wonka, shouting, 'Wait for us! Wait for us!' It was amazing how fast they were running across the floor of the great Chocolate Room. Mr Wonka and Charlie and the others stood staring at them in wonder. They leaped across paths and over little bushes like gazelles in spring-time, with their bare legs flashing and their nightshirts flying out behind them.

Suddenly Grandma Josephine put the brakes on so hard she skidded five yards before coming to a stop. 'Wait!' she screamed. 'We must be mad! We can't go to a famous party in the White House in our nightshirts! We can't stand there practically naked in front of all those people while the President pins medals all over us!'

'Oh-h-h-h!' wailed Grandma Georgina. 'Oh, what *are* we going to do?'

'Don't you have any clothes with you at all?' asked Mr Wonka.

'Of course we don't!' said Grandma Josephine. 'We haven't been out of that bed for twenty years!'

'We can't go!' wailed Grandma Georgina. 'We'll have to stay behind!'

'Couldn't we buy something from a store?' said Grandpa George.

'What with?' said Grandma Josephine. 'We don't have any money!'

'*Money!*' cried Mr Wonka. 'Good gracious me, don't you go worrying about money! I've got plenty of *that*!'

'Listen,' said Charlie. 'Why couldn't we ask the helicopter to land on the roof of a big shop on the way over. Then you can all pop downstairs and buy exactly what you want!'

'Charlie!' cried Mr Wonka, grasping him by the hand. 'What *would* we do without you? You're brilliant! Come along everybody! We're off to stay in the White House!'

They all linked arms and went dancing out of the Chocolate Room and along the corridors and out through the front door into the open where the big helicopter was waiting near the factory gates. A group of extremely important-looking gentlemen came toward them and bowed.

'Well, Charlie,' said Grandpa Joe. 'It's certainly been a busy day.'

'It's not over yet,' Charlie said, laughing. 'It hasn't even begun.'